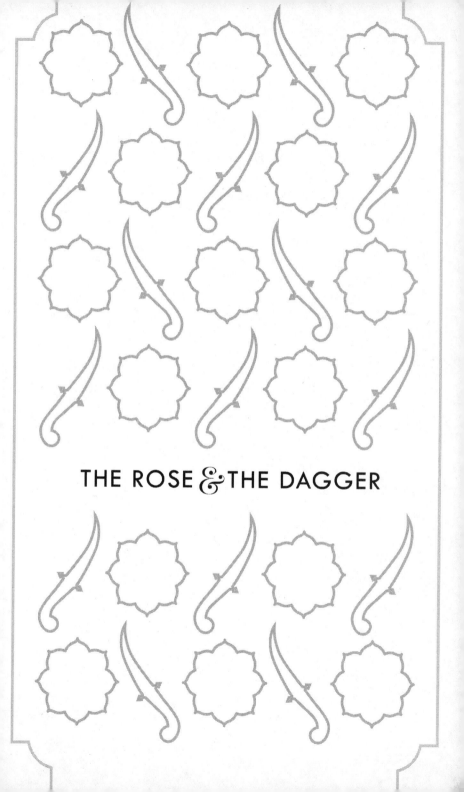

# THE ROSE & THE DAGGER

*Also by Renée Ahdieh*

The Wrath and the Dawn

# THE ROSE & THE DAGGER
## ·RENÉE AHDIEH·

G. P. PUTNAM'S SONS

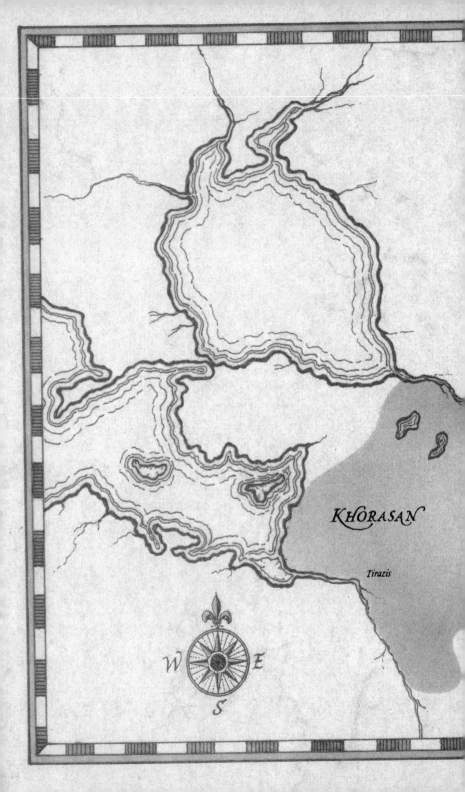

KHORASAN

Tirazis

W · E

S

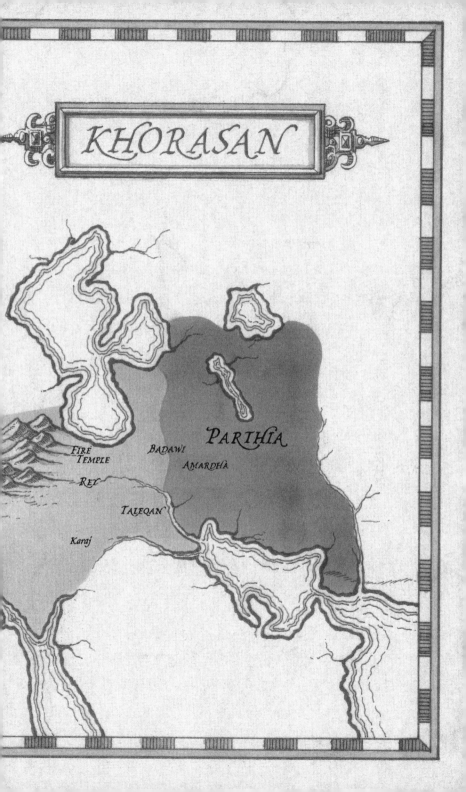

G. P. Putnam's Sons
an imprint of Penguin Random House LLC
375 Hudson Street
New York, NY 10014

Copyright © 2016 by Renée Ahdieh.
Map illustration copyright © 2015 by Russell R. Charpentier.
Cover photography: Raul Rodriguez.
Cover photo illustration & frontispiece: Michelle Monique.

G. P. Putnam's Sons is a registered trademark of Penguin Random House LLC.

Library of Congress Cataloging-in-Publication Data is available upon request.

Printed in the United States of America.
ISBN 978-0-399-54663-1
3  5  7  9  10  8  6  4

Text set in Italian Old Style MT Std.
This is a work of fiction. Names, characters, places, and incidents either are the product
of the author's imagination or are used fictitiously, and any resemblance to actual
persons, living or dead, businesses, companies, events, or locales is entirely coincidental.

*To my sisters:*
*Erica, Elaine, and Sabaa—*
*This book would not be possible without each of you.*
*And to Victor, always.*

*The rose's rarest essence lives in the thorns.*

Jalal al-Din Rumi

# PROLOGUE

The girl was eleven and three-quarters.

Three very important quarters.

They'd been of consequence when her father had left her in charge this morning, with an important task to accomplish. So, with a world-weary sigh, she pushed up her tattered sleeves and heaved rubble into the nearby wheelbarrow.

"It's so heavy," her eight-year-old brother complained, as he struggled to move a piece of debris from their home. He coughed when a cloud of soot rose from the charred remains.

"Let me help." The girl dropped her shovel with a *clang*.

"I didn't say I needed help!"

"We should work together, or we won't finish cleaning everything before Baba returns home." She braced her fists on her hips while glaring down at him.

"Look around you!" He threw his hands in the air. "We'll *never* finish cleaning everything."

Her eyes followed his hands.

The clay walls of their home were ripped apart. Broken. Blackened. Their roof opened up to the heavens. To a dull and forlorn sky.

To what once had been a glorious city.

A midday sun lay hidden behind the shattered rooftops of Rey. It cut shadows of light and dark across angry stone and scorched marble. Here and there, smoldering piles of rubble served as a harsh reminder of what had taken place only a few short days ago.

The young girl hardened her gaze and stepped closer to her brother.

"If you don't want to work, then wait outside. But I'm going to keep working. Someone has to." Again, she reached for her shovel.

The boy kicked at a nearby stone. It skittered across the packed earth before crashing to a halt at the foot of a hooded stranger standing by the remains of their door.

Tensing her grip on the shovel, the girl eased her brother behind her.

"May I help you . . . ?" She paused. The stranger's black *rida'* was embroidered in silver and gold thread. The scabbard of his sword was finely etched and delicately bejeweled, and his sandals were cut from the highest-quality calfskin.

He was no mere brigand.

The girl stood taller. "May I help you, *sahib*?"

When he did not answer right away, the girl raised the shovel higher, her brow taut and her heart hammering in her chest.

The stranger stepped from beneath the sagging doorjamb. He threw back his hood and raised both palms in supplication. Each of his gestures was careful, and he moved with a liquid kind of grace.

As he strode into a weak slice of light, the girl saw his face for the first time.

He was younger than she expected. No more than twenty.

His face approached beautiful. But its angles were too harsh, his expression too severe. The sunlight on his hands revealed something at odds with the rest of his finery; the skin of his palms was red and cracked and peeling—evidence of hard labor.

His tired eyes were a tawny-gold color. She'd seen eyes like that once. In a painting of a lion.

"I didn't mean to startle you," the stranger said softly. His eyes shifted around the ruin of their one-room abode. "May I speak to your father?"

The girl's suspicion gripped her once more. "He's—not here. He went to stand in line for building supplies."

The stranger nodded. "And your mother?"

"She's dead," her brother said, stirring from behind her. "The roof fell on her during the storm. She died the next morning."

There was an unassuming quality to his words that the girl did not feel. Because to her brother, the words were not yet real. For after they'd lost nearly everything in last year's drought, the storm had taken its final toll on their family.

And her brother had yet to grasp this most recent loss.

The stranger's severity deepened for an instant. He looked away, and his hands fell to his sides. After a beat, he looked back at them, his eyes unwavering, despite his white-knuckled fists. "Do you have another shovel?"

"Why do *you* need a shovel, rich man?" Her little brother marched up to the stranger, accusation in each of his barefooted steps.

"Kamyar!" His sister gasped as she reached for the back of his ragged *qamis*.

The stranger blinked down at her brother before crouching on the packed-earth floor. "Kamyar, was it?" he asked, a trace of a smile adorning his lips.

Her brother said nothing, though he was barely able to meet the tall stranger's eyes.

"I—I apologize, *sahib*," the girl stammered. "He's a bit insolent."

"Please don't apologize. I rather appreciate insolence, when it's dispensed by the right person." This time, the stranger did smile, and his features softened.

"Yes," her brother interrupted. "My name is Kamyar. What is yours?"

The stranger studied her brother for a moment.

"Khalid."

"Why do you want a shovel, Khalid?" her brother demanded again.

"I'd like to help you repair your home."

"Why?"

"Because when we help one another, we are able to accomplish things faster."

Kamyar nodded slowly, then canted his head to one side. "But this isn't your home. Why should you care?"

"Because Rey is my home. And Rey is your home. If you could help me when I needed help, would you not wish to do so?"

"Yes," Kamyar said without hesitation. "I would."

"Then it's settled." The stranger stood. "Will you share your shovel with me, Kamyar?"

For the rest of the afternoon, the trio worked to clear the floor of charred wood and waterlogged debris. The girl never gave the stranger her name and refused to call him anything but *sahib*, but Kamyar treated him like a long-lost friend with a common enemy. When the stranger gave them water and *lavash* bread to eat, the girl dipped her head and touched her fingertips to her brow in thanks.

A flush rose in her cheeks when the almost-beautiful stranger returned the gesture, without a word.

Soon, the day began bruising into night, and Kamyar wedged himself into a corner, his chin drooping to his chest, and his eyes slowly falling shut.

The stranger finished arranging the last of the salvageable pieces of wood by the door, and shook the dirt from his *rida'* before pulling the hood of his cloak back over his head.

"Thank you," the girl murmured, knowing that was the least she should do.

He glanced over his shoulder at her. Then the stranger reached into his cloak and produced a small pouch cinched shut by a leather cord.

"Please. Take it."

"No, *sahib*." She shook her head. "I cannot take your money. We've already taken enough of your generosity."

"It isn't much. I'd like for you to take it." His eyes, which had appeared tired at the outset, now looked beyond exhausted. "Please."

There was something about his face in that moment, hidden as it was in the play of shadows, in the lingering motes of ash and dust . . .

Something about it that signified a deeper suffering than the girl could ever hope to fathom.

She took the small pouch from his hand.

"Thank you," he whispered. As though he were the one in need.

"Shiva," she said. "My name is Shiva."

Disbelief flared on his features for an instant. Then the sharp planes of his face smoothed.

"Of course it is." He bowed low, with a hand to his brow.

Despite her confusion, she managed to respond in kind, her fingers brushing her forehead. When she looked up again, he had turned the corner.

And disappeared into the wending darkness of night.

# THE WATER LIES

Iᴛ ᴡᴀs ᴏɴʟʏ ᴀ ʀɪɴɢ.

Yet it signified so much to her.

Much to lose. Much to fight for.

Shahrzad lifted her hand into a stream of light. The ring of muted gold flashed twice, as if to remind her of its mate, far across the Sea of Sand.

*Khalid.*

Her thoughts drifted to the marble palace in Rey. To Khalid. She hoped he was with Jalal or with his uncle, the *shahrban.*

She hoped he was not alone. Adrift. Wondering . . .

*Why am I not with him?*

Her lips pressed tight.

*Because the last time I was in Rey, thousands of innocent people perished.*

And Shahrzad could not return until she'd found a way to protect her people. Her love. A way to end Khalid's terrible curse.

Outside her tent, a goat began to bleat with merry abandon.

Her temper mounting, Shahrzad flung off her makeshift blanket and reached for the dagger beside her bedroll. An empty threat, but she knew she should at least fight for a semblance of control.

As if to mock her, the shrill sounds beyond her tent grew more incessant.

*Is that a . . . bell?*

The little beast outside had a bell around its neck! And now the clanging and the bleating all but ensured the impossibility of sleep.

Shahrzad sat up, gripping the jeweled hilt of her dagger—

Then, with an exasperated cry, she fell back against the itchy wool of her bedroll.

*It's not as though I'm managing to sleep as it is.*

Not when she was so far from home. So far from where her heart longed to be.

She swallowed the sudden lump that formed in her throat. Her thumb brushed against the ring with two crossed swords— the ring Khalid had placed on her right hand a mere fortnight ago.

*Enough. Nothing will be accomplished from such nonsense.*

Again she sat up, her eyes scanning her new surroundings.

Irsa's bedroll was neatly stashed to one side of the small tent. Her younger sister had likely been awake for hours, baking bread, making tea, and braiding the contemptible goat's chin hair.

Shahrzad almost smiled, despite everything.

Her wariness taking shape in the gloom, she tucked the dagger into her waistband, then stretched to her feet. Every muscle in her body ached from days of hard travel and nights of poor sleep.

Three nights of worry. Three nights spent fleeing a city set to flame. An endless fount of questions without answers. Those three long nights of worry for her father, whose battered body had yet to recover from whatever damage it had incurred on the hilltops outside Rey.

Shahrzad took a deep breath.

The air here was strange. Drier. Crisp. Soft bars of light slanted through the tent seams. A thin layer of fine silt clung to everything. It made her tiny world appear as though it were fashioned of diamond-dusted darkness.

On one side of the tent was a small table with a porcelain pitcher and a copper basin. Shahrzad's meager belongings were perched beside it, wrapped in the threadbare carpet given to her by Musa Zaragoza several months ago. She knelt before the table and filled the basin with water for washing.

The water was tepid, but clean. Her reflection looked strangely calm as it stared back at her.

Calm yet distorted.

The face of a girl who had lost everything and nothing in the stretch of a single night.

She slipped both hands into the water. Her skin looked pale and creamy below its surface. Not its usual warm bronze color. She fixed her gaze on the place where the water met the air, on the strange bend that made it seem as though her hands were in a different world beneath the water—

A world that moved more slowly and told stories.

*The water lies.*

She splashed some water onto her face and dragged her damp fingers through her hair. Then she lifted the lid from the small wooden container nearby and used a pinch of the ground mint, white pepper, and crushed rock salt stored within to cleanse her mouth of sleep.

"You're awake. After you arrived so late last night, I didn't think you would rise so early."

Shahrzad turned to see Irsa standing beneath the open tent flap. A triangle of desert light silhouetted her sister's slender frame.

Irsa smiled, her gamine features coming into focus. "You never used to wake for breakfast before." She ducked into the tent, securing the tent flap closed behind her.

"Who can sleep with that damnable goat shrieking outside?" Shahrzad flicked water at Irsa to divert her inevitable onslaught of questions.

"You mean Farbod?"

"You've named the little beast?" Shahrzad grinned as she began plaiting the tangled waves of her hair into a braid.

"He's quite sweet." Irsa frowned. "You should give him a chance."

"Please tell Farbod that—should he persist in his early morning recitals—my favorite meal is stewed goat, served in a sauce of pomegranates and crushed walnuts."

"Ha!" Irsa took a long stretch of twine from the pocket of her wrinkled *sirwal* trowsers. "I suppose we shouldn't forget we're now in the presence of royalty." She bound the length of twine around the end of Shahrzad's braid. "I'll warn Farbod not to further offend Khorasan's illustrious calipha."

Shahrzad glanced over her shoulder into Irsa's pale eyes.

"You've gotten so tall," she said quietly. "When did you get so tall?"

Irsa wrapped both arms around her sister's waist. "I've missed you." Her fingertips grazed the hilt of the dagger, and she pulled back in alarm. "Why are you carrying—"

"Is Baba awake yet?" Shahrzad smiled overbrightly. "Can you take me to see him?"

The night of the storm, Shahrzad had ridden with Tariq and Rahim to a hilltop outside Rey, in search of her father.

She'd been unprepared for what they'd found.

Jahandar al-Khayzuran had been curled in a puddle around an old, leather-bound book.

His bare feet and hands were burned. Red and raw and abraded. His hair was falling out in clumps. The rain had gathered them in the mud, smashing the strands against wet stone, like so many discarded things.

Her sister's dappled horse was long-since dead. Its throat had been slashed. The blood had drained in rivulets from a vicious wound at its neck. Veins of mud and drifting ash had melded with the crimson to form a sinister tracery across the hillside.

Shahrzad would never forget the image of her father's huddled body against the red-and-grey slope.

When she'd tried to pry Jahandar's fingers away from the book, he'd cried out in a language she'd never heard him speak before. His eyes had rolled back into his head, and his lashes had fluttered closed, never to open again, not once in the four days since.

And until they did, Shahrzad refused to leave him.

She had to know her father was safe. She had to know what he had done.

No matter what—or whom—she'd left behind in Rey.

"Baba?" Shahrzad said softly, as she knelt beside him in his small tent.

He shuddered in his sleep, his fingers wrapping tighter around the ancient tome clutched in his arms. Even in his delirium, Jahandar had refused to relinquish the book. Not a soul had been permitted to touch it.

Irsa sighed. She stooped next to Shahrzad and handed her a tumbler of water.

Shahrzad held the cup to her father's cracked lips. She waited until she felt him swallow. He muttered to himself, then turned back on his side, tucking the book farther beneath his blankets.

"What did you put in this?" Shahrzad asked Irsa. "It smells nice."

"Just some fresh mint and honey. Also a few tea herbs and a bit of milk. You said he hasn't eaten anything in a few days. I thought it might help." Irsa shrugged.

"It's a good idea. I should have thought of it."

"Don't scold yourself. It doesn't suit you. And . . . you've done more than enough." Irsa spoke with a wisdom beyond her fourteen years. "Baba will wake soon. I—know it." She bit her lip, her tone lacking conviction. "Calm is needed to heal his wounds. And time."

Shahrzad said nothing as she studied her father's hands. The burns there had blistered alongside bruised purples and garish reds.

*What did he do on the night of the storm?*

*What have we done?*

"You should eat. You barely ate anything when you arrived last night," Irsa interrupted Shahrzad's thoughts.

Before she could protest, Irsa removed the tumbler from Shahrzad's hand, hauling her to her feet and dragging her into the dunes beyond their father's tent. The scent of roasting meat hung heavy in the desert air, the smoke above them an aimless cloud. Silken grains of sand sifted between Shahrzad's toes, just near too hot to bear. Harsh rays of sunlight blurred everything they touched.

As they walked, Shahrzad glanced around the Badawi camp through slitted eyes, studying the hustle and bustle of mostly smiling faces; people carrying bushels of grain and bundles of goods from one corner to the next. The children seemed happy enough, though it was impossible to ignore the gleaming assortment of weaponry—the swords and axes and arrows—lying in the shadow of curing animal skins. Impossible to ignore them or their unassailable meaning . . .

Preparations for the coming war.

*"And I shall take from you these lives, a thousandfold."*

Shahrzad stiffened, then drew back her shoulders, refusing to burden her sister with these troubles. Such troubles were meant for those with unique abilities.

Those like Musa Zaragoza, the magus from the Fire Temple.

Though it took effort, Shahrzad shrugged off the curse's interminable weight. She walked with Irsa through the enclave of tents toward the largest, at center. It was an impressive structure, patchworked though it was: a hodgepodge of sun-worn colors, with a faded pennant at its apex, gamboling about in the breeze. A hooded sentry cloaked in roughspun stood at the tent's entrance.

"No weapons." The soldier's hand clamped down on Shahrzad's shoulder with the force of a lifelong aggressor. The sort who enjoyed his role far more than he should.

Despite her wiser inclinations, Shahrzad's response was immediate and automatic. She shoved his hand away, her scowl set.

*I am in no mood for boorish men. Or their warmongering.*

"Weapons are not permitted in the sheikh's tent." The soldier reached for her dagger, his eyes glittering with an unspoken threat.

"Touch me again, and I'll—"

"Shazi!" Irsa moved to placate the soldier. "Please excuse my—"

The soldier pushed Irsa back. Without a moment's thought, Shahrzad slammed both fists into his chest. He staggered to one side, his nostrils flaring. Behind her, she heard men begin to shout.

"What are you doing, Shahrzad!" Irsa cried, her shock at her sister's recklessness etched across her face.

Enraged, the soldier took hold of Shahrzad's forearm. She braced herself for the coming fight, her toes curled and her knuckles clenched.

"Let go of her immediately!" A tall shadow loomed upon the soldier.

*Perfect.*

Shahrzad winced, a flash of guilt warring with her fury.

"I don't need your help, Tariq," she said through gritted teeth.

"I'm not helping you." He strode closer, aiming a brief but quelling stare in her direction. His unconcealed pain was raw enough to rob her of mettle.

*Will he never forgive me?*

The soldier turned to Tariq with a deference that would, under normal circumstances, irritate Shahrzad immensely. "Apologies, *sahib*, but she refused to—"

"Release her at once. I didn't ask for excuses. Follow orders or be met with the consequences, soldier."

The soldier released her with reluctance. Shahrzad shoved off his grasp. Steeling herself with a breath, she faced those nearby. Rahim stood at Tariq's shoulder; several young men were at his opposing flank. One was a reed-thin boy sporting the guise of a much older man. His beard was growing in patches over a long, lean face, and his comically stern eyebrows were cut over ice-cold eyes.

Eyes that watched her with abject hatred.

Her fingers shifted toward her dagger.

"Thank you, Tariq," Irsa said, since Shahrzad had yet to offer a shred of gratitude.

"Of course," he replied with an awkward nod.

Shahrzad chewed at the inside of her cheek. "I—"

"Don't trouble yourself, Shazi. We're beyond such things." Tariq knocked the cowl of his *rida'* back and ducked through the entrance of the tent, sparing himself more of her company. The boy with the ice-cold eyes glowered at Shahrzad before following suit. Rahim paused beside her, his expression grim, as though he had expected better. Then he stepped closer to Irsa, his head tilted in question. Her sister sent half a smile his way. Sighing softly, Rahim trudged past them into the tent, without a single word.

Irsa elbowed Shahrzad in the ribs. "What's wrong with you?" she admonished in a whisper. "We're guests here. You can't behave in such a manner."

Chastened, Shahrzad nodded curtly before striding through the cavernous hollow.

It took her eyes time to adjust to the sudden darkness. A series of brass lamps hung at lazy intervals from the wooden rafters above, their thready light pale after the desert sun. At the far end of the tent was a long, low table, crafted of roughhewn teakwood. Worn woolen cushions were thrown about in haphazard piles. Screaming children scurried past Shahrzad, blind to all but their single-minded quest for the most esteemed position at the breakfast table.

Seated at the very center of this teeth-rattling tumult was an old man with a keen pair of eyes and an unkempt beard. When he saw Shahrzad, he smiled at her with a surprising amount of warmth. To his left was a woman of similar age with a long braid of muted copper. At his right sat Shiva's father, Reza bin-Latief. Shahrzad's stomach tensed, her flash of guilt resurfacing. She'd seen him last night, but in the clamor of their arrival the exchange had been brief, and she was not yet certain she was ready to face Shiva's father.

So soon after failing to exact revenge for the murder of his daughter.

So soon after falling in love with the very boy who had murdered her.

Deciding it was best to avoid unwanted attention, Shahrzad kept her head down and took the cushion beside Irsa, across from Tariq and Rahim.

She avoided the gazes of those around her, especially that of the boy with the ice-fire eyes, who took every opportunity to burn through her with the heat of his discomfiting stare. The desire to draw attention to his behavior was always at the forefront of her mind, but Irsa's earlier admonition continued to ring true: she was a guest here.

And she could not behave in such a reckless manner.

Not with the welfare of her family at stake.

A leg of roasted lamb was placed at the center of the well-worn table. Its serving platter was an immense affair of hammered silver, dented on all sides from age and use. Thick slices of *barbari* bread, coated with butter and rolled in black sesame seeds, were left in baskets nearby, alongside chipped bowls of whole radishes and slabs of salted goat cheese. Squabbling children reached for the radishes and tore hearty chunks of *barbari* in half before grabbing at the meat with their bare hands. Their elders crushed stems of fresh mint before pouring dark streams of tea over the fragrant leaves.

When Shahrzad chanced to look up, she found the old man with the keen eyes studying her, another warm smile pooling across his lips. The gap between his two front teeth was pronounced, and, at first glance, it made him appear almost foolish.

Though Shahrzad was not the least bit fooled.

"So, my friend . . . *this* is Shahrzad," the old man said.

*To whom is he speaking?*

"I was right—" The old man cackled. "She *is* very beautiful."

Shahrzad's eyes flitted down both sides of the table. They stopped on Tariq.

His broad shoulders were rigid; his chiseled jaw was tight. He exhaled through his nose and lifted his gaze to hers.

"She is," Tariq agreed in a resigned voice.

The old man quirked his head at Shahrzad. "You've caused a lot of trouble, beautiful one."

Despite the reassuring hand Irsa placed atop hers, Shahrzad's ire rose like embers being stoked to flame.

Aware she lacked grace in that moment, Shahrzad chose to say nothing. She rolled her tongue in her mouth. Pinched her lower lip between her teeth.

*I am a guest here. I cannot behave as I desire.*

*No matter how angry and alone I may feel.*

The old man smiled again. Ever wider. Ever more gap-toothed.

*Infuriating.*

"Are you worth it?"

Shahrzad cleared her throat. "Pardon?" she said, keeping tight rein on her emotions.

The boy with the ice-fire eyes watched with the rapt attention of a hawk.

"Are you worth all this trouble, beautiful one?" the old man repeated in maddening singsong.

Irsa wrapped a pleading hand around Shahrzad's fingers, cold sweat slicking her palm.

Shahrzad could not risk her sister's safety. Not in a camp filled with unknowns. Unknowns who could just as soon as toss her family into the desert for an errant word. Or slit their throats at a misread glance. No. Shahrzad could not put her father's dubious health in jeopardy. Not for all the world.

She smiled slowly, taking time to subdue her fury. "I think beauty is rarely worth the trouble." Shahrzad gripped Irsa's hand tighter in sisterly solidarity. "But *I* am worth a great deal more than what you see." Her tone was airy despite the veiled rebuke.

Without hesitation, the old man threw back his head and laughed. "To be sure!" His face shone with merriment. "Welcome to my home, Shahrzad al-Khayzuran. I am Omar al-Sadiq, and you are my guest. While within these borders, you will always be treated as such. But bear in mind: a calipha in silk or a beggar in the street makes no difference to me. Welcome." He dipped his head and brushed his fingertips along his brow with a broad flourish.

Shahrzad released a pent-up breath. It escaped her in a rush of air, taking with it the tension from her shoulders and stomach. Her grin stretching farther, Shahrzad bowed in return, touching her right hand to her forehead.

Shiva's father watched their exchange with a blank expression, his elbows folded against the table's weathered edge. "Shazi-*jan*," he began in a somber tone.

He caught her just as Shahrzad reached for a piece of *barbari*. "Yes, Uncle Reza?" She lifted her brows in question, her hand hovering above the breadbasket.

Reza's features turned pensive. "I'm very glad you are here— that you are safe."

"Thank you. I'm very grateful to everyone for keeping my family safe. And for taking such excellent care of Baba."

He nodded, then leaned forward, steepling his hands beneath his chin. "Of course. Your family has always been my family. As mine has always been yours."

"Yes," Shahrzad said quietly. "It has."

"So," Reza said, lines of consternation bracketing his mouth, "it pains me greatly to ask you this—as I thought you might have been remiss when you arrived last night—but I have swallowed your insult for as long as I can endure it."

Shahrzad's entire body froze, her fingers still poised above the bread. The tension renewed its grip on her body, guilt coiling around her stomach with snakelike savagery.

"Shahrzad . . ." Reza bin-Latief's voice had lost any hint of kindness; any warmth in the man she'd considered a second father was gone. "Why are you sitting at this table—breaking bread with me—wearing the ring of the boy who *murdered* my daughter?"

It was a cutting accusation.

It sliced through the crowd like a scythe through a sea of grain.

Shahrzad's fingers pressed tight over the standard of the two crossed swords. Tight enough to cause pain.

She blinked once. Twice.

Tariq cleared his throat. The sound echoed through the sudden stillness. "Uncle—Uncle Reza—"

No. She could not let Tariq save her. Not again.

Never again.

"I'm . . . I'm sorry," she said, her mouth dry.

But she wasn't. Not for this. She was sorry for a hundred things. A thousand things.

An entire city of untendered apologies.

But she would never be sorry for this.

"Don't be sorry, Shahrzad," Reza continued in the same cold voice. The voice of a stranger. "Decide."

Mumbling her regrets, Shahrzad pushed to her feet.

She didn't stop to think. Clinging to the remains of her dignity, she stumbled away from the table and into the blazing desert sun. Her sandals caught in the hot sand, hefting it behind her, striking her calves with each step.

A large, calloused hand took hold of her shoulder, halting her.

She glanced up, shielding her eyes from the blinding light.

The soldier. The lifelong aggressor.

"Get out of my way," she whispered, fighting to leash her wrath. "Now."

His lips curved upward with a leisurely kind of malice. He refused to move.

Shahrzad grabbed his wrist to shove it aside.

The rough-spun linen of his *rida'* rolled up to his elbow, revealing a brand seared into his inner forearm.

The mark of the scarab.

The mark of the Fida'i assassins who had stolen into her chamber in Rey and tried to kill her.

With a gasp, Shahrzad ran. Clumsily, mindlessly, her only thought, of escape.

Somewhere in the distance, she heard Irsa's voice calling for her.

Still, she refused to stop.

She ran into their tiny tent, throwing the door fold shut with a resounding slap.

Her shallow breaths rebounded across the three walls. Shahrzad raised her right hand into a shaft of light filtering through a tent seam. She watched it catch on the muted gold of her ring.

*I don't belong here. A guest in a prison of sand and sun.*

*But I need to keep my family safe; I need to find a way to break the curse.*

*And return home to Khalid.*

Alas, she did not know whom she could trust. Until Shahrzad knew who this Sheikh Omar al-Sadiq was and why a Fida'i assassin lurked in his camp, she must remain careful. For it was clear she did not have an ally in Reza bin-Latief as she once had had. And Shahrzad refused to put her burdens on Tariq. It was not his place to keep her or her family safe. No. That duty remained with her, and her alone.

Her eyes flashed around before fixing on the pool of water in the copper basin.

*Exist beneath the water.*

*Move slowly. Tell stories.*

*Lie.*

Without a thought for sentimentality, Shahrzad yanked the ring from her finger.

*Breathe.*

She closed her eyes and listened to the silent cry of her heart.

"Here." Irsa dropped the tent flap and moved to Shahrzad's side. She needed no direction. Nor did she offer any kind of reproach. In a trice, she'd unraveled the length of twine binding Shahrzad's braid. The sisters locked eyes as Irsa took the ring from Shahrzad's hand and fashioned a necklace from the twine.

Wordlessly, Irsa secured the necklace behind Shahrzad's throat and tucked the ring beneath her *qamis*. "No more secrets."

*"Some secrets are safer behind lock and key."*

Shahrzad nodded to her sister, Khalid's words a low whisper in her ear. Not in warning. But in reminder.

She would do whatever needed to be done to keep her family safe.

Even lie to her own sister.

"What do you want to know?"

# ALWAYS

H<small>E WAS ALONE.</small>

And he should take advantage of the time, before the demands of the day stole these moments of solitude from him.

Khalid stepped through the sands of the training courtyard.

As soon as he reached for his *shamshir*, he knew his hands would bleed.

No matter. It was of little consequence.

Moments spent in idleness were moments left to thought.

Moments left to memory.

The sword separated from its sheath with the soft *hiss* of metal on metal. His palms burned; his fingers ached. Still, he gripped the hilt tighter.

When he turned toward the sun, the light struck his eyes, searing his vision. Khalid cursed under his breath.

His growing sensitivity to light was a recurring problem of late. An unfortunate effect of continued sleeplessness. Soon, those around him would become all too aware of this issue. He was too comfortable in the dark—a hollow-eyed creature that slithered and slunk through the broken hallways of a once-majestic palace.

As the *faqir* had cautioned him, this behavior would be construed as madness.

The mad boy-king of Khorasan. The monster. The murderer.

Khalid squeezed his burning eyes shut. Against his better judgment, he let his mind drift to memory.

He recalled being a boy of seven, standing in the shadows, watching his brother, Hassan, learn the art of swordplay. When his father had finally permitted Khalid to learn alongside Hassan, Khalid had been surprised; his father had often disregarded such requests in the past.

"You might as well learn something of value. I suppose even a bastard should know how to fight." His father's scorn for Khalid seemed endless.

Strangely, the one and only time his father had ever shown pride in him had been the day, several years later, when Khalid had bested Hassan with a sword.

But the following afternoon, his father had forbidden Khalid from studying alongside Hassan any further.

He'd sent Hassan to study with the best. And left Khalid to fend for himself.

That night, an angry eleven-year-old prince of Khorasan had pledged to become the best swordsman in the kingdom. Once he had, then perhaps his father would realize the past did not give him the right to deny his son a future.

No. That would take a great deal more.

And the day he held a sword to his father's throat, his father would know it.

Khalid smiled to himself as the memory brought back with it the bittersweet taste of childish fury.

Yet another promise he'd failed to keep.

Yet another failed revenge.

He did not know why he was remembering these things on this particular morning. Perhaps it was because of that boy and his sister from yesterday.

Kamyar and Shiva.

Whatever it was that drew Khalid to their door had also bade him to stay and help. It was not the first occasion on which he had done such a thing. Since the storm, there had been several times Khalid had ventured into sections of his city, cloaked in the anonymity of silence and shadow.

The first day, he had wandered into a beleaguered quarter of Rey, not far from the souk. While there, he had given food to the wounded. Two days past, he'd helped repair a well. His hands—unaccustomed to the harshness of physical labor—had bled and blistered from the strain.

Yesterday was the first time he had spent in the company of children.

At first, Kamyar had reminded Khalid of Shahrzad. So much so that, even now, it brought the beginnings of another smile to Khalid's face. The tiny boy was bold and insolent. Unafraid. The best and the worst of Shahrzad.

Then, as the hours had passed, it was the girl who'd brought to mind Shazi's spirit the most.

Because she hadn't trusted him. Not in the slightest.

She'd watched Khalid out of the corner of her eye. She'd waited for him to betray her—to shed his snakeskin and strike. Like a wounded animal, she'd warily taken food and drink, never dropping her guard, not even for a moment.

She was smart, and she loved her brother with a fierceness Khalid almost envied.

He'd appreciated her quiet honesty the most. And he'd wanted to do more for their family. So much more than clear their tiny home of destruction and leave behind a pittance in a leather pouch. But he'd known nothing would ever be enough.

Because nothing could ever replace what they'd lost.

Khalid opened his eyes.

With his back to the sun, he began his drill.

The *shamshir* cut through the sky in swooping arcs. In flashes of silver and streaks of white light. It whistled around him as he tried to quiet the clamor of his thoughts.

But it wasn't enough.

He put both hands on the hilt and twisted it in two.

The blades were forged of damascene steel, tempered in the Bluefires of Warharan. He'd commissioned them himself. None were their equal.

A sword in either hand, Khalid continued moving across the sand.

Now, the sound of dully shrieking metal rasped about his head with the fury of a desert sirocco.

Still, it wasn't enough.

A trickle of blood slid down his arm.

He felt nothing. He only saw it.

Because nothing hurt like missing her.

He suspected nothing ever would.

"Has it come to this?"

Khalid did not turn around.

"Have Khorasan's coffers been so depleted?" Jalal continued to jest, though his tone sounded oddly forced.

His back to his cousin, Khalid wiped his bloodied palms on the ends of his crimson *tikka* sash.

"Please tell me the Caliph of Khorasan—the King of Kings—can still afford to procure a set of gauntlets or, at the very least, a single glove." Jalal sauntered into view, a dark eyebrow crooked high into his forehead.

Khalid returned his *shamshir* to its sheath and glanced at the captain of his Royal Guard. "If you need a glove, I can procure one for you. But only one. I am not made of gold, Captain al-Khoury."

Laughing, Jalal propped his hands on the hilt of his scimitar, his grip tight. "Procure one for yourself, *sayyidi*. It appears you are sorely in need of it. What happened?" He nodded at Khalid's bloodstained palms.

Khalid tugged his linen *qamis* back over his head.

"Does it have anything to do with you disappearing yet again yesterday?" Jalal pressed, his agitation becoming all the more evident.

When Khalid failed to respond a second time, Jalal stepped before him.

"Khalid." All pretense at lightheartedness was gone. "The palace is in shambles. The city is a disaster. You cannot continue disappearing for hours on end, especially without a detachment of bodyguards. Father cannot continue lying to everyone about where you are, and I . . . cannot continue lying to him." Jalal ran his fingers through his wavy mop of hair, further setting it into disarray.

Khalid paused to study his cousin.

And was alarmed by what he saw.

Jalal's usual veneer of smug self-satisfaction was absent. A scraggly beard shadowed his jawline. His ordinarily pristine cloak was wrinkled and smudged, and his hands seemed on an unending quest for something to grasp—a sword hilt, a sash knot, a collar loop . . . anything.

In all his eighteen years, Khalid had never known Jalal to fidget.

"What's the matter with you?"

Jalal guffawed loudly. Too loudly. It rang so patently false that it only succeeded in disturbing Khalid further.

"Are you in earnest or in jest?" Jalal crossed his arms.

"In earnest." Khalid took a cautious breath. "For now."

"You want me to confide in you? I must confess, I'm galled by the irony."

"I don't want you to confide in me. I want you to tell me what's wrong and stop wasting my time. If you need someone to hold your hand, seek out one of the many young women who pine outside your chamber door."

"Ah, there it is." A bleak expression settled on Jalal's face. "Even you."

At that, Khalid's irritation reached a breaking point. "Take a bath, Jalal. A long one." He began striding away.

"I'm going to be a father, Khalid-*jan*."

Khalid stopped short. He turned in place, his heel forming a deep divot in the sand.

Jalal shrugged. A rueful smile tugged at one corner of his lips.

"You . . . unconscionable imbecile," Khalid said.

"That's kind."

"Are you seeking permission to marry her?"

"She won't have me." He tugged his fingers through his hair again. "It appears you aren't the only one to have noticed the harem of women outside my chamber door."

"I like her already. At the very least, she's wont to learn from her mistakes." Khalid leaned into the shadows against the stone wall and shot a daggered glance at his cousin.

"That's also kind."

"Kindness is not among my celebrated virtues."

"No." Jalal laughed drily. "It's not. Especially not of late." His laughter gave way to a sobering pause. "Khalid-*jan*, you do believe me when I say my only thought was to keep Shazi safe when I told that boy—"

"I believe you." Khalid's voice was soft yet sharp. "As I said before, there is no need to discuss it further."

The two young men stood in awkward silence for a time, staring into the sand.

"Tell your father." Khalid pushed off the wall to take his leave. "He'll make certain she and the child are provided for. Should you need anything else, you have only to ask." He began walking away.

"I love her. I think I want to marry her."

Again, Khalid stopped short. This time, he did not turn around.

The words stung—the ease with which they fell from his cousin's lips. The realization of Khalid's many shortcomings when it came to Shahrzad. The reminder of all the lost possibilities.

His chest tight, Khalid let Jalal's words settle on the breeze . . .

Waiting to hear if they had the tenor of truth to them.

"You think?" Khalid said finally. "Or you know."

The slightest hesitation. "I think I know."

"Don't equivocate, Jalal. It's insulting. To me and to her."

"It's not meant to be insulting. It's my attempt at honesty— a trait I know you hold in high esteem," Jalal retorted. "At present—with no knowledge of her true feelings on the matter— it's the most I can manage. I love her. I think I want to be with her."

"Be careful, Captain al-Khoury. Those words mean different things to different people. Make sure they mean the right things to you."

"Don't be an ass. I mean them."

"When did you mean them?"

"I mean them now. Isn't that what matters?"

A muscle worked in Khalid's jaw. "Now is easy. It's easy to say what you want in a passing moment. That's why a harem waits outside your door and the mother of your child won't have you." He strode back toward the palace.

"Then what *is* the right answer, *sayyidi*? What should I have said?" Jalal called out to the sky in exasperation.

"Always."

"Always?"

"And don't speak to me of this again until it is!"

# STORIES AND SECRETS

I RSA CLAPPED BOTH HANDS OVER HER MOUTH, STIFLING a cry.

She watched in amazement as her sister trailed the tiny, shabby rug around the center of their tent, using nothing but the tips of her fingers as a guide.

The magic carpet swirled through the air with the languid grace of a falling leaf. Then, with a gentle flick of her wrist, Shahrzad sent the floating mat of wool back to the ground.

"Well?" Shahrzad said, staring up at her with a look of worry.

"Merciful God." Irsa sank down beside her. "And the magus from the Fire Temple was the one to teach you this?"

Shahrzad shook her head. "He merely gave me the carpet and said Baba had passed along his abilities to me. But I need to speak to him further about it, very soon. I have . . . many important questions for Musa-*effendi.*"

"Then you intend to seek him out?"

"Yes." She nodded firmly. "Once I determine how best to travel to the Fire Temple without being seen."

"Perhaps"—Irsa hesitated—"perhaps when you go, you could

speak to Musa-*effendi* about Baba as well? In the event that he . . ." She trailed off, unwilling to finish the thought she knew they were both most concerned with at the moment.

The thought that their father would never awaken from the effects of whatever foul misdeed had befallen him the night of the storm.

What would happen to them if Baba died? What would happen to *her*?

Irsa folded her hands over her knees and chided herself for such selfish thoughts amidst such suffering. This was neither the time nor the place to worry about herself. Not when there were so many others to worry about. Most especially Baba.

As Shahrzad leaned forward to stow the magic carpet beneath her belongings, the twine around her neck slipped into view.

The ring stayed safely hidden, but its story still begged to be told. And Irsa could not help but pry.

"How could you forgive him, Shazi?" Irsa asked softly. "For what he did to Shiva? For—everything?"

Shahrzad's breath caught. In one quick motion, she turned to Irsa.

"Do you trust me, *Jirjirak*?" Shahrzad took Irsa's hands in her own.

*Cricket.* Ever since she was a little girl, Irsa had hated that nickname. It hearkened back to a time when she'd been cursed with reedy legs and a voice to match. Shahrzad was the only one who could use the dreaded sobriquet and not elicit a cringe—or something worse—from her.

For the tenth time in as many moments, Irsa studied her

34

sister's face, seeking an answer she hoped to understand. Her sister was just as lovely as ever, though her features had changed in the few short months she'd been at the palace. Not by much, and not in a way most people would notice. Her cheeks had lost some of their roundness, and the bronze of her skin had lost a bit of its glow. Thankfully, her chin was just as stubborn, her nose just as pert. But a shadow had fallen over her face; some kind of weight she refused to share. Her hazel eyes looked almost lucent in the nearby lamplight. Their colors had always been so changeable. So unpredictable. Much like her sister's moods. One moment, she was bright and full of laughter, ready for any kind of mischief. The next, she was stark and serious, prepared to battle to the death.

Irsa had never known what to expect from Shahrzad.

But trust had never been an issue. At least not for Irsa.

"Of course I trust you," she said. "But can you not tell me—"

"It isn't my secret to tell, Irsa-*jan*."

Irsa bit her lower lip and looked away.

"I'm sorry," Shahrzad said. "I don't wish to hide these matters from you. But if anyone were to discover that you knew of such things, they might hurt you to learn the truth, and . . . I couldn't live through that."

Irsa drew back. "I'm not as weak as you think I am."

"I never said you were weak."

Irsa's smile was small and fleeting. "Some things do not have to be said. You didn't have to tell me you were in love with Khalid Ibn al-Rashid. And I didn't have to tell you I cried myself to sleep for weeks after you left. Love speaks for itself."

Shahrzad pulled her knees to her chest and blinked at Irsa in silence. Sighing to herself, Irsa collected her satchel of tea herbs and reached for a sprig of fresh mint. "Are you coming with me to see Baba?"

With a brisk nod, Shahrzad unfurled to her feet.

A dry desert wind circulated through the Badawi camp. It blew spirals of sand around the warren of billowing tents. Irsa tucked her braid into her *qamis* to prevent its tail from lashing her face.

Shahrzad unleashed a colorful stream of curses when the end of her plait whipped against her cheek, tousling her hair loose. Black waves coiled above her head in a wicked tangle.

"Oh my." Irsa suppressed a grin at her sister's language. "Who taught you to say such things? Was it the caliph?"

"I hate it here!"

Though Shahrzad's unwillingness to answer even the most innocuous question stung, Irsa ignored the twinge. "Give it some time. You'll find it's not so terrible." She linked arms with her sister and pulled her close.

"Of all places, why are we in this godforsaken desert? Why has the old sheikh granted us refuge?" Shahrzad spoke in as low a voice as the wind would permit.

"I am not privy to the details. I only know he sold Uncle Reza horses and weapons. His tribe trades in both. Perhaps that is why we are allowed to stay." She paused in thought. "Or perhaps it is merely a result of his closeness with Tariq. The sheikh treats him as though he were a son."

"So then, has he not joined forces with Tariq and the other soldiers? Is he not involved in the war effort?" Shahrzad's brows drew together in confusion.

"I do not think so," Irsa retorted. "But when I attend the next war council, I'll be sure to gather more details for you."

Shahrzad shoved tendrils of hair behind an ear and rolled her eyes.

As they continued crossing the sands toward their father's tent, Irsa watched her sister make a slow scan of their surroundings. Her eyes trailed Shahrzad's until they fell upon a thin figure in the distance, mirroring their measured study.

A bony elbow jabbed Irsa's side. "Who is that boy?"

"Ouch!" Irsa jabbed back. "You mean Spider?"

"What?"

"Oh, I call him Spider, on account of his gangly limbs and his tendency to lurk. He arrived with the Emir of Karaj. I believe he's the emir's distant relative. I think his name is Teymur or Tajvar or something of the sort." She waved a dismissive hand.

"He has a . . . disconcerting look about him."

Irsa frowned. "He's a bit odd, but he's harmless, Shazi."

Shahrzad pinched her lips together and said nothing.

Irsa pulled back the flap, and they ducked inside their father's tent. In the arid heat of the afternoon, the darkness within had grown even more stifling. They lit an oil lamp and prepared another tumbler of water, fresh mint, and tea herbs. Their father choked down the mixture as he had that morning, still muttering and clutching the ridiculous book in his arms.

Shahrzad fanned herself with both hands. "He's drenched in sweat. We should change his wrappings and wash his face and neck."

Irsa poured water into an earthen bowl and removed clean strips of linen from her satchel. She bent to swirl the cloth in the cool water. "Are you going to tell Baba about the magic carpet? He would be so excited to learn he's passed his abilities on to you." Smiling to herself, Irsa wrung out the cloth.

"Ba—Baba?" Shahrzad began. Shahrzad was leaning over him, looking perplexed. A flash of something passed across her face. Alarm?

Irsa dropped the linen and swiveled to her father's side. "What's wrong?" Irsa asked. "Did he open his eyes?"

Shahrzad shook her head. "I—no. I thought I heard something outside, but I must have been mistaken." The ends of her lips turned into the beginnings of a smile. "I know the desert enjoys playing tricks on a weary mind. If you'll start with Baba's face, I'll wash his arms."

"Are you quite certain?" Irsa pressed.

"Quite." It was a firm rejoinder, one that could not be ignored.

And though Irsa set about working in silence with Shahrzad to cleanse their father's skin of sweat and grime—

She knew her sister was lying.

"What happened?" Irsa whispered, the instant their father's tent flap fluttered shut behind them. "Tell me the truth, Shazi, or I'll—"

Shahrzad wrapped a hand around Irsa's wrist to pull her near. "I thought I heard something outside the tent," she replied in a hushed tone. "And I didn't want anyone to overhear us speaking about matters of import."

"You think someone is *spying* on us?" Irsa couldn't imagine why anyone would care to listen to their conversation.

"I don't know. It's possible."

Tugging the strap of her satchel tight across her body, Irsa quickened her pace. Her gaze drifted from side to side. For the few weeks she'd been here, she'd never felt unsafe. Not even for a moment. She spent most mornings with Aisha and the children, and in the afternoons Rahim was teaching her to ride horses more proficiently.

Who would threaten two young girls of common birth?

As Irsa cut a sideways glance at her sister, she remembered.

Shahrzad was no longer the mere daughter of a lowly keeper of books.

She was the Calipha of Khorasan.

An asset for any enemy of Khalid Ibn al-Rashid.

Of which there were many.

In the same instant the realization dawned on her, Irsa banished the thought.

Shahrzad had been here for only a day. Her sister was being ridiculous. Paranoid. Clearly the result of living alongside a monster and fearing for her life on a daily basis.

Irsa bent through the opening of their tent.

A clammy hand grabbed her by the neck and flung her inside.

She squealed.

Long fingers gripped her by the nape. Hot breath washed across her skin.

"It wasn't supposed to be you," a low voice rasped in her ear. "I'm sorry."

She blinked hard and fast, forcing her eyes to adjust to the dim light.

Spider?

"What are you doing?" Irsa cried.

"Let her go." Shahrzad stood at the entrance, one hand on the jeweled dagger at her waist. Her features were impassive. But something savage moved deep in her eyes. As though she had expected such a threat.

The thought chilled Irsa to the marrow of her bones.

"Is that an order, my lady?" Spider spat in Shahrzad's direction.

"No. It's a promise."

"A promise of what?"

Shahrzad angled her head ever so slightly. "That, if you let my sister go, I'll stay here with you. I'll listen to your grievances. Whatever I can do to rectify them, I'll do. I promise."

He blew another hot spate of air against Irsa's neck. "I don't believe you." She could feel him trembling behind her.

"You should." Shahrzad took a step forward. "Because I wasn't finished. It's also a promise that, if you don't let my sister go, *you* will be the one to hear *my* grievances. And mine are not of words, but of fists and steel."

Spider rasped a laugh. "Fitting. As you are the whore of a bloodthirsty monster."

Shahrzad flinched. And in that tiny flicker of pain, Irsa saw a wellspring.

Outraged, Irsa began struggling against him. He banded

his forearms tighter around her waist and neck. She started to choke.

"Irsa!" Shahrzad held up her hands in surrender. "Let her go!"

"Give me your dagger."

"Let her go, and I'll give you my dagger." Shahrzad removed the blade from her waistband.

"Your dagger first!" Spider said, his fingers digging into the tender skin beneath Irsa's ear.

"Sha—Shahrzad!" Irsa croaked.

A bead of sweat trickled down Shahrzad's brow. "I'll give it to you. Just let Irsa go. Your quarrel is with me."

"Drop it first, and she can leave. But if she goes to get help— if I so much as hear the White Falcon outside this tent—I'll kill you."

"She won't get Tariq." The dagger plinked by her sister's feet. "She won't do anything."

Irsa felt him relax in the same instant her chest pulled tight from within.

Shahrzad thought her incapable of *anything*.

Completely and utterly useless.

And, in truth, what had she done to prove otherwise?

Spider loosened his hold on her neck. "Kick it toward me, and I'll let her go."

Shahrzad gave Irsa a small smile of reassurance, then toed the dagger in his direction.

He released Irsa and shoved her toward the entrance.

When Irsa looked back at Shahrzad in hesitation, her sister spurred her onward with a warning glance.

Irsa wanted to stay. Wanted to beg Spider to see reason.

But she was afraid. She'd already cost Shahrzad her dagger and didn't know what assistance she could provide beyond a poignant plea.

So she burst into the desert sun, her heart clamoring in her chest and her pride laid waste at her feet.

Frantic, she began searching for help. The eyes she most needed to find belonged to a tall boy with broad shoulders and the easy smile of a summer afternoon. A boy who had loved her sister since they were children.

A boy who would thrash first and ask questions later.

Tariq would know what to do. Tariq would wring Spider's scrawny neck.

Irsa stumbled through the sand toward Tariq's tent, the blood roaring in her ears.

"Irsa?"

She tried to ignore the familiar voice nearby. The voice of the boy she most *wanted* to find. A boy whose kind face she found herself searching for time and again. No. Irsa did not need *Rahim*. She needed Tariq—a boy of determination and action.

"Irsa?" Rahim fell into step beside her, his gait unfaltering. "Why are you running through—"

"Where is Tariq?" she gasped.

"On a scouting expedition to a nearby emirate." He angled into her path, his eyes narrowing. "Why? Is something wrong?"

Irsa shook her head, her fear spiking in a hot flash. "No, I just—I need Tariq!" Her gaze darted every which way, frantic.

"Why?"

A rush of air flew from her lips. "Because I have to do—*something*." She pushed past him. "You don't understand. Shazi—"

He took her by the shoulders, his touch strangely soothing. Strengthening. "Tell me what you need."

No. Neither of them was a leader. She'd always known Rahim to be a boy who followed. Just as she was a girl who ran. A girl who failed to do anything, save spare her own skin.

She should have grabbed Shahrzad's dagger. Or done *something*.

The guilt clawed at her stomach. Irsa began to tremble, even beneath the sweltering sun. She felt Rahim's grip tighten on her shoulders.

Offering more strength.

Irsa stood straight, clenching her fists.

Shazi would not give up. She would not give in to fear. Nor would she waver in the sand, like a ridiculous ninny. She would take action. Fight to the death. And be smart about it, as only Shahrzad could.

Though Irsa continued to shake, she kept her voice steady as she worked through the beginnings of a plan. "Did Tariq take his falcon with him?"

"No." A flicker of puzzlement passed across Rahim's face. "Zoraya scouted the terrain in advance this morning, so he left her behind to rest."

"Rahim"—Irsa took a breath—"will you do something for me?"

He did not even bother to reply. He simply held out his hand.

And Irsa took it.

# AN INDELIBLE LINE

Shahrzad REFUSED TO BE COWED BY THE GANGLY boy standing before her.

In another world—in another life—she might have pitied him.

But he'd threatened Irsa. An indelible line had been drawn.

And, despite his best efforts to conceal it, she could see his fingers shaking around her dagger.

*Move slowly.*

"What is your name?" she began in a quiet tone.

He sucked in a sharp breath. "I'll be the one to ask the questions."

She stood still as he paced around her in a circle.

His agitation was worsening.

"How?" With every erratic footfall, streams of light bounded across his face, casting his patchy beard in sinister shadow.

Shahrzad clasped her hands before her. "Pardon?"

"How did you survive?"

She chose her next words with care. "I told stories."

He halted midstep. His disdain was clear before he even spoke.

"You told *stories*? You expect me to believe that monster kept you alive because you *amused* him?"

Shahrzad leveled a withering stare in his direction. "Believe what you choose to believe. But the proof stands before you, all the same."

He made a sound of choked disbelief. She almost recoiled from its harshness. "Are you trying to provoke me? Are you truly that big a fool?"

For the second time, Shahrzad lifted her palms in a placating gesture. "I'm not trying to provoke you . . ." She waited patiently, hoping the boy would take the bait.

"Teymur. My name is Teymur."

"Teymur." Shahrzad curved her lips into a careful smile. "I'm not trying to provoke you," she repeated. "I'm trying to understand you."

A poor choice of words. Shahrzad realized it as soon as they passed into comprehension.

"*Understand* me?" Teymur snarled. "You couldn't possibly understand me!"

"Please just tell me—"

He charged at her. Long fingers closed around her throat like a cuff. Shahrzad wrapped both hands around his wrist, trying to stay his grip. She stared back into his flame-filled eyes, determined not to flinch.

She was not afraid. This boy—this skinny man-child—was far more afraid than she would ever be. The sweat fell in steady trickles down either side of his face.

"How could you possibly understand?" He was shaking so hard it made his voice quake. "You're *alive*. The monster let you live!"

With his other hand, he placed the tip of her dagger beside her chin. The blade was still ensconced in its jeweled sheath.

"Where did you get this?" Teymur examined the delicate etchings carved into the scabbard. He ran his thumb along the seed pearls and the tiny garnets embedded in the hilt. The emeralds at its base flashed with an evil light.

"Teymur—"

"Is it his?" His gaze moved from the dagger back to Shahrzad. "Did he give it to you?"

She said nothing.

"Answer me." He shook her by the throat. "You promised me answers!"

"Yes. He gave it to me."

"And if I kill you with it?" His voice drained to a whisper. "Like he killed my Roya."

Shahrzad swallowed thickly. She knew that name.

One of so many. One in a sea of scattered letters.

In a storm of remembrances.

"I'm so sorry."

"Don't you dare apologize!" The tips of his fingers pushed into her skin.

His pain radiated through Shahrzad, from his hand to her heart, touching an old wound that would never fully heal.

*Shiva.*

"What do you want from me?" she asked, her eyes squeezed shut, barring him from her pain, if only for a moment more.

"The truth."

She swallowed again. "What do you wish to know?"

"Where your loyalties lie. Do you matter to Khalid Ibn al-Rashid?" He spat the name as though it were a curse. "Does he care for you?"

"I cannot speak to his feelings. He guards them well." A half-truth. She could manage this, if pressed further. The blood returned to her clenched fingers in a rush.

"Then speak to your own. Does the monster matter to you?"

*Lie.*

"No." Shahrzad locked her jaw. "He does not."

"So you belong to the White Falcon still?"

"I belong to *me*."

"Where is your heart, Shahrzad al-Khayzuran?" His voice was coarse in its insistence.

*In an alley by the souk. In a night of oblivion.*

*In the promise of tomorrow.*

"With . . . Tariq Imran al-Ziyad." The lie burned on her tongue. "Where it always will be." She kept her eyes closed, knowing they might betray her.

Teymur took in a harsh breath. It rattled in his chest, then filled the space between them, hot and fetid. In, then out. Twice more.

At his silence, a sense of unease kindled within her.

He pulled her close. Too close. His warm breath prickled her forehead.

"Did the monster . . . hurt Roya?"

In his sudden closeness, she understood his meaning.

And was horrified by it.

Her eyes flashed open. "He didn't touch her."

He studied her in awful stillness. So very close. Her pulse ratcheted in her throat, pounding with a restless incessancy.

"You told him stories. As you are telling me stories now."

His resolve firmed as he spoke. And Shahrzad knew she could no longer stand idle. Knocking his arm aside, she rammed into his shoulder and made to flee.

With vicious precision, Teymur seized her tight, taking her feet out from under her and slamming Shahrzad to the ground. All the air was knocked from her chest. She gasped once, the pain in her side searing as she struggled to catch her breath.

For the first time, a cold wave of fear coursed down her back.

This skinny weasel of a boy was stronger than she. He was tall and wily. And she could not fight him off forever. Nor could she reason with him.

But perhaps there was another way. A way of diversion and lies.

A surge of fury chased after the fear. Shahrzad gripped the wrist at her throat, digging her nails into his skin.

Whatever lingering pity she might have had for him melted in her rage.

The indelible line had deepened to a chasm.

He was preying upon the basest of fears. A fear Shahrzad had long held in the darkest recesses of her mind.

"What are you doing, Teymur?" She fought to keep her voice steady.

The two sides of the man-child battled for control as he glared down at her. He was so very afraid, blustering and shuddering through this hard-won triumph.

She would not lie here in silence as he warred with his convictions.

"Are you going to rape me," Shahrzad demanded, "or are you merely trying to frighten me with the thought? And what do you hope to achieve by such uninspired villainy?"

Teymur winced at her boldness. Her nerve at bringing his shameful intentions to light.

Shahrzad knew her taunts were foolish. Knew they might further provoke him. But she could not—would not—comply in the face of such cowardice.

Not while there was still breath left in her body.

For a moment, Teymur seemed to waver. Then he clenched his jaw, bracing himself above her. With surprising deftness, he unsheathed the dagger and positioned the blade beside her face again. "You must matter to him, or he wouldn't have let you live."

The feel of the cold steel against her skin did not frighten her. She clung to rage instead. "Khalid Ibn al-Rashid values precious little in life. I amused him for a time. Do not seek reason beyond that. You said it yourself: he is a monster." She spoke in clear tones, her barely leashed fury underscoring each syllable.

"You're still lying to me. Do you mean to tell me the Caliph of Khorasan would not care if harm were to befall you?"

"As I said before, I cannot speak to his feelings."

Teymur sneered down at her. "You expect me to believe the mighty King of Kings wouldn't be angry for what has transpired today?"

*No.*

*Khalid would break every bone in your body for what you've done.*

Shahrzad stared up at him coolly. "If you think Roya would condone your actions in this moment, nothing I can do or say will matter." She choked back the rising bile. "But I can't imagine any girl with real love in her heart would ever approve of such a thing."

His hold on her neck flagged as his face fell to despair. Each of his features wilted into the next. In that instant, Shahrzad saw how much Teymur had loved Roya.

How much he'd lost of himself when he'd lost her.

But it was no excuse. There would never be an excuse for this.

Successful in achieving a distraction, Shahrzad now sought to disarm him.

Ever so cautiously, she shifted one hand from around his wrist. While Teymur contended with his inner demons, Shahrzad let her hand drop to search the ground for a potential weapon. A rock, a tumbler, a bowl, a stick, anything . . .

As her fingers scrabbled for purchase, they fell upon—

*A piece of dried meat?*

Teymur remained lost in thought, his fingers loose at her throat, so Shahrzad let her gaze drift sidelong in one quick pass of the tent.

Even in the dim light, she could see that several strips of dried meat had been slid under the bottom of the tent in her direction.

They were the type of dried meat Tariq usually fed to Zoraya.

*Tariq can't want me to bait his falcon . . .*

This did not seem at all like something Tariq would have devised. If Tariq knew what was transpiring within the tent's walls, he would have ripped it from the ground and used its ropes to hang Teymur in the wind. Tariq—brash at every turn—would have been loath to drum up a stealth attack of any sort. And definitely not one involving Zoraya.

*If not Tariq, then who devised such a harebrained scheme?*

Shahrzad's eyes combed the walls of the tent.

*And where is that accursed falcon?*

One thing was for certain: if this plan was intended to provide a distraction, it would prove to be an interesting one.

Shahrzad curled her fingers around the strip of dried meat.

Like a mongoose to a cobra, her hand shot up to the collar of Teymur's *qamis*. She lodged the strip in the hollow behind his neck. Momentarily stunned, he released the dagger and slapped both his hands to his nape as though he were trying to quash a marauding insect.

In a flurry of feathers and flashing talons, Zoraya came screeching through the entrance of the tent, straight for Teymur's collar. He screamed and toppled sideways off Shahrzad. The falcon continued attacking him, her wings spread wide. Shahrzad seized another piece of dried meat while Teymur tried in vain to fend off Zoraya's onslaught.

Before Shahrzad had a chance to form a coherent thought, Rahim al-Din Walad burst into the tent with Irsa on his heels. Strips of dried meat were clasped in Irsa's fists. Rahim grabbed Shahrzad by the arm and hauled her to her feet.

"Go! Both of you." He ripped his scimitar from its scabbard, his expression stern.

"I will not," Irsa replied, her voice surprisingly strong and steady. "Not until I know you and Shazi are safe."

Shahrzad, too, refused with a pointed glance. When Rahim began to protest, she turned a deaf ear his way. He muttered a curse and moved to one side, his scimitar held at the ready.

"Zoraya. Stop this, at once!" The falcon ignored the command, so Shahrzad whistled softly.

Zoraya squawked in reply, but ceased her assault. Stooping to collect her discarded dagger, Shahrzad stepped before a cowering Teymur. His neck and hands were scratched bloody, and the front of his trowsers was soaked. An acrid tang filled the air. Utterly indifferent, Shahrzad held the piece of dried meat before her. The falcon took it in her talons and landed beside Shahrzad's feet, her blue-grey feathers spread in protective shadow.

Shahrzad glowered down at Teymur. "If you ever touch me again, I'll rip off your sorry excuse for manhood and feed it to the falcon."

Then she stepped closer, brandishing her unsheathed dagger.

"But if you even *look* at my sister again, I'll kill you outright."

# A GATEWAY BETWEEN WORLDS

SHAHRZAD KNEW SHE WAS DREAMING.

Knew it and did not care.

For she was home.

Her bare feet trod upon cool stone as they made their way down the cavernous corridors toward the doors of her chamber. With her heart in her throat, she took hold of one handle and pushed it open.

It was dark. A deep-blue dark. The kind that brought the cold with it, no matter the temperature.

The marble floor was covered in a gently curling fog. It pooled waist-deep, like thick white smoke, from wall to wall. As she took a slow step forward, it parted around her like a ghostly sea, cleaved by the prow of a haunted ship.

A warm light began to glow in the center of the chamber. It hung above her bower—a silent sentinel, surrounded by a veil of diaphanous silk.

In the middle of a platform of cushions sat a lone figure, shrouded in shadow.

"Khalid?"

Shahrzad moved through the fog at a quicker pace, her eyes squinting through the blue darkness and the gossamer veil—

Struggling to catch a glimpse of the face she so longed to see.

The figure shifted. Moved aside a swath of spider-silk.

"No, Shazi-*jan*. I am not he. But I hope you'll forgive this intrusion." The figure smiled at her with the knowing smile of secrets past, present, and future.

And Shahrzad stumbled, barely squelching a cry.

A bubble of laughter burst from the jewel-toned cushions, so familiar and so full of light that it tore at Shahrzad's heartstrings.

How many times had she wished to hear that sound just once more?

She'd been willing to kill for it.

"Shiva?" Shahrzad whispered in disbelief as she rounded the foot of the bed and reached for the silk curtain.

"Come!" Shiva said, patting the space beside her.

Shahrzad's hands shook as she pushed aside a pane of gossamer and knelt onto the cushions. As if in a trance, she stared at her best friend, waiting for her to disappear.

Waiting for the crushing emptiness that was sure to follow.

Shiva smiled, impish and full of life. A single dimple marred her left cheek, as perfectly imperfect as always.

The image tore at yet another heartstring. For just as Shahrzad knew this to be a dream, she knew she would have to wake at some point.

And face this for the lie that it was.

The dimple appeared again as Shiva hooked a fall of dark hair behind an ear. "Silly goose. Just because we're in a dream doesn't mean this is a lie."

"So you're in my head now?" Shahrzad retorted.

"Of course! I've always been here." Shiva rested her chin on one knee. "I've just been waiting until you needed me."

"But"—Shahrzad caught herself, surprised by a sudden wash of anger—"I've needed you so many times, Shiva."

"No, you haven't. I've watched you. You've done splendidly on your own." The edges of Shiva's eyes crinkled with pride.

"But I haven't," Shahrzad continued. "I've made so many mistakes. I fell in love with the boy responsible for your death!"

"You did. And that was difficult to watch, at times. Especially the morning you almost died."

"I betrayed you."

"No, you goose. You didn't betray me. I told you; I was here the whole time. And I have a confession to make . . ." Shiva's eyes drifted sideways, sparkling with sly awareness. Filled with vibrant light. "The moment I saw him running toward you that morning, I knew you were going to save him, just as he saved you." When Shiva reached a hand toward hers, Shahrzad jumped at its warmth.

It felt so real. So achingly alive.

Again, Shiva smiled, her slender shoulders easing forward with lissome grace. "It feels real because you remember me this way. And it's lovely to be remembered as warm and perfectly imperfect." Shiva laced her fingers through Shahrzad's and held tight.

For a moment, the tension in Shahrzad's throat made it

difficult to speak. "I'm—so sorry for loving him, Shiva-*jan*. So sorry for not being stronger."

"What a ridiculous thing to apologize for!" Shiva's fine-boned features looked doll-like in her outrage. "You should know better. Never apologize for such nonsense again. You of all people should know what happens when you disobey me." She shook a fist, laughing teasingly as she brought to mind their many childhood squabbles. Shahrzad could not help but join in her laughter, until its chorus filled the space around them.

"I don't want to wake up." The laughter died on Shahrzad's lips, its echo calling back to her from beyond the double doors. From a gateway between worlds.

"And I don't want you to wake up," Shiva said. "Yet, when the time comes, you will wake up, all the same."

"Perhaps we should just stay here."

"I think not." Shiva's mouth crooked into a melancholy smile. "After all, you were not looking for me when you first arrived. You were looking for him." It was not an accusation. Merely an observation. Shiva had always been like that—incapable of withholding the truth but incapable of cruelty. A rare kind of person. The best kind of friend.

Shahrzad averted her gaze. "I—don't know that I can ever look for him again. Not with the curse—"

"Then you must break it," Shiva interrupted. "That is beyond question. What remains is how you intend to go about doing so. Have you made a plan?"

Though Shahrzad had intended to seek Musa Zaragoza soon for this exact purpose, she could not answer Shiva. She wasn't yet sure how to proceed. Even as a child, she'd gone through much of life on instinct. That and sheer nerve.

It was Shiva who had been the planner. Shiva who had always thought ahead of what was to come.

"See?" Shiva said, her forehead smoothing. "This is why I came to you tonight, my dearest love. You're lost. And it simply will not do."

Shahrzad watched as the fog spread toward the ceiling, wrapping its wraithlike arms around the platform and curling about the single taper above. "I don't know where to begin," she admitted, her voice fading into the fog.

"Why don't you start by saying aloud what it is you wish for?"

Could she even dare to say such a thing? After all the death and bloodshed and senseless destruction, it seemed like the worst kind of selfishness.

To build her world upon a bower of bones.

"So tiresome." Shiva nudged her in jest. "This is *your* dream, you goose! If you cannot say what it is you desire in your own dream, then where can you dare to say it?"

Shahrzad saw herself reflected in Shiva's gaze.

It was a shell of the girl she knew. A girl hunched forward, reticent. A girl absent—from life, and of life.

She squared her shoulders. "I want to be with Khalid. I want my father to be well. And . . . I want the curse to be broken."

"There she is," Shiva said, amusement leavening her tones.

"But are such things possible?" Shahrzad countered. "For they do not seem so."

"Then how does one go about making the impossible, possible?"

Shahrzad shrugged, her expression morose. "You'd have better luck asking me how to make a goat fly."

"Very well, then." Shiva nodded, an air of solemnity about her. "How does one make a goat fly?"

"Tie it to a very large kite."

"It wouldn't get far, as it's tied to a string."

"Be serious."

"I'm very serious!" Shiva laughed, letting the sound carry beyond the encroaching fog and past the silent sentinel above. "What if you were to put the goat on your floating carpet? Perhaps it would fly then?" Her eyes shone with a suspicious light.

"Don't be ridiculous."

"It was just a thought." Shiva waved a hand through a whorl of white smoke. "But, if you ask me, the best way to go about flying is to cut the strings tying you down . . ." Her words began to sound muffled, as though she were underwater, yet her smile continued to burn bright.

"Cut the strings, Shazi. *Fly.*"


Shahrzad woke with a start.

Their tent was awash in black. Her sister's breaths had long ago lapsed into the rhythm of a deep sleep, and the sound of a lulling desert wind buffeted the stitched walls.

Her throat was dry, but her heart was full.

She waited for the crushing emptiness to follow when she realized her dream had ended with so many things left unsaid.

It never came.

For the first time since she'd fled the city of Rey nearly a week ago, she didn't feel lost and quite so alone. She had found a means to achieve her purpose. And her purpose had a weight she could bear.

Something she could truly fight for.

*"Cut the strings, Shazi. Fly."*

*Thank you, Shiva.*

Careful not to disturb Irsa, Shahrzad stepped into her sandals to take in some air. She stole her sister's *shamina* and draped the long triangle of cloth over her head to shield herself from a chilly desert night. Then she made her way to the entrance of the tent, securing its flap shut behind her—

Before sprawling across the body lying in wait outside.

*"Uff!"* Shahrzad rolled into the sand.

Strong hands grabbed her, pinning her down. A vision of a hooded soldier flashed through her mind. An angry soldier with a scarab brand and a weapon meant for war.

She struck out against a wall of muscle. Slapped at a face hewn from stone. Stared back into eyes the silver of sharp knives.

Tariq's heart pounded over hers.

"Get off me!" she said, dismayed to feel her cheeks flush.

He pushed to his feet, taking her with him in one lithe movement.

"What are you—"

"What the hell—"

She shoved away from him, crossing her arms.

He knocked the sand from his hair with a vicious swipe of a hand.

"You first," Tariq said in a sullen voice that brought to mind a much younger version of himself. One with a lazy smile and a penchant for pranks.

One Shahrzad much preferred at that moment.

"That's quite gallant of you. After you've ignored me for the better part of a week, like a boy half your age with twice your charm."

His lips stayed poised between silence and speech for the span of several breaths.

"You—are awful, Shazi. Just awful." He rubbed a palm across his face, but not before Shahrzad saw the look of aggrievement he failed to mask.

She squeezed her elbows, refusing to reach out and comfort him. No matter how much she wanted to. No matter how natural it felt to comfort the boy she'd loved for so long.

"I know I'm awful. So it begs the question: Why are you here?"

"I've asked myself that same question, several times . . . especially as I lay in the cold sand, keeping watch over an awful girl. One with little sense of gratitude and no sense of loyalty."

It was as though he'd doused her with icy water.

Fending off a fresh wave of guilt, she whirled away, her cheeks aflame.

Tariq chased after her, taking hold of her arm.

Shahrzad threw him off. "Don't touch me, Tariq Imran al-Ziyad! Don't you *dare!*" She was horrified to feel the sting of tears behind her eyes. Not once had she cried in the past few days. Not when they'd found her father's huddled figure on a cloud-darkened slope. Not when she'd turned to take in a final glimpse of her burning city behind her.

Not even when she'd learned Tariq had promised Jalal never to bring her back.

Tariq drew her close without a second thought.

"Stop it." She splayed both hands against his chest as angry tears began to well. "I don't need you!"

*You deserve someone who will feel you at her side without needing to see you.*

*And I've only felt that way about one boy.*

"Stop trying to hurt me, you awful girl," he said grimly. "It won't work. At least not in the way you hope it will."

Hot tears slipped down her face. Yet she refused to lean on him. Refused to succumb to such weakness.

With a weary sigh, Tariq wrapped his arms around her.

They felt solid, certain, safe.

They felt like everything she'd ever loved about being young and free. The scent of sand and salt on his skin; the wild feeling of falling and knowing someone would always be there to catch her or, at the very least, tend to her wounds; the newness of all things . . . and of love, especially.

"Rahim told me what happened." Tariq's fingers shifted to the nape of her neck as they had so many times before, so many years past. He lowered his voice; it rumbled, rich and resonant against her, almost decadent. A luxury she no longer needed nor deserved. "I'll beat that boy bloody for even thinking such things."

*No.*

Shahrzad pushed away from him. "It isn't your place. I've already spoken to Teymur. He won't pursue the matter further."

Tariq's eyes flashed. "My *place*?"

"I've handled the matter, Tariq. Do nothing, as it would serve no purpose, save to shed more blood. And I've had enough of that." She shouldered her way past him.

He cut her off, his jaw jutting forward, his fists at his sides. "Would you shackle the boy-king in such a manner?"

"Don't compare yourself to Khalid. It's childish and beneath you."

Tariq winced, but stood his ground. "Answer me, Shazi. Would you tell him it wasn't his place to rage against this boy for what he did to you?"

She paused. "Yes."

"And he would listen to you?" His brows gathered in disbelief.

"He . . . would listen."

*Then do exactly as he pleased.*

"You're lying," Tariq scoffed. "I don't believe for a moment that butcher you call a husband would let that boy see another dawn after what he did to you."

"What Khalid would do is none of your concern." She was dangerously close to shouting. "And I'm finished discussing this incident and my *butcher* of a husband with you!" Shahrzad sliced a hand through the air with finality.

"So now you think it's your place to control what happens in this camp?" Tariq said. "Is that why that sniveling boy was returned to his people, like a child to be scolded? Did you honestly think—"

"I honestly thought nothing would be served from shedding more blood. Teymur was taken to the Emir of Karaj's tent to be dealt with accordingly. And it *is* my place to decide how to deal with this matter. It is *not*"—she jabbed a finger into his chest—"your place to dole out justice on my behalf!"

"Do you truly believe the emir will punish him for what he did today? He won't. And now I have no idea where Teymur is. For I doubt that fiend was sent away to be dealt with, as you'd so like to believe. He's gone and, with him, all sense of justice!" Tariq threw his arms wide, his face marred by exasperation. "Did you know Teymur was set to marry into the emir's family? It's possible the emir even put him up to the task."

"You will not seek revenge on my behalf, Tariq Imran al-Ziyad. I forbid—"

He grabbed her by the shoulders. "I will do as I damned well please, Shahrzad al-Khayzuran!" His voice was raw in its torment. "I denied myself what I wanted once out of principle, and not a day goes by that I don't regret that decision with every fiber of my being!"

The sound of his anguish spiraled up into a desert night, across a vast spread of tiny stars.

Through Shahrzad's very skin.

Without a word, Shahrzad took his hand and led him into the desert, far beyond the enclave of tents. When she finally turned to face him, Tariq appeared to have aged a decade in a matter of moments.

They stared at each other across a small sea of glittering sand. Across years of friendship and trust, seemingly lost in an instant.

"Do you ever think about that night?" Tariq could not meet her eyes as he posed the quiet question.

For a time, she was unsure how to respond.

"You did the right thing," Shahrzad said, studying the infinite grains as they slid around her toes. "I put you in an impossible situation. An inappropriate one."

"That's not what I asked you."

She lifted her gaze. "Yes. I've thought about it."

He shifted from one foot to the other, this boy who was never awkward, hurting her heart with his uncommon awkwardness. "May I ask why you came to my room that night?"

Tariq deserved her honesty. For all those stolen kisses in shadowed corners. For all those years of unfailing love.

For starting a war to save her.

She held his gaze, though the ache in her chest made her want to run far and fast.

"Because I wanted to feel."

"Shahrzad—"

"I wanted—no, *needed*—to feel something." There was a gentle resolve to her words. "I thought that, if I lost myself in your arms, I might feel something again. Then I could mourn for Shiva and move on. But you were right to turn me away. I never resented you for it. Please believe me when I say that," she finished in a soft tone.

Tariq was silent for a long while. She watched the pain in his eyes fade, replaced by bitter resignation. "I believe you. It doesn't change the fact that I've resented myself almost every day since." He took two steps toward her and stopped, hesitant.

Shahrzad sensed his indecision. Her fingers gripped the folds of Irsa's *shahmina*.

*He's waiting for me to ask him why.*

*And he's afraid of what will happen when I do.*

Her toes curled within her sandals, grinding the silt against her skin. "Why have you resented yourself?"

Tariq pressed his lips into a thin line. The muscles in his neck leapt out as he swallowed hard. He appeared to be arranging his words before speaking, again so uncharacteristic of her first love.

Then his eyes found hers and held them, fierce in their conviction. "Because I know that, had I given us both what we wanted that night, you would be my wife now, instead of his."

Her head snapped back, aghast. "Is—is that what you thought I was doing?" Shahrzad managed to sputter. "That I went to your room as the daughter of a poor librarian, planning to leave as the wife of a future emir?" She glared up at him, propping her arms akimbo. "It was not my intention to force you into marriage, you arrogant ass! Had I shared your bed that night, I would *never* have expected you to propose marriage the following day!"

"My God, is that what you think I'm saying?"

"What else am I supposed to think when—"

He shot forward, covering her mouth with his hand. Silently pleading for a stay of execution.

After a beat, Shahrzad nodded, though her indignation hummed through the air. Tariq removed his palm and she detected the faintest hint of amusement in his expression. A trace of the boy she'd always known. And greatly missed in the past few days.

With a deepening frown, Shahrzad seized the edges of Irsa's

*shamina* and folded them across her chest. "Well, then, what did you mean to say?"

"I meant to say," he began anew, "that if you'd stayed with me that night, I would have gone to see your father the next morning—"

She opened her mouth to protest, and he resumed his silent entreaty.

Then he stepped closer. "But it would not have been because I felt obligated to go," Tariq said, his hands coming to rest on her shoulders, tentatively at first, then with a decisive weight. "It would have been because I did not want to wait a single day more . . . and it would have been *wrong*. My cousin had been murdered a fortnight before. My aunt had thrown herself from her balcony three days later. How could I go to your father—to my parents—and ask to marry you?"

His features had softened while he spoke, though his voice had lost none of its intensity. In that moment, Shahrzad was reminded of how all eyes managed to stray toward him in a room, unbidden. Of how he took up too much space and never seemed to notice.

His hands fell loose at his sides as he waited for her to collect her thoughts and speak.

When she did, it was her turn to feel awkward and at a loss. "I—would never have expected you to do such a thing."

Again, a trace of amusement flashed across his face. "You continue to wound me, you awful girl. Because I know. Had I spent a single night with you, I would never have wished for us to be parted from that day forward."

Shahrzad wanted to stop him from speaking further. From saying anything he might regret.

*What can I do to spare him any more pain?*

But Tariq took her by the chin, resolute in his course, tipping her gaze to his.

"Ever since the afternoon I watched you fall from the battlements at Taleqan, you've felt inevitable to me. That's how much I love you." His words were effortless. Just as always. "But you can no longer say the same about me, can you?"

She could not look him in the eye.

"Please answer me, Shazi," he said. "It's time I heard the truth. I . . . deserve to hear it."

When Shahrzad studied his face, she realized that—over the course of the last few days—he'd been bracing himself for this moment.

Though it would not make it any easier for either of them.

She exhaled slowly.

"I do love you, Tariq." With great care, Shahrzad settled a palm against his cheek. "But . . . he's where I live."

Tariq covered her hand with one of his. Nodded once. The only acknowledgment beyond this was the smallest movement of muscle along his jaw. A staving-off of emotion that betrayed him far more than any onslaught of tears ever would.

"I'm so sorry for hurting you," Shahrzad whispered, the ache in her chest flooding into her throat. She pressed her free palm to his other cheek, conveying her regret through touch. Silly, she knew, but she could not fathom how else to make amends for such betrayal.

Tariq eased back, his expression oddly distanced. "I knew you were in love with him when I saw you together in Rey. But . . . I've been a fool, clinging to misbegotten hope."

"Please know—" Shahrzad pressed her lower lip between her teeth, certain she would draw blood. "I never meant to cause you pain."

"My pain was my own fault. Rahim told me what you said to Teymur today—that your heart was with me, as it always would be."

The taste of copper and salt struck her tongue. "I—"

"You lied to save yourself. I understand," he said in a flat tone. "But you must know that Teymur will tell the Emir of Karaj, and the rumor will spread."

She blinked at him, bewildered by this sudden change of tack. Gone was any sign of vulnerability. In its place was a severe brow and a set demeanor.

An abrupt return to the distance of before.

"You'll be safer in this camp—especially among the butcher-king's enemies—if we keep up appearances," he finished.

Though she had little intention of staying at the camp for long, Shahrzad knew she should say something. If not in defense of herself or of Khalid, then at least in defense of Tariq.

She shook her head, gripping the *shamina* even tighter. "I can't ask you to do that. I *won't* ask you to do that. It isn't fair."

"No, it isn't," Tariq agreed. "But you have yet to ask me to abandon this war."

Her eyes went wide in surprise. "Would you do that? Is such a thing even possible?"

"Even if it were, I would not." Tariq did not hesitate in his response. "When I set out to do something, I do not go about it lightly. And shirking my responsibility would not only be a failure to those around me, but a failure to myself."

"To those around you?" Anger flared within her, sudden and bright. "Do you know what kind of men are around you, Tariq?" She thought of the sentry outside the tent that morning. Of the Fida'i brand seared into his skin. "You've surrounded yourself with mercenaries—hired outlaws and assassins from all walks of life—in an attempt to overthrow a king you know nothing about! Khalid is not—"

"Hired outlaws and assassins?" Tariq laughed caustically. "Listen to yourself, Shazi! Do you know who your husband is? Have you not heard the stories about the Caliph of Khorasan? The murdering madman? Did he or did he not kill Shiva—your *best friend*?" He drew out the last two words, enunciating their meaning.

Articulating her treachery.

She bit back her retort. "The truth is not that simple."

"Love has blinded you to the truth. But it will not blind me," Tariq said, though his eyes pooled with feeling. "There is only one remaining truth of import: Is he responsible for my cousin's death?"

Shahrzad stared at him in injured silence. "Yes."

For no matter the tale, it was the truth.

"Then it is that simple."

"Tariq, please." She reached for him. "You said you love me. I beg you to reconsider—"

He backed away. Trying so hard to conceal his pain. "I do love you. Nothing will change that. Just as nothing will change the fact that he killed my cousin and stole the girl I love from me." Shahrzad watched in horror as his hand fell to the hilt of his scimitar, gripping it tight.

Though he nearly tripped in his haste to retreat, Tariq's voice did not waver.

"Make no mistake—the next time I see Khalid Ibn al-Rashid, one of us will die."

# WILLING TO LEARN

He HAD MADE MISTAKES. THIS HE KNEW BEYOND ALL doubt.

Mistakes in judgment. Mistakes in planning. Mistakes in understanding.

Perhaps it could be said that he was guilty of mistaken pride.

Foolish conceit, even.

But Jahandar had not meant for things to transpire as they had.

When he'd first called upon the power of the book, he'd thought he could control it. He'd thought he was its master.

That had been the first of his many mistakes.

For the book had no intention of being controlled. And every intention of forcing its will upon Jahandar al-Khayzuran. Alas, its will remained veiled behind the poetry of an ancient language, sealed shut with a rusted lock and key.

A part of Jahandar knew that by all rights the book should be destroyed.

Anything capable of the destruction he'd witnessed that

fateful night of the storm should not be allowed to exist in the world of man.

And yet . . .

Jahandar curled his fingers tightly around the book. Its warmth seeped into his skin, pulsing at the blisters on his hands.

The living heat of a beating heart.

Perhaps he could control it now. Now that he knew what kind of creature it was.

Was it the height of foolishness to think such a thing? Further evidence of his misplaced conceit?

Perhaps.

He could try. Only something small, at first. Nothing like the mistakes he'd made on the outskirts of Rey. He knew better now.

Now that he'd seen what it was capable of, he'd wade into the book's waters with greater care. With far more consideration than he'd espoused on the hilltop.

The night he'd witnessed the book put an entire city to ruin.

He shuddered as he recalled the bolts of lightning that had sliced across the sky and struck at the heart of Khorasan's most prized gem.

The city where Jahandar had raised his daughters and curated his beloved library.

The city where he'd buried his wife after watching her fall to a wasting disease.

The city of his most resounding failures.

He recalled the many times he'd proven powerless to those around him—powerless to prevent his wife from succumbing to her illness; powerless to keep his post as a vizier following her death; and powerless to prevent his daughter from striding down the palace halls toward certain doom.

Powerless to effect any change at all. A casual observer to life. Useless.

Again, he clutched at the book, grateful that both his children had escaped the storm unscathed . . .

When he suspected so many others had not.

Jahandar cracked open his eyes in the stifling dark of his tent.

As it had when they'd arrived the night before, guilt crushed his chest, making it difficult to breathe. His nails dug into the cover of the book as he struggled to take in air. To stanch the flood of remorse welling in his eyes.

To drown out the memory of the screams in his ears.

It wasn't his fault!

He hadn't meant for it to happen. He'd only meant to provide a distraction. Rescue his beloved daughter. And perhaps find his true calling—

As a man of power. A man to be respected. A man to be feared.

But Jahandar could fix it. He knew how to fix it.

He'd passed along his gifts to his daughter.

Irsa had said as much today, when she'd mentioned a magic carpet. It had taken all his self-control to lie still when he'd heard the words. To keep silent in the face of such possibility.

Shahrzad was special. Just like Jahandar.

And she was strong. Even stronger than he was. He had felt it whenever Shahrzad's hands had brushed the book; it had welcomed her presence.

It had acknowledged her capacity for greatness.

His chance for redemption.

Once he regained full use of his body, Jahandar would return to his studies.

This time, he would master the book. Become truly worthy of its power. He would not permit it to control him again.

No. Never again would he make such mistakes.

He would teach his daughter to use her powers. Then, together, they would put right all that had gone wrong.

For a mistake was only a mistake if it was left to remain so.

And Jahandar was a lifelong scholar.

It was the one thing he had always prided himself on being—

Willing to learn.

# THE BUTTERFLY AND THE BRUTE

K HALID DID NOT LIKE SURPRISES.

Even as a child, he had been wary of them.

He could not recall a single time when he'd been pleased with a surprise. In his experience, surprises were often a prelude to something much more insidious. Like a slow poison masked by a fine wine. Served in a bejeweled cup.

No.

He hated surprises.

Which was why, when Khalid walked into Vikram's chamber and found Despina sitting at his bodyguard's bedside, he was most displeased.

How had she managed to learn of the Rajput's recovery so soon? Khalid had received word only at dawn, less than an hour ago.

Indeed, the handmaiden's eyes and ears were quite vast. They were among the chief reasons she had always made such an excellent spy. No doubt it came from her ability to make friends and gain confidences with the ease of a butterfly. As she'd made friends with those of influence around the palace.

As she'd made friends with Shahrzad.

The handmaiden rose to her feet and bowed, pressing the tips of the fingers of her right hand to her forehead. "*Sayyidi.*"

"I'm impressed." Khalid remained at the foot of the bed, his features tight.

Despina smiled, her eyes sparkling even in the weak light filtering between the window slats. "Forgive me for saying so, *sayyidi*, but you don't look it."

A single cough emitted from Vikram's lips, meant to conceal what, in the Hindustani warrior, passed for amusement.

Khalid turned to him without preamble. "Your shoulder?"

There had never been a need for formality between them. They'd trained together for years. Bled together. Fought together. The Rajput had been his bodyguard since the day Khalid had been crowned king. His friend since before that.

Vikram did not answer. His black gaze held fast to a nondescript corner above while Khalid took in the reddened bandages and the foul-smelling poultices wrapped around the copper skin of his left shoulder. When Vikram sat up to reach for the tumbler of water on the low table beside him, he could not suppress a twinge of pain. Despina bent to assist him, ignoring his deepening scowl.

"You just missed the *faqir, sayyidi*," she said as she replaced the tumbler on the low table. "He came to say—"

"That whelp's arrows shattered my breastbone. And the bone in my shoulder," Vikram said in a gruff tone. A tone that promised a fierce reprisal in the near future.

Despina blinked, at a loss for words. Then recovered in a flash of white teeth. "But the *faqir* also said—"

Vikram silenced her with a glance. Pouting, Despina returned to her stool and looped her arms across her chest.

The pitiless side of Khalid felt strangely appeased by this exchange—the sight of the twittering butterfly being silenced by the towering brute. Were Shahrzad here, Khalid suspected she would have added greatly to his satisfaction with a sharp quip that would have bettered yet worsened the situation all at once.

He strode from the foot of the bed to Vikram's side. "Is there anything you need of me?"

Vikram leaned back against the pillows and eyed him with his usual uncompromising stare. "A new arm."

At this, Khalid almost smiled. "Alas, I need both of mine."

"For what?" Vikram grunted, affecting a look of disdain.

"To fight."

"You lie. Like the posturing peacock you are."

Khalid's eyebrows rose. "I never lie."

"A lie." The Rajput's mustache twitched, his gaze dark.

"*Never* . . . is perhaps the wrong word."

"*Seldom* is better."

"Seldom, then." Khalid offered him the hint of a smile.

Vikram exhaled, smoothing his right hand across his short beard. "I cannot fight anymore, *meraa dost*." It was a difficult admission. His eyes closed for an instant.

"Now *that* is a lie," Khalid said without hesitation. "The *faqir* told me your shoulder would heal in time. It may not return to what—"

"I cannot feel anything in my left hand."

Truly, Khalid hated surprises. With the fire of a thousand suns, he abhorred them.

His gaze drifted to Vikram's left hand, lying prone atop the linen sheets. It looked the same as always. Merciless. Inveterate. Invulnerable.

Yet not.

He knew words of reassurance were unnecessary. Vikram was not a fool, nor was he in need of coddling. Nevertheless, Khalid could not ignore his inclination to state the obvious.

"It is too soon to pass judgment on the matter." He refrained from speaking in a gentle tone, for he knew Vikram would despise it. "Feeling may return to your hand in time."

"Even if it does, I will never fight as I once did." There was no sentiment behind the response. Just a simple statement of fact.

Despina shifted in her seat—the second sign of discomfort Khalid had seen from the handmaiden since his arrival.

Though this puzzled him, Khalid granted Vikram's words their requisite consideration. "Again, it is too soon to pass judgment on the matter."

"That whelp used obsidian arrowheads." Vikram's fury cut dark fissures across his forehead and deep valleys down the sides of his face. "They shattered the bones. Beyond repair."

Despite his wish to fan the flames, Khalid tamped down his ire. It would serve no purpose to fuel rage. Instead his features fell into a mask of false composure. A mask he wore well.

"I heard as much."

"I cannot serve as your bodyguard with only one good arm," Vikram ground out in pointed fashion.

"I disagree."

"As I knew you would." He frowned. "But it matters not, *meraa dost.*"

"And why is that?" Khalid said.

Again, the handmaiden shifted in her seat.

Vikram eased farther into his pillows, the edges of his expression smoothing. "Because I will not be less than what I am. And you will not force me to be less." He did not even bother to challenge Khalid with his unyielding stare.

"What is it you need of me, my friend?" Khalid repeated his earlier query, though it sounded entirely different now.

The Rajput paused. "I wish to leave the city. To start a life of my own."

"Of course." Khalid nodded. "Whatever you need."

"And to take a wife."

More surprises. Would it never end?

"Is there someone you have in mind?" Khalid's expression remained careful. Controlled.

Vikram leveled an almost mocking gaze at his king. Then his features shifted slowly to the pouting butterfly at his bedside.

To Khalid's best spy.

Apparently, Khalid's abhorred surprises were only beginning.

Try as he might, Khalid could not hide the look of disbelief etching its way across his face. "And are you amenable to this marriage?" he asked the handmaiden in a voice barely above a whisper.

When her pretty lips started to pucker into an amused moue and her eyes began to shimmer like wells full of unshared secrets, it took all of Khalid's willpower not to lose his temper and turn from the room in a mindless rage.

"Very well, then. Far be it from me to understand the machinations of love." Khalid shook his head, banishing all evidence of his incredulity. "Is there anything else?"

"There is . . . one thing more," the Rajput grumbled, almost as an afterthought.

Khalid waited, hoping it was not another surprise.

"Despite my choice of a wife,"—the warrior eyed his future bride, who returned his look with a knowing smile—"I do not wish to become the subject of rumors."

"I understand," Khalid replied. "I will not discuss these matters with anyone. You have my word."

Vikram nodded curtly. "We will depart in two days. After that, all else is in the hands of the gods."

A sudden pang of loss shot through Khalid. He was not bothered by its presence. Merely by its keenness. "I shall miss your company, my friend."

"A lie." Vikram coughed, his good shoulder quaking with repressed humor. "You shall be the finest swordsman in Rey. Finally."

"The finest swordsman in a fallen city," Khalid countered, holding back the beginnings of a grin. "Fitting." He looked away, rubbing a palm along his jaw.

"*Meraa dost?*"

It was the first hint of indecision Khalid had heard in Vikram's voice.

He glanced back at his friend.

"Are you truly not going to bring her back?" the Rajput asked.

"What's this?" Khalid finally grinned, though it was with a heavy heart. "After all your early protestations?"

"Despite all, I find I . . . miss the little troublemaker. And how she made you smile."

As did Khalid. More than he cared to admit to anyone.

"She is not safe in Rey, Vikram," Khalid said. "I am not for her."

"And the whelp is?" The lines across the Rajput's forehead returned.

Along with Khalid's simmering rage. "Perhaps. At least he can make her smile."

"And you cannot?" Vikram's eyes cut in half. Flashed like pieces of flint.

Like the obsidian in Tariq Imran al-Ziyad's bone-shattering arrowheads.

Khalid's blood pooled thick with anger. Thick with unjustifiable wrath.

After all, he had been the one to let Shazi disappear with Nasir al-Ziyad's son. He had not gone after her, as he'd first wanted to do. He had not ordered Jalal to bring her back, despite the wishes of his heart.

It had been Khalid's decision to let her go.

Because it was best she not suffer alongside him—alongside Rey—anymore.

For at what point could he reconcile his faults with his fate?

It was no longer possible.

Despite all his attempts to avoid his destiny, it had found its way to him. Had slashed its way across his city. Set fire to all he held dear.

And he could not watch Shahrzad burn with him.

He would burn alone—again and again—before he would ever watch such a thing.

"I cannot make her smile," Khalid said. "Not anymore."

The Rajput ran his hand through his beard, lingering in contemplation.

"It is too soon to pass judgment on the matter."

Khalid bowed deeply, touching his fingertips to his brow. "I wish you happiness, Vikram Singh."

"And I you, *meraa dost*—my greatest friend."

## NOT A SINGLE DROP

C*UT THE STRINGS, SHAZI. FLY.*"

The words were whispers in her ears, carried on the air like a secret summoning.

"*Fly.*"

Shahrzad sat in the center of her tent, ignoring the commotion outside. Sounds of the newest contingent of soldiers arriving in camp. Sounds of impending war. Instead she focused on the dusty ground, her knees bent and her feet crossed at the ankles.

Before her lay the ugliest carpet in all of creation.

Rust colored, with a border of dark blue and a center medallion of black-and-white scrollwork. Fringed on two sides by yellowed, woebegone tassels. Seared in two corners.

A rug with a story of its own . . .

Albeit a small one. It was barely large enough to hold two people, sitting side by side.

Shahrzad canted her head in contemplation. Took a measured breath. Then she pressed the flat of her hand to the rug's surface.

A prickly feeling, like that of losing sensation in a limb, settled around her heart. It warmed through her blood, spreading into her fingertips.

Though she knew what to expect, it still took her by surprise when a corner of the carpet curled into her hand.

She removed her palm and swallowed. The rug fell flat.

*"Cut the strings, you goose. Did you swallow your ears just now, along with your nerve?"*

"I heard you the first thousand times, you rat!" With a small grin for Shiva's memory, Shahrzad reached for an empty tumbler and the pitcher of water on the low table nearby. Catching her tongue between her teeth, she filled the tumbler halfway and placed it within the center medallion of the ugliest carpet in all of creation.

"Now for the true test," she muttered.

Shahrzad returned her palm to the carpet. Just as before, the strange feeling unfurled around her heart before tingling down her arm. The edges of the rug bowed in on themselves, then the rug took to the air. Soon, there was nothing beneath it but empty space. She lifted onto her knees, moving with caution. The tumbler had not stirred from within the medallion; not a single drop of water had spilt. Exhaling through her nose, Shahrzad floated her fingers to the right. The rug followed along at shoulder level, the water's surface as calm as an unruffled lake.

Shahrzad decided to take the enterprise a step further.

She stood without warning, her hand spiking toward the steepled ceiling of the tent. Shahrzad expected the carpet to careen out of control, but—though it lifted in the mere blink of an eye—it refused to be buffeted about on such a graceless tide.

Instead, it rippled as though it were under the spell of the lightest of breezes. Trailing her fingertips, it rose above her head—a series of small waves upon an invisible shore—before spiraling back to the ground at her command. She repeated the motions twice. Up. Down. And back again. Not once did the carpet break contact with her skin. Not once did it lose control. It bore the cup as its weightless passenger, from ceiling to floor like clouds upon the air.

The most Shahrzad ever saw was the water loll from brim to brim, never spilling, simply swirling about, as though it were dancing to a languorous music it alone could hear.

Her eyes wide, she let the magic carpet circle back to the earth.

In her ears, the voice of her best friend—the voice behind the secret summoning—began to laugh, lyrically, beautifully.

Teasingly.

*Your turn, you goose.*

Shahrzad smiled to herself. Tomorrow night she would test the magic carpet again.

Without the tumbler.


Baba looked better this morning. At least, that was what Irsa thought. He didn't seem quite as wan or quite so withered. And he had swallowed his mixture of water and herbs with a bit more relish than he had yesterday.

Perhaps he would wake soon.

Irsa made a face as she blew the sticky strands of hair off her forehead. She was certain she was starting to resemble one of Rey's innumerable street urchins. Replete with dirt along the collar and sand behind the ears. With a huff, Irsa lifted her chestnut braid and twisted it into a knot at the nape of her neck.

Merciful God! Why was her father's tent so much hotter than her own? It felt like a bakery on a summer afternoon. How could Baba stand it?

Irsa studied his sallow complexion once more, then finished mopping the sweat from his forehead. "Please wake up, Baba. It's my birthday today. And it would be the best gift of all to hear your voice. Or see your smile." She pressed a kiss to his brow before collecting her things and striding to the entrance of her father's tent.

Lost in thought, Irsa failed to notice the lanky figure standing just outside.

"Irsa al-Khayzuran."

She stopped short. Turned. Almost tripped over a sandaled heel. Then raised a hand to shield her eyes from the searing rays above.

"I waited a long time in the sun for you . . . so that I could make sure all was well after yesterday's ordeal," Rahim al-Din Walad stated quietly. "But I suppose I'm rather easy to ignore?"

Heat rose in her neck. "No. I mean, yes. I mean, I didn't mean to—"

His attempt at laughter sounded like anything but. "I'm only teasing, Cricket."

Irsa cleared her throat. "Well, don't." Rahim knew she hated that nickname.

He managed a soft laugh. It sounded kind of dry, like parchment being torn in two, but Irsa felt strangely soothed by it. Odd things had always soothed her in such a way.

Like the peculiar expression on Rahim's face.

"As you can see, I'm quite well." Color sprang into her cheeks. "Did you need—something else?"

"Do people only talk to you when they need something?"

Why did he always ask so many questions? And why did it irritate her so? "No. They only talk to me when they need to. Or when they think *I* need something, as you usually do," she retorted. "But I suppose you're waiting in the hot sun for your health?" As soon as the question rolled off her tongue, Irsa wanted to clap her hand over her mouth.

What was wrong with her? After all Rahim had done for her recently! Teaching her to ride horses on sweltering afternoons when he could have been with Tariq or the other soldiers. Then helping her to rescue Shahrzad just yesterday.

Truly, there was no conceivable reason for her to be so awful to him.

Beyond complete stupidity.

Another dry rasp of laughter. "If I recall correctly, Shazi was also a bit of a wretch on her fifteenth birthday."

Rahim knew it was her birthday?

"I—did Shazi tell you?" Irsa stammered, all too aware of his nearness, her pulse starting to pound in her ears. She felt the same warmth that had brushed across her hand only yesterday, when he'd given her the reins.

"No." Rahim pressed his lips together as a gust of wind blew a shower of sand through his tightly marcelled curls. "You thought I would forget?"

"No. I thought no one would remember."

He stared down at her, unblinking. His look the same—strangely soothing.

The blood rose in Irsa's cheeks again. She swiped the sweaty hair back from her face—

And suddenly remembered that her braid was in a disheveled knot at the back of her neck. That she resembled a ragamuffin of the highest order. Her eyes wide, she unwound her braid and tried to arrange the sticky chaos atop her head.

"What are you doing?" Rahim finally blinked, his eyelashes as thick as brushstrokes across a canvas.

"Trying not to look like a street urchin."

"What?" Tiny vertical lines formed along the bridge of his nose. "Why?"

"Because—I—girls should be beautiful!" Irsa shot back, dabbing her forehead with her sleeve. "Not sweaty, stinking disasters."

"Is that a rule?"

"No, it's—you're . . . troubling." Irsa couldn't help it. He truly was. With his unceasing questions. And his unwavering warmth.

A light caught within his eyes. "So I've been told."

Rahim had never looked at her like that before.

"I brought you something," he said after several moments of steady deliberation.

"What?" She stepped into his shadow and dropped her hand from her brow. "Why?"

He reached into the brown linen of his *rida'* and removed a scroll bound by hemp cord. "I borrowed it from Omar. So you have to return it. But . . . I thought you might like it." He shrugged, then held the weathered bit of parchment out to her.

Still taken aback, it took her too long to reach for it.

Rahim waited, unperturbed, though she could see another question forming on his lips.

She beat him to it. "What is it?"

"Omar told me how you thought to put tea herbs and milk in your father's water. This is a scroll on plants and their healing properties. I thought you might like it. I'll bring some parchment and ink for you tomorrow. Perhaps you can transcribe it." He shrugged again. "Or . . . I can do it for you. Though my handwriting leaves a great deal to be desired."

Irsa was flabbergasted. Of all the things she'd expected sensible Rahim to do or say, it was not this.

He'd brought her a gift?

"I—well—I suppose I could do that. Yes. I mean, I'll transcribe it. Not you."

"You're welcome." He laughed; again, the sound was brittle in the air yet warm on her skin. When he turned to leave, Irsa felt a sudden urge to ask him to stay.

But to what end?

As though he could sense her consternation, Rahim looked over his shoulder. "Are—are you coming to the gathering following the war council tonight?"

Irsa started to nod, then stopped herself. "Will Shahrzad be allowed to attend?"

"I cannot see why anyone would object. Not with Tariq at her side. Nothing of import will be discussed around the fire. And everyone is rather curious about her. But, if she decides to come, it won't be easy. All eyes will be upon her," Rahim warned, ever the vigilant friend.

"I'll be sure to keep her apprised. And . . . I'll make certain nothing happens to her." Irsa lifted her chin, meeting his gaze. Steady. Stalwart.

At least she hoped that was how she appeared. She could very well appear mad, for all she knew—sweaty-haired and clutching a scroll of curatives to her chest.

"I expected nothing less." Again, Rahim paused in consideration of her. "*Tavalodet mobarak*, Irsa al-Khayzuran. May you have a hundred birthdays to come."

"Thank you, Rahim al-Din Walad."

He bowed with a hand to his forehead. When he straightened, he smiled that same almost-smile, as though he alone were aware of something important. "What you said earlier? You have nothing to worry about."

"What do you mean?"

"You're better than beautiful." Rahim took a careful breath. "You're interesting. Never forget that."

# AS A ROSE UNFURLING

He WOULD NEVER SAY IT. NOT EVEN AT KNIFEPOINT.

But Jalal may have been right.

The Caliph of Khorasan should not disappear for hours on end, without word or explanation.

But Khalid refused to remain at the palace, day in and day out. There were too many stories there. Ugly stories of blood and wrath and betrayal. The only places where Khalid had ever sought solace had been destroyed by the storm.

Or harbored memories he was not ready to relive yet.

At least beyond the palace walls, the stories were alive and real. Even if they were raw—even if they tore at his compunctions— he could face them.

He could fix them.

And, after a morning spent dealing with countless scrolls and tedious affairs of state, Khalid needed to see results. Something tangible he had done with his time.

Besides fending off an impending war.

Alas, it was possible he'd erred today.

The sun shone bright on the steps of the city's library.

Too bright.

Painfully so.

As the day wore on, small distortions began to swim across his sight. His headache worsened to a near-debilitating degree. It had always been there, but the morning hours spent staring at tiny script on unending reams of parchment, followed by an afternoon of hefting hot granite down uneven steps, had not helped matters at all.

Khalid paused a moment to pull his cowl lower and wipe the sweat from his brow.

It was not mere happenstance that he had chosen to help repair the city's oldest library. Though there were many others assisting in this undertaking, he had felt drawn to the crumbling stone structure for several days.

The place where Shahrzad's father had worked, before her family fled Rey.

A place Shazi had loved, if her affinity for storytelling was any indication.

It was clear the building had fallen into disrepair long before the events of the storm only a week ago. The steps leading to its vaulted doorway were cracked and misaligned, the once-vivid sandstone darkened to a mottling of greys and browns.

The storm had merely brought to fruition the inevitable.

Prodded by its winds, several pillars had collapsed on themselves, falling to ruin under the weight of time and neglect. Now the main entrance to the library was completely barred by their remains.

Khalid had already sent his engineers to the site to brace the sagging rafters. Today he was working alongside several careworn laborers, forming a line to haul away the debris.

The hood of his *rida'* kept him safely anonymous. For who would ever suspect the insidious Caliph of Khorasan of hauling stones before the city's library on a sweltering summer's day?

Khalid swore under his breath as the sweat on his palms nearly caused him to lose grip on his burden. Indeed, who would ever expect of him such a beneficent act, for it was clear he was quite ill equipped to perform meaningful labor of any sort. What good were all those endless drills with swords—all those endless lessons in supposed strategy—if he couldn't even transport rocks from a building?

When the stone in his hands fell to the ground with a sudden *thud,* it missed his foot by a hairsbreadth.

Khalid swore loudly and foully and without a care.

"Watch it, boy!" A near-toothless man edged a rock past him, his sun-worn face in a perpetual snarl. "You're liable to lose every last toe that way."

Khalid dipped his head in wordless acknowledgment. Then he stooped to collect the stone.

His right hand was bleeding again, a gash of brilliant red across his palm. He wiped it on his black *tikka* sash, hoping to stanch the flow.

"You'd better clean that. And wrap it in something, before it worsens." The toothless man pushed past him again, moving with uncanny efficiency for someone so slight. "There's usually water in pails at the side of the building." He nudged his chin toward the shadows.

Khalid adjusted the front of his *rida'* so he could address the man without impediment. "Thank you."

"Don't thank me. I still don't understand why a boy with leather sandals that fine is troubling himself with work like this." He regarded Khalid with a critical stare.

"Perhaps I have a strange affinity for old books."

"Perhaps." But he looked doubtful. "In any case, clean your wound. If it festers and you perish of a fever, your rich father will not be pleased."

With a small smile, Khalid bowed, then proceeded to the side of the building to take heed of the man's advice.

A rabble of children played amongst pails of water. Several boys fought over a rusted tumbler perched above a questionable fount, littered with ash and debris. One enterprising young girl hovered near a large bucket, its contents fastidiously clean. Not a single twig or a smattering of dust could be seen. She glanced up at Khalid, a smile alighting her features as she took in the fine sword hanging from his hip.

"Some water on a hot day, *sahib*?" The bit of colorful twine around her wrist slid down her skinny arm as she held up a hollowed-out gourd.

Khalid could not help but grin back. "How much for the pail . . . and the gourd?"

"For you, *sahib*?" Her smile turned mischievous. "Only two dinars."

Barely able to contain her exulting crow when Khalid handed over the coins, the girl raced into the streets, her day's work considered done. The other children scurried after her, eager to partake in her winnings.

Though he'd been soundly fleeced, Khalid thought it money well spent.

He crouched by the pail and let the lukewarm water wash across his stiffening palm. As he splashed some onto his face, he allowed himself the luxury of lowering his hood before dipping the gourd beneath the surface and ladling water onto his head.

Khalid let it drip down into his eyes. The water stung at first, so he pressed his thumb and forefinger into the bridge of his nose, trying to allay the burn. When he stood, he rolled back his shoulders, basking in this temporary reprieve.

"You ungrateful cur."

There was not even a moment to process the insult before two hands grabbed Khalid by the hood of his cloak and flung him face-first against the roughhewn wall of Rey's oldest library. His foot caught on the pail, sloshing water onto the stone.

Though his sight remained blurred, he'd recognize his cousin's voice anywhere.

"What the hell are you doing?" Khalid demanded, struggling for breath.

Jalal wrapped a fist in Khalid's *rida'*, spinning him around. "I knew you were angry with me, but I never thought you capable of this." His voice was choked by rage. "Truly, I never thought you could be this vile. I suppose I should have known better. I've always put too much stock in family."

Khalid blinked hard, seeking a point of sanity in the madness taking shape around him. "Step back before you make an irrevocable mistake, Captain al-Khoury."

"There's no one to save you, Khalid-*jan*," Jalal said, with a look to shrivel a cloudless sky. "And it's your own damned fault. No Vikram. No bodyguards. For once, we're going to fight fair, and I'm going to give you the beating you've been due for over a decade, you thankless bastard."

Though his words were clipped and precise, Jalal's features were haggard. He still had not managed a proper shave. Weariness pooled in the shadows beneath his eyes.

Weariness tinged by fury.

"You can try, by means fair or foul," Khalid shot back in a cool tone, despite his unsettled state. "But I insist you reveal your reason for such behavior before I soundly trounce you, as I'd like to know what I'm supposedly guilty of—beyond having the bad luck to call you cousin."

At that, Jalal reared back and punched Khalid in the face.

Khalid had been born the son of a king. An eighth-generation al-Rashid. As such, it was only the third time in his life anyone had ever struck him with such unmitigated force. With such visceral hatred.

First his father. Then Shahrzad.

And now Jalal.

Khalid reeled to the ground, his fingers clawing at the dirt. Blood thundered in his brow, excruciating in its force. The chained beast in his head bayed, thrashing about, its claws raking across his eyeballs.

Still, Khalid pushed himself up to his knees . . .

And launched into Jalal's torso.

They landed in the dirt like two angry schoolboys, in a jumble of arms and legs and clumsy scabbards. Jalal lobbed a fist in Khalid's direction, even while struggling to right himself. It glanced off Khalid's jaw. In response, Khalid shoved the side of his cousin's face into the dirt and pressed a knee to Jalal's stomach. He managed to land several unforgiving blows to Jalal's head and chest before Jalal kicked him off, spitting a mouthful of blood and elbowing Khalid without mercy near his brow once—

Then twice more.

A crowd of curious onlookers had begun to gather, surely wondering what had prompted two well-dressed young men to come to such wicked fisticuffs.

Khalid clutched his skull, trying to crush away the agony. Needles of light cut the edges of his vision. Stabbed his temples. Enraged by his cousin's inexplicably brutal attack, he rolled to standing and reached for his *shamshir*.

Jalal's eyes went wide. Then, without a second thought, he scrambled to his feet and unsheathed his scimitar. "Draw!" A line of crimson dripped down his chin.

Khalid's fingers tightened around the hilt. Yet he refused to unsheathe his sword.

Refused to engage a loved one in a battle of lethal force.

"Do it, you coward!" Dirt marred one side of Jalal's face, coating his skin in an eerie dash of glittering dust.

Even from where he stood—even in a silence fraught by nerves—Khalid could see a suspicious mist forming over Jalal's eyes.

It iced the blood in his veins.

"You think I can't beat you?" Jalal strode closer, brandishing his scimitar. "Or is this guilt? Finally a show of guilt for someone besides yourself?"

"Guilt for what?" Khalid took in a ragged breath, fighting to maintain his preserve. "What did I *do*?"

The silence stretched inexorably thin.

Jalal licked his bleeding lip. "You never did forgive me for sending her away, did you?" His voice was hoarse, scratched. Defeated. "For asking that boy to take her with him?"

At that, Khalid's hand dropped from his *shamshir*. Though this was a far cry from explaining his cousin's behavior, at least they were no longer on the cusp of disaster.

"I told you there was nothing to forgive. And I meant it."

"Then why did you do it?" Jalal's sword fell to his side, but his face remained knotted by anger.

"What are you talking about?" Any more of these continued vagaries, and it would be a struggle for Khalid to keep his temper.

Jalal considered Khalid, clearly searching for signs of artifice.

"Despina."

Everything around Khalid stilled. Even the very air around him swirled to a sudden halt.

"You sent her away," Jalal whispered, his tone hollow. "After I confided in you. You must have known of whom I was speaking. Or my father must have asked you to send her away. And you did it. Without question." He took a slow step forward. Then another. "In the end, family is nothing to you. I . . . am nothing to you."

Something flared in Khalid at these words. "I never—"

Jalal's eyes darkened to a muddy haze. "Don't start lying to me. Not now."

"I'm not. I would never lie to you."

"Then it's a coincidence?" He cast Khalid an arch glance. "That—mere days after I tell you I want to marry the girl carrying my child—she's sent away from the palace, without explanation?"

"I didn't send her away. She asked to leave." The truth in its entirety stood poised on the tip of Khalid's tongue. He wanted to tell his cousin what had happened. But now the circumstances seemed so . . . odd. Now that Khalid knew what had transpired— and the true identity of Jalal's love—Despina's hasty marriage to Vikram appeared more than a little suspicious.

More than a little convenient.

Especially for a girl so versed in secrets and lies.

Khalid made another quick study of Jalal al-Khoury's face.

At the poorly hidden pain marring his cousin's features.

He would not risk causing Jalal any further pain. Not until he had answers.

Not until he knew what Despina was hiding.

Khalid closed the distance between them and placed a tentative hand on Jalal's shoulder. "Especially if I'd known your true feelings, I would never have sent Despina away. Even if Uncle Aref had made such a request, I would not have done so. Jalal—"

"Why not?" Jalal's lips thinned, his eyes going chillingly blank. "I sent away the girl you love. So it stands to reason that you would send away the girl I love as punishment. You've always had a bad temper. I just never knew you possessed such a mind for revenge as well."

At that, Khalid felt his temper rise in a hot spike. "I do not possess a mind for revenge."

Perhaps he had in the past. But he didn't now. Not anymore.

Not since Shahrzad.

The pain on Jalal's face dissolved in a scoff of disbelief. "It appears you're more like your father than I thought."

"I am nothing like my father." Though he fought to keep his temper at bay, Khalid's fingers balled into fists. "I thought you knew that. You've spent most of your life trying to convince me of it."

"And you've spent most of yours trying to convince me otherwise. Congratulations. You've finally succeeded." Jalal clapped with pejorative slowness, the hilt of his scimitar caught between his hands. "What was it you used to say in moments of poetic fancy? 'We are as a rose unfurling, becoming more clearly ourselves?'" he jeered, his anger making him reckless. His anguish making him foolish. "You lost something you love. I suppose you thought it only fitting that I lose something I love. Unfortunately in this case, I lost *two* things—an entire family."

His accusation hung in the small space between them, bitter and broken in tone.

Though no less harsh for its brokenness.

No less effective.

Khalid knew Jalal spoke from a place beyond reason. Still, he could not ignore the sharp stab each of his words inflicted upon him . . . and the responding desire to return his cousin's efforts with some spite of his own.

After all, if he was to be accused of monstrous behavior irrespective of proof, should he not rise to the occasion?

Khalid cut his eyes, peering down his nose at Jalal. "If she left you, it is not my fault," he said, in that softly condescending manner his cousin so despised. "If you loved her, it was your responsibility to marry her. Your responsibility to care for her. *Your* responsibility to tell her you loved her."

Laughter rolled from Jalal's lips, the sound as caustic as vinegar.

"As you told Shazi?"

Four more stabs. Each so effective.

"She knows how I feel." Despite the cool efficiency of his retort, the air was leached from around Khalid once more, and his fists drew even tighter against his sides.

"And now, so do I. Keep watch over your shadow, Khalid-*jan*. Because, for the first time in eighteen years, I won't be there to watch it for you."

# THE FIRE

T HERE WAS FAR TOO MUCH ANGER IN THE AIR. FAR too much hatred.

Such emotions made it difficult to think rationally. Not that actual sense seemed of import to any of the brash fools present.

Omar al-Sadiq frowned at the gathering of men in his tent.

Frowned and remained silent.

Their war council was not going well. It was clear there was too much at stake for all involved.

Nevertheless, Omar listened as Reza bin-Latief shared reports about the boy-king of Khorasan. His peculiar disappearances. And the sorry state of his ravaged kingdom.

Many of the caliph's Royal Guards had died the night of the terrible storm. A large portion of his standing army had either perished or fled Rey. Now Khalid Ibn al-Rashid was calling on his bannermen to help rebuild and refortify the city.

Rey—and its ruler—were vulnerable.

At this revelation, a collective outcry arose from many of the young men present.

"Now is the time. We must strike at the heart of Khorasan!"

"Kill the bastard while he is weak!"

"Why are we sitting here idling about? We should attack the city with all haste!"

Omar's frown deepened. Still he said nothing. He did not so much as move from his cushioned seat in the corner. Even while he witnessed the clamor rise to a feverish pitch.

It did not behoove Omar or his people to raise objections now. It was best for him to remain unseen and unconcerned. A casual observer of this crisis. Omar did not yet have all the facts. And he needed to know more about the war that would likely transpire at his border.

The war that might put his people at risk.

The request Omar had recently made of Reza had not been met with glad tidings. Only moments before, he'd asked Reza to remove his soldiers from the borders of Omar's camp. This was to be the last war council in his tent. His last chance to witness the seeds of this discord. He'd already risked too much by assisting them with the provision of horses and weapons.

The Badawi people could not be associated with this uprising. Not yet.

Not when Omar had yet to choose which side to take.

It was true he felt genuine affection for the young *sahib* Tariq and his uncle Reza bin-Latief. But Aisha continued to warn him that neither of these men was to be trusted. One was lovelorn and reckless. The other hid behind secrets and sellswords.

And when it came to such things, his wife was never wrong.

The outcry around him grew even more uncontrolled, tearing Omar from his musings. The soldiers stamped their feet and waved their arms in the air, demanding to be heard.

Finally Reza stepped into the center of the tent.

At his flank stood two hooded soldiers, muscled and menacing. When a surge of men moved forward, the lackey to Reza's right barreled into their path, a hand on the hilt of his scimitar.

The scarab brand on the soldier's forearm flashed into view for an instant.

The mark of the Fida'i.

Omar leaned farther back into his cushions and ran his fingers along his beard.

Hired assassins. In his camp. Aisha was right. Such a thing could not be tolerated beyond tonight. His family. His people. There was simply too much at risk.

"My friends!" Reza raised both hands in the air, awaiting silence. "Though it may seem that now is the best time to attack Rey, it will all be for naught if we fail to secure the border between Khorasan and Parthia first. We must seize control of the lands between the two kingdoms, so that we may have strongholds we can rely on for supplies. I urge you to temper your rage—at least for the time being." A smile coiled up one side of his face. "Save it for when it is most needed. For when justice will finally be served on the boy who dares to call himself a king."

The cheers began anew. Frenzied in their fury.

Omar toyed with his mustache and swallowed a sigh.

His list of questions for Reza grew with each passing moment.

For it had not escaped Omar's notice that Reza seemed disturbingly at ease with warmongering. As well as ever-flush with gold. Alas, the identity of Reza's nameless benefactor continued to elude Omar.

To deepen his suspicions.

The presence of Fida'i in Omar's camp only made matters worse. As did the recent attack on the Calipha of Khorasan. Especially since Omar had not been granted the courtesy of meting out justice. Not even on his own land.

Omar refused to lose control. The calipha and her family were his guests. These were his lands. His people.

He wanted Reza's men out of his camp. He wanted to keep those in his charge safe. It pained him greatly that he did not yet know from whom.

As he glanced across the way, Omar saw another face sporting a frown to match his own. Though he'd noticed this face for its troubled silence earlier, it rather surprised him now. For it was a face that failed to conceal its confusion . . . and the many questions lurking beneath.

The frowning boy stood in a place of esteem on Reza's far right. He did not partake in the angry revelry. He did not say a word. Nor did he seem pleased with the news that his enemy's position had weakened.

When Omar leaned forward to study the tang in the air between the boy and his uncle, he sensed brewing consternation. A strange uncertainty.

Perhaps a struggle for power. Or a lack of understanding.

Omar should speak to Tariq Imran al-Ziyad soon.

This had been a poor decision on Shahrzad's part.

But it was too late now. If she left, the whispers would trail after her. The vitriol would spew in her wake.

Her escape would prove their point. Would prove she was afraid of them.

That their stares and their hatred had taken root.

Fear was a currency these soldiers understood well. A currency Shahrzad could ill afford at this time. Especially if she wanted to learn how best to sneak through the camp tomorrow night. And make her way to Musa Zaragoza.

So she sat with her feet to the fire. With a multitude of eyes glowing like embers in her direction. Like circling wolves, awaiting their alpha's command.

Shahrzad's gaze drifted around the ring of men seated near the crackling flames. Drifted past them to note the position of the sentries posted about the camp. Their position and their number. How often they wandered past.

The flickering flames threw everything into chaotic relief. Into distorted patterns of light and shadow.

Shadow that would hold her secrets. She hoped.

Irsa's left knee bounced at a feverish pace, her chin in her palm and her fingers tapping her cheek. "We should go."

"No." Shahrzad did not move her lips, nor did she look her sister's way. "Not yet."

A steady stream of men trickled from the sheikh's tent toward the immense blaze in the center of the encampment. As they took their places beside the fire, the men passed around pitchers of spiced wine with a liberal ease—an ease that spoke of recent discord and a pressing need to forget.

Apparently their war council had not gone well. And though Shahrzad was eager to discover why, she was not foolish enough to believe anyone would tell her.

Instead she watched the *ghalyan* coals being placed atop an iron brazier, while a gnarled-fingered old man packed several water pipes with sweet-smelling *mu'assel*. Their silk-wrapped hoses were kept carefully coiled beyond the reach of any sparks. A group of young women sat beside the towering *ghalyans*, giggling amongst themselves as they waited for the coals to catch flame. Their bright-colored *shahminas* hung loose about their shoulders, shielding their backs from the cool breeze of a desert night as the fire bathed the air before them in bristling heat.

Rahim lumbered from the depths of the Badawi sheikh's tent, his face crimped into a scowl, Tariq on his heels. Without once breaking his stride, Tariq took up a pitcher of spiced wine and knocked it back. He wiped his mouth with his free hand, then moved toward the fire, the pitcher dangling from his fingertips. As always, Tariq wore his every emotion like ill-advised regalia. Sadness. Frustration. Anger. Bitterness. Longing. For the first time, Shahrzad seriously considered fleeing, but instead lifted her chin and met Tariq's gaze.

Again, he did not falter.

Nor did he look away.

Shahrzad barely noticed when Rahim dropped beside Irsa, stirring up a cloud of sparks and grousing all the while. Though it took a great deal of effort, Shahrzad managed to curb her desire to pull away when Tariq took his place to her right—too close to be mistaken for a friend—his shoulder pressed against hers and a hand resting in the sand behind her . . .

Positioned with a cocky, proprietorial air.

Her body tensed; her eyes tapered to slits. She wanted to rail against him. And shove him away.

Tariq knew better. He knew how much she loathed this kind of behavior.

But she could not mistake the change around her.

The circling wolves—the eyes of judgment that had been upon her—continued their silent appraisal, but their hostility had diminished.

As though Tariq had willed it so.

While Shahrzad resented the insinuation that Tariq Imran al-Ziyad was her saving grace, she could not deny this change.

*They listen to him.*

Was Tariq the one behind the attack in Rey? Had he dispatched the Fida'i assassins to her bedchamber that night?

*He could not have . . . done such a thing.*

No. Even though Tariq despised Khalid, his love for her would bar him from resorting to such violence. From putting her at such risk.

From hiring mercenaries and assassins to achieve his goals.

Wouldn't it?

A flare of doubt formed in Shahrzad's chest. She banished it with a breath.

Shahrzad had to believe in the boy she'd known and loved for so long.

Beside her, Irsa's leg continued its nervous twitching. Just when Shahrzad had decided she had to put an end to it—before it drove her mad—Rahim reached for Irsa's knee.

"You're shaking your luck away, Irsa al-Khayzuran." He squeezed her knee still. "And we might need it soon." His eyes drifted back toward the still-emptying tent. Back to the site of the recent war council and its unspoken meaning.

Rahim's hand did not leave Irsa's knee.

Flickering firelight or no, Shahrzad could see the tinge of pink on her sister's skin.

And the odd slant of Rahim's lips as he glanced down into the sand.

*Dear God. Irsa and . . . Rahim?*

Shahrzad snatched the pitcher from Tariq's hand.

The heat from the fire had warmed the wine. Had heightened the spiciness of the cloves and cinnamon. The bite of the ginger. The rich sweetness of the honey, and the sharp citrus of the cardamom.

It tasted strong and delicious.

Heady and potent.

She swallowed more of it than she should have.

"Shazi." It wasn't an admonition. It was a warning.

When she glanced at Tariq, he was staring at her sidelong, his thick eyebrows set low across his forehead.

"Why are you permitted to drink to your heart's content, yet I am not?" she countered, clearing her throat of the wine's sting.

Tariq reached for the pitcher. "Because I have nothing to prove."

"Ass." She held it just beyond his grasp. "You are not my keeper, no matter how much you may wish it." Though she'd meant the words as a rejoinder, she regretted them the instant they passed her lips. For she saw Tariq draw back into himself.

"I thank the stars for that," he said in a hollow tone.

Shahrzad leaned closer, wanting to apologize but uncertain of how best to do so.

Without warning, Tariq snaked his arm around her. His hand shot forward, his long fingers taking hold of the pitcher.

"Let go of it this instant, or I'll dump its contents on your head and leave you to wallow in honeyed misery," he whispered in her ear, his amusement as plain as his threat.

Shahrzad froze, his breath tickling her skin.

"Do it and I'll bite your hand," she said. "Until you scream like a little boy."

He laughed—a rich susurrus of air and sound. "I thought you were tired of bloodshed. Perhaps I'll toss you over my shoulder. In front of everyone."

Refusing to comply without a fight, she pinched his forearm until he grimaced.

"This isn't over." Nevertheless, Shahrzad relinquished the pitcher.

Tariq grinned. "It never is." He took a celebratory swallow of wine.

Though she'd ceded this battle, a small part of her felt lightened by the exchange. It was the first time in almost a week—indeed, the first time since they'd left Rey—that they'd spoken to each other without the hint of anguish hanging in the air between them.

Without her betrayal in the forefront of their minds.

It also marked the first occasion Shahrzad believed their friendship might survive all that had transpired.

This newfound hope easing the weight on her heart, Shahrzad looked up at the starlit sky above. It was a deep blue, with a crescent moon wrapped in a fleece of passing clouds. The sky seemed to stretch on without end, its horizon curving to meet the sand on either side. Its blinking stars were a study in contrasts, some flashing in merriment, others winking in wicked suggestion.

The stars in Rey were never so bright.

For a moment, Shahrzad was reminded of something her father used to say: *"The darker the sky, the brighter the stars."*

Just as she began to drift into thoughtful solitude, a burst of nearby laughter jarred her into awareness.

The young women sitting beside the *ghalyans* were being entertained by a host of young men with pitchers of spiced wine.

"Despite the old sheikh's request tonight, it matters not where we set up camp. What matters is that we're close to laying siege to Rey," an inebriated young man proclaimed. "And, when we do, I will be the first to piss on the grave of Khalid Ibn al-Rashid!" He lifted his pitcher skyward.

The girls tittered. One stifled a cackle. The other young men joined in the toast, their pitchers raised high and their voices raised even higher.

Their shared joy was like the tip of a cold blade against Shahrzad's spine.

"That monster doesn't deserve a grave," another young man chimed in. "His head belongs on a pike. He'll be lucky if we offer him a dram of water before we sever it from his body." A rousing chorus of approval. "After he murdered those innocent young girls, a clean death is too good for him. I say we tear him apart and leave him for the carrion crows. Better still if he continues to draw breath while the crows pick at him."

At this next cheer, the group of men grew in number, as more were drawn to the clamor like bees to nectar.

The blood roared through Shahrzad's body. The tiny hairs on her skin stood straight up.

*Khalid.*

With nothing but their drunken threats, these foolish boys had managed to burn brutal images onto her mind. Brutal images that would not soon be forgotten.

Her strong, proud king. Her beautiful, broken monster.

The boy she loved beyond words—

Torn to pieces.

She would *never* let them near Khalid.

She would say whatever lie needed to be said, exist beneath hate-filled waters forever . . .

Until she drowned in their enmity, if need be.

It was not fear that drove her to such reckless thoughts.

It was fury.

*I will destroy the next one who dares to speak. The next one to utter his name.*

She could feel Tariq's eyes on her. Like the eyes of the wolves about the fire.

He pulled her close. Tried to shield her. Not simply out of concern.

But out of pity.

She knew it the instant she felt his hand in her hair, smoothing it from her face, silently assuring her of—

"Let's ask the White Falcon!" The first young man turned to Tariq. "The *supposed* leader of our host." The men around him did not even bother to hide their amusement at the slight. "How would you like to see the monster meet his end?"

Tariq stiffened at the taunt, then relaxed. He tilted his head back, affecting a look of ease. His fingers ran through Shahrzad's dark waves, in full view of those around them.

*Please show me you are not driven solely by hatred, Tariq.*

*Show me there is honor behind your actions.*

*That I can still reach you.*

"I am not necessarily in agreement," Tariq began in a solicitous tone that managed to quiet the restless din around them. "For I do think Khalid Ibn al-Rashid deserves a dram of water."

Shahrzad's pulse slowed in time with her breath as Tariq held up a hand against a slew of protests.

"And his body deserves a proper burial . . ." Again, he silenced the crowd with a gesture.

"*After* I put his head on a pike for all the world to see."

The sound of the cheering was lost in the bitter rage echoing through Shahrzad's ears. The strangled screams of a wrecked heart.

As the men continued carrying on with their pitchers and their puffs on the *ghalyans* around them, Tariq handed Shahrzad his spiced wine, his expression bleak. Vaguely apologetic.

Yet determined.

Shahrzad drank, staring into the fire—

Watching it burn her newfound hope to ash.

"I don't need your help." Shahrzad pushed Tariq away, then proceeded to lurch to one side.

"A likely story, you awful girl." He threaded his arms across his chest, watching Shahrzad sway through the Badawi camp on unsteady feet, in the opposite direction of her tent.

Tariq was honestly surprised she was able to remain upright at all. Even hours later, he still felt impeded by the effects of the wine, and he'd never known Shahrzad to drink spirits of any kind before.

By all rights, Tariq knew he should fall down laughing at his current predicament. The irony. Shackled to the one person he hoped to avoid. This was not at all how he'd wished to end the night. He'd hoped the wine would dull his frustrations. With Shahrzad and his uncle's continued evasions. With the soldiers' veiled taunts as to his irrelevance. It was becoming clearer every day that he was nothing beyond a name. After all, when had his uncle given him anything more than nominal power?

Tariq felt uneasy around these men who were willing to destroy what remained of Rey without question. Willing to shed innocent blood for their cause.

Blood Tariq was not ready to spill.

When Shahrzad pitched to one side again, Tariq shot forward and caught her, though the sudden motion nearly launched him into the sand. Fighting for balance, he reached for a nearby pole, its waning torchlight glowing thinly around them.

"I told you, I don't need your help!" she slurred, though she gripped at his *qamis* in an attempt to stand straight.

Her delicate hands were against his chest. She smelled of spiced wine and springtime. Her hair was a tangle of invitation. Everything about her was utterly beguiling. Enchanting in that way only she could be—a girl who wielded her wiles without intent.

A girl who, despite his wiser inclinations, ensnared him still.

When she peered up at Tariq with a question on her perfect lips, it was all he could do not to answer it with a kiss.

"Was it you?" she whispered.

"What?" Tariq said, shaken from his trance.

Shahrzad grasped tightly the linen near his throat. "Did you send the Fida'is?"

"What are you talking about?"

"You wouldn't do that, would you? No matter how much you hated him? You wouldn't do that to *me*." She clenched the fabric even tighter, a plaintive note in her voice.

He blinked, trying to clear his mind of the wine's lasting haze. "Shazi—"

"You have too much honor for that." She shook her head while looking away, as though she were speaking to herself. "I could never love a boy without honor."

"Yet you love him." Tariq's rancor could not be missed.

Nor could he miss the opportunity to strike out at her.

Shahrzad's eyes focused on his. For a moment, he saw the heat of anger shine through the muddle of colors. "Khalid has honor, Tariq. If you'd only—"

"I don't want to hear you make excuses for him." Tariq shoved off the pole, determined to return Shahrzad to her tent and be done with this night, once and for all.

She stumbled after him. "If you would just listen—"

A group of soldiers rounded the corner, stalking into the light. Judging by their comportment, Tariq guessed they were intoxicated, but they didn't seem to be glad of it. They seemed to be looking for something, their shoulders caged, their fists at their sides.

The type of drunks on the hunt for a fight.

Tariq pulled Shahrzad back against the pole, concealing her in what appeared to be a lovers' embrace. He made certain to stand just beyond the weak circle of radiance cast by the torchlight. When Shahrzad raised a halfhearted protest, Tariq muffled her words against his chest.

Better the soldiers not see her.

Better these men on a hunt for a fight not find their match in the young Calipha of Khorasan.

For it was unlikely Shahrzad would be gracious with them, either.

Her body slackened against his as they waited for the soldiers to pass. The desire for battle was slowly leaving her as the wine continued to exert its influence. When she rested against him and he saw her eyes flutter closed, Tariq took a deep breath.

The ache of loss for something not yet gone was sharp. Sharper than anything he'd ever felt before.

"You need to sleep," he murmured.

"*Mmm.*"

Tariq exhaled, mentally cursing himself. "I'll take you to your tent."

Her head slumped forward in a nod. "Check their arms."

"What?"

"Look for the scarab," she said. "Don't trust the scarab."

"I won't." He rolled his eyes, glancing over his shoulder to make certain the soldiers were out of sight. Then he lifted Shahrzad from the sand, nearly thrown off-kilter by her weight, slight though it was. The wine did him no favors. Staving off its effects, Tariq staggered toward her tent.

Her arms circled around his neck. "I'm very sorry, you know."

Tariq could hardly hear her. "For what?" Again, he almost laughed at the absurdity of her apology. Now, of all times.

"That you have to see me. And do this. It isn't your pl—" Her eyes flew open, the crown of her head almost smacking him in the jaw. "Where is Irsa?"

"With Rahim."

Irritation marred her brow. "I shall beat him to death's doorstep. Make no mistake."

"What?"

"That gangly imbecile," she mumbled, her cheek falling against his chest. "I won't stand for it. I'll send the Rajput after him. He'll chase him down with his fiery *talwar* . . ."

With a shake of his head, Tariq pushed through the opening

of Shahrzad's tent, nearly dropping her in the process. He left the tent flap wide, allowing the moonlight to brighten the relentless dark of the space.

True to form, Irsa al-Khayzuran's bedroll was neatly bundled and stacked to one side. Shazi had not bothered to put hers away; it remained in the center of the small tent, her blanket askew, her pillow bunched in a fitful heap.

With barely concealed amusement, Tariq placed Shazi on her bedroll, not even bothering to drag her blanket across her body. She stirred when he tried to lift her pillow.

"Don't." She put a hand on his arm, her eyes slivering open.

"Or what?" he whispered, his lips twitching. "Empty threats do not move me, Shazi-*jan*."

She wrinkled her nose, then curled into a ball, pressing a palm to her forehead.

Again, he tried to lift her pillow and place it beneath her head. After a time, he realized the futility of such efforts and decided the best course of action was to let her sleep off her stupor.

As Tariq moved to stand, he noticed a piece of parchment that had fallen from the folds of Shahrzad's clothing. Most likely jarred loose when he nearly dropped her.

He lifted it into the moonlight.

It was creased in the manner of something that had been folded and unfolded numerous times.

Something with contents that mattered a great deal to someone.

He glanced down at Shahrzad's sleeping form. Wavered for the span of a breath.

Then unfolded the parchment.

*Shazi,*

*I prefer the color blue to any other. The scent of lilacs in your hair is a source of constant torment. I despise figs. Lastly, I will never forget, all the days of my life, the memories of last night—*

*For nothing, not the sun, not the rain, not even the brightest star in the darkest sky, could begin to compare to the wonder of you.*

*Khalid*

With great care, Tariq refolded the letter along its creases, his fingers longing to crush it in his fists.

To tear it asunder. To burn it into nonexistence.

He knew Shahrzad loved the boy-king. He'd known it since Rey.

And he'd known the boy-king cared about Shahrzad.

But he had not known the boy-king truly loved her. Despite what the captain of the guard had said the night of the storm, Tariq had not wanted to believe the murdering madman capable of loving anything or anyone. At least not in a way Tariq could ever understand.

This?

Tariq understood.

Completely.

In a rather short letter, the Caliph of Khorasan had managed to put to words exactly how Tariq had always felt about the only girl he'd ever loved. Had always felt but never managed to say with quite such simple eloquence.

These were not the words of a madman.

For the first time, Tariq saw what Shahrzad saw when she looked at Khalid Ibn al-Rashid.

He saw a boy. Who loved a girl. More than anything in the world.

And he hated him all the more for it.

# BOUNDLESS

SHAHRZAD PAID DEARLY FOR HER SILLY SHOW OF bravado with the spiced wine.

She spent the better part of the next morning with her face in a basin, emptying her stomach of its contents. Her insides were a jumble of knots; the dullest stream of light made her wince. There were moments she swore the very roots of her hair howled in protest.

Were it not for Irsa, Shahrzad felt certain these symptoms would have endured all day. When Shahrzad complained of feeling as though she were on a rolling ship in the midst of a storm, Irsa rummaged through her neat little pile of things and unraveled an old scroll. After scanning its contents, Irsa left their tent and returned with a tonic brewed from ground gingerroot and the peel of a dried lemon. Though Shahrzad protested at first—the concoction smelled quite strong and tasted rather bitter—she could not deny it helped in settling her stomach.

At Irsa's behest, Shahrzad remained in their tent, nursing her wounds and forcing down more of the bitter tonic. Ordinarily, she would have disliked wasting an entire day in bed while Irsa sat at their low table, transcribing scrolls by the light of an oil lamp. But on this particular day, Shahrzad did not protest.

For on this day, these circumstances suited her just fine. If everyone thought her ill, they would be even more likely to leave her to her own devices.

Even more likely not to notice when she snuck out after dark . . .

With her magic carpet in tow.

It was time to find Musa Zaragoza.

Time to see what she—and the magic carpet—could do.


In stealthy silence, Shahrzad tucked her dagger into her waistband and skirted past her sleeping sister. She secured a *shahmina* about her shoulders before grabbing the magic carpet. Once outside, she stayed to the tent shadows, her heart beating like a caged bird.

If someone found her creeping about at night only days after her arrival, they would suspect her of trying to flee or perpetrating something more insidious. It would not help quell the suspicions those in the camp harbored against her. And it would be even worse if she came across another boy like Teymur.

Her skin crawled at the thought.

With careful steps, Shahrzad moved between patches of darkness, avoiding any stretches of light. Her gaze went to the sentry posts she'd noted the night before. She allowed herself to breathe freely when she cleared the edges of the Badawi camp and strode into the endless sweep of sand beyond.

As luck would have it, she'd chosen a night without wind—a night in which every sound she made would be distinct. If she fell or yelped or did anything that might attract attention, her secret would be a secret no more; her detractors would have proof their doubts were rooted in fact.

And they might send her away, along with her injured father and her innocent sister.

At the very least, they'd find Shahrzad alone in the desert, with a dagger and a rug. Everyone would suspect her of treachery. They would be unlikely to leave her to her own devices again.

It could not be helped. She had waited long enough.

Though her first instinct was to go to Khalid, Shahrzad knew it would only be more difficult to leave Rey once she returned. And now was not the time to place her wants above the needs of her family.

Especially the needs of her father.

Shahrzad had to find Musa. After Baba, he was the only person she knew with any aptitude for magic. It might be beyond the realm of possibility, but perhaps he would know how to help her father.

Or how to break a terrible curse.

She wandered farther into the desert, trying to find a place where a rise of sand would conceal her from prying eyes.

Soon, Shahrzad came across a large dune that should suit her needs. Still, she felt silly when she unfurled the threadbare carpet onto the silken sand.

She took a step back. Reconsidered the small rectangle of tattered wool.

*What am I doing? How . . . ridiculous. This is utterly ridiculous.*

Her gaze hardened.

*I'm being a goose. Shiva would not approve of such indecision.*

*Nor would Khalid.*

Her eyes fell shut.

*"You are boundless. There is nothing you can't do."*

His words in her ears, Shahrzad removed her sandals and threaded them through her *tikka* sash. Then she secured her braid a final time and sat on the carpet.

There was no time for her to worry further about the ridiculousness of this endeavor.

No time for anything at all, really.

Shahrzad had thought she would need to press her hands to the rug's surface. But as soon as her bare feet grazed the worn wool, the sensation around her heart flared, warm and bright.

"Oh!" she cried softly as she dropped onto the carpet, her knees to her chest. The feeling flashed through her limbs with a sudden, burning brilliance. The carpet lifted into the air, its corners curving upward. It hovered above the sand, rising like a kite on an errant breeze.

Two emotions battled within Shahrzad.

The first was fear.

The second she would not yet dare name.

As the carpet continued its slow rise, the warmth flooded through Shahrzad's body, into her arms and legs, through the very tips of her fingers. It tingled in her nose and pulsed along the ridges of her ears.

Power.

Of a kind she'd never known before.

When she looked down again, she was high above the silver sands. As high as the highest turret of Taleqan.

The fear remained, but it was soon surpassed by that other as-yet-unnamed emotion.

Before she even had a chance to consider it, she knew with an innate kind of certainty how to direct the carpet, as a fish born in water knows how to swim.

*"Let it take you where your heart longs to be."*

*Home. To Khalid.*

Shahrzad gripped the carpet tight with determination. "No. Take me to Musa Zaragoza," she whispered. The prickling warmth around her heart blazed brightly, then seared through the rest of her, tearing another cry from her lips.

Along with an unexpected smile.

The carpet swooped in a lazy arc, rising even higher. To the height of the highest parapet of Rey. As soon as it turned, it took off into a light-studded sky. The world below her disappeared in a rush of flickering fire.

Fear lost its battle.

Exhilaration won.

Shahrzad laughed into the night, a current of air at her feet. She rose onto her knees. Let her arms spread wide in the wind. Let the whistling chill wash over and past her, but not through her. Never through her.

Never for a moment did she think the carpet would let her fall.

She was the water in the tumbler, swirling and dancing to a music she alone could hear.

And up here—higher than she'd ever thought she could be—the wind blew alongside her, while all else vanished in a blur.

Still, there was no fear.

For up here, Shahrzad chased the wind.

The ground did not exist. Nor did the sky.

Here, she was truly boundless.

Fear would never overtake her again.

# THE BOY BY THE SEA

SHAHRZAD FLEW OVER THE DESERT, TOWARD A mountain range.

When she saw the sea sparkling on the horizon, her eyes widened in shock.

She'd traveled an astonishing distance in a rather short amount of time.

The magic carpet began to slow as it neared a low promontory overlooking a pale strip of sand. The moon still hung high in the sky, its shifting light glancing over receding waves. A lace of foam collected along the shore. Shahrzad took a deep breath. The air was thick and heavy, filled with the tang of salt. As the carpet circled above the cliff, a pillared structure with a dome of brindled stone emerged from behind a wall of grey rock. Marble columns capped by tongues of fire stood sentry at the corners. A wide set of stairs descended to a rectangular pool of water near the edge of the promontory.

The magic carpet floated alongside the pool, poised just above a smooth stone rise. Shahrzad eased a bare foot off the woolen surface.

And the carpet landed with a careful *whuff*.

She donned her sandals and made a slow scan of her surroundings.

The pool was enclosed on two sides by rows of cusped arches. Between those arches were marble statues of men and women pouring gilded streams of water or wielding strange contraptions Shahrzad had never seen before. One was an orb filled with what appeared to be swirls of fire—or perhaps it was wind? Another looked to be spinning a vortex made of . . . sand?

Burning incense rose from squat copper pots flanking the pool. Blue-grey smoke seeped into the air above them, the scent of peppery-sweet myrrh strong. Set against the tan stone was a mosaic border of bright blue lapis lazuli.

Shahrzad rolled up the rug with care. She strapped it to her back using her *shahmina* before taking a tentative step forward.

The pillared structure seemed to be a temple. Given the hour, it was no shock to see very few signs of life around her. Still, Shahrzad kept a hand near her dagger as she passed the pool and its copper pots of smoking incense, walking cautiously toward the wide set of stairs ahead.

Her gait did not falter when a familiar figure appeared at the top of the staircase.

He was quite tall and dressed in a cloak that fell to his feet in a chaos of colors. Leather *mankalahs* were wrapped around each wrist. His head was completely shorn of hair, and his deep brown eyes glowed like beacons of warm light.

"I was wondering when you would visit me." Musa Zaragoza

grinned down at her, his smile bright. He held out his hands to her, signaling her up the stairs. A boy and a girl near her age materialized from behind the fire-capped columns to Musa's right. The girl raised a trio of tapers in a rosewood holder, the wax dripping in creamy rivulets beside her wrist.

Both the boy and the girl were armed with short, hooked swords at their left hips.

Shahrzad halted near the bottom step. Without a second thought, she reached for her dagger.

Musa smiled broadly, his features smoothing in understanding. "You're among friends here, my star. I can assure you of precious little in this world, but in this, I can rest my life: here, you are safe."

"Forgive me, Musa-*effendi*," she said, though her fingers did not move from her side. "But there are times I forget what being safe feels like."

He waved a dismissive hand. "There is nothing to forgive."

Shahrzad's gaze flicked back to his silent sentries. "I hope I have not offended anyone. Or caused any undue trouble by coming here tonight."

The girl's head of spiraling curls tilted in Shahrzad's direction, her eyes wide. Inquisitive. The boy yawned, his stick-straight hair mussed on one side, as though he'd just risen from a nap.

"You have caused no trouble. Parissa and Masrur are on guard duty this evening. As usual, Mas would rather be asleep, but Parissa's curiosity has won out over all else. She is quite fascinated, as she's heard a great deal about you." Musa laughed, and it crinkled the dark skin around his eyes. He glanced over his shoulder at the boy and girl in question.

"I apologize for visiting in the middle of the night." Shahrzad offered them a wary grin as she started up the steps, her hand finally falling from her dagger. Parissa held her tapers high, illuminating the path for Shahrzad, while Mas remained as drowsy as ever.

"We suspected you were on your way." Musa's smile turned knowing. "The stars told Parissa to expect a visitor late this evening, and she relayed the message to me earlier."

Startled by this news, Shahrzad almost missed a step. "The stars?" Her eyes shot to the doe-eyed girl hovering on her left.

*She can read the stars.*

Shahrzad had heard of those who could do such a thing. But she'd never had occasion to meet someone with this rare ability.

Parissa was no longer looking at her. She was studying the carpet lashed to Shahrzad's back, with a troublingly covetous gaze.

One that gave Shahrzad decided pause.

"Why don't you join us inside for some tea, and I will answer all of your questions," Musa said, his voice quiet and soothing, like a brook weaving between uneven stones.

Shahrzad tarried a beat, her foot coming to rest on the final step. "I'm afraid I don't have time for tea. I must return before dawn breaks."

*Before my absence is discovered.*

She swallowed, hoping to convey her need for discretion in nothing but a glance.

"I see." The sharply attuned magus nodded, though his eyes narrowed in question. "Is there something—"

"I need your help, Musa-*effendi*." She met him atop the staircase, squaring her shoulders without concern for pride or propriety. "For my father . . . and for Khalid."

Unseemly though it was to begin with demands, Shahrzad knew it could not be helped. She did not have time for anything more than complete candor.

Neither did those she loved.

Thankfully, Musa did not press further. He took her hand without the slightest pause. "What is it you need, my star?"

At Shahrzad's wordless behest, Musa relieved Parissa and Masrur of their posts and sent them to sleep. Mas gave her a grateful look, though Parissa appeared rather miffed. She eyed the magic carpet a final time before leaving, a trail of wax dribbling in her wake.

Musa listened to Shahrzad's story while sitting on the stone steps of the Fire Temple, his face stark. Only twice did his expression soften. Once when Shahrzad mentioned her father's book. Then again when he heard her speak of Khalid. The moment Shahrzad confessed how much she'd come to care for Leila's son—the son who'd watched his beloved mother die at the hands of a cruel father—Shahrzad suspected she had much more than an ally in the otherworldly magus.

After Shahrzad finished her tale, Musa paused to ruminate on the dancing flames at the top of the marble column nearby.

"Did you know these things would come to pass?" Shahrzad asked when she could stomach the silence no longer. "Did Parissa read the stars and reveal my future?"

He shook his head, a smile playing at the edges of his lips. "That is not the way of it. Your future is not set in stone, my dearest star. A coin turns on itself a number of times before it lands."

Shahrzad exhaled protractedly. "How I wish I believed that were true, Musa-*effendi*. But recent events have proven it is not. Khalid's future appears to be set in stone. And with it, mine."

Musa leaned forward, his elbows settling upon his knees. "So you've come here in hopes I might break this fearful curse?"

"Is it possible?" she whispered, gripping the fabric of her trowsers tightly.

"Alas"—he gazed at her sadly—"magic in our world can be a mysterious gift. One not so easily controlled, and not without great cost. I have no notion of the magic that was used to enact this evil, and even if I did, there are not many powerful enough to fend off a curse. The most I could do is offer some kind of talisman to ward away Khalid's sleeplessness for a short time. But I am not powerful enough to counteract a curse, dearest one. The only way I know to break a curse is to fulfill it."

Shahrzad's face fell, the bleakness taking hold.

"But I might be able to do more for your father," Musa continued. "Especially with regard to the book he keeps with him. You said he has many burns on his hands? That this book gives off an unusual amount of heat?"

"Yes, it nearly burned me when I came near it the other day." Shahrzad's mouth thinned as she recalled the peculiar wave of heat she'd felt whenever she'd drawn close to the tome in her father's arms.

"And he spoke in an unfamiliar language when you found him on the hill outside Rey?"

Shahrzad nodded.

Musa pressed a forefinger to his lips in momentary contemplation. "I know you are averse to involving anyone else in these matters, but I do feel as though we need to consult with another individual."

"Is there someone you know who might be able to help?" A thread of hope tugged at Shahrzad's heart.

"Perhaps. There is someone here who may know more than I. If my suspicions are correct, he would, at the very least, be able to answer questions about this book, though it may prove to be an . . . interesting task gathering answers from him."

Shahrzad shifted uncomfortably, her palms resting against the cool stone beside her. "Can I—can we—trust him? Save you, I have told no one about the curse, and I do not wish to tell anyone else. Such information would be dangerous in the wrong hands."

"Trust is an interesting matter when it comes to Artan. He will not give it to those who do not offer it first. In any case, I leave the decision to you." Bemusement washed across his features for an instant, then vanished in a burst of certitude. "But regardless of your choice, he will not betray you, of that I am sure." He rose from the steps and reached out a hand to her. "Come with me, my lady."

Shahrzad trailed after Musa as he made his way down the steps, past the rectangular pool of water. Though she remained doubtful, she continued following the magus as he walked toward the edge of the promontory.

When he made a sharp turn near the brink of the cliff, another set of stairs emerged before them, descending into utter darkness. Carved straight from rock, they were jagged and precarious. Without a railing. Without any handholds to speak of. She assumed they led to the stretch of sand below, but she could not see exactly where, as the trail vanished in another sharp turn a stone's throw away.

A staircase that gave new meaning to faith.

*One would think they'd have a torch nearby.*

*Especially at a Fire Temple.*

Unperturbed, Musa smiled back at her. "Would you rather use the magic carpet?"

"Or why not a bridge made of moonbeams?" she grumbled.

He laughed heartily and held out his hand for hers. Without a word, she let him lead her down the perilous stone steps into the cavernous void below.

The sound of crashing waves grew louder as they neared the shoreline.

At first, Shahrzad could not fathom why they were crossing a dark beach in the dead of night. The shafts of moonlight dancing off the waves did not indicate the presence of any other besides her and the colorfully robed magus before her.

But as they crossed the ripples of sand, Shahrzad noticed a small outcropping of rocks jutting into the sea.

Stretched across a flat stone in its center was the lone figure of a young man.

A small wave struck the base of the stone, bursting white spray into the air, drudging seawater onto his trowsers. Yet the young man did not stir from his spot.

Musa came to stand near the edge of the lapping water, a few paces from the boy. The magus proceeded to wait, assuming a stance of serene silence.

After a time, Shahrzad grew impatient. The boy on the rocks was being quite rude to Musa-*effendi*. For he had to know they were there. The half-moon behind them cast their shadows onto his face, long and lean and unmistakably present.

She coughed twice.

Still, the boy did not move a muscle, save to blink. And to sigh.

Which, of course, meant he was not dead.

*Scapegrace.*

Musa took in a great breath of briny air. "Artan?"

The boy propped a foot on one knee and placed a hand beneath his head. Then he yawned loudly. Prodigiously.

"Artan Temujin," Musa tried again. It was not a forceful entreaty. Clearly, the magus had the patience of twenty men. And the serenity of many enlightened souls.

By contrast, Shahrzad was tempted to shove the boy off the rock. To watch the waves toss him about for a while.

But there was a possibility she would need his help.

What happened next all but caused Shahrzad to fall face-first into the waves herself.

The boy lifted a hand into the air above his chest. He twisted his fingers, and a spinning ball of fire the size of a fist appeared above his open palm. He flicked the rapidly rolling blaze higher, so as to see Shahrzad in a better light. Then he tossed the fireball into the waves with a flip of his wrist. It fizzled in the sea before disappearing in a whorl of white smoke.

All the while, Shahrzad could barely suppress a gasp.

*I will not be impressed by this scapegrace. No matter how impressive he may be.*

When the boy sat up, she noticed him sway to one side. He slid from the rock with a splash into knee-deep waters—

Before tipping over altogether with a wry chortle.

*He's drunk!*

Shahrzad folded her arms, curbing her indignation. She glanced at Musa, who did not seem at all disturbed by the boy's condition. He seemed resigned.

As though he'd expected as much.

When the boy sat back and lifted his face into the starlight, Shahrzad detected many things of note.

Like Musa, the boy's head was completely bald. The lobes of both ears were pierced with small gold hoops. His skin was a light sable color, and his eyes were sloe-shaped and elegantly hooded, distinctly of the Far East. He was not classically handsome, but he was striking in his own way. For his beauty lay in the sum of his faults—an all-too-prominent jaw, a nose broken and healed in several places, a diagonal scar through his lower lip. From where she stood, the rest of his skin looked as smooth as the surface of a looking glass. He wore no shirt, and slender pants that had been fine many moons ago. Now they appeared tattered and without a care.

Just like the boy who wore them.

Once he found his footing, Shahrzad discovered he was not

much taller than she, though his torso was wide—he was barrel-chested and strong.

"She's pretty," the boy slurred with a slight accent. His mouth tugged to the side in a cutthroat grin.

Without thinking, Shahrzad returned one in kind.

He let out a wild laugh. "But not pretty enough."

"How fortunate your talents lie elsewhere. And that you are not a judge of beauty," she said with another biting smile.

"Ah"—he held up a long forefinger—"but I am. I happen to be the preeminent judge of beauty this side of the Shan K'ou river. There was a time I had to choose which of four enticing virgins was the most—"

"Artan." Musa tsked, canyons of disapproval forming around his mouth.

The boy laughed again, falling back into the water. He proceeded to float on an idling current, his arms outstretched and his legs spread wide.

"He's drunk," Shahrzad murmured through pursed lips. "And a liar."

"That's true." The boy didn't flinch. "They weren't virgins." He winked at her. "Though *liar* is a bit of a stretch. I merely enjoy embellishing the truth."

Musa rubbed a hand across his face. "Please sit up for a moment. As a favor to me, act in a manner befitting your heritage."

At that, the boy let out another overly emphatic round of laughter.

"I'm sorry, Musa-*effendi* . . . but he is not in a state to provide us with any help. And I do not have time to wait." Shahrzad turned on a heel, frustrated she'd even hoped to gain assistance from such a lazy, rude boy.

"Shahrzad-*jan*—

The boy lurched to his feet in a squelch of seawater. "*That* cheeky snipe is the Calipha of Khorasan?" It was the first sign of a frank reaction to anything they'd said thus far.

*He knows who I am?*

Shahrzad turned back to the boy. "And just who are you?" she asked, her fists on her hips.

"Artan Temujin." Though he nearly toppled over in the process, the boy gave her a taunting bow.

She hooked a slender brow at him, trying to invoke some restraint. "Who is that *exactly*?"

"Give me your hand and I'll tell you." Sly treachery laced his every word.

"I'd sooner kiss a snake."

"Smart girl!" He laughed. "But you've kissed a murdering madman . . ." Beads of water rolled down his barreled chest. "Is that not the same thing?"

"You—" Shahrzad started after him, no longer able to contain herself.

With a satisfied smirk, Artan yanked her into the water beside him. Torn off her feet, she caught herself on his left arm.

Several things stunned her all at once.

He was overly warm, as though he were quite fevered, despite his recent stint by the sea. Up close, the skin of his palms was rough and calloused, and one of his forearms was monstrously scarred—

Just like Baba's hands.

But the most startling thing of all was the jolt that raced through her blood at his touch. Almost akin to the sensation of the carpet. A crackling around her heart that flashed through the whole of her.

"Well, well, well . . ." Artan paused, his dark eyes boring holes into hers. "It appears you were not wrong, Musa-*abagha*."

Shahrzad thought she heard the magus sigh behind them.

"Take your hands off me," she bit out at Artan, determined not to show how unnerved she felt. When he failed to relinquish his hold, she shoved his chest. He tilted to the side before grasping her wrists in one of his hands.

"What a temper!" He laughed appreciatively. "I should warn you, little snipe: the last girl who tried to thrash me into submission found her sight quite addled the next day." Artan beckoned her closer, as though she had a choice. "I made her eyes point in two different directions."

"Ha!" Shahrzad snorted. "In order to achieve such a feat, would you not need to stand straight first?"

"You should truly be afraid on the days I can stand straight. Why, there was a time I put to rout an entire fleet of—"

"Enough!" Shahrzad pushed him away. "I tried to be patient with you, since Musa-*effendi* said you might be of assistance, but I no longer believe that to be possible. Just answer this one question, and I'll leave you in peace. Do you or do you not know anything about a book that burns to the touch?"

Artan blinked, taken off guard. "What—does it look like?"

"Old. Battered. Bound in rusted iron and dark leather."

"With a lock around its center?" He cleared his throat, still fighting for focus.

"Yes."

He paused. When deep creases appeared across the even skin of his forehead, Artan seemed almost . . . fierce. Dangerous. "Has someone opened it?"

Under his abruptly severe gaze, Shahrzad suppressed the need to shudder. "I think my father may have."

"Does your father speak Chagatai?"

"I—don't know."

"That must wound your pride to admit," Artan said, his tone derisive.

Shahrzad looked away, a flush creeping up her neck.

*I should accept his criticisms. For now.*

"Is your father an idiot?" he continued.

"No!" Outraged into temporary speechlessness, Shahrzad merely stared at him.

"Only an idiot would open a book like that," Artan said, cold and merciless. "It's old, dark magic. Blood magic. The kind you pay for, many times over . . . if your idiot father hasn't paid already."

Shahrzad turned to Musa. "Why would this horrid boy be—"

"My ancestors wrote that book," Artan interrupted without a trace of the smugness Shahrzad would have expected from such an admission. "If your father is in trouble, my family are among the only ones who will know what to do."

Her heart shuddered to a stop.

*Holy Hera. He may actually be of help.*

Shahrzad worried the inside of her cheek.

She might have pressed her luck too far already with Artan Temujin.

*Khalid was right. My mouth never ceases to cause me woe.*

Shahrzad knew she had to try to win this scapegrace over, despite her behavior thus far. When she glanced at the boy standing across from her, he was watching her with a distressingly keen air about him, especially for someone so addled by drink.

It was a face marred by indolence. Riddled by insolence.

But an interesting face. That she could not deny.

"Would you—could you take me to see your family?" she asked, trying her best to affect an air of humility. In such a situation, perhaps even begging was not beyond her.

"No, Queen of a Land I Care Nothing About." Artan laughed at his own joke. "I won't."

"Artan, son of Tolu . . ." Musa Zaragoza's sonorous voice rang out from along the shore.

It was not loud, nor was it demanding.

Nevertheless, Artan rubbed his nose with the back of one hand, frowning with frustration. He groaned, the sound much louder than the situation warranted.

It was only a series of names. Yet it seemed to signify so much.

"Please," Shahrzad said, shrugging away her confusion. She took a step toward the boy. "I need your help."

Artan pressed a palm into his forehead, exasperated. "I shouldn't help you. And I have no desire to take a snipe like you anywhere."

She gnawed at her lip. "Please—"

"At least not until you learn to defend yourself. You're like a newborn colt; I can see everything you're capable of doing, which is a great deal of nothing, save run your mouth." He snorted. "Come back tomorrow night. Once you learn to control basic magic, I'll take you to see my aunt. She won't help anyone she doesn't respect. And she'll laugh you out of the room. Before burning you out of existence." Artan scowled once more at the shoreline, then kicked at the water, sending a salty mist high into the air.

Still at a loss, Shahrzad watched as the boy continued to exert his irritation on the hapless sea.

"Thank you," she said softly. "After my less-than-gracious behavior earlier, I know I don't deserve—"

"Oh, I intend to exact revenge upon you for this, make no mistake." Artan eyed her askance. "And I always get what I want."

Something about the way he looked at her made Shahrzad regret the decision to ask him for help. That same sense of danger intensified about him. Like the feeling right before falling. "Why—what exactly made you change your mind?"

"Because Musa-*abagha* asked me. And Musa-*abagha* asks for very little in return for offering me a safe haven." He sneered, sharp and biting. "Don't worry; I have no interest in you. I like nice girls, and you are not nice at all. You're selfish and spiteful."

Startled by this pronouncement, Shahrzad began to protest. "I'm not—"

"Don't misunderstand me. I'm pleased by it. It means we can be friends one day."

"Why in God's name would I want to be *your* friend?"

Artan fell back into the water with a strangely contented smile. "Because I'm just as selfish and spiteful as you are."

# WHERE THERE IS RUIN

THE FIREBALL HURTLED THROUGH THE DARKNESS, streaking across the sand.

Right toward her face.

Shahrzad tried.

Truly. She did.

But, at the last moment, all she could manage was to throw herself into a patch of glimmering powder at her feet.

"Useless!" A deep voice cracked out at her like a whip. "Just a complete waste of time."

*I . . . hate him.*

Gritting her teeth, Shahrzad clenched fistfuls of sand, wanting desperately to fling them into Artan Temujin's smug face.

"Are you angry, little snipe?" Artan continued. "Good. So am I. This makes the second—no, wait—*third* night in a row you've arrived at the temple and ruined my evening with the moon."

She unfurled to her feet, dusting off her palms. "Pardon me for ruining what would have been an otherwise productive evening."

"I'm pleased you agree with me. For the moon would surely

have offered me more entertainment than your pitiful attempts at magic." He snorted. "Such gifts . . . wasted on such tripe."

*Bastard!*

A rush of blood heated her cheeks. "If I had a fireball, I'd send it straight between your legs. But I worry there would be little to burn."

Artan laughed, loud and without a care. "At least your sense of humor offers something to recommend you. Though I've never been one for skinny, angry girls." He cast her a questioning glance. "Does the Caliph of Khorasan like the way you look?"

"Of course he does!"

"Wretched dolt." He leaned back on his heels. "Beauty fades. But a pain in the ass is forever."

"Ha! I suppose you would know."

Another fireball blazed to life in his palm. "That I would." Artan grinned, waggling his brows. "And I would take heed, if I were you."

When she broke into a run again, Artan groaned behind her. "The old adage is true, Shahrzad al-Khayzuran: we only run from things that truly scare us!"

"Then I am truly afraid of fire, Artan Temujin!"

Another loud groan. "Cease with being afraid. And begin doing something about it!"

Despite her distress, Shahrzad tried to conjure the feeling of warmth that flared to life whenever her skin came in contact with the carpet.

But she couldn't. It was impossible.

Like grasping for the stars.

She'd tried now for two consecutive nights. The only conclusion she could come to was this: her power did not arise from within her. Instead, she absorbed it from things around her.

When she'd first offered this suggestion to Artan, he'd laughed, his head thrown back and his mouth a fathomless chasm. Then he'd proceeded to attack her with a controlled volley of fire. He'd wanted her to—at the very least—defend herself.

Artan wanted her to toss aside *spinning balls of fire*. Or move other objects into their path to repel them.

With naught but the wish to do so.

It had been her turn to laugh, head thrown back in equally exaggerated fashion.

Artan believed that, if she were pressed by the thought of immediate danger, perhaps her body would react on instinct. So, for the past two nights, they'd been confined to the beach. He'd begun by threatening her with small, slowly swirling circles of flame. Shahrzad had run from them in a near panic. Indifferent, Artan had proceeded to actual churning spheres of death—which were decidedly harder to avoid.

All Shahrzad had to show for it were multiple bruises from the many times she'd thrown herself into the sand.

All Artan had to show for it was mounting frustration.

"You're a terrible teacher," Shahrzad cried. "This method was flawed from the beginning!" She neared the lapping waves, slowing her strides.

"If you're suggesting I'm flawed, then you're correct."

Stopping in her paces, Shahrzad leaned forward, gasping for breath. "Lesson concluded for the evening."

"Not quite."

She turned around, more than a little unsettled by his tone.

Sure enough, Artan began firing another series of shots directly at her. Orb after orb of rolling flames flew from his outstretched palms.

Shahrzad panicked. There was no way she could dodge them all.

"Don't run," Artan shouted. "Make them run from *you*. Make me believe I'm not taking a sheep to be sheared by wolves when I take you to my aunt!"

"I can't," she shrieked, aghast at the number of fire spheres spinning toward her. Not knowing what else to do, Shahrzad made a dash for the water and dove beneath the waves. She held her breath for as long as she could, treading beneath the churning surf. Then she kicked for the surface and emerged in waist-deep water, sputtering for air—

"Shahrzad!"

She peeled back a curtain of hair just in time to see a final ball of fire spin toward her.

There was no time to react.

It crashed against her, burning through her *qamis* and into her stomach.

For a moment, there was nothing but shock.

From the shoreline, Shahrzad heard Artan shouting in a strange language. The ball of fire turned back on itself and disappeared in a feather of smoke.

She couldn't even manage to scream. Around her, the smell of burning flesh mingled on the sea breeze. Her knees started to tremble as a wave collided against her.

The salt water on her bare skin stunned her back into feeling. Into agony.

Shahrzad fell toward the sea, a cry caught on her lips.

"Idiot." Artan gathered her in his arms and dragged her from the foaming surf back onto the shore. "Absolute fool," he muttered.

The shaking spread from her legs into her arms. Her teeth began to chatter.

"It's—it's on f-f-fire." Shahrzad dug her fingers into his wrist. "My—my skin. It's—it's . . ."

Kneeling along the shore, Artan pushed her back against the hard sand. "Complete moron."

"S-s-stop. I c-couldn't—"

"I'm not talking about you!" Without another word, Artan stripped back the scorched bits of linen around her stomach.

That time, Shahrzad managed a scream.

"Shut up, shut up!" Artan tugged at an earring, his expression pained. "Lie still, and I'll fix it. I swear I'll fix it."

Though his words were wrong, his face was strangely right. His jaw was fixed. The diagonal scar through his lip, white. He pressed both hands to her shoulders in an attempt to steady her quaking. A jolt blazed through her.

The dark centers of Artan's eyes spread, like a drop of ink through water. His hands moved from her shoulders to hover above her stomach.

From the tips of his fingers bloomed an unsteady light.

But it wasn't a warm light.

Something viciously cold tugged at her center. Tugged through her skin. A tremor rolled down her spine, as though the very air around them was prickly and alive.

The ink in Artan's eyes began to change color. Began to brighten to a stormy grey.

He swallowed a cry of pain. Then fell back onto his heels.

When Shahrzad sat up, she glanced down at her stomach. An ugly red welt remained. But it was nothing like the burn she'd expected, the pain nothing worse than that of a few days in the hot sun.

It took her only a moment to realize what had happened.

For on Artan Temujin's bare stomach, in the exact same spot, was a burn like hers.

Except his was far worse.

His was blistered. Sores formed along its length.

The sores she should have had.

Somehow, Artan had transferred the worst of her injury onto his skin.

"You—didn't have to do that," she sputtered, a salty lock of hair caught on her lips.

It was a ridiculous thing to say. An obvious thing to say. Yet she felt it should be said, nonetheless.

His mouth bent into a smile resembling a scythe. "You're welcome."

"Thank you," Shahrzad replied, still at a loss.

After a beat of unsettling calm, a shudder racked through him, and Artan collapsed into the sand. "We always seem to do things hind over end, don't we?"

"It appears so."

His chest heaved from exertion. "This"—he motioned between their matching burns—"isn't working."

"No." She leaned up on an elbow, her expression morose. "It's not."

"Such a pity." Artan remained prostrate along the shore, lost in thought, regarding the night sky above. "My aunt will eat you alive."

"Why—why do you think your aunt will eat me alive?" Shahrzad asked haltingly. "And if you know this, why did you agree to take me to her?"

*What is the real reason you are helping me, Artan Temujin?*

When Artan finally deigned to speak, his gaze remained fixed on the stars.

"Have you ever heard the story 'The Girl Who Grasped the Moon'?"

"Of course. Every small child has heard it."

"Tell it to me as you heard it."

"To what purpose—"

"Humor me." Artan pointed at his blistered stomach. "This once."

Shahrzad's brows pinched together. "Just this once." She turned her gaze toward the sky. "There was a girl who lived in a stone tower, surrounded by white dragons that did her every bidding. When she desired a sticky pastry, she had but to ask. When she wished to sleep, they turned the sky to night with the beat of their wings. The sun to moon with a simple roar. Though the girl wanted for nothing, she continued to want—more and more of everything and anything. But more than anything, the girl wished to be powerful. To her, the dragons always possessed more power than any being in the world, because they were able to make her every wish come true."

Artan heaved a breath, holding it for a spell. At this odd behavior, Shahrzad's confusion swelled further, and she stopped speaking.

When Artan eyed her sidelong, Shahrzad continued. "One night, when one of her dragons brought her a thick gold necklace she'd requested from a distant land, the girl smelled the strange perfume adorning its silken wrappings and decided she could no longer live with wanting this power. She had to have it. The girl demanded the dragon take her to its magic's source. The dragon turned to the full moon, its distress plain on its horned face. The girl did not care. She insisted the dragon take her to the moon so that she might harness its power. They flew toward it, a volley of stars collecting in their midst. The girl gathered the stars and from them fashioned a rope. Then—though the dragon roared a final warning—the girl threw a ring of stars around the moon, all while laughing like a bell tolling in the night."

Shahrzad stopped to glance at Artan. "But, like so many things of power, the moon refused to be contained."

At this, Artan smiled. But it was not a smile of amusement. It was a smile of something much darker and deeper.

"The moon began to glide through the sky. Torn from her dragon's back, the girl clung to the rope of stars. She cried out, asking the moon to grant her wish or release her. Like a chilling breeze, the moon's reply chased across her skin: 'You wish to be powerful? Then I will make you into my shadow. A moon to command the lost stars. But know that such a thing will come at a cost.' Without hesitating, the girl trilled with laughter. 'I care not about cost. Take all my worldly possessions, for I have no need of them once I possess such power.' The moon's words wafted through the night air, colder than a first snow. 'Very well, girl. I have long desired a true companion.' Then, in a swirl of stardust, the moon turned the girl into its shadow, bereft of all light. Tethered to it for all time. This shadow moon—the new moon—was granted power only a few nights a year. But never power enough to free itself from its bonds."

"This is why the moon we know seems to disappear," Artan finished quietly. "Overshadowed. Eclipsed."

Shahrzad nodded once. "Always chasing the true moon."

Their voices fell silent as the waves crashed in the distance.

"Why are you here, little snipe?" Artan began. "Is it really for your father?"

"Yes." Her response was swift.

"Nothing more?"

At this, Shahrzad hesitated. Of course she was here for her father. But she was also here for another reason. A reason that needed to remain shrouded in mystery. "Why do you ask?"

Artan turned his head to hers. "Because I know there's more. I know you're queen of a broken city and of a kingdom on the brink of war. That your king is a monster."

Shahrzad said nothing. Her fingers moved to the bare skin of her stomach, tentatively grazing her wound. It felt hot to the touch. Her mind's eye returned to only moments ago, when Artan Temujin's face had lost all hints of pretense.

When signs of true remorse—signs of richer emotion—were all too evident.

*"Trust is an interesting matter when it comes to Artan. He will not give it to those who do not offer it first."*

Perhaps it was time to put a small measure of trust in this boy. "Khalid is—not a monster. Not at all." Her heart lulled for a beat in the warmth of memory.

"Truly?" Artan studied her further. "Then what is he?"

"Why are you so curious?" Her eyes narrowed. "Why did you agree to help me, Artan Temujin?"

Artan did not reply immediately. "That story about the girl? It's about my family."

"What?" Trying to conceal her shock, Shahrzad turned to face him.

"Don't misunderstand me. Facets of your story are ridiculous. Heavily embellished by time. But its core is rooted in truth. One of my ancestors stole a powerful bringer of light to become an equally powerful wish-granter. In return, her maker trapped her. Bound her to him forever. A powerful genie, trapped in a hollow sword." His expression was equal parts bitter and blithe.

For a moment, Shahrzad was filled with disbelief. "I—"

"You wanted to know why I agreed to help you. It's mostly because Musa-*abagha* asked me to. And because I am bound by my ancestor's foolishness. Bound to be a trapped granter of wishes. Musa-*abagha* has kept me safe these many years. Safe from those who would enslave me. Make of me a dragon who does nothing but bring gold necklaces to thankless little girls." He laughed bitterly. "Musa Zaragoza protects me from my family's curse; he keeps us—me, Parissa, Mas, and the others—hidden and teaches us to control our powers. Protects us all here at the Fire Temple. Here, when we are asked to use our abilities, it is always our choice. Here, we are never slaves to our magic."

"But why would Musa-*effendi* need to protect you from your family?"

"My family is every bit as power-hungry as the girl who grasped the moon. They are monsters imbued with strange magic. My aunt safeguards them in a mountain fortress. But"—Artan paused, his face grim—"she's made mistakes before. My parents were casualties of her arrogance. They left the fortress, seeking a way to destroy their bonds. The magic they leaked into the world brought about terrible consequences. As a result, my aunt expects me to stay near and do as I'm told. Serve whom I'm told. So I ran away." Artan watched her closely as he spoke. "I find my aunt's control to be another form of slavery."

Shahrzad mirrored his scrutiny, taking care in preparing her next question.

"Is your aunt—very powerful?"

He snorted. "She could set fire to this temple with a single belch. And light every candle in Khorasan with the mere hint of her flatulence."

"Be serious."

"She's powerful." Artan laughed without guile. "And, like you, completely devoid a sense of humor."

Shahrzad let another small stretch of time pass, the sound of waves crashing upon one another growing louder, much like her thoughts. "Is she powerful enough to cure the sick?" She gnawed her lip. "Powerful enough to—break a curse?"

"Ah." He cut her a glance, all signs of humor gone. "There it is. Are you the one cursed?"

Shahrzad closed her eyes, then shook her head.

"Well, she'd need to speak with the one cursed," Artan replied. "And she would need to know what kind of magic was used."

"What if we don't know?" she whispered.

He brought both hands behind his neck, weaving his fingers through one another. After a time, Artan responded, his words soft. "You'll have to bring him, Shahrzad. Your king. He'll have to speak with my aunt if she's to help him."

Fear gripped her chest. Though she'd meant for him to help her—which entailed him knowing the truth—it didn't trouble her any less to hear it spoken aloud.

"Sometimes you make it so difficult to despise you," Shahrzad mumbled.

"I know." Artan grinned, still staring up at the stars.

They continued observing the night sky in companionable silence until the sound of footsteps swished in the sand nearby.

"Shahrzad-*jan*?" Musa's deep voice rang out in the darkness.

She stood, a sharp pang zinging from the burn at her waist. "Yes?"

"If I could speak with you for a moment—" He reached into the folds of his cloak. "I've brought something for you."

In his hand was a square of jade half the width of his palm, strung onto a slim circle of dark leather, meant to be worn about the neck. The surface of the polished green stone was covered in intricate markings.

"The talisman we spoke of," Musa said quietly.

*The one to ward away Khalid's sleeplessness.*

"I'm not certain it will do much," Musa murmured. "Again, it will likely only stave off the effects for a short while. But I thought to help, in whatever small way."

Artan yawned loudly at this. Shahrzad glared at him before glancing up at the tall figure before her. His black brows were stippled in white, furrowed by concern. "Thank you, Musa-*effendi*. This is far greater than anything I could have hoped for."

Musa nodded. "Please tell Khalid—I'm sorry I wasn't stronger those many years ago. I'm sorry for leaving him alone. But I'm here now, should he ever have need of me." With that, he placed the talisman in her hand and bowed deeply, his fingertips grazing his forehead.

As her thumb brushed over the etchings carved into the jade, Shahrzad tried her best to ignore the undeniable weight settling around her heart.

The weight of realization.

And the thrill of certainty.

*I'm going home.*

# A MOUSE'S CALL TO ARMS

THE MOON WAS A HALF DISC OF ALABASTER. IN THE distance, the clouds churned in tenebrous suggestion.

Just like the twist of nerves in Irsa's stomach.

Alas, she was not a good sneak. For her toes seemed to snag on everything in sight.

Twenty paces ahead, Shahrzad moved from shadow to shadow with a sure-footedness Irsa would have envied, were she not so aggravated.

Were she not so angry.

Irsa drew her cloak tighter about her—

And caught her ankle on another tent binding.

Muttering one of Shahrzad's choicest epithets, Irsa tore her sandal loose, then squinted through the dark.

Her sister had disappeared.

Without a moment's pause, Irsa broke into a run.

As she rounded the curve of the next tent, a hand darted from a pool of shadow and snared her wrist.

"Why are you following me?" It was both a demand and accusation.

Irsa gasped. Shahrzad's eyes flashed through the gloom.

Shocked from its temporary stupor, Irsa's pulse began rampaging through her body. Hot on its heels raced her indignation.

Irsa ripped her arm from Shahrzad's grasp. "Where are you going?" Fury dotted every word.

Shahrzad's jaw dropped.

Clearly, Shahrzad had not expected Irsa to be cross with her.

"I—" Shahrzad hardened her gaze. "I asked you first."

"I don't care! Tell me where you're going. Have you not learned anything? After what happened with Teymur, don't you know it's dangerous for you to disappear alone like this? I can't understand why you would—"

Her sister reached for Irsa, pleading and conciliatory. "Irsa—"

"No!" Irsa said. "I don't want a long-winded excuse. I want you to tell me where you're going and why. *Now.*"

Shahrzad sighed. "Of all nights, I wish you hadn't followed me tonight, Irsa-*jan*." She glanced into the desert with a wistful look. "Would you please let me go this once? I promise I'll take you with me tomorrow. I swear I will."

"I—I don't believe you." Irsa's eyes began to well. She bit back the tears, cursing her wretched sensitivity. "Why should I believe you? You didn't even go to see Baba today. Not once. Did you know he opened his eyes when I fed him his broth this afternoon? It was only for a short while, but he looked for you . . . and you weren't there! I had to lie for you while you slept, Shazi. Just like yesterday. And the day before that."

"I'm so sorry." Shahrzad took her hand and squeezed.

"You can't keep doing as you please and expecting everyone to wait for you. As though we have nothing better to do. As though we are capable of nothing else."

"I know. That was never my intention." Shahrzad chewed her lower lip. "But—can we please speak of this tomorrow?" Her eyes darted into the desert again, and Irsa felt the heat of resentment rise anew, pricking at the corners of her eyes.

"Go." She shook off her sister's grasp. "Go to wherever it is you're disappearing. To wherever it is that is more important than here and now."

Her sister reached for her hand again. "I promise I'll—"

"From now on, only make promises you intend to keep. And be safe, Shazi. Please. Stay safe."

Shahrzad paused, her features tight before she slipped into the shadows ahead without so much as a glance over her shoulder.

Irsa's feet felt leaden as she made her way back through the encampment. Each step seemed involuntary. She dragged her toes, making patterns in the sand. When she looked up again, Irsa realized she'd stopped outside a tent that was not her own.

What was she doing?

Irsa stood outside Rahim al-Din Walad's tent like a ninny absent purpose.

Absent reason.

Then she made a decision. And cleared her throat.

"Rahim?"

It sounded like a mouse's call to arms.

Irsa stood taller and tried again.

"Rahim."

Better. But still not exactly the roar of a lion.

She jumped and wheeled when his tent opened in a burst of lanky appendages.

"What's wrong?" Rahim swiped at the sleep crusting his eyes.

What *was* wrong?

Why had Irsa even come here?

"Aisha told me a story," she blurted without thought. "Do you want to hear it?"

"What?" He scrubbed at his disheveled scalp, his gaze incredulous. "Irsa, you can't be serious," he said. "It's the middle of the night."

"Never mind." The mouse returned, only to take its leave.

"Wait, wait." Rahim reached for her elbow. "Tell me."

Irsa stared up at him, lost in heavy lids and ink-black eyelashes. Had he always been so . . . tall? "She—she told me this desert was once a sea." Irsa paused to steady her voice. "That it was filled with all kinds of fish that danced in shining waters and swam beneath a perfect sun. Until one day a disgruntled little fish decided he was tired of swimming and wanted to fly. So he went to the Sea Witch, who asked him to collect all the white flowers along the farthest reaches of the sea and bring them to her. From their petals she would fashion him wings. When the little fish brought the Sea Witch a woven nettle filled with white flowers, she cast a spell, and a black shadow bloomed across the sun. It was as though night had fallen for all time. The sea dried up, and all the beautiful fish began to disappear, save for the lone fish with his white-petal wings. When the sun finally reappeared, the little fish felt such guilt for what he had done that he flew into its scorching light, his wings bursting into a thousand pieces. Now when you look across the desert and along the shore, you can still see how he paid for his wings—the lovely white shells with the flowers etched onto their surfaces." She finished the tale in a rush of words, all spoken in a single breath.

Rahim smiled at her patiently.

"I'm not a good storyteller," Irsa whispered, the remnant of a tear sliding crookedly down her face.

He reached forward and caught it with his thumb.

Embarrassed, Irsa pulled back.

It was a mistake to have come here.

Wasn't it?

A faint gust of wind blew around them, enveloping her in the scent of linseed oil and . . . oranges?

Rahim must have eaten oranges before falling asleep. How—wonderful.

"What's wrong, Irsa-*jan*?"

"She keeps leaving me behind," Irsa said softly. "Everyone keeps leaving me. And I'm worried about her. But—mostly—I'm alone."

Without a word, Rahim sat before the tent and patted the sand beside him.

She took the spot, tucking her knees to her chest.

Rahim looked at her, his eyes unwavering.

"You're not alone now."

Smiling, Irsa rested her cheek against his shoulder.

And it was enough.

# A PERFECT BALANCE

T HE RAIN STARTED TO FALL WHEN THE GATES OF REY appeared along the horizon. Fat, unwieldy drops began to *plink* on Shahrzad's shoulders and *splat* on the corners of the magic carpet.

She'd felt the storm's threat as she soared beneath the gathering clouds. The metallic scent had woven through the wind, toying at the ends of her tresses—

Spurring her onward.

All the while sending her blood surging through her body.

*Khalid.*

As Shahrzad neared the city gates, a current of air buoyed the carpet, taking her past the torchlit battlements, beyond the sights of any wandering sentries.

The slumbering city was as she remembered it . . .

Yet not.

Sections of Khorasan's crown jewel looked as though a giant fist had smashed down upon its surface. Others were scorched beyond recognition. For a few breaths, a feeling of despondency slid its hold around Shahrzad's heart.

Then, as she directed the carpet lower, she saw signs of hope.

The light color of newly hewn granite against old. The smell of sap from freshly milled wood. The piles of organized debris. The stink of burning refuse.

Around her was a city all but forsworn.

Half in ruin.

Yet half reborn.

Her heart swelled, shaking off despondency's grip. The people of Rey had not tucked tail and run.

Nor had Khalid.

Shahrzad sent the carpet higher. Toward a broken palace of granite and marble glistening in the first flush of a summer's rain.

Toward the broken palace she called home.

A trill of apprehension snaked through her, igniting a flurry of questions.

*Khalid is just as stubborn as I am. What if he refuses to trust Artan, or Artan's family?*

*What if he rejects their offer of help? What if he's resigned to living out his days with this curse?*

Then the most selfish question of all—the one she'd refused to allow herself to consider—began echoing through her mind:

*What if he's furious with me for leaving Rey?*

*For leaving him without a word.*

The fat droplets grew long and lean as they started to multiply. Without warning, the clouds burst, showering a sweet silver rain upon the city. A hazy mist formed above the earth as the water sizzled onto the stone and soaked through the parched soil.

Shahrzad landed on the balcony outside Khalid's antechamber.

She waited in silence for a time, her pulse drumming in her ears. Her emotions ran a wild gamut, and she trembled, despite the warm summer breeze.

He was so close. Almost within reach.

But Shahrzad couldn't bring herself to slide open the carved screens in front of her.

She'd left him. Even if she'd done it to protect him—to protect the love they shared—she'd left him alone. And she'd made the decision to do so without him.

Khalid had not run from his obligations. That much had been quite evident to her, as she'd flown over Rey. She'd seen his mind for organization—his quiet intelligence—in every aspect of the restoration. In the logical engineering. In the careful attention to detail.

He was everywhere. Even if no one else saw this simple truth, Shahrzad did.

She was the one who'd left behind a burning disaster, without so much as a glance back. Left the boy she loved to manage an insurmountable task without her.

Would he look at her with eyes of betrayal? Eyes of judgment?

Or would they be the same eyes as always?

Eyes that had been for her and no other.

She was soaked to the bone now. The sweet-smelling rain had drenched her hair and was dripping from its ends. Her *qamis* clung to her body, and her deep blue *tikka* sash trailed against the onyx stone beside her sandaled feet.

How much time had she wasted being afraid on the balcony?

*Enough.*

Squaring her shoulders, Shahrzad started for the screens—

And they slid open.

She halted in her tracks, refusing to look up.

Shahrzad knew it was Khalid. She sensed rather than saw him.

As always. As ever. As a rose to the sun.

Her knees shook. A chill ran from the nape of her neck to the soles of her feet.

"Shahrzad?"

Low and unassuming. Unmistakable. When Shahrzad met his gaze, everything around her melted away. Even the driving rain came to a sudden standstill.

A moment suspended in time. A pair of amber eyes across a balcony.

And there was no more fear. No more worry. No more judgment.

Her knees no longer shook. Her heart steadied in her chest.

In that moment of perfect balance, she understood. This peace? These worries silenced without effort?

It was because they were two parts of a whole. He did not belong to her. And she did not belong to him. It was never about belonging to someone.

It was about belonging together.

Shahrzad walked toward him, her head high.

Khalid did not blink.

"Shazi."

"Yes," she replied, her voice clear and strong. Just as she felt.

His eyes narrowed infinitesimally. As though guarded in their disbelief. As though undeserving of their truth. The gesture was so achingly familiar that Shahrzad wanted to launch herself into his arms.

But she was soaked, and Khalid looked as pristine as always. His black hair was faultless. The sharp planes of his face brought to mind a hawk in flight. Piercing, yet coolly aloof. As though he could gauge a man at a glance, had he the care to do so. The fine linen of his garments hung across the trim figure of a seasoned warrior.

His eyes gleamed molten gold. And they said all without a word.

Shahrzad drew her sodden waves to one side, splashing water by his feet.

"I'm sorry!" She wrinkled her nose. "That was—"

He pulled her in to his chest, a hand tangling through her hair. The beat of his heart rang loud and true against her cheek. The only measure of time that mattered.

She exhaled fast only to inhale deep. To breathe in his scent. The scent of sandalwood and sunshine. Her fingers moved across his skin, making memories of their own. The hands of a master swordsman. The lips of her greatest love. The heart of a king.

"Khalid."

Following their embrace, Shahrzad saw Khalid carefully maintain his distance.

Though it frustrated her, she understood why.

It was not to punish her. It was to protect her. She knew him well enough to realize this. And Shahrzad had yet to divulge why she'd returned.

Perhaps talking *was* of greater importance.

*For now.*

Khalid listened—the stern set of his eyebrows high in his forehead—as Shahrzad told him about the magic carpet. As she told him about the strange new ability she had yet to fully control. But, save for that initial display of emotion, he offered nothing further on the matter.

Instead, Khalid procured a change of clothes for her and—infuriatingly—turned away while she stripped off her drenched garments.

At that, Shahrzad was forced to swallow a rather cheeky comment.

They were *married*, after all.

Alas, she understood this behavior as well.

This time he was protecting himself.

So, despite Shahrzad's desire to challenge Khalid's resolve with a verbal assault, she chose a less direct approach, opting to wear the loose linen *qamis* he'd provided for her . . . and nothing else. After all, the *sirwal* trowsers were much too large. Both garments were cut for a man. The *qamis* covered more than enough, for its hem fell close to her knees.

More than appropriate.

*For now.*

Shahrzad found herself smothering a rather *in*appropriate grin.

When Khalid turned around, his eyebrows shot into his forehead again.

Then he sighed, long and low.

"Is something wrong?" Her voice sounded innocent, though her expression conveyed a sentiment far less so. Shahrzad sat on the edge of his platformed bed, tucking her legs to one side.

"*Wrong* is not exactly the right word." His retort was brusque, but there was a note of humor beneath it.

Khalid strode through his poorly lit chamber, his movements fluid, like those of a shadow limned in smoke. Shahrzad followed him with her eyes, aware she likely resembled a predator stalking prey.

He removed a cushioned settee from behind his ebony desk and brought it before the bed. When Khalid sat down, he made a point of the distance between them—

A point Shahrzad was not meant to mistake.

At this, she frowned. "That's taking matters a bit far, don't you think?"

"If I intend to think, then no. One could argue it's not far enough." Khalid leaned against the settee, his eyes flashing. Focused. Unflinching.

No. Shahrzad was not the predator. Not anymore.

*Well, then.*

Flustered, she made a motion to stand. "Really, I—"

"Shazi." Khalid lifted a hand to stop her. "You can't . . . you . . . you shouldn't stay."

She'd never known Khalid to struggle with words before.

"I'm—not staying."

Khalid sank lower into the ivory silk. Then he nodded.

"But I have every intention of staying—eventually." Shahrzad raised her chin with an imperious air. "In fact, I intend to do far more than stay. I intend to flourish. Once we break the curse." She let her statement carry through the vast chamber, defying the very walls to rise up and challenge her.

Even in the weak light from the latticed lamp above, Shahrzad saw Khalid's face soften. "If I thought there was a way to break this curse—"

"There may be," she interjected. "But I need you to trust me. And not be angry with me for what I'm about to tell you."

"I do trust you."

"But will you be angry?"

He said nothing. His eyes merely constricted at the edges. Undoubtedly weighing their options. Or forming their strategies. *Some things do not change.*

"You must know you have an abominable temper," Shahrzad said with reproach.

A smile ghosted across his lips. "As do you, my queen."

"We are not discussing *my* shortcomings." She sniffed. "Promise me you won't lose your temper until I finish talking?"

Again, he said nothing.

"Khalid?"

He dipped his head once in acknowledgment.

"I went to the Fire Temple to see Musa Zaragoza."

Khalid stiffened. Already Shahrzad could see him assembling his objections, so she barreled forward before he could begin.

"I know you harbor bitterness toward him because of what happened with your mother. Of his . . . failure to come to her aid. But he wishes to help now. And he was the one who gave me both the knowledge and the means to travel here unseen."

"I appreciate him helping you, Shahrzad. A great deal."

But he didn't sound as though he did. Save for the breath Khalid used to speak her name, the rest of his words were rote in tone. Cold and perfunctory.

Disappointed by his inability to forgive Musa, Shahrzad leveled a withering stare in his direction. Khalid met her—glare for glare—until he exhaled in defeat, giving her leave to continue.

"One of his students at the Fire Temple has a relative who professes to be a powerful sorceress. It's possible she can offer us a way to undo the curse."

Khalid's response was immediate, his posture unyielding. "This kind of magic comes with a price. One I am not willing to pay."

"Please." Shahrzad sat up, her damp hair falling over one shoulder. "At least come with me and learn what that cost might be."

"No." His pronouncement was final.

But Shahrzad refused to be swayed. "Khalid—"

"I do not know these people; therefore, they cannot be trusted."

"You said you trusted me."

"I trust you implicitly. But it would be irresponsible of me to trust Musa Zaragoza or his so-called students with my life," Khalid said cuttingly. "And I doubly do not trust them with yours."

"Stop being so stubborn!" Her bare feet fell to the onyx floor. "Do not make me beg you. Because I won't. I'll merely lose my temper or cry. And I have always secretly despised those who cry to wheedle their objectives. But if you force me to do it, Khalid Ibn al-Rashid, I will. And I cry *beautifully*." She crossed her arms and pursed her lips.

A corner of his mouth twitched. "You do not cry beautifully."

"Liar!"

"I'm not lying." He held her gaze. "I rarely lie."

She'd long suspected this to be the case. Yet Shahrzad could not resist pressing Khalid further. "You've never lied to me?"

He paused. "Once."

"Oh?" She peaked a slender brow. "And when was that?"

"In the souk. When you asked if I remembered my last dream. I said I did not."

"And you did?"

Khalid nodded.

Shahrzad took a cautious breath, wondering if it would be wiser not to push the matter. "Will you tell me what your dream was about?"

"At the time, it was less a dream and more a recurring nightmare." Khalid regarded her for a beat. "I dreamed of sleeping beside a girl in my chamber. I don't remember her face. Nor do I remember anything about her. I only remember how I felt."

"How did you feel?"

"As though I'd found peace." His gaze grew even more intent. Even more pointed.

"Oh." Shahrzad looked away, toying with the sleeve of the borrowed *qamis* to conceal the flush in her cheeks.

*That night at the souk, Khalid lied because he thought this dream was about me.*

"The last time I had this dream was the night before you came to the palace," he continued. "I remember it well because I woke suddenly, searching for something that . . . wasn't there." His eyes drifted to the alabaster wall; he was lost in thought.

Lost in a familiar wasteland. A wasteland Shahrzad hoped never to see again.

She walked toward him, resolve firming her steps.

"That peace you seek is here," Shahrzad whispered. "Fight for it. I'll fight for it with you. I'll do whatever it takes." Her hands clenched around her sleeves. "When I was in the desert, I woke each day and carried on with my life, but it wasn't living; it was merely existing. I want to live. *You* are where I live."

Khalid stared up at her, his features inscrutable—

His eyes inciting her heart to riot.

"I've missed the silence of you listening to me." Shahrzad attempted a weak smile. "No one listens to me as you do."

His expression turned quizzical.

"You don't wait to speak," she clarified. "You truly listen."

"Only to you," Khalid replied gently.

At that, Shahrzad reached a hand toward him. Stopped just before his brow, as if seeking permission. He bent forward, and her fingers sifted through the black silk of his hair. Khalid reached behind her knee, drawing her closer.

"Fight with me," she said.

At his silence, Shahrzad tugged his hair back, forcing him to look her in the eye. "I want a life with those I love around me, safe and happy. What do you want?"

"To live . . . fiercely."

"What else?"

"To taste every breath." Khalid skimmed a hand down her leg. A frisson of heat shot up her spine.

"What else?" Her voice shook.

"To fall asleep each night with you by my side."

Shahrzad took his face between her palms.

"Then fight for it."

His careful control shattered. Khalid stood suddenly, catching her to him.

"Will you go with me?" she gasped as his hands moved higher.

He nodded.

Then Khalid pulled her close and crushed his mouth to hers. His tongue edged past her lips, and she breathed his name while he strode toward the bed, pouring their bodies onto the dull silk.

She would never cease to be astounded by this—

The flawless awareness behind every look, every whisper, every sigh.

His words were a spark cast in oil. His touch was a fire against her skin.

Shahrzad tugged the length of linen over her head, and Khalid rose to his knees and removed his *qamis*. He glanced down at her—

Then everything stilled with an awful precipitousness.

His jaw flexed. His knuckles turned white.

He was furious.

Beyond furious.

His face was a lesson in rage. The quiet, all-consuming sort. It was at its worst when he was this quiet.

As Khalid stared down at her body, she realized why.

The bruises. The burn.

"Khalid—"

"Who did this to you?" His voice was soft. Deathly soft.

Its brutal assurance sent a shiver down her back.

*Never forget: Khalid is not a forgiving man.*

*To him, violence begets violence. And likely always will.*

"Don't," Shahrzad said gently. "Don't ruin our time together with anger. I am not hurt. And these injuries are my own fault. Ones I would gladly take again and again, because they've made me stronger. They've led me to you."

"Shahrzad—"

She reached up to trace the mark on his collarbone. The faint bruise along his jaw. Then she shifted her fingers to the newest cuts on his hands. To the gash across his palm that had not yet healed.

"I hate your scars, too," Shahrzad murmured. "But skin is skin, be it a man's or a woman's. And pain is pain. Don't lament mine more than I do yours. And trust that—if ever there comes a time when an injustice is done to me—you will be the first to know." She pressed a kiss to his injured palm. "And I will stand by your side as *we* right it."

Shahrzad took his hand and placed it on the wound on her stomach. "I promise it doesn't hurt." She grinned almost teasingly.

He frowned. "Liar."

At that, Shahrzad pushed him onto his back.

Her hair scarving about her throat, she moved over Khalid. "I may be partial to roses, but I am not a fragile flower."

"No." Khalid's mouth arced upward ever so slightly. "You are not."

"Do you know why I adore roses?" Shahrzad untied the knot

of his *tikka* sash with deliberate slowness. "I've always loved them for their beauty and their scent, but—"

"It's because of their thorns." His muscles tensed at her touch. "Because there's more to them than first meets the eye."

She smiled down at Khalid, tracing her fingers along the curved hollows at his hips. "Do you know how much I missed you?"

Khalid inhaled sharply. "I do." He grazed a thumb across her lower lip. "And do you know you make my life a thousand times worth living?"

"Yes." Her throat went dry. "I do."

Khalid's eyes fell upon the stretch of twine hanging from her neck. His fingers shifted to coil around the ring.

"I couldn't wear it on my hand anymore," Shahrzad explained. "But I didn't want to—"

He pulled her toward him by the necklace, kissing her silent.

Their lips soon found a rhythm. And their bodies met, seeking the same.

Seeking a moment of perfect balance.

A moment that held everything.

And in that moment, they lost all consideration for anything beyond themselves. For in that moment, there was no pain. There were no scars. And a curse was a worry of a bygone era.

Here, the only thing that mattered was before each of them. Here and now.

"I love you," Shahrzad breathed. "You are all that I am."

"And you are all that I will be."

For here, they existed beyond time.

Here, they could no longer feel the place where she ended and he began.

"It's late," Khalid said. "You should sleep."

"What are you talking about? I'm not doing anything."

"Stop smiling and go to sleep."

"How do you know I'm smiling? You're not even looking at me."

"I can feel you smiling, Shazi."

The warm sound of her laughter stole through Khalid's skin, heating the coldest reaches of his soul.

He lay on his stomach with his eyes closed, trying to dispel the torturous ache in his head. That his pain would choose now to trouble him was merely further proof of his endless misfortune.

Or perhaps further proof of fate's twisted humor.

The cushions rustled around him. Shahrzad eased onto his back, draping her small form over his. He felt the press of her cheek between his shoulder blades. Then, with a featherlight touch, she ran both hands up his arms to the nape of his neck.

"Do you want me to stop?" she asked when she realized her attempts to soothe were to no avail.

"No."

"What *do* you want?" Her tone bordered on playful.

Khalid thought for a moment, trying to banish the images her words brought to mind. "Perhaps a story." He smiled to himself, despite the thudding in his brow.

"Any story?"

Khalid nodded, his eyes still closed.

She leaned close to whisper by his ear. "A young man was strolling through the wood when he came upon a honey-tongued dove. He paused to listen to the sweet melody of its song and was amazed when the dove stopped singing and began *speaking* to him."

It was as though she were from a dream. One from which Khalid never wished to wake.

He felt her smile again. "The dove said, 'Young man, you seem to have good taste! I'd like to share a secret with you. If you take this path here, you will come across a lacquered red door with a wooden handle. Before it, you will find a tribe of Weeping Men. Ask them not why they weep; merely pass through the door, and you will find riches beyond your wildest dreams!' The young man was so surprised to encounter both a talking dove and the promise of riches beyond his wildest dreams that he eagerly followed the honey-tongued dove's directions through the wood."

"The foolishness of youth," Khalid murmured.

Shahrzad laughed softly, and the sound rolled down his spine. "Just as the dove had said, the young man came into a clearing with a single door of red lacquer, latched shut by a wooden handle. Before it sat a tribe of Weeping Men. The young man ignored the Weeping Men and proceeded straight to the door. He pressed on the wooden handle, then stepped across the threshold. Before him was a hanging garden. But it was not a garden of flowers or fruit; it was a garden of brilliant jewels. Where there should have been an apple orchard, there was instead a copse of emeralds. Where there should have been berries, he found rubies the size of his thumb. Bright yellow jasper gleamed in place of oranges.

178

Glittering amethysts dripped in place of hyacinths. Diamonds and pearls lay shimmering on branches of jessamine. The young man stuffed his pockets full of jewel-fruits and flower-gems, laughing until his sides hurt."

She twined her fingers through his. "When he finished walking through the hanging garden, he arrived at a beautiful village, overlooking a crystalline sea. He immediately bought the most magnificent home he could find. After he'd traversed the whole of this village, he came across another lacquered door with another wooden handle. He pressed it open and traipsed into the market of a grand city, filled with the sights and sounds of trade and the smells of delicacies. In no time at all, he had amassed a sizable amount of gold. The quality of the gems he possessed was unparalleled, and his knack for trading knew no bounds. It seemed no matter where he turned, luck was on his side! When he happened upon yet another door with a wooden handle, he pushed through it, only to cross paths with the loveliest young woman he had ever beheld. Hand in hand, they made their way across another stunning vista, filled with verdant valleys and sparkling springs. Never once did the young man look back. Ever forward. Ever toward the next door.

"Then, many years later, when the young man could no longer call himself young, he came across another door with another wooden handle and, without the slightest hesitation, he stepped through it, heedless of where it might lead."

The only sound in the room was that of their shared breaths.

Shahrzad's voice took on a melancholy note. "He found himself wandering through a wood. Stepping into a familiar clearing.

Surrounded by a tribe of Weeping Men. The lacquered door before him did not have a handle. In that moment, the not-so-young man understood. So he sat beside his tribe . . . and began weeping."

The silence stretched thin for a time. "Why did you choose that particular story?" Khalid finally asked.

Another stretch of silence. "Sometimes . . . I worry I want too much," Shahrzad said.

"It's not possible. For you deserve everything you want and more."

She shifted to rest her chin on his shoulder, causing Khalid to wince.

"Does it hurt that much?" Her concern was all too evident.

A part of Khalid knew he should lie to spare Shahrzad worry. But he simply did not see the point. To him, lies rarely served their intended purpose. Except in necessitating more lies.

"Yes," Khalid admitted. "But I'll live."

"I have something that might help." Shahrzad placed a suggestive kiss in the middle of his back.

Despite the siege in his forehead, Khalid considered her offer. Her dark hair was a shining veil against his shoulder. The smell of rain clung to every curl. Even now, he could picture the way her lips parted when he kissed the hollow at her throat. The way her soft breath washed across his skin. The way her slim hands—

Khalid almost groaned in defeat. "I am more than willing, but I believe we've tried that remedy tonight. More than once."

Another lilting spate of laughter filled the air. She slid off his back, leaving him cold. Khalid cracked open his eyes to see Shahrzad step to her pile of discarded garments.

When she returned, she held a square of green stone in her palm, strung onto a leather string. "It's a talisman. Musa-*effendi* said it might help to ward away your sleeplessness."

"Musa-*effendi*?" Khalid rolled over in protest. The last thing he desired was a gift from the cowardly magus he'd known as a boy. The coward who'd stood by and watched his mother drown in her own blood.

"Enough." Shahrzad raised a hand to his chest, staying his objections. "Take help when it is offered, Khalid-*jan*. True strength isn't about sovereignty. It's about knowing when you need help and having the courage to accept it."

Though his eyes burned, Khalid studied her as she spoke. As though he were forming an imprint, forever indelible in his mind. Her impudent chin. Her jewel eyes and vagabond hair. No one could deny that Shahrzad was beautiful. But it was not simply her beauty that captivated Khalid beyond compare.

It was the way she carried herself with such poise.

Such strength.

"You're very wise, Shahrzad al-Khayzuran. Perhaps you should rule Khorasan. And leave me to languish in your chamber, until you have need of me."

"Perhaps I should." She lay alongside him. "But I was not born a boy."

"I've long thought such a thing should not matter." Khalid draped one of her legs around his.

"Will you at least see if the talisman works?"

In place of a response, Khalid buried his face in her dark waves, taking in the fragrance of lilacs and rain. She blew an exasperated puff of air above his head.

"You—"

"I'll try it," he said into her neck. "Now go to sleep."

Shahrzad turned away from him, burrowing into the crook of his arm.

"Khalid?"

He fought back the beginnings of a smile. "Yes?"

"You don't need to say you love me. I know you do. But . . . may I ask why you won't?"

Though it was posited nonchalantly, Khalid felt the beat of Shahrzad's heart between her shoulder blades. Felt it quicken. And it pained him to know he'd given her cause to doubt his affections. But he'd known for some time that he owed her an explanation.

In truth, he owed her much more than that.

Of course she wanted to know why. She was a girl who freely spoke her mind and generously bestowed her sentiments on those she found deserving. After all Khalid had done—and everything he'd failed to do—it would forever amaze him that she still found him to be one of the deserving.

Khalid pulled her closer. "At Ava's grave, I swore I would spend my life *showing* those I loved how I felt, and never resorting to words. I promised I would do for others what I'd failed to do for her. Not to profess love. But instead to act upon it."

They lay in silence for a time. Though he was unable to see her reaction, Khalid knew she was thinking. Knew she was taking his promise into consideration.

Perhaps it was foolish of him to hold fast to it. A promise to a girl who no longer lived. A girl who had suffered so greatly in life. And died with his lie blistering her ears.

A lie of love. The one thing she'd asked of him.

The one thing he'd never attempted to give.

In all things, Khalid had failed Ava. In this, he wished to succeed.

And he did not make promises lightly.

"I understand," Shahrzad said.

"Shazi—"

"Since you can't say it, will you at least tell me how much you love me?"

Khalid ran the tip of his nose beside her ear, a grateful smile upon his lips.

"From the stars, to the stars."

## ONCE AND FOR ALL

SHAHRZAD SNUCK BACK INTO HER TENT JUST AS DAWN was cresting along the horizon.

She felt fortunate to have managed the return journey unseen. In truth, she'd left Rey with not a moment to spare. Though she'd desperately wanted to stay with Khalid and watch the sky catch fire around them, she could not risk being seen.

And she knew she had to answer for how she'd left things with Irsa the night before.

As soon as their tent fell shut, Shahrzad turned to see her sister sitting up in her bedroll, her eyes red-rimmed and bloodshot.

Clearly, Irsa had not slept well. And might even have shed a tear or two.

Shahrzad stifled a sigh. "Irsa, I—"

"I told Rahim you were gone." A note of insolence punctuated her raspy whisper.

"What?" Shahrzad almost dropped the bundle containing the magic carpet.

Irsa bit her lip. "Since you've missed breakfast almost every morning, he already suspected you were up to something, so I—"

"So you simply told him I was gone?"

"After you left, I went to speak with him, and—" Irsa cleared her throat while toying with the edge of her blanket. "And he knows you're not sick. He already knew something had been occupying your time these past few nights. So, when he walked me back to our tent and saw that you weren't here . . ."

Shahrzad could not be angry with her sister. She *would* not be angry with her. Irsa had done so much to be a bastion of strength for Shahrzad. To offer understanding and support, when no one else would dare to do so. And Shahrzad had done little to deserve it. All those times Irsa had desired her confidence, Shahrzad had demurred from giving it, knowing her secrets were too dangerous for a girl so earnest and tenderhearted.

Here was proof Shahrzad had been wise to withhold it. When pressed, Irsa had been incapable of lying to Rahim as to Shahrzad's whereabouts. Had Irsa truly known where Shahrzad was, she would undoubtedly have told him.

What might have happened then? Shahrzad shuddered to think.

No. Shahrzad would not be angry with her sister for this lapse in judgment. It could not have been helped.

It was just the way Irsa was—honest to a fault.

Even still, when Shahrzad glanced down at her sister, her temper started to rise.

"I know you're angry with me," Irsa continued, a quaver entering her voice. "But I did not intentionally divulge your secret to Rahim. In truth, this is—your own fault. What did you expect? You've missed breakfast for almost a week. I don't know what's come over you of late. You've become careless. Distracted."

185

The flare of anger spiked even higher. Even wider.

"Are—are you planning to go out again tonight?" Irsa asked. What started as a squeak finished wrapped in steel.

"Yes." Shahrzad's own answer was dangerously defiant.

"Even though it grows more difficult each day to hide your secret?"

"You don't have to lie for me."

"Of course I do." Irsa threw back her tattered blanket and stood tall. "You're my sister. But your friends are worried about you, and soon their worry will turn to suspicion." Lines of concern pleated her brow. "Please don't go out again tonight. I beg you."

Shahrzad thought quickly. She had already made plans to take Khalid to the Fire Temple to meet with Artan and Musa Zaragoza. If she did not return to Rey as promised, Khalid would undoubtedly worry. And those at the Fire Temple would be left waiting for them; she was without means to deliver word to either side.

She swallowed hard, knowing these issues paled in comparison to the larger matter at hand.

*Be honest.*

In truth, Shahrzad had no intention of denying herself a single moment with Khalid, simply to mollify her sister. She knew it was selfish. But his absence had become a lasting presence. And Shahrzad was tired of doing nothing to change circumstances. Of merely waiting in the desert for life to happen to her.

All that would end tonight. Destiny was for fools. Shahrzad would not wait for her life to happen.

She would make it happen.

"I'll go to breakfast with you now, and then we'll spend the afternoon with Baba," Shahrzad said. "I'll make sure everyone sees me. Will that help lessen your worries?"

The lines across Irsa's forehead stretched even farther. Shahrzad could see her warring with herself. "Is what you're doing really of such import?"

"Yes." Shahrzad did not falter in her response.

Her sister looked to the floor, wrapping the end of her chestnut braid around her fingers. "Tonight is . . . a dangerous night to be taking chances."

"Why is that?"

Irsa paused a final time, still prevaricating. Then she leveled her gaze on Shahrzad. "Come with me." She took her hand and led her outside.

They rounded the maze of tents until they stood at the fringes of the encampment. There—in the distance where the soldiers had moved their camp—Shahrzad saw a large band of men saddling their horses.

Assembling their weapons.

At the head of this cadre sat Tariq astride his dark bay stallion, his cloak billowing in the breeze. The banner of the White Falcon flew beside him.

"They're going out on their first raid," Irsa said. "They plan to leave by midday."

"What?" Alarm crept into Shahrzad's stomach, tangling her insides in a coil of knots.

*A—raid?*

"Tariq is leading a contingent of troops toward a nearby stronghold tonight . . . with the intention of overthrowing its emir and seizing control," Irsa said quietly.

"How do you know this?" Shahrzad cried.

"Rahim told me."

"Which stronghold?"

"He didn't tell me that," Irsa confessed. "I do still share a tent with the Calipha of Khorasan, after all."

Once more, Shahrzad's thoughts flitted through her mind like stones across a pond. If Tariq was leading a band of soldiers on a raid along the nearby border of Khorasan and Parthia, they were likely trying to seize control of that border.

Which would leave the border at risk. Leave it vulnerable to outside attack.

Vulnerable to Salim Ali el-Sharif, the power-hungry Sultan of Parthia.

*Perhaps that's their intention.*

A sudden chill ran through her blood.

Shahrzad had to tell Khalid at once. She had to travel to Rey tonight and prevent the possibility of war with Parthia, before even more innocent people died without cause.

As her mind raced, a renewed sense of guilt crashed down upon her. Shahrzad was responsible for this impending disaster as well. Were it not for her, Tariq would never have engaged in this foolhardy pursuit for justice.

This foolhardy quest to avenge his love.

"Shahrzad?" Irsa took hold of her shoulder, shaking her from the tumult of her thoughts. "Have you been listening to a word I've said?"

"What?"

"It's not—dangerous, is it?" Irsa asked. "What you're doing—it's not dangerous?"

Shahrzad laughed, but the sound did not ring true. She spun away from the soldiers with their gleaming swords. The two sisters returned to their tent.

Without a word, Shahrzad poured water from the pitcher into the copper basin. Her hand shook, causing her reflection to waver. Setting her jaw, Shahrzad tugged her wrinkled *qamis* over her head, determined to wash and go about her day.

To stay the course, whatever may come.

"Shahrzad!" Irsa's outcry came from a face drained of all color.

*Curse these damnable bruises. As well as Artan Temujin.*

She brushed aside her sister's worry with a flick of a wrist. "Don't concern yourself. These are not serious injuries." But Shahrzad could see her words falling on deaf ears. And dubious eyes.

Should she simply tell Irsa how she had sustained them? Confess all and hope her sister would keep quiet for just a short while longer?

*When goats fly.*

It was too risky. Especially now that Irsa was confiding in Rahim. If Irsa misspoke, Rahim might say something to Tariq. And Tariq, of all people, could not know anything about her visits to Khalid.

The risk was simply too high. The hatred simply too rife.

No. It was best Shahrzad not say a word of it to Irsa.

Shahrzad turned her back on her sister and began scrubbing water and a gritty bar of *Nabulsi* soap along her body.

When she lifted her arm, the lingering scent of sandalwood rose from her skin.

*Khalid.*

Fear stole its way into her heart. Her throat swelled tight.

Clenching her teeth, Shahrzad fought back the rush and continued bathing.

*Now is not the time for cowardice.*

After all, if everything went to plan, they would have answers soon. Once Shahrzad and Khalid knew what to do about the curse, all could be revealed.

Then everyone would know the truth.

They would all know that the boy Shahrzad loved was not the monster they believed him to be. That he was—and would be—the great king their kingdom so desperately needed. The great king Shahrzad saw when she flew over their city.

Until then, she had to stay silent. For it would not help matters if the boy-king everyone so despised was cursed to rule a forsaken kingdom. The army massing against Khalid would only be spurred to action if they knew the tides of fortune had turned against him as well.

But once Shahrzad found a solution, she could tell Tariq the truth.

Perhaps then, his hatred for Khalid would begin to dissipate.

And reconciliation could begin.

For ending this curse was not simply about ending their suffering.

Shahrzad had to put a stop to the war she'd set in motion.

It was not just a matter of love. It was a matter of life.

And she meant to right it, once and for all.


Jahandar permitted one eye to sliver open. Then shut. Then open once more.

He silently cursed himself when he realized his error.

"Are you awake, old friend?" A warm voice rang out in the darkness.

Jahandar tried to remain still, hoping the man at his bedside would leave.

Low laughter rumbled nearby.

"I saw your eye open just now," the voice continued. "And I know you woke yesterday and earlier today. Come now, Jahandar. I am not here to cast judgment. I only wish to speak with a dear friend."

Jahandar took a wary breath, vexed with himself for stirring in the first place. He'd felt someone enter the tent a moment ago, and he'd thought it must be Irsa or Shahrzad, so he'd woken from his fallacious slumber, eager to speak with his children again. But he was not ready to speak with anyone else.

Much less Reza bin-Latief.

Nevertheless, he'd already made his blunder. Jahandar supposed he had to own up to it, lest anyone suspect the truth behind his mysterious ailment.

Or, rather, the lie behind it.

Jahandar let both his eyes drift open. His friend of many years sat before him, a lamp of polished brass glowing nearby.

Reza sent a patient smile his way. "You look terrible."

Jahandar's shoulders were racked by laughter that ended in a series of coughs. "The years have been kinder to you, without a doubt. But not by much."

It was true. The last time Jahandar had seen Reza bin-Latief was not long after his wife and daughter had perished within days of each other. A tragedy no man should have to endure. One that had clearly taken its toll.

Reza had lost weight. His hair had thinned on top while greying at the temples. His mustache was fuller, and he'd begun to grow a beard. He no longer had the appearance of a man who found much joy in life. The lines along his face were not lines drawn by delight or satisfaction.

They were lines drawn by thought. Or perhaps calculation?

"What time of day is it?" Jahandar asked, his voice cracked and dry.

Reza handed him some water. "Almost dinnertime."

Jahandar took an absentminded sip. "My daughters will be by shortly." As soon as the words fell from his tactless lips, Jahandar wanted to catch them.

How thoughtlessly cruel!

But Reza did not seem to notice. "You are a lucky man. Such devoted children. I'm told Irsa comes to see you quite frequently."

"Shahrzad has been by twice today." Jahandar took another sip.

Reza propped a hand beneath his beard. "That's good to hear. I was told she's been ill the last few days."

"Ill?" Jahandar's brows gathered on his forehead.

"Old friend . . ." Reza paused to smile, then leaned closer. "I've not come to waste your time or trouble you unnecessarily. I know you're still recovering. And there is a pressing matter I need to attend to this evening. But may I ask you a question?"

"Of course."

"I've heard—many conflicting rumors of what occurred the night of the storm in Rey."

Jahandar stiffened. His free hand drew tight over the book. It still felt warm to the touch, though it no longer burned with the same fervor. The cold metal of the key around his neck weighed him down, like an anchor dragging along the seafloor.

Reza observed his reaction in silence. Then he pressed on, without missing a beat.

"Can you not tell me what happened?"

"I—I do not remember." Jahandar's broken nails dug into the worn leather of the book.

"Truly?"

Jahandar nodded.

Reza sighed with obvious reluctance. "I am not one of the shiftless masses, Jahandar-*jan*. We've spent many years of friendship together. I was there when Irsa was born. And I was there when . . . Mina died." His voice grew soft. "I did all I could, and I always wished I could do more."

Jahandar's heart caught in his throat. It was true. Reza had brought his own personal physician to Jahandar's wife's sickbed, though his efforts had been for naught. And Reza had cared for Shahrzad and Irsa in the days following, when Jahandar had been . . . unable to do so.

"I know, old friend," Jahandar whispered. "I will never forget what you did."

Reza's smile was sad and small. "Alas, such trying times can never be forgotten. But I'd rather we recall what friends are capable of in our times of need." He paused for emphasis. "Just as I know what *you* are capable of, even if there are only a handful of people who are aware of it."

This, too, was true. Reza had always known that Jahandar possessed unique abilities.

Reza steepled both hands beneath his chin, letting his gaze fall upon Jahandar's smooth scalp. "Old friend, did you do something the night of the storm?"

Could he confide in Reza bin-Latief? Could he trust him with his secret?

"If you did," Reza pressed in a low voice, "please know I will not judge you. In fact, I will *celebrate* you. For I know you did not mean to do anything wrong. And, if you did do something, it must have been a remarkable feat."

Jahandar swallowed.

"One we would have a tremendous use for," Reza finished.

Use? Reza had a use for Jahandar?

"If you accomplished such an astounding feat alone," Reza said quietly, his brown eyes bright in their fervor, "can you imagine what you could accomplish with a force of soldiers at your back? With the strength of an army at your beck and call?"

Jahandar's gaze flitted across Reza bin-Latief's face. Across the lines drawn by deep thought. And obvious calculation.

He saw it. He knew what Reza was doing.

Knew it . . . and did not care.

Jahandar realized that for the first time in many years—for the first time since Mina had died and he had lost his position in the palace—Reza truly *saw* him. Saw the man he'd first met those many years ago. A vizier to the Caliph of Khorasan.

A man of power and influence.

A man worthy of Reza's consideration.

In low tones, Jahandar began talking. And did not stop.

Not until Reza bin-Latief smiled with satisfaction.

Just like old times.

# THE WINGED SERPENT

$S$HAHRZAD HAD NOT INTENDED TO TORMENT KHALID with the magic carpet.

Not at first.

But he brought it on himself. Truly, he did.

The moment the Caliph of Khorasan said—with coolly regal arrogance—that only a child would be afraid to fly, Shahrzad knew it was a challenge she was meant to take on.

Meant to see fall to glorious pieces.

After all, even she had been afraid at first. But Khalid need not know that.

As soon as he settled onto the carpet, Shahrzad coaxed it into the air without a word of warning.

A volley of expletives flew from Khalid's mouth. They only became more foul as Shahrzad urged the carpet high above the city, in a twist of whistling wind. Laughing into the darkness, she spurred the magic carpet even faster, then rose to her knees. When Khalid tried to tug her back down—his eyes flashing—she sent a look of mocking scorn over one shoulder.

"Get down," Khalid yelled over the wind, taking tight hold of her waist.

"Don't be a bore!"

"You'll fall."

"No, I won't." She spread her arms wide.

"How do you know that?"

"I just do!"

"Get down," he insisted, his jaw rigid. "Please!"

"Why?"

"Because you're killing me, by degrees!"

Grumbling, Shahrzad eased back onto the carpet. Khalid pulled her into his chest, his breath fast against her neck.

A small part of her felt guilty.

The rest felt smug.

*Serves him right. Perhaps the King of Kings won't be so arrogant next time.*

She grinned to herself. Khalid ceasing to be arrogant was just as unlikely as her ceasing to provoke him. It was simply too easy. And much too much fun.

"Are you finally starting to breathe in a normal fashion?" Shahrzad teased. "I must confess I find your behavior rather odd, considering you said only a child would be afraid to fly."

"I wasn't afraid." Khalid wrapped a forearm of corded muscle around her.

She slanted a disbelieving look his way. "You just lied to me."

"I wasn't afraid," he repeated. "I was terrified."

When she laughed, Shahrzad was rewarded with one of his

uncommonly effortless smiles. The kind that changed a face of shadows into one of light.

The kind that made her want to forget how small the magic carpet happened to be.

"You're beautiful," Shahrzad commented softly.

Khalid's hand tightened around her waist. "Are you not stealing the words customarily reserved for a man?"

"You're welcome to say other, less customary things." Though her tone was airy, her pulse stuttered.

"Such as?"

"You're a smart man. I'm sure you'll think of something."

"I already have." The touch of Khalid's lips trailing below her ear sent a swirl of desire through her.

*It's a shame we're otherwise occupied at the moment.*

Or else she would definitely act upon it.

They traveled over a stretch of desert near an expanse of mountains. Above them, a few lonely stars flickered, stitched across a dark fabric of night. Khalid soon grew accustomed to the rush of wind against his face, the tense set of his shoulders slackening. After a time, the air began to thicken with the scent of salt, and the sea glimmered along the horizon.

The carpet slowed as they neared the promontory before landing by the pool of water set against the cliff. Shahrzad secured the magic carpet to her back while Khalid unsheathed his *shamshir*, his movements like that of a prowling jungle cat.

Though she'd behaved in the same manner only a few nights ago, Shahrzad rolled her eyes. "That's unnecessary. Not to mention insulting."

"Forgive me for not feeling welcome wherever I go," he muttered. "And for not taking any chances."

With a shake of her head, Shahrzad reached for his free hand, threading her fingers through his.

"Shahrzad-*jan*?" Musa emerged from between the strange statues at the opposite side of the pool.

Again, Khalid did not miss a beat. Though he recognized the magus, he tugged Shahrzad closer and raised his *shamshir*.

Musa smiled at Khalid, his teeth like pearls set against ebony. "I did not think you would come."

It took Khalid a moment to reply. "My wife can be very persuasive." His sword remained vigilant.

The magus's eyes crinkled at the corners. "It is good to see you. It has been so long."

Khalid said nothing.

Musa strode closer. He appeared to be studying Khalid. Perhaps trying to see traces of the boy he'd known in the young man before him. "You look—"

"Like my father," Khalid finished in a clipped tone. "Many have told me."

"You do. But I see your mother in you. Most especially in your eyes."

"You have no cause to flatter me. Lies do not become you."

"I am not lying." Musa rounded the pool. "Your eyes may be the same color as your father's, but I can tell they see the world as Leila did. They see all. Your father"—he failed to forestall a grimace—"saw very little."

Khalid's eyes narrowed to slits. "My father saw enough."

The meaning behind his rejoinder was evident.

*A father who saw enough to destroy a small boy's world.*

"No." Musa stopped before them, his colorful cloak swaying above the tan stone. "He saw what he wished to see. And he never gave anyone the chance to show him otherwise."

There was obvious meaning to the magus's words as well.

"I did not come here to be lectured by my mother's tutor," Khalid countered. "Nor did I come here to grant you the chance to win me over, Musa Zaragoza."

Musa nodded. "I did not expect to win you over in a night. But—"

"Do not expect to win me over," Khalid said coldly. "Ever."

"Khalid-*jan*," Shahrzad whispered. She tugged on his hand in silent censure.

Though he did not appear the least bit remorseful, Khalid squeezed her palm in acknowledgment.

Musa's smile turned wistful. "I am so very sorry, little *pahlang*. For everything."

Shahrzad felt Khalid's body go rigid beside her.

Little *pahlang*. Little tiger.

"You do not have permission to call me that." Khalid's features were drawn and tight. "I am the Caliph of Khorasan to you. Nothing more."

In that moment, everything about Khalid hearkened back to a time when Shahrzad had lived in fear of the dawn. When all she knew of him was a boy of ice and stone, who murdered his brides without cause or apology.

A time when all she had were stories fueled by hatred.

It pained her to see Khalid returning to this. A shell of what he was.

A shadow of what he could be.

Musa bowed, his fingers to his forehead. "A thousand apologies, *sayyidi.*"

Glaring at Khalid, Shahrzad shook off his grasp. "Musa-*effendi,* please do not—"

"I am not offended, my dearest star," Musa replied. "I know why the young caliph despises me so. I did nothing when he begged for help. It has haunted me for many years."

"There was nothing you could have done," Shahrzad cried. "Had you tried to help, you likely would have been killed as well!"

"No." Musa canted his mouth to one side. "When we are faced with our darkest fears, inaction is for the weak or the hopeless. There is *always* something to be said or done. Though words alone—"

"Are mere scratchings on a page," Khalid finished, his voice even colder. "The power behind them lies with the person."

Musa stood completely still. "You remember." A careful smile broke across his face. "That gives me a great deal of comfort. Though I do not deserve it, I thank you."

Khalid's chest rose and fell in steady consideration. "And I . . . thank you. For all you have done for Shahrzad."

Musa bowed again. "*Sayyidi.*" He turned his attention to her, his expression undisguised in its warmth. "Your impatient tutor waits for you in his usual spot, my lady."

The creature waiting on the beach was most definitely not Artan Temujin.

It was easily five times as long as a man. And twice as thick. But these particulars did not give rise to Shahrzad's distress. What alarmed her most was that it resembled a snake. Covered in darkly iridescent scales. Replete with a giant hood.

And . . . wings?

Shahrzad swallowed a strangled scream. Khalid drew his sword with a quick rasp.

"Where have you been?" Artan demanded, suddenly emerging from behind the slithering monstrosity.

"What the hell is that—thing?" Shahrzad tried not to yell. The creature coiled around itself while she spoke, a rainbow of colors torquing across its scales, its leathery wings gleaming in the moonlight.

"Who? Shesha?" Artan grinned with wicked humor. "He's harmless."

The snake bared its black fangs, as though it understood. And disagreed, rather wholeheartedly.

"He's just a silly winged serpent." Artan waved a flippant hand. "Who enjoys frightening people. And—like any good tyrant—much of his appearance is for show. He's really very sweet . . . most of the time."

Throughout this entire exchange, Khalid had not shifted position. His *shamshir* had stayed poised at his side, his body between Shahrzad and that of the snake—

His eyes trained on Artan.

Now, both the sword and its master turned toward the bald-headed boy, with unflinching intent.

Artan snorted. "I suppose this is the *cursed* husband?" He laughed to himself.

*Did this fool not hear a word I said about Khalid's temper?*

Before Shahrzad could interject, Artan bounded over the serpent's tail and onto the sand.

"You really are as humorless as she let on," he continued, eyeing Khalid askance. "But there's little I can do to remedy that."

*The second offense.*

"Should I call you Khalid?" he pressed. "Because you're not technically *my* king. No matter. I'm Artan Temujin, and—after much persuading—I've come to rescue you from your fate. But only after your wife begged me. On her knees, of course." He snickered. "I do so prefer her when she grovels."

It was not the barrage of taunts that sparked a reaction. It was the sight of Artan's burned forearms that registered on Khalid's face. Shahrzad winced when she saw it. Only someone who knew Khalid well would notice.

The slightest twinge beneath an eye. It appeared and disappeared in a flash of recognition.

In an instant of understanding.

*Oh, God.*

Then Artan made the lamentable decision to wink at Khalid. And clap him on the shoulder.

*The final offense.*

The *shamshir* flashed through the darkness toward Artan's throat—

Stopping a hairsbreadth from its mark.

Smiling the entire time, Artan brought both hands beside his face, as though he meant to surrender. Then the center of his palms promptly burst into flame.

"I'll admit I was trying to provoke you," Artan said without a hint of fear. "It's a pastime of mine. Shahrzad told me you have a temper. But things have escalated a bit faster than I might have intended. Why don't we—"

"Was it you who burned her?" Though a bead of sweat slipped down his neck, Khalid did not flinch from the whirling spheres of fire.

Artan's eyes grew wide. Unlike Khalid, he was unable to mask his reaction. Guilt rippled across his features, causing his bare scalp to flush red. "Well, uh—"

"Stop it, both of you!" Shahrzad grabbed Artan by the back of his shirt and yanked him away from Khalid. "What are you doing?" For a moment, she considered punching Artan square in the nose. "Are you completely deranged?" Then she whirled on Khalid. "And *you* have been nothing short of abominable this entire evening. First with Musa-*effendi*, and now with Artan. They're trying to *help* us, Khalid!"

Despite her condemnations, the *shamshir* stayed at the ready. And the spheres of fire continued spinning.

"Put them away at once, you miserable louts!" Shahrzad

insisted. "This is why the world would be a far better place in the hands of women."

"By far better you mean far less interesting." Artan grinned once more, though he extinguished his weapons. "Wouldn't you agree, O King of Kings?"

Khalid lowered his sword, but kept his icy stare fixed on Artan.

"Hmm." Artan paused in consideration. "If not for our brief but charming exchange, I'd almost be worried you'd married a mute, my dear little snipe. I'd understand, given how much *you* talk, but I have to say I'm a bit surprised."

"He's not mute," Shahrzad said. "He just doesn't suffer fools."

"Therefore he must have very little to say around you." Artan winked, flinging an arm about her shoulders and pulling her close.

Shahrzad placed a hand in his face, shoving him back. "He speaks when the company merits it, you ass."

"However does he survive, being surrounded at all times by such fools?"

"One stab at a time," Khalid said quietly, sheathing his sword with a pointed *snap*.

At that, Artan threw back his head and laughed. "Oh, I like him, little snipe. He doesn't say much, but he speaks true. He can stay."

"Stay?" Shahrzad said. "I thought we were going to see your aunt."

"We are, we are!" Artan tugged on an earring. "It's just that Shesha's being a bit—uncooperative at the moment." He pivoted in the sand and moved toward higher ground. Then he tossed two fur-lined robes back at them. "Find a way to secure these to that tiny carpet; you're going to need them."

Shahrzad eyed the thick piles of fur at their feet. "Artan . . . where are we going?" Her voice dripped with suspicion.

"To a hidden fortress." He waggled his brows. "Carved into a mountain."

# THE DARK SIDE OF A MIRROR

THIS WAS THE FARTHEST SHAHRZAD HAD EVER FLOWN on the magic carpet.

Before, her journeys had taken no more than an hour. True, she'd traveled faster than she'd ever believed possible—the ground had blurred beneath her, and the stars had stretched thin on either side—but she'd always had a vague sense of where she was going.

This time, she had not the slightest notion.

The carpet soared eastward for more than two hours. Then, when an expanse of mountains—far higher and far more imposing than those in Khorasan—appeared on the horizon, the carpet began to rise.

The air began to grow crisp and cold.

Without a word, Khalid draped one of the fur-lined cloaks around them and held her close. The chill had not seeped through Shahrzad's skin—it never did, thanks to the warmth of the magic in her veins—but she was not one to shy away from the chance to feel Khalid's body against hers. A smile curved across her face as she settled in to his chest and traced an idle fingertip along his palm, all while surveying the mountains silhouetted in the distance.

Shahrzad had commanded the carpet to follow the winged serpent, but she still felt strange watching the slithering beast cavort through the clouds. She'd never seen such an odd creature before. Though she'd heard tell of such things, Shahrzad had always considered them as one might consider a faraway star. Or a tale of old.

In the starlight, Shesha's long silver whiskers trailed on either side of his pointed snout, like slender ribbons streaming in a soft breeze. His whiskers were whimsical in their bent, and his eyes were unnerving, for they glittered with the bloodred menace of the finest Hindustani ruby.

Soon, Shesha swerved to the left, toward a snowcapped peak in the distance. This mountain was of the peculiar sort. Its west-facing expanse was sheared flat, as though a giant sword had cleaved down one side of it. The stone itself was a deep blue-grey. Under cover of a cloud-darkened sky, it appeared black. So black that it seemed to absorb all the light around it. Not a single stitch of snow clung to its smooth surface.

As they rounded the strange mountain's apex, Shahrzad saw that its east-facing side curved upward in jagged peaks, almost like a set of fingers fanning straight into the sky.

Shesha veered toward the lowest outcropping, then dove suddenly, his leathery wings pulled tight against his scales. The magic carpet followed, and an icy wind whipped against Shahrzad's face, all but stealing the very breath from her body.

Between the thumb and forefinger of the mountain rose a

tiered building, carved straight from the rock. Had she not known to look for it, Shahrzad would have missed it entirely. Its four gabled roofs were stacked one on top of the other in graduated height. A wooden sign in a language of golden slashes hung above the entrance.

As they landed in the small courtyard before the building, a gust of wind riffled a set of brass chimes dangling from the timber eaves. The melody was of the eerie, doleful sort. The sort that clung to one's bones, long after its notes were lost on the breeze.

It was in step with the empty, ice-laden expanse around them. And the single stone bowl of fire lying squat in the middle of the courtyard. A sputter of blue and orange amid a stretch of black and white.

"Charming, isn't it?" Artan remarked as he tugged the fur-trimmed hood of his cloak over his bare head.

"It's . . . different." Shahrzad pulled her own cloak tighter about her.

"You should see it in winter."

At that, Shahrzad saw Khalid subdue a smile.

The trio strode toward the entrance, leaving Shesha to slither toward the fire. A set of low doors with a high stone threshold stood before them. Artan removed his sandals, and Shahrzad and Khalid followed suit.

Not a soul had come to greet them.

Which did not bode well with Shahrzad.

The floors were covered in a thick lacquered paper, polished smooth. Their surface was strangely warm. As though a fire burned beneath them. A faint scent of mint floated through the air. At least Shahrzad thought it was mint. Mint mixed with lemons. Or perhaps it was aloe wood?

Artan moved through the narrow hallways with the swift ease of years past. Slender lanterns covered in waxy parchment lit the way before them. They proceeded up a set of stairs and into another set of hallways. As they entered a shadowy corridor—

A creature sprang from the darkness, hissing at Artan.

It was white and lizardlike. Around the size of a small jungle cat. With sharp talons and a smattering of dark spots across its back. The spiked fan along its spine was turned up, and its tail whipped about in warning. As it hissed, drops of saliva struck the lacquered-paper floor, burning holes through its surface. Thin trails of silvery smoke curled in their wake.

"Get back, you tiny menace!" Artan threatened the creature with an upturned, outstretched palm.

Though nothing happened, Shahrzad thought she heard the sizzle of a spark catching flame. The lizard continued spitting in Artan's direction, its spine arching higher and its yellow eyes glowing.

The soft sound of a woman's laughter emanated from the other end of the corridor.

"Has Tolu's son finally returned?"

The woman's voice was not pleasant. But it was not displeasing, either.

Shahrzad stepped closer to Khalid. His fingers wrapped around the hilt of his sword.

Artan snorted. "Relieve your pitiful excuse for a sentry of her duty, and I'll tell you."

A harsh word Shahrzad did not recognize split through the gloom. The lizard retreated. But not without hissing once more at Artan, and spitting near his bare foot for good measure.

"Is it safe for me to proceed, Aunt Isuke?" Artan said, his amusement still evident.

Her low laughter resonated once more. "As safe as you'll ever be, son of Tolu."

After exchanging a wary glance, Shahrzad and Khalid followed Artan into a large room with teakwood beams running across its ceiling. A floor of woven rushes extended before them. Seated near a low table in its center was a slender woman who reminded Shahrzad of a bird. Not a bird of song or a bird in flight.

But rather a bird of prey.

Her back was as straight as an arrow, and her eyes were two pieces of flint. Her hair was long and hung about her shoulders like a cape of polished pewter. One thin braid fell behind an ear. Threaded through it was a string of colorful glass beads. Her tunic was trimmed in fur and tied across her chest with a leather cord.

She did not smile when she saw them. She merely quirked her head with interest. Her sloe-eyed look was alert and unwavering.

"You've brought friends." Her gaze drifted to Khalid first. When he remained stone-faced, Isuke turned toward Shahrzad, her eyes lingering.

"I think of them as friends." Artan grinned. "They may not."

"The girl agrees," Isuke confirmed. "The boy does not." She sniffed the air as though she could discern their thoughts through scent. "Yet."

"I gathered as much." Artan laughed.

"Then again"—Isuke cocked her chin in the other direction—"the boy cannot have friends. He does not permit himself the luxury." She blinked slowly. "For he is shrouded in darkness."

Khalid's hand tightened around Shahrzad's. She swallowed, her eyes meeting Artan's.

"Don't be so impressed, little snipe," Artan teased. "I could have told you these things within a moment of meeting your king. He hates smiling and never laughs. It's not a stretch to assume he lacks friends."

"Why have you brought them to me?" Isuke demanded. "Are they an offering?"

At that, Shahrzad placed a hand on her dagger, readying to bolt, while Khalid unsheathed his *shamshir* without hesitation.

Artan sighed loudly.

"Don't bother, boy," Isuke said to Khalid, her tone imbued with sinewy softness. "If I wanted to kill you, you'd be dead already. You came in the company of my nephew. That alone makes you worthy of interest. But the girl has a mystic's blood in her veins, and you have a black cloud around your soul. I would hear you out before I make a decision as to what to do about you."

When Khalid still did not lower his sword, Artan turned to look him in the eye. "I promise no harm will come to Shahrzad while we're here." Solemnity hardened his expression. "On my father's grave, I swear it."

Isuke's shoulders stiffened.

Artan's promise had offended her. Or intrigued her. Shahrzad could not be certain. But neither possibility gave her much reassurance.

Yet it appeared Khalid was not of the same mind. He returned Artan's unflinching stare for a time, and—just when Shahrzad had decided the situation had taken a turn for the worse—Khalid relaxed. The muscles along his jaw ceased to ripple.

His sword fell to his side.

"Why have you brought them, son of Tolu?" Isuke's voice had gone even softer. Dangerously so. The flint in her eyes darkened to obsidian. "And why are you making such promises on their behalf?"

"The boy is cursed, Aunt Isuke. They want your help to rid him of it, as well as to find a means to restore her father's health." Artan paused. "I would consider it a favor to me if you would hear them out."

"A favor?"

"Yes."

"They are that important to you?" Isuke glanced back at Shahrzad with renewed interest.

"I told you: they are my friends." Artan hesitated for the barest of instants. "And they may possess . . . knowledge of my parents' misdeeds."

Though it was carefully worded on Artan's part, Shahrzad started at this revelation. Khalid eyed Artan, his expression darkening.

A strange flash of emotion passed across Isuke's face. It was gone before Shahrzad could place it. "Very well. As a favor to you,

I will hear them out." Her features hardened. "But I expect the same courtesy when I make a request of you in the future."

Artan gave her a curt bow in response. Then Shahrzad took a position on the woven rushes opposite Isuke, with Artan kneeling to her left. She glanced up at Khalid expectantly, and he finally sat beside her, his *shamshir* close.

The sorceress listened as Shahrzad relayed the sad tale of Ava and Khalid. Of their arranged marriage and the heartbreaking loss of their child. Of Ava's desolation and eventual death. Of Ava's father luring Khalid to his home, where he took his own life in exchange for the dark magic to enact the curse upon Khalid.

When Shahrzad finished, she turned to Khalid. In a terse voice, he recited the curse's terms, sharing how he had begun to fulfill it, but could no longer be subjugated to the whims of a vengeful madman.

The entire time, the sorceress's only reaction was the same birdlike tilt of her head. When they were done, she removed a sheaf of papers from her desk with calculating slowness.

"A curse is payment for a debt owed—a deal made, however unfairly," Isuke began. "In this case, a man's life was given as payment for its magic. If the magic is to be rendered powerless, an offering of equal weight must be made."

"Then . . . I must die." Khalid spoke as though he were resigned.

As though he had expected it.

Every muscle in Shahrzad's body pulled tight. A litany of protests formed in her throat.

Isuke's mouth curved downward in what she must have considered a smile. "No. I did not say that. If it were that simple—a life for a life—this curse would have ended many dawns ago. Curses are rarely that simple." She placed an oval mirror the size of two hands on the table. Then she laid both palms beside it.

The mirror seemed to rise of its own volition. It turned to reflect Shahrzad and Khalid before it began to spin very slowly, as though it were hanging from the ceiling on an invisible string.

"I am saying," Isuke continued, "that magic mirrors itself, both in power and intent. Like every mirror, all magic has a dark side. A side that can be tricked into seeing what it wishes to see." For a moment, she seemed amused by her own words. "In magic and in life, deceit is often the best way to defeat one's enemies."

The mirror spun. Slowly. Lazily. It flashed silver as it met Shahrzad's face, before catching Khalid's reflection. Then the mirror's dark side passed, whirling around in another play of light and shadow.

Shahrzad blinked. When she glanced to her right, she noticed Khalid's brow had furrowed in concentration. As though the mirror had become a complex riddle he intended to solve.

Isuke's voice faded to a languid drone. "Thus, if you wish to determine an appropriate counterpoint for this curse, you must delve beneath its surface."

*I don't . . . understand.*

The revolving mirror caught Shahrzad's attention once more. Flashing before making another slow turn. Light and dark. Shahrzad, then Khalid. Again. And again.

Shahrzad grew dizzy. The scent of lemons and mint filled her nostrils and spread into her chest. Her eyelids began to droop. A heaviness slid around her like a second skin, as though she were on the verge of falling asleep. Or drifting in that space between dreams, where she was aware of what was happening around her, but had no control over it.

In that moment of suspended weightlessness, an unwanted presence entered her mind.

It was as though a hooded figure had ambled into the haze of her bedchamber, rummaging through her things like a thief in the night. When it failed to find what it was looking for, it turned in her direction.

Shahrzad gasped.

It did not have a face. Where there should have been features was instead a blank oval of ivory, like a polished eggshell. The faceless intruder glided toward her, then led her into a misty corridor, glancing through open doors to its left and right.

The rooms within were filled with Shahrzad's memories. All the times she'd fought with Shiva or Irsa. Made a point to return Rahim's good-natured grumbling. Listened to her mother recite stories. Disappeared for a stolen embrace with Tariq. Read books alongside her father. Cried alone in her room.

The intruder dwelt on some of the moments she'd shared with Khalid. Many of the nights she'd told him tales by lamplight. Contended with him over matters of the heart, while tearing bread into tiny pieces. All the times she'd kissed him—in darkened alleys and behind veils of shimmering gossamer. The interloper lingered for a spell on their first kiss in the souk.

As though it had come to the same understanding as they had in that instant.

Her intruder soon developed a keen interest in any memory of her father. It watched without eyes as Jahandar presented Shahrzad with the single budding rose from his garden, the afternoon she'd first come to the palace at Rey. It leaned in closer—eager—while Jahandar coaxed the rose to life, only to bring it past death with an unwitting turn of his wrist.

After that, the intruder searched with purpose through the misty hallways for Jahandar al-Khayzuran. Soon, it came across the memory of the day before, when Shahrzad had pressed her father for information on what had transpired the night of the storm in Rey.

On what Jahandar had done to his hands. To his hair. To Irsa's horse.

To the very storm itself.

His eyes aflame, Jahandar had shown her the book he'd kept pressed to his chest all this time. He'd removed a black key from around his neck.

And unlocked the tome . . .

To shine a slow-spreading silver light upon his face.

From beyond the white haze, the faceless intruder reached a cold hand to tightly clench Shahrzad's wrist.

Tightly enough to draw pain.

Shahrzad stifled a cry.

"Aunt Isuke!" Artan thundered. "That's enough!"

The sound of broken glass scattered the weightless drift in Shahrzad's mind, bringing everything back into stuttering focus.

Her eyes flashed open. She was brought out of a world of hazy white smoke.

The first thing she noticed was the imprint of a hand on her wrist. Red and throbbing and real. Shahrzad blinked hard. When she glanced up, her heart plummeted into her stomach.

Both Khalid and Artan were on their feet.

Khalid's sword had been hurled across the room. It was embedded in a far wall at an odd angle, its jeweled hilt still shuddering from impact.

Isuke's ominous mirror was in pieces around them.

Shahrzad knew Khalid had shattered it. Somehow, he had managed to break whatever control the sorceress had over him and had destroyed her mirror in an attempt to stop her. In response, the sorceress had flung Khalid's sword far out of reach.

Now Artan stood between Khalid and his aunt.

*He did nothing while his aunt stole into my mind. Where do Artan Temujin's loyalties lie?*

She initially thought Artan had stepped between Khalid and his aunt to prevent Khalid from attacking her.

But Shahrzad realized she might have been mistaken. Artan seemed inclined to side with them, not with his aunt. His back was to Khalid, and only a fool would turn his back on his enemy. Artan was not a fool. At this moment, his expression revealed a complicated mixture of resolve and remorse. As though Artan knew he had erred.

So Artan had not stepped before Khalid to stop him; he had stepped before him to *save* him.

He had chosen to side with a boy he barely knew over his own family.

*But why?*

Shahrzad's gaze drifted to the sorceress seated across from her.

*It's clear Isuke meant to rob me of my thoughts. To what purpose?*

The sorceress remained with her back as straight as an arrow and her hands upon the table. Unapologetic.

"You promised," Artan said, his voice laden with accusation. "You promised it would be nothing more than a search for the book. You prom—"

"I did not make any promises." Isuke's reply bordered on serene, despite its biting undertone. "You did. In any case, the girl is not hurt."

"You're lying," Khalid replied in a savage whisper. "She cried out."

"I'm not hurt. I was . . . startled," Shahrzad said. "But I demand to know—"

"Your demands are of little consequence to me," Isuke interrupted. "But the book your father has—he cannot be allowed to keep it."

Confusion settled across Shahrzad's brow. "I don't understand. Is it the reason my father—"

"Your father's wounds will heal in time. But he has unleashed something much more destructive on your world." The only change in the sorceress's affect was a shift in eye color, from flint to obsidian, then back again. "If you destroy the book for me, I will lift the curse from the boy you love so dearly. I will render its debt repaid."

Though Shahrzad longed to ask all the questions collecting in her mind, she chose the most pressing one. "Why must the book be destroyed?"

Shahrzad had to know the sorceress's reasons, for she did not trust her motivations. Nor did she have any intention of trusting someone who knew everything about her and had yet to offer anything in return.

Isuke paused in consideration of her. "That book offers nothing but tragedy to its bearer. You should be proud to bring about its demise."

"Forgive me, but that's not an answer," Shahrzad said in equally cutting fashion. "What does this book have to do with you?"

"My reasons should not matter so long as you achieve your goals, but I will say this: the book involves Artan's parents. When you destroy it, you will free him of their debts."

"These debts—of what sort are they?" Khalid said, looking Artan's way.

"That book has brought about untold suffering and destruction. Death in its most grievous form," Isuke answered, her eyes flashing. "When it was gifted to a foolish king many years ago, we thought it had been lost and were glad of it. Now I would have it gone, once and for all."

Her mind brimming with suspicion, Shahrzad studied the birdlike woman across from her. "If you now know where the book is, why would you not destroy it yourself?"

Isuke almost smiled. "As I learned from entering your thoughts, you are not as big a fool as I first surmised."

"No." Artan laughed, though he did not sound the least bit amused. "She is not."

"I cannot destroy this book," Isuke confessed. "Nor can any member of my family. It is a book fashioned from the magic running through our veins. Blood *freely given* must be what destroys it. But it cannot be our blood."

"So it must be mine." Shahrzad nodded in grim understanding. "And I must do it willingly."

"No," Khalid interjected, the angles of his profile sharpening even further. "I will not—"

Shahrzad turned toward Khalid, prepared to meet him with resistance of her own. "If there is a way to break the curse, then I will do it. And you will not stop me."

"Shazi—"

"This is not your choice to make, Khalid. It is mine, and mine alone."

"It is your choice to do as you please." His hands balled into fists. "Just as it is mine. There is no cause for you to go about this alone and—"

"The choice does in fact lie with you, boy." Isuke's mouth curled downward again as she summoned her strange smile. "For, ultimately, *you* must be the one to destroy the book, as the curse resides within you. The girl must steal it from her father, along with the key to open it. Then she must deliver them to you, so that you may destroy the book and put an end to your curse."

Shahrzad bit her lower lip. "And—how must he go about do-ing that?"

"The curse was a curse paid for in blood," Isuke replied. "So blood must be paid in kind. Both now and at the time of the book's destruction. But you needn't worry; the blood offering is significant in meaning, not in quantity. And first I will need a way to carry it out . . ." She eyed the blade at Shahrzad's waist. "Give me your dagger, girl."

With reluctance, Shahrzad passed her dagger to the sorceress. Isuke unsheathed the blade and began muttering to herself. The metal took on a white-hot glow. As the sorceress continued whis-pering in a tongue that sounded vaguely familiar to Shahrzad, tiny symbols began working their way around the blade.

Once the symbols had managed to sustain their eerie glow, Isuke shifted her gaze to Khalid. "Give me your hand."

Shahrzad's teeth stayed on edge as Khalid extended his palm. He did not flinch as Isuke used the glowing blade to slice a thin gash above the existing one. As the drops of crimson struck the dagger's surface, the metal changed from a white-hot blue to a fi-ery red. It pulsed with a heartbeat of its own, its symbols rippling with the light of a passing star.

Everything around them darkened with the same sudden intensity.

Her face devoid of emotion, Isuke wiped the blood away and restored the blade to its jeweled sheath. She started to return the dagger to Shahrzad, but did not relinquish her hold on it.

When Shahrzad's hand brushed across the metal sheath, it felt as cold as death.

"Use the key to open the book, but only when you are ready to destroy it," the sorceress said to Khalid in furtive tones. "Repeat the same ritual you just saw: use this dagger to slice open your skin, and drip your blood onto the blade. Then pierce the dagger through the book's pages before setting it aflame." She stopped as if in consideration. "The book will fight you. It will scream. Do whatever must be done to set torch to it. For the fire will take your curse with it as the book's ashes are scattered to the winds. This I swear to you, by my name and the name of my ancestors before me."

Isuke's fingers curved like claws over Shahrzad's wrist, where the mark from earlier remained. Then and only then did she show any sign of emotion. Her lips drew back over her teeth in a sneer. Two vertical lines appeared at the bridge of her nose.

"Do what must be done, girl. Destroy the book and free us of a terrible burden. But fail, and its weight will no longer be my family's alone . . ." The sorceress's eyes bled into pools of obsidian. "But yours as well."

# TO SLEIGHT AND FEINT

$S$HAHRZAD WAS AT A LOSS.

She'd tried for three days straight.

For three days, she'd feigned interest in her father's book. She'd sat alongside him in his tiny tent and listened while he explained the origins of its magic. She'd smiled as he'd tried to tell her how he'd gone about painstakingly translating its pages. Painstakingly memorizing its contents.

All under the pretext of saving her.

*Saving her?*

A likely story.

Especially now that Shahrzad knew his reasons for prizing the book so highly. For protecting it, even through his fog of delirium. Now that she realized how its evil paled in comparison to its possibilities.

The power to smite a kingdom.

To lord over others with impunity.

Before, Shahrzad would never have believed her father could be so enraptured by the thought of power. But the proof sat before her, day in and day out. Her father's eyes pooled with a feverish light, his scarred palms stroking over his bare scalp, as if seeking a reminder of all that had occurred.

All that his actions had brought about.

Though Jahandar had said he did not intend for such death and destruction to strike at the heart of Rey—that all he'd intended to do was save her—Shahrzad could not shake the feeling of doubt that settled upon her.

For her father could not meet her eyes when he said these things.

As such, it had taken all her efforts to conceal her horror when her father revealed that Reza bin-Latief had requested his help with future endeavors.

*Future endeavors? Of what sort?*

Her skin crawled at the thought.

Tariq's forces had already managed to secure two nearby strongholds along the border between Khorasan and Parthia. Shahrzad had warned Khalid last night, and though he'd begun to rally his bannermen to Rey several weeks ago, the city's beleaguered state made the possibility of organizing a force to retake the border a difficult one. Rey's standing army remained in shambles. It would take time for Khalid to launch a counteroffensive.

Time they did not have.

So Shahrzad continued to try to inveigle her father to turn over his book.

To rectify the curse's blight in advance of the war.

Alas, Jahandar refused to let it out of his sight. He slept with the book pressed to his chest and its key hanging from a thin chain around his neck.

How was she ever to take the book from her father and deliver it to Khalid if he would not part with it, even for a moment?

*I should simply tell Baba the truth. And ask him to give me the book.*

Shahrzad had considered this many times. Especially that first day. A part of her had wanted to believe her father would be willing to do anything to give his daughter the love and happiness life had so often denied him.

But when she looked in his eyes as he spoke of the book in such reverent tones—as he discussed the sense of purpose its magic had given him—she knew he would not easily part with it. Even if it cost Shahrzad her happiness.

This realization pained her more than she cared to admit.

For her father had always been a good man. A kind man. A smart man.

A man with so much to be proud of. Daughters who loved him. And a life still left to live. But Shahrzad knew her father's mind had fallen prey to itself. Had begun to believe its own lies.

So on this particular afternoon, Shahrzad went about preparing bread for the evening meal in a haze of worry.

"Shazi?" Irsa said from beside her.

"Hmm?"

Her sister sighed with practiced patience. "What are you doing?"

"Preparing the dough for *barbari*."

"I can see that. But . . . you're using the flour for *sangak*."

When Shahrzad looked down and realized her error, she almost hurled the sticky mass into the patchwork fabric of the tent.

But she knew it would do little to mollify her and only create more work in the end. So, instead, Shahrzad dumped the batch of not-bread onto the floor in one fell swoop. At least that particular mishap could be remedied in a trice. It was childish, but the dough did make the most satisfying *splat* as it struck the ground.

Irsa tsked. "I suppose we could both use a moment of rest."

With that, Irsa reached for two cups and a few sprigs of mint, which she passed along to Shahrzad. Then Irsa walked behind a table laden with root vegetables. She ducked beneath a trellis strung with drying herbs before reemerging with a small platter of tiny round cakes made from ground almonds and candied apricots, covered in a dusting of sugar.

The two girls sat on the floor beside the lump of failed dough. Shahrzad mashed the sprigs of mint into the cups and poured two streams of tea. Then she snagged a tiny almond cake.

"What's troubling you?" Irsa said before breaking a crumbly cake in two.

"Nothing." Shahrzad's reply was unusually sullen.

"Fine. Nothing is troubling you." Irsa licked the sugar dust from her fingertips. "One day, I will no longer ask, and it will be your own fault."

"You're becoming quite prickly. Perhaps you should stop spending so much time around Rahim al-Din Walad." Shahrzad almost grinned.

"And you're becoming quite the liar." Irsa shot Shahrzad a pointed glance. "You've made so many promises to me. Promises you've yet to keep."

Shahrzad took a deep breath. Everything Irsa had said was

true. She'd long been denying Irsa her confidence. But her intentions had only ever been well meaning. As such, it seemed wrong to include Irsa now that Shahrzad was mired in a quandary of her own making.

But in the recent past, such pride had nearly proven to be Shahrzad's downfall. Her refusal to see the truth through the tales had almost cost her Khalid's love. If she confided in her sister now, perhaps Irsa could provide the assistance she so desperately needed. Perhaps two heads would prevail where one had failed, as their mother had so often said.

Or perhaps Shahrzad would rue the day she'd put her sister's life at risk for her own selfish gain.

Shahrzad took a slow sip of tea and tried to swallow her doubts in a swirl of mint and sugar.

*I can't continue in such a manner. Something must change.*

*Perhaps that something is me.*

"I need to take Baba's book and key from him . . ." Shahrzad did not look away from her sister as she began.

Irsa's eyebrows pulled together in quizzical fashion.

"Without him knowing I've taken them," she finished. "At least not immediately. Can you think of a way?"

Irsa chewed on almond cake as she thought. "There's a sleeping draught in the scroll of curatives Rahim gave me. Do you think that would work?"

Shahrzad pursed her lips in consideration.

*It's risky. But I have been unable to come up with a better solution for the whole of the past three days.*

"It might."

"However, I should caution you," Irsa continued. "I think it will take time for Baba to fall asleep. And I don't know how effective the draught is, as I've yet to try it." She sipped her tea. "Why do you need his book, Shazi? And why can you not simply ask him for it?"

Shahrzad settled her face into a mask of false composure. It would be imprudent of her to tell Irsa everything she had learned. Imprudent to trouble her sister with such painful details about her father's sad exploits. "Why I need it is not—"

"No." Irsa's mouth thinned. "If you want my help, I want you to tell me your reasons. Tell me the truth."

"The truth is not—"

"Pretty? Easy? As it would seem?" Irsa scoffed, almost stiffly. "How old do you think I am, Shazi? A mere babe in swaddling? Or a young woman able to concoct a sleeping draught. For you cannot have both."

Shahrzad blinked, taken aback by the simple truth of her sister's words. Irsa was right. Shahrzad could no longer pick and choose what she saw in her. Nor could she continue protecting her. No matter how much she might wish to do so.

If Irsa was old enough to help her—old enough to while away the hours with Rahim al-Din Walad—then she was old enough to know why Shahrzad needed their father's book.

"You're right. No matter how much I wish to deny it, you're no longer a child. It's time I told you the truth." Shahrzad breathed deep and began.

This time, she left nothing out. In a voice so soft it could barely be heard, Shahrzad told her sister the story of the curse.

Of everything the boy she loved had been forced to do to protect his people. Of all they now had to do to end a reign of terror perpetrated by a grief-stricken madman.

Irsa listened in wide-eyed shock.

When it came time to hear of the daunting task before them, Irsa leaned closer and cut her eyes in concentration.

"So I must take the book from Baba while he sleeps, then collect Khalid from Rey so that he may destroy the book and end the curse, along with this needless war," Shahrzad finished, her shoulders falling forward from the burden of all she'd divulged.

Irsa remained silent for a time. "This is a tremendous risk. Especially with so many unfriendly eyes upon you," she finally said. "And things might progress more smoothly if you had help. Why don't you let me take the book from Baba while you travel to Rey?"

"No." Shahrzad shook her head. "It's too dangerous."

"No," Irsa insisted. "It isn't. It makes sense for me to do it. He won't suspect me of having any interest in the book. Let me give him the sleeping draught in his evening tea. I'll wait for him to fall asleep, then meet you in the desert."

"I couldn't bear it if something were to happen to you."

"What could happen to me?" Irsa frowned. "It's not as though I'm fighting at the vanguard. I'm only transporting a book," she said with unassuming brevity. "Why don't we meet by the well, east of the encampment? It's a short ride from here. I'll borrow Aisha's horse, then bring both the book and the key there, and in doing so save you the trouble and the time. You can leave for Rey once I've given Baba his tea." Her voice had grown more fervent as she spoke, her words grounded in their surety.

Shahrzad chewed the inside of her cheek, still unwilling to relent, but warming to the idea.

*It does make sense. And it would be nice to work together, for a change.*

"Don't worry, Shazi." Irsa grinned good-naturedly. "I am merely waiting for Baba to fall asleep, then delivering a book to you. There's no danger in this."

Despite her wiser inclinations, Shahrzad smiled back.

Perhaps her sister was right.

They were taking charge of their destinies. Refusing to allow fate to dictate their futures. Perhaps the reason Shahrzad had been struggling so much of late was because she'd been fighting against a raging current. Perhaps she should swim alongside it, for a change.

"All right," Shahrzad agreed. "Let's do it."

"Together." Irsa smiled wider.

Shahrzad nodded. "Together."

Tariq wasn't sure what could have possessed him to follow Irsa al-Khayzuran tonight.

Of all the things he should have been doing, he should not have been secretly following Irsa. He should have been planning their next raid. Or at least forming the beginnings of a strategy with his uncle, despite his growing unease as to Reza bin-Latief's objective.

Instead here he was with Rahim, trudging through the desert on horseback . . .

Trying to keep silent.

Indeed, they were fortunate Irsa was such a poor sneak. As well as a decidedly poor lookout. For any soldier worth his salt would have noticed them trailing at a distance.

Would have forgone this ridiculousness long ago.

But Tariq had been worried about Shahrzad for some time. These past few days, he'd tried to keep tabs on her whereabouts. Earlier this evening, Tariq had seen her steal into the desert, carrying a rolled bundle. Before he'd been able to break away from his soldiers and follow her, Shahrzad had disappeared without a trace.

Now Tariq was forced to do the next best thing and follow Irsa. For if anyone knew what Shahrzad was up to with this strange disappearance, it would be her younger sister.

Tariq was more than willing to resort to subterfuge if it meant learning the explanation behind Shahrzad's recent behavior. More than willing to steal into the desert, in pursuit of a hooded figure beneath a moonlit sky.

And Rahim?

It was becoming abundantly clear Rahim would follow Irsa al-Khayzuran anywhere.

All Irsa had in her possession was a tiny parcel wrapped in a length of dark linen, pressed against her chest. She was not dressed for traveling. The light *shahmina* about her shoulders would not protect her from much.

Tariq found this strange because Irsa al-Khayzuran was usually quite sensible. Usually not a cause for concern. She never had been. Was not the type ever to be.

She was predictable. Pleasant. Agreeable.

Everything Shahrzad was not.

All the same, Tariq kept his recurve bow at the ready.

For whatever might lurk ahead.

After half an hour of riding, they neared the well and the abandoned settlement where Tariq had first met Omar al-Sadiq several months ago. He briefly recalled the way the elderly sheikh had shrunk back from Zoraya's flashing talons. For once, Tariq was glad to have left the falcon behind, as she would have undoubtedly given away their presence by now.

Rahim and Tariq dismounted from their horses, concealing themselves behind one of the cracked stone buildings. They lingered in a pool of shadow while Irsa tied her steed to a post near the well.

Despite all, Tariq had to admit he was somewhat curious.

Who was little Cricket meeting?

For Tariq could see no trace of Shahrzad anywhere nearby.

Rahim inhaled through his nose. Even from an arm's length away, Tariq could sense his friend's budding apprehension as though it were his own.

"Why are you so concerned?" Tariq whispered.

Rahim eyed the slender figure of Irsa al-Khayzuran in the distance.

Tariq smothered a smirk. "She's not in any danger. Obviously she's meeting someone she knows. Are you worried it might be another boy?"

"Why would I care if she were meeting another boy?" Rahim shot back. "I only want to make sure she's not in danger."

"Of course you wouldn't care if it was another boy." Tariq rolled his eyes. "That's why you're following her in the middle of the night, like a cuckolded husband."

A sound of exasperation rolled from Rahim's throat. "We both know why we're here, and it has nothing to do with—"

Tariq cut him off with a hand to his shoulder.

Two figures were approaching Irsa. One was easily recognizable. Tariq would know its shape anywhere. He'd spent the better part of his life memorizing its lines. Small and slight. With a messy braid, recently tousled by strong winds.

The other was tall. Hooded. Male.

Less easily recognizable.

Yet Tariq knew—even before the figure pulled back the cowl of his *rida'*, even before his hand moved to the small of Shahrzad's back—who it was.

The hate flew to Tariq's fingers. Coiled through his stomach. His own words echoed in his ears.

*"Make no mistake—the next time I see Khalid Ibn al-Rashid, one of us will die."*

Tariq did not pause to reflect. He did not stop to reconsider.

Love would not blind him to the truth.

His fury rising, Tariq shoved away Rahim's blind attempt to stop him—

And reached for an arrow.

Shahrzad did not like this place.

When she and Khalid had first flown above the settlement surrounding the well, a strange sense of foreboding had washed over her.

As they strode through it now, the feeling only worsened.

All the buildings around them were abandoned. Many of the mud-thatched roofs had collapsed in on themselves, forming craters that lent an even greater sense of menace to the space . . . warning any and all who dared to tread near that time would not look kindly on those who lingered.

Worse, despite all her sister's earlier reassurances, Shahrzad could tell Irsa was nervous. Her sister paced in a tiny circle by the well, clutching a linen-wrapped bundle to her chest. Shahrzad watched as Irsa wore a smaller and smaller ring into the sand by her feet—

Knowing she felt the same menace in the air about her.

The only thing that gave Shahrzad the sense that all would be righted soon was the reassuring presence of the hand at her back.

The warm, solid presence of the boy at her side.

*Khalid sees everything. He never fails to notice the most insignificant detail.*

*He won't let anything happen to Irsa.*

Shahrzad squared her shoulders. Soon, Khalid would destroy her father's book. Then they could begin to right the many wrongs around them. And she would never have such cause to worry again.

As they strode toward the well, a sudden breeze cut through

the horseshoe of abandoned buildings, slicing through the stone hollow in a frenzy of air and sound.

A familiar noise ricocheted in its wake.

Shahrzad stopped walking.

*Was that a . . . horse?*

For a moment, she thought she'd heard the clatter of hooves in the distance.

Beside her, Khalid paused as well. Then he moved past her, as though he were trying to puzzle it out. Irsa's horse stood nearby, tethered to a post.

And no one else knew where they were.

The breeze died down. The whorls of sand fell to her feet.

But all was not right. That much was evident.

Shahrzad felt it on the air.

Just as she saw the distinct shift of shadows near a building on the far right.

And she knew. She knew with the same sort of paralyzing certainty as one who dangles from a precipice.

For she'd trained in the art for years. Now was the perfect moment.

The wind had just fallen. Down and to the left. She could almost feel the feathered fletchings between her fingertips. The *twang* of the bowstring as it was pulled tight.

The *snap* as the arrow was loosed.

Without a second thought, Shahrzad shoved Khalid aside.

# AN ARROW TO THE HEART

THE ARROW ZINGED THROUGH THE DARKNESS, whistling past Irsa on its deadly trajectory.

The world around her seemed to slow all at once.

She saw her sister leap toward the Caliph of Khorasan, trying to push him aside.

In the same instant, the caliph grabbed her, wanting to shield her with his body. Two stubborn lovers, protecting each other from the very same threat.

Fighting the very same losing battle.

He grabbed her as she pushed him. And all was lost.

The arrow buried itself in Shahrzad's back.

Then, just as quickly as the world slowed, it sped forward in a sudden rush.

Irsa watched the caliph catch Shahrzad tight against his chest. Though his face was blank, his eyes were a summer storm. A fiery sun besieged by churning thunderclouds.

A belated cry of surprise escaped her sister's lips.

At the sight of the arrow quivering from Shahrzad's back, Irsa screamed.

The sound split the night sky in two.

"Shazi!" Irsa rushed to Shahrzad's side.

Her sister's fingers were wrapped in the folds of the caliph's black *rida'*. Neither of them had yet to utter a word, their eyes fixed upon the other's. Whatever silent conversation they shared was not one Irsa understood. They sank to the ground, the caliph still holding Shahrzad tight against him. Irsa knelt in the dirt nearby, her heart clamoring in her chest.

"We—we have to do something!" she cried. "We need to—"

A rush of movement behind them spurred the caliph to action. He passed Shahrzad to Irsa and stood in almost the same motion. Irsa held Shahrzad, frantically studying the blossoming wound on her sister's shoulder, wondering what she should do, wondering what she *could* do . . .

The grate of a sword being drawn from its sheath yanked Irsa from her tempest of thoughts. For the first time since the arrow blurred past her, she paused to truly look up at the Caliph of Khorasan.

The madman of Rey. The murderous boy-king.

Her sister's husband.

He was tall. Not as tall as Rahim, but taller than she'd expected. There may have been a time someone else would have found him attractive. But it was not now. Now his features were punishing in their severity. Ruthless in their intent. The only emotion Irsa could discern was fury.

And the promise of death hung in the air about him.

He was truly terrifying.

Truly a monster.

The sight of him looming above her—his sword poised to kill—made Irsa want to cower in a corner, like the useless mouse she'd laid claim to in the worst of her nightmares.

How could Shahrzad love *him*?

Before Irsa could take in a breath to think, the caliph positioned the hilt of his sword between his palms and twisted it in two. Now he held mirror images of one sword in either hand. Twin weapons to wreak twice the destruction. His eyes never straying from their lethal task, he moved before Shahrzad and Irsa, shielding them from view.

Beyond him, footsteps raced through the sand.

"Shazi!"

"Merciful God!"

Irsa turned in shock at the sound of the two voices.

Rahim and Tariq? What were they doing *here*, of all places? How had they—

Shahrzad reached up to seize Irsa's *shahmina*, her hands shaking.

"Shazi?" Fending off her confusion, Irsa bent closer to hear what her sister was trying to say.

"Irsa," Shahrzad choked, her fingers winding around the thin fabric of Irsa's shawl. Her lips had lost all color, and her voice was more breath than sound. "You have to stop him."

"What do you mean?" Irsa cried.

"He'll kill them." The trembling had progressed from Shahrzad's limbs into her core. Her sister's body had begun to quake, and Irsa's hands felt sticky from Shahrzad's blood.

"I—what do I—"

"Make them stop," Shahrzad gasped. "You have to make them stop!"

Rahim had drawn his scimitar to take position before Tariq. A quiver of arrows dangled from Tariq's shoulder.

*Tariq* had fired an arrow at them? *Tariq* was responsible for this? But he must have been aiming at the caliph! Only to strike *Shahrzad*. Merciful God! How had this happened?

How was she supposed to stop them? It had taken her weeks to get her own sister's attention! How was she to stop a brash boy like Tariq, armed to the hilt with dreams of blood and glory?

Much less stay the hand of a cold monster like the Caliph of Khorasan.

"P-please," Irsa cried. A mouse's call to arms. "Don't!"

Tariq's face had taken on a greyish hue. "Is she dead?" he asked the caliph, tugging his fingers through his hair in anguish.

It was then that Irsa realized Tariq was defenseless, save for the quiver of arrows lashed to his back. No bow to speak of. No scimitar at his side. Not even a dagger tucked in his sash.

Utterly useless to fight a monster wielding two swords.

Alas, Irsa knew this did not matter to Tariq. Not in the slightest.

For it was as clear as rain he was beyond all rational thought.

The Caliph of Khorasan said nothing in response. He merely brandished both swords in punishing arcs of precision. Arcs that only too well demonstrated his intent.

He stepped forward.

Without a word, Rahim moved to defend Tariq.

Irsa shrieked as the caliph raised both weapons against Rahim. She felt her sister struggle to catch her breath, struggle to sit upright, struggle to protest . . .

"Is she dead?" Tariq's grief caused his voice to crack through the blue darkness. "Just answer that question, you bastard, and you may do as you please with me."

"Why would I do anything for you?" the caliph replied, low and vicious.

"Because if she's dead, I don't care what happens to me!"

"Then we agree on at least two things." With that, the caliph shifted his attention toward Rahim, his swords glinting on a moonbeam.

"Please!" Irsa screamed. "Please don't—"

"Irsa." Shahrzad yanked her closer, still struggling, her face contorted, her words a ragged whisper. "You have to . . . yell at Khalid. Get up. Make him stop! Do *something*."

Irsa shook her head. He was the Caliph of Khorasan! Could a mouse even dare?

"Irsa!"

The clash of swords rang out in the desert, the ring of metal on metal pulsing through the air.

Yet Irsa remained motionless with fear. As though every cogent thought within her had been swallowed in a breath.

It was over in four strokes. There was no contest to be had. The Caliph of Khorasan was a demon, trained to wield blades forged in the Bluefires of hell itself.

Rahim tumbled into the sand, scrambling for his lost sword.

Irsa's heart flew into her throat.

Every part of her tingled with awareness. With inescapable realization.

It would not be enough for the caliph to disarm Rahim. Not in his current state. The monster of Rey would kill Rahim to get to Tariq.

To destroy Tariq for what he had done to Shahrzad.

And Irsa could not live in a world—*refused* to live in any world—where she had let such a thing come to pass.

So in the end, it wasn't the pleading whispers of her sister. It wasn't the fear that coursed through Irsa's blood. No. It was never the fear. It was so much more than that.

It was older than the desert, this feeling. And it forever put an end to the mouse's reign. Once and for all.

"Khalid Ibn al-Rashid!" Irsa roared. All eyes whipped back in her direction. "Stop this immediately. For if you do not, I promise Shahrzad will never forgive you!"

Her chest heaved as her gaze fell on the boy lying in the sand.

The boy who always asked the right questions. The boy who made her feel better than beautiful. The boy who gave her the strength to be a lion.

"And if you hurt Rahim, I will never, *ever* forgive you," Irsa finished, truth imbuing her words with a steel no sword could strike down.

Even the very grains of sand seemed to yield to her. Seemed to sigh back in relief.

The Caliph of Khorasan gazed at her for an unblinking moment. His features lost a measure of their severity. He stood straight.

And lowered his swords.

Then, as though nothing of import had occurred, the caliph strode back toward Irsa, restoring his blades to a single sword as he walked. Rahim clambered to his feet and retrieved his scimitar before carefully following in the caliph's footsteps, with Tariq in tow.

The caliph knelt beside Shahrzad and tried to lift her. She grimaced, the tension banding across her face. Her coloring had worsened considerably, her skin sallow, her forehead damp with sweat.

"We—have to take her back to the encampment," Irsa said, determined to remain calm despite the recent tumult. "For I don't think it's wise to remove the arrow here. The wound does not seem to be terribly deep, but she's still losing a great deal of blood, and Tariq uses—"

"Obsidian arrowheads." The caliph's eyes rippled with the remnants of a passing fury.

Irsa nodded. "It's likely to worsen the more she moves. We have to do something. Soon."

"Shazi?" The caliph reached for Shahrzad, and his suddenly gentle disposition had a strangely disquieting effect on Irsa. It was as though another person had settled into his skin. "I have to separate the shaft from the arrowhead before we move you."

Her sister nodded once into the fabric of Irsa's *shahmina*.

The caliph paused. "It will hurt."

Shahrzad licked her lips. "Simply do it and stop talking about it, you lout," she muttered in a barely audible tone.

Irsa was almost as astonished by her sister's fearlessness as she was by the sight of the caliph's mouth tugging upward with shadowed amusement. He drew Shahrzad closer, again with great care. With a quick snap, the caliph broke the shaft of the arrow as near to her skin as he could manage. Shahrzad muffled a cry against him, and her shaking continued with renewed vigor.

"She's unlikely to remain conscious for long," the caliph said to Irsa in a quiet voice. "Seasoned soldiers have been known to quail long before this."

"S-s-stop talking about me as though I weren't here," Shahrzad rasped through chattering teeth.

"We're only a short ride from our encampment," Irsa said. "If we—"

"Take one of our horses," Rahim said from behind them. "Then ride back to the Badawi camp with Tariq. No one will question you if you return with Tariq, so long as your face is covered. I'll ride back with Irsa."

The caliph glanced over his shoulder at Rahim. Rahim did not flinch from his cool appraisal. After a beat, the caliph stood with Shahrzad in his arms. He did not say a word as they waited for Tariq to retrieve the horses. When Tariq moved to help with Shahrzad, Rahim stayed him with a hand to his chest before assisting the caliph himself. Soon, the caliph sat astride a dark bay stallion with Shahrzad's pale figure tucked before him.

Still in complete silence, the caliph pulled the hood of his *rida'* low onto his head and directed the horse forward, as though he intended to proceed without them. Then he swiveled Tariq's horse back in their direction. His eyes glowed down at them like embers in a fire.

"Tariq Imran al-Ziyad?" the caliph began, his thinly veiled anger giving the name the rancor of an oath.

Irsa saw Tariq's fists clench tight.

"Lead the way . . . before I rethink the matter and kill you outright."

# A BROTHER AND A HOME

IRSA DID NOT KNOW WHAT TO MAKE OF HER SISTER'S
husband.

He was a confusing mixture of extremes, cloaked behind a
black *rida'*.

With everyone else, he was chipped ice on a mountain. With
her sister, he was a summer breeze across the sea.

Alas, this did little to change the fact that Irsa remained terrified of him. For she was quite certain he'd almost killed Tariq no
less than three times since returning to the Badawi camp.

The first incident occurred not long after they arrived at
Tariq's tent. Though on that score, Irsa supposed the caliph's enmity was somewhat warranted.

As soon as they concealed themselves within the tent, Irsa
tried to remove Shahrzad's bloodstained *qamis*, so as to better see
the wound in question. *Of course* it was not appropriate for Tariq
to assist her with this. Especially in the presence of Shahrzad's
husband. Surely Tariq could not have thought it was. Irsa was not
quite certain why he'd even attempted to do so.

Foolish at best. A death wish at worst.

And in the face of a murdering madman?

A death likely to come about in any number of colorful ways.

Then, once the wound was cleaned, she and the caliph attempted to remove the arrowhead. Since neither of them was versed in such matters, it proved to be a challenging task, especially with Shahrzad's combativeness coming to the fore. In the end, they were forced to consult with Tariq, as he had been the one to fashion the arrowhead in question.

With the purpose of exacting a great deal of damage.

With the intention of shredding skin and shattering bone.

Irsa was certain the caliph meant to murder Tariq at this admission. Unfortunately, it did not much help Tariq's cause when he was the one to extract the arrowhead. After all, he was the one with the strongest understanding of its design. Not to mention the steady hands of a skilled archer. He managed to remove the arrowhead intact, which Irsa had been most grateful to see, despite the difficulty accompanying the effort.

Shahrzad bit down on a piece of worn leather while it was being done, and tears stained her cheeks for the duration. Though they all witnessed Shazi curse Tariq quite soundly afterward—which implied all was on its way to being mended—Irsa was still sure the caliph intended to do Tariq physical harm in the near future.

The last incident in which Tariq narrowly escaped an early demise occurred not long after Irsa cleaned Shahrzad's wound a final time with a mixture of old wine and warm water. Not long after Irsa realized the wound would not stop bleeding anytime soon.

When she knew it would have to be sealed shut with a hot blade.

Shahrzad was not a girl to flinch away from such a thing. Nor was she a girl to lament a scar.

But Irsa knew this would not be a small thing to stomach. Nevertheless, it had to be done. Shahrzad had already lost a fair amount of blood. Any more and it would no longer be a matter they could successfully conceal from the rest of the camp. When Irsa brought her suggestion to light, Shahrzad agreed it was not to be further debated.

In the end it was done using the slender tip of Rahim's *khanjar* dagger, so as to ensure the smallest scar. The caliph was the one to do it. At her sister's behest.

Shahrzad lost consciousness in the process. In truth, Irsa was glad of it. For the smell of burnt flesh alone was enough to sicken her.

Again, Tariq nearly escaped death. Of that Irsa was quite certain.

For after the wound was sealed shut—when it was clear Shahrzad had lost all sense of herself—the caliph seized the front of Tariq's *qamis* with his left hand, still clutching the hilt of the red-hot dagger in his right. Irsa felt the hatred gather in the space between them as sure as she felt the weariness take hold of her bones. The only thing stopping the caliph from seeing his wishes come to fruition was Rahim.

Rahim pulled Tariq away. Forced him to leave. Then followed him, an apologetic glance thrown over a shoulder.

Tariq had been quick to oblige, disappearing into the darkness, his face a storm of regret. But—thanks to Rahim—at least Tariq was still alive.

Now it was just Irsa and the caliph alone with Shahrzad. Alone in Tariq's tent.

Irsa, alone . . . with an infamous murderer of young girls.

She finished wringing out the bloodied linen in a bowl of lukewarm water and stood, trying to stave off the settling fatigue. The caliph remained beside Shahrzad, studying the wound in her back and the fresh wrappings draped over it.

"When she wakes, I'll bring her some barley tea with valerian root. It should help fend off the fever and let her sleep through the worst of the pain." Irsa bit her lip, briefly lost in thought.

The caliph did not respond, nor did he look her way. Instead he remained focused on Shazi, his expression unreadable.

Irsa could not ignore her compulsion to fill the torturous silence with sound. "Though it seems foolish to say so," she babbled. "I'm—grateful the arrow struck at such an odd angle, for the wound is not terribly deep. She'll be sore for a few days, and I'm certain her shoulder will hurt her for a while, but . . . it could have been much worse."

The caliph finally shifted his gaze from Shahrzad to regard Irsa with a set dispassion. "Yes," he agreed. "It could have been much worse." His eyes narrowed. "Had you not been there, many things could have been much worse. I thank you for that, Irsa al-Khayzuran."

A nervous flush bloomed across her cheeks. After all, it was not every day the Caliph of Khorasan considered her as though she were a question he sought to answer. "Rahim . . . brought you a change of clothes." Irsa took a calming breath. "There's clean water in that pitcher there, and—should you need more—there's a trough not far from here. I'm sure you'd like to wash away all the—blood. I can step outside if you wish . . . *sayyidi*."

At that, the caliph waited to respond, as though he were gathering his thoughts. It was impossible for Irsa to tell, for he was impossible to read.

Impossible in every which way.

"There's no need for you to call me that."

A flare of surprise shot through Irsa, stilling her hands of their fidgeting. "But—"

"I'd like for you to call me Khalid." The caliph braced his elbows on his knees. "Since you've already scolded me in typical al-Khayzuran fashion, it shouldn't be too difficult." An odd trace of humor flickered across his face.

Irsa's flush spread from throat to hairline. "I—I apologize for that. I wasn't in my right mind."

"I disagree. I think—of all of us—you were the only one precisely in your right mind."

The intense way the caliph looked at her—as though he could see past her eyes into her very mind—only deepened Irsa's feeling of awkwardness. She brushed back the strands of wispy hair that had fallen into her face. "I suppose you were a bit . . . hot-tempered."

The suggestion of a smile played across his lips. "A fault for which I'm sure to be reprimanded in the near future." He glanced down at the sleeping figure of Shahrzad. "Deservedly."

"Yes." Irsa smothered a grin, despite her unease. "You probably will be—though how Shahrzad can manage to reprimand anyone for possessing a bad temper, I will never understand."

At that, the caliph truly smiled. The gesture managed to soften all the edges of his profile, rendering him almost . . . boyish. Almost beautiful.

Absolutely less monstrous.

The realization caught Irsa off guard. It was the first time she truly grasped the fact that the Caliph of Khorasan was still only a few years older than she.

Still only a boy in his own right.

And perhaps a boy with a bit more to him than the stories foretold.

Irsa wove her braid between her fingers in careful consideration of this fact.

Once again, they both fell silent.

"I understand your discomfort around me," the caliph said quietly. "My behavior earlier was reprehensible. And I'd like to apologize for it."

When Irsa's face reddened a second time, it was for an entirely different reason.

"I hope you'll be able to forgive me one day," he continued.

She nodded, still searching for the right words.

The caliph rubbed his neck, then angled himself away from the light. Almost hesitating. "May I ask where your father's book is?"

Though he spoke in hushed tones, Irsa looked to the tent's entrance before answering. "It's here," she whispered. "In my satchel."

The caliph's expression lost a hint of its starkness. He returned to studying Irsa, his face creasing and uncreasing with his unspoken thoughts. "I don't"—he inhaled through his nose—"I've never had a sister." His thick brows flattened, casting a darker shadow above his eyes. "And there's never been a time I've stopped to form an opinion on the matter. Have you ever stopped to think what it would be like to have a brother?"

"Well, I—I don't have a brother."

But in truth Irsa had always wanted one. Ever since she was a little girl, she'd considered what it would be like to have someone to look up to, as a sister would a brother. Someone to tease her, as only a brother could. Someone to watch over her and needle her when it was both necessary and unnecessary.

For many years, Irsa had thought to find this brother in Tariq. But Tariq had always been occupied by other, grander things—bows and arrows and bets and falcons. Grander things that befit a boy such as he. Much like Shahrzad. And Irsa had never truly resented it. For she'd always hoped things would change as they grew older.

That Tariq would see Irsa as his sister. And become a true brother to her in time.

The caliph inclined his head contemplatively. "Today when you yelled at me—it was the first time I realized what it might be like. To have a sister."

"And what did you think?" Irsa whispered.

"I rather liked it."

Her mouth fell ajar. "Even though I yelled at you?"

"In truth, that might have made all the difference."

252

"Really?" Irsa blinked, astounded. "Goodness, but you're odd. Has anyone ever told you that?"

His smile appeared again, just as mystifying as before. Then—

The Caliph of Khorasan laughed.

And it was not at all like she would have expected.

It was relaxed. Soft and melodic. Though it was definitely not a sound that appeared to have been much practiced, it was also not a self-conscious laugh. It was simply a laugh that spoke of a better time. A time when a small boy laughed at better, brighter things.

Irsa had the distinct feeling she was bearing witness to a rather extraordinary event.

"I'm sorry," she said, trying her best to be respectful, though she knew her behavior had already surpassed the notion. "I didn't mean to insinuate that you were odd."

"You did far more than insinuate; you said it outright." The caliph's eyes gleamed, but Irsa could detect no hint of menace in them.

"Yes." She fiddled with her sleeve. "I suppose I did."

"In any case, I am far from offended. In all things, I find myself grateful to you. I should probably say as much."

Her gaze widened. Would she never cease to be surprised by him?

"Thank you . . ." His mouth slanted, as though he were still deliberating something. "Irsa."

Irsa, too, found herself lost in a moment of deliberation. Then she came to a sudden, irrevocable decision.

"You're welcome . . . Khalid."

She aimed a crooked smile at him, and disbelief began warming its way through her. Before the color could rise into her cheeks, she collected the change of clothes Rahim had provided and passed them to the—to *Khalid*.

He stood and tugged the stained *rida'* from his shoulders. Then he glided toward the pitcher of water, without a word.

Flustered by the budding understanding of why her sister might have chosen to love this supposed monster, Irsa fumbled for her satchel. She passed the linen-bound book to Khalid in a flurry. Then Irsa raced from the tent, her mind a muddle of thoughts.

She turned the corner into utter darkness.

And found Rahim pacing outside.

"What are you doing?" she gasped, drawing back.

He came up short at the sight of her. "I—I was . . ." He dragged a hand along the scruff at his jaw with a *scritch*. His voice had a gravelly quality to it. Even more so than usual. As though he'd been yelling to the heavens for an age.

"I guess I'm waiting for you," Rahim finished, firming both his tone and his countenance. When he blinked, his ink-black lashes fanned against the soft skin of his eyelids with an almost sultry kind of slowness. "Waiting to see if you're all right."

"Oh." Irsa tried not to sound eager. And failed miserably.

"Oh?"

She twisted her braid around her fingers. "Why didn't you just come in?"

At that, Rahim shot her a morose smile. "He doesn't like me."

"I don't think he likes many people."

"He likes you." His smile stayed fixed.

"You think so?"

Rahim nodded. "I'm sure of it. He listened to you. And he doesn't strike me as the sort of king who does that often." He opened his mouth to say more, then shut it as though he'd reconsidered the matter.

Irsa could no longer stomach it. Could no longer stomach not knowing all Rahim meant to say. Everything he thought, at any given time. She knew it was beyond the pale, but she wanted to know everything he ever wished or wanted, at all times.

At least now the reason behind such desires had a name.

Love.

Irsa had all but confessed her feelings in the desert. And she thought Rahim at least returned a measure of her sentiments. Or at the very least cared for her a great deal.

But he had yet to say a word on the matter.

Irsa wet her lower lip with the tip of her tongue, her throat suddenly dry. "Was there—something you wanted to tell me?"

He took in a breath through his nose. "There was . . . and yet there wasn't."

"What do you mean?"

"That's just it." Rahim sighed. "When I'm around you, you make me forget."

"Forget?" Irritation began to gather at the bridge of her nose.

"At the same time you make me remember."

"You're confusing me, Rahim al-Din Walad." Irsa crossed her arms as though that would conceal the sudden *thrum* of her heart.

Grinning, he scrubbed a palm over his tightly marcelled curls, knocking loose a shower of sand. "I should want to say a great many things to you, Irsa al-Khayzuran. I should want to thank you for saving me today. To thank you for saving my best friend. But"—Rahim took a slow step toward her—"that's not what I want to do."

"What—what do you want to do?" she breathed.

Another step. Too close and yet still so far away. "I want to ask you something."

"Then ask it." The warm scent of linseed oil and oranges reached out to Irsa, beckoning her even closer. Asking her to stay.

When Rahim swallowed, the heavy knot in his throat rose and fell.

"May I kiss you?"

"Why are you asking permission?" Irsa murmured. "Doesn't that—ruin the moment?"

"No." He smiled, but its edges wavered with a deeper meaning. "Because it's not just a kiss."

"Why is that?"

"Because when I kiss you, I want yours to be the first . . . and last lips I ever kiss."

"Oh," she said for the second time. For the last time.

It was a sigh and an acknowledgment, all at once.

"So"—Rahim reached up to push the hair back from her face—"may I kiss you, Irsa al-Khayzuran?"

Her heart stopped, then started anew, faster and more fervent than ever before.

"Yes."

His face solemn, Rahim bent toward her, tipping her nose

upward with his. She felt him tremble as he brushed a tentative kiss to the furrow of her lips, so soft at first. Then he settled his mouth fully against hers, and Irsa finally understood.

Understood what it meant to feel at home wherever you were. To feel as though you belonged in any moment, at any place, in any time.

Because at that moment, with the press of Rahim's lips to hers, with the touch of his tongue sending wildfire through her veins, she knew she would always be home here.

With this boy. In this moment. In this time.

And that her heart would never be lonely again.

Tariq had wandered the whole of the Badawi camp twice. Both treks had been completed in a trance. All the while, his emotions had been a flurry of remorse and resentment. Of anger and anguish.

He did not know what to do.

The last thing Tariq had ever wanted to see was the girl he loved more than anything fall beneath his arrow. Fall to the blindness of his own rage.

And Tariq had watched. He'd watched all of it.

He'd been unable to turn away.

Because it was his fault.

Tariq had realized it the moment he'd released the arrow. The instant he'd loosed it from the sinew.

He'd wanted to take it back.

Of course Shahrzad had leapt to save the boy-king. She had always been one to give all to those she loved. Just as she'd been willing to risk all to avenge Shiva. In the end, it should have surprised no one—least of all Tariq—that Shahrzad had reached for the Caliph of Khorasan without a second thought.

But Tariq had not counted on the boy-king acting in kind. He'd not counted on him putting his life before hers. Without a moment's hesitation.

Yet Tariq had watched him move to shield her with his own body.

Just as Tariq would have done.

Tariq knew then—as he'd known when he'd read the letter Shahrzad kept tucked in her cloak—that this was not an ordinary love born of a passing fancy.

In truth, Tariq had known even then that he could not win. That this was not a battle to be won.

Only a fool would have continued to think otherwise.

Yet Tariq had chosen to be a fool.

And he knew it now, with a cold, unwavering kind of certainty. The same kind of certainty he'd felt beneath the Grand Portico when he'd first realized Shahrzad loved the boy-king. He'd ignored the truth that fateful afternoon. But now, despite all Tariq's rash dreaming, all his desperate thoughts that, one day, if Shahrzad and the boy-king were parted from each other long enough . . . Tariq knew his wishes would never come to pass.

Shahrzad would never return to Taleqan with him.

For she no longer belonged there.

She belonged in a palace of marble and stone. A queen, in her own right. With a boy-king who loved her, as she loved him. The boy-king she'd turned to tonight, at all times. First when the arrow had struck her, then when she'd been in immeasurable pain, and even when the question of a hot blade against her skin had been suggested in hushed tones—

Shahrzad had sought the solace of only one person.

It ached. It tore at every selfish part of Tariq's soul. It ripped in two every memory of the years they'd shared together. Every day he'd waited for her to return. To see that they were meant for each other.

To realize the boy-king meant nothing.

Shahrzad and the Caliph of Khorasan had been together for only a few months. Apart for less than that. Yet each was willing to die for the other.

While Tariq had been willing to kill the boy-king, at nothing more than a glance.

How had their lives descended to this?

Love for hate, in the mere blink of an eye.

Again, the memory of Shahrzad crumpling beneath his arrow flew to the forefront of his mind. Tariq shuddered to a stop. In that moment, he'd made a thousand careless promises to a thousand faceless gods.

Among these promises, he recalled one that burned with a sudden, shining fervency: *If you let her live, I'll do anything you ask.*

A heedless promise made as Tariq had hurled his bow aside and raced toward Shahrzad, unconcerned with anything beyond the girl lying before him.

Unconcerned with all—even the lasting memory of his own hatred.

Tariq paused before his tent. He had to speak with the

boy-king—the caliph. He had to understand what it was Shahrzad understood. To know what she saw in Khalid Ibn al-Rashid. For a monster could not love as the Caliph of Khorasan loved. Could never care for Shahrzad with the tenderness Tariq had witnessed tonight.

Of that, he was certain.

His resolve hardening, Tariq ducked within his tent.

Irsa was inside, sitting next to Shahrzad's motionless figure, a single taper casting a golden glow through the yawning darkness.

The caliph was nowhere to be found.

"Tariq." Irsa glanced about nervously.

"Where is he?"

"He went to wash not long ago." Irsa unfurled to her feet. "I just gave Shahrzad some tea to help her sleep." She continued to look about with obvious unease while rubbing her shoulder. "I don't think it's wise for you to remain here. Khal—the caliph will likely return soon . . ." She trailed off, her meaning as clear as the intention behind it.

Though Tariq knew she meant well in warning him, he ignored it. "She's asleep, then?"

Irsa nodded.

Stifling a weary sigh, Tariq crouched beside his raised bed pallet—the bed pallet Shahrzad now occupied, her chin tucked into his pillow, her wound covered in poultices. Irsa knelt across from him, her eyes fraught with a mixture of pity and frustration.

After a time, Tariq met her gaze. "I'm so sorry this happened, Cricket. Please believe me when I say I never meant for any of this to occur."

"I know you didn't. But I am not the one who deserves to hear your apology," Irsa said quietly.

"I know."

"If you know, I think it would be wise for you to take the knowledge and act upon it in the future." With that, Irsa reached for the packets of herbs she'd used to brew Shahrzad's tea and stepped aside.

Tariq took hold of Shahrzad's hand. He wove his fingers through hers. The skin of her palm was soft, save for the calluses he recognized from her years of training in archery. The years he'd spent training alongside her. Encouraging her to defy the odds. To be more than the wife everyone expected her to be. To command attention wherever she went, as only she could. As only she had, from the day Tariq realized there was—and would be—only one girl in the world for him.

Only one. Always.

Even though Tariq knew it was wrong, he brushed a thumb across her forefinger. He knew he would never again have a chance to touch her like this. But he wanted to.

One last time.

"I'm so sorry, Shazi-*jan*," he murmured. "God, if I could change that moment, I would not have done it, not for the world. I would take a thousand arrows for you." Tariq bent his head closer to hers. "When I thought you were dead, there was nothing I wanted more than to take it back. I'm so sorry, my love. I can't swallow my hatred as you can. I'm not like you. But I can swear I will listen to you next time. No matter how distasteful I find your words to be. I will listen, Shazi."

Tariq rose to standing, then stooped to kiss her temple. "I swear on my life, you will never be hurt by me again," he said in her ear as he brushed aside a wayward curl.

A muted yelp from the corner jostled him straight. Tariq turned. Irsa al-Khayzuran's face was frozen in a mask of fright. Her eyes were locked on the entrance of the tent.

Where the Caliph of Khorasan stood by the open tent flap—

Watching him.

Tariq could find nothing in his expression. Not a hint of emotion. Not the slightest sign of awareness he'd heard a single word. The caliph waited a beat before walking inside. Once he'd made certain his face was concealed beneath his *rida'*, he gathered Tariq's recurve bow and quiver of arrows in unhurried silence.

Then waited by the entrance.

Without a word, Tariq followed him out into the desert. The caliph paused to hand him his bow and arrows before striding twenty paces away.

As calm as the eye of a storm, the caliph withdrew his *shamshir* and twisted it in two.

"Three arrows," he began in a voice that managed to carry over the distance, though Tariq could not detect any sentiment behind the words. "Three shots, Tariq Imran al-Ziyad. There is no one here to stop you. No one here to defend me. I'll give you three arrows. Three chances to finish what you started by the well."

"Why three?" Tariq mirrored the caliph's impassive tone as he shifted his quiver onto his shoulder.

"One for your cousin." The caliph thrust a sword into the sand before him, its jeweled hilt swaying in the moonlight. He flourished the other in a glittering sweep. "One for your aunt. And one for your love."

Tariq returned his fixed stare.

Even from this distance, the caliph's strange eyes possessed an otherworldly glow. "But when you fail—and you will fail—you will never again repeat what I just saw."

"Then you are jealous?" Tariq called out, loud enough to echo across the cool sands.

A thin stream of pale purple clouds drifted above, moving too fast for comfort, yet too slow to convey anything of significance.

Tomorrow's storm would come without warning. If at all.

"Jealousy is a childish, petty emotion." The caliph switched the single *shamshir* to his left hand in a single, fluid motion. "I don't feel jealousy. I feel rage."

Tariq waited a beat. The boy-king's words were in stark contrast to his actions. Was this finally a weakness? Finally something that made him seem less like a monster and more like a man?

"Do you worry about me, Khalid Ibn al-Rashid?"

The caliph hesitated, and that said more than words ever could. "There was a time I did. But the fact that you waited until Shahrzad slept to touch her shows me you know she would not approve. You will not disrespect her in such a manner again. Nor will you disrespect me."

Tariq let his recurve bow dangle by his feet. "I did not do it to disrespect her. I am not trying to win her back." He took a measured breath. "I know I've—lost."

The single *shamshir* flashed through the air once more. "Yet you still wish to kill me." It was not a question.

But Tariq chose to answer it, all the same. "Of course."

"Then here's your chance."

"It's not much of a chance, since you say I will lose."

"You will." The caliph wrenched the other *shamshir* from the sand and brandished both swords. "For you're a fool if you think I would choose to fight a battle I could not win."

"Is that why you have yet to meet me on the battlefield, you arrogant bastard?"

The caliph's mouth slid into a wry smile. "Partly."

"And what are the other reasons?" Tariq removed an arrow from his quiver.

"Because I do not yet know my enemy, Tariq Imran al-Ziyad. And, unlike you, I do not willingly fight the unknown."

"I know who you are," Tariq ground out.

"No. You think you know who I am."

"Perhaps you should endeavor to change my mind."

"Perhaps I should." Again, the caliph turned his swords in elegant arcs. "You have three arrows. Aim true."

Tariq inhaled. He nocked the arrow to the sinew. Then pulled back.

He should aim for the bastard's heart. For, despite the boy-king's pompous effrontery, no man could escape three arrows, fired in rapid succession. Perhaps he could dodge one. Knock aside the second with a well-timed swing of a sword.

But not a third. He could not be *that* gifted a swordsman. No one was. The thought was simply ludicrous. Filled with the sort of bold audacity that routinely caused Shahrzad such trouble.

They were alike in that respect. Shazi and the boy-king.

Arrogant. Audacious.

Yet oddly steadfast in their convictions. Oddly honorable.

Tariq should aim for his heart. And take him down. For Shiva. For his aunt.

For himself.

Anger coursing through his blood, Tariq pulled the arrow even farther back. He heard the sinew tighten beside his ear. The goose feathers between his fingers felt so familiar in their softness; they almost whispered a promise on the wind.

The promise of an end to his suffering.

He could do it. The boy-king's arrogance made him weak. Made him believe Tariq incapable of such violence. Or unable to espouse the necessary skill.

Tariq stared down the needless sights to the end of the arrow. The obsidian point gleamed back at him, menacingly beautiful in the light of the moon.

The last arrowhead Tariq had seen was the one he'd removed from Shahrzad's back. Stained crimson with her blood.

Dripping red with the blood of the only girl he'd ever loved.

It seemed only a moment had passed since Tariq had promised he would never hurt Shahrzad again.

A moment and a lifetime.

And this? What Tariq was about to do? This would do far more than hurt her. This would destroy her. Beyond words. Beyond time. As Shahrzad had once said of his own death. On a night not so long ago when she'd worried Tariq might perish at the hands of the Caliph of Khorasan.

There would never be an end to this.

Unless someone chose to end it.

Tariq lowered his weapon. "The wind is not right."

"The wind should not matter to a master archer such as yourself."

"It should not," Tariq replied simply. "Yet it does."

The caliph dropped his swords to his sides. "Perhaps you are not the archer I thought you to be."

"Perhaps." He cut his gaze at the boy-king. "Or perhaps I'm merely waiting for a more favorable wind."

The boy-king's expression darkened in response, a muscle working in his jaw. "Never forget, Tariq Imran al-Ziyad—I gave you this chance. Today you fired upon me . . . and in turn struck that which matters more than life itself. The next time you attempt such a thing in her presence, I will flay you alive and leave the rest for the dogs."

Tariq's brows shot into his forehead. "And here I was on the cusp of believing you might not be a monster."

"I'm my father's son—a monster by blood and by right." The caliph's voice remained cool, despite the heat of his words. "I do not make empty threats. You would do well to remember that."

"Yet you wish for me to trust that you deserve Shahrzad. That you are what is best for her." Tariq refrained from sneering.

"I would never presume such arrogance. And rest assured; the day I concern myself with your good opinion will be the day the moon rises in place of the sun. But know this: I will fight for what matters to me, until my last breath."

"She matters to me, too. I will never love anyone or anything as much as I love Shahrzad."

At that, the caliph's smile returned, mocking in its bent. "I disagree. You love yourself more."

Resentment simmered through Tariq's chest, roiling to a slow burn. "Do not—"

"Until you can learn to let go of your hatred, you will always love yourself more."

Laughter burst from Tariq's lips, dark and scathing in tone. "Can you honestly claim not to hate me?"

The caliph paused. "No. I do not hate you. But I deeply resent your past, more than I can put to words." He restored his blades to a single sword and began pacing toward him. "Do you know how many times I could have killed you, Tariq Imran al-Ziyad? How many times I've wished, in the blackest reaches of my soul, that you were no more? I've known who you were—who your family was—for a long time. My father would have killed you simply for looking at Shahrzad the way you do. For myself, I would have killed you. But for her, I didn't." He sheathed his sword with a quick *snap*. "And I never would have, but for the events of tonight," he said, almost as an afterthought.

Tariq clenched a hand around his bow-grip, taking the caliph's confession into consideration. As difficult as it was for Tariq to admit, he did not believe the caliph to be lying. For he did not seem prone to deceit. Which put to question many other suspicions Tariq had long harbored against him. Suspicions that had long begged for answers.

Tariq's hatred could no longer remain festering in their shadow.

"Why did you murder my cousin?" he asked in a terse voice.

"Because I thought I didn't have a choice," the caliph responded with care. "I believed it was taken from me by a man who wished for me to suffer as he suffered. A man who sought to"—he took a halting breath—"curse me for my heedlessness. To curse the families of Rey with the deaths of their daughters each dawn. And in so doing, the man cursed the whole of Khorasan." A trace of anguish flickered across the caliph's gaze—an anguish that hinted at an untold amount of suffering. He answered as though he expected to answer for many years to come. As though he knew no answer would ever be sufficient.

"A . . . curse? You killed my cousin because of a *curse*?" Incredulity flared through Tariq. His eyes grew wide, blurring his sight to all around him for an instant.

"I was wrong to believe I didn't have a choice," the caliph said quietly, continuing to make his way toward Tariq. "So very wrong. And I can never right this wrong. Nor can I right the wrongs to your family. But I can promise to make amends, if you will grant me the chance."

Tariq gritted his teeth. Despite this revelation—despite the realization that this must have been what Shazi had been trying to tell him all along—the caliph's answer was truly not an answer. It was merely a string of hollow reassurances.

Nothing of substance.

"Your promises are but empty words," Tariq shot back. "Said all too late."

"My promises are not empty words." The caliph stopped a body's length away from him. "Though a promise means little without a measure of trust."

Tariq's jaw set. "The sheikh of this camp once told me trust is not a thing given; it is a thing earned. You have not yet earned mine."

The caliph's mouth curved into a reticent smile. "I think I'd like to meet this sheikh."

A spell of awkward silence passed before Tariq responded, his words equally reticent. "Though I'm loath to admit it, I suspect he'd like you."

"Why do you say that?"

"He likes a good love story." Tariq sighed resignedly.

"I'm not yet certain if this is a good love story."

At this quiet pronouncement, Tariq caught sight of a vulnerability buried deep beneath the arrogance. More of the man behind the monster.

Tariq paused to consider the boy-king he'd so long despised. So long wanted to see die a thousand slow deaths at his willing and eager hands.

For the second time, Tariq saw the hint of something . . . more.

Not something he liked. Perhaps not something he could ever like.

But perhaps something he no longer hated.

"For your sake, it had better be a good love story," he whispered.

At that, the Caliph of Khorasan bowed to Tariq Imran al-Ziyad, a hand to his brow.

After a moment, with the slightest twinge behind his heart—Tariq returned the gesture.

# AWRY

WHEN SHAHRZAD AWOKE THE NEXT MORNING, IT was with a spinning head and a leaden shoulder. Her tongue felt thick and heavy, and every muscle in her body ached.

But she was warm. Warmer than she could ever remember being.

For the first time in her life, she woke wrapped in someone else's arms.

Khalid was asleep beneath her.

She was on her stomach, strewn across him, their limbs an unwieldy tangle.

For a moment, she froze, thinking she might still be lost in a dream, concocted by one of Irsa's foul-tasting tonics.

*How is Khalid asleep?*

She stared at him, confusion warring with the traces of slumber. Then she noticed a sliver of leather mingling with a length of metal about his throat.

He was wearing the talisman Musa Zaragoza had given her.

Shahrzad had rarely seen Khalid look anything other than

pristine. The sight of him appearing in a state beyond his control was . . . intriguing, to say the least.

He looked like a beautiful disaster.

His dark hair was in complete disarray. There were smudges of dirt beneath one eye. They'd gathered in the creases formed by the scar beside it. His *qamis* did not fit him, for it was obvious it did not belong to him. It was too tight across his chest and too long in the arms.

Shahrzad stared at Khalid's sleeping form in watchful silence. The steady rise and fall of his chest beneath her could almost lull her back into sleep, if she would but let it.

Instead she set her chin on her stacked palms and continued her careful study.

Khalid at rest was a fascinating prospect to behold. Awake, every shadow, every hollow appeared pronounced by the icy apathy he displayed for all things—the proud and petulant mask he wore to conceal the world of sentiments beneath. At rest, everything was softened. Molded as if from the finest clay. His lips were slightly parted. Begging to be touched. His eyebrows— usually set low and severe on his forehead—were smooth and without the looming threat of his judgment. His lashes were long and thick, curving darkly over the skin of his cheekbones.

*So very beautiful.*

"A painting would be better."

Her breath caught.

Khalid's lips had barely moved while he spoke. His eyes had remained closed.

She cleared her throat. "I do not need a painting. Nor do I

want one." Though she strove to sound indifferent, the husky rasp of her voice betrayed her.

Perhaps she could attribute it to the hour. Or to the recent ordeal.

Or to any number of—

"Liar."

The blood rising in her cheeks, she turned away from him . . . and gasped sharply.

A searing pain bloomed from her shoulder and across her back. Shahrzad bit her lower lip hard.

Immediately, Khalid's eyes flew open. He caught her chin in one hand, his gaze skimming across her face. Then he reached for a tumbler beside the bed pallet and passed it to her.

"What is it?" she asked, clearing her throat.

"Something your sister left to ease any discomfort."

Shahrzad swallowed the liquid, its bitter taste coating her throat. She made a face. Though Irsa had obviously tried to mask the tonic's unpleasant tang with honey and fresh mint, it still possessed a rather dreadful flavor.

While she drank, something stirred from the shadowy corners of the opposite side of the tent. Tariq soon appeared, his hair mussed and his eyes still heavy with sleep. "Is something wrong?"

"No," Khalid replied. "Nothing beyond morning mulishness."

Shahrzad frowned. "No one asked you."

"As a matter of fact, I did ask him." Tariq yawned through his words. "For I'd be much more likely to get an honest response from him than from you."

Shahrzad cut her eyes at Tariq, more than willing to battle

with him, despite her condition. "So now you're talking to him instead of trying to kill him?"

"Be kind, Shazi," Tariq retorted, the portrait of ease. "After all, I did let him sleep in my tent."

*We're in Tariq's tent. And we managed to survive the night here.*

Shahrzad could scarcely believe it. Again she wondered if she might still be suffering from the aftereffects of last night's ordeal. For surely there could not be a note of humor in Tariq's voice. And she had yet to detect even a hint of tension in Khalid.

*It's clear something of note happened between them.*

*Beyond their attempts to murder each other.*

But Shahrzad could not be certain whether all was indeed as it appeared.

Wariness settling between her shoulders, Shahrzad glanced from her husband to her first love. Then back again.

What had made Tariq no longer wounded to the core by the mere existence of Khalid? And what had made Khalid no longer of a mind to destroy Tariq on sight?

*I will never understand men.*

But she would not question her good fortune. Not now, at least.

"What is the hour?" Shahrzad asked, her voice still thicker than usual. It appeared the tea she'd consumed at Irsa's behest was clouding her faculties. Or perhaps it was the tonic left by her bedside. Whatever the case, she could not fault either draught much. Whatever she'd consumed had lessened her pain, which should by all rights be considerable.

Tariq studied the weak light filtering through the tent seams. "I believe it's just near dawn."

She closed her eyes. "Oh."

"But I don't think he should remain in the camp for much longer," Tariq said in a thoughtful tone. For a moment, indecision seemed to hover about him. As though he himself were unsure of his course. "For I cannot continue to guarantee his safety, should anyone discover his identity. After all"—he turned somber—"this is not an army rallied in his support."

Shahrzad braced herself for one of Khalid's blistering replies. Something low and curt that was sure to provoke Tariq.

When Khalid said nothing, Shahrzad took the opportunity to answer with a quick nod. "He's right. We should return to Rey with all haste, Khalid." Biting back a gasp, Shahrzad shifted to one side, preparing to stand.

"I can travel there myself," Khalid replied.

"No," she said. "No one knows you left, and the *shahrban* will be incensed if he believes something has happened to you. Not to mention Jalal. We should return quickly."

*And the magic carpet is the best way to do so.*

"My uncle will be angry with me regardless. And Jalal—will be unlikely to notice." At the mention of his cousin, Khalid's body tensed ever so slightly.

"Of course he'll notice."

"I would not be so certain."

The sudden tension—along with the hint of dejection in his voice—made Shahrzad turn back to look at him. Even in the early-morning shadows, the change in his disposition was unmistakable . . . provided one knew what to look for.

*What has happened between Khalid and Jalal?*

When she saw the look of warning Khalid passed in her direction, Shahrzad decided not to discuss the matter further. At least not in Tariq's presence.

Instead, she endeavored to sit straight, stifling a cry at the shooting pain that traveled down the length of her arm. The entire right side of her body was stiff. She clenched and unclenched her fist in an attempt to restore movement to her fingers.

"Shazi"—Tariq started toward her, concern marring his face— "I don't think you should—"

"Don't presume I care what you think." She glared at him while waving him off with her uninjured arm. "Especially since you're to blame for this."

Tariq winced. "I'll not protest on that score. And though it's a feeble thing to say, I *am* sorry. More sorry than I can put to words."

"I know you're sorry. We're all very sorry any of this ever had to happen," she said in a peevish tone. "But now is not the time to tell me what to do, especially in the face of all your mistakes." With a cutting glare, Shahrzad returned to her task of restoring movement to the right side of her body, despite the searing ache behind each motion.

"Are you not going to stop her?" Tariq said to Khalid, his exasperation all too evident.

"No," Khalid replied in an unruffled manner, still lying on the bed pallet in studious silence. "I'm not."

Shahrzad shot Tariq a triumphant look.

"But will you lend me a horse and enough provisions to journey to Rey?" Khalid said to Tariq, rolling to standing with unaffected grace. Almost mocking Shahrzad for her inability to stand straight.

"Khalid!"

He swiveled to face her. "I won't stop you from doing as you please. Just as you will not stop me."

Tariq grinned, clearly more than a little amused to see Shahrzad thwarted. "I'd be happy to lend you a horse and provisions. But I expect full repayment in the future. With interest, for you can undoubtedly afford it. Also don't expect to take my horse. Not this time." He paused. "Or ever again, for that matter."

"I agree to your terms." Khalid stood before Tariq, the former half a hand shorter than the latter, yet the two appearing to be on strangely equal footing.

A king on par with his nobleman.

Nodding at Khalid with an almost affable expression, Tariq glanced back at Shahrzad. "I'll gather the necessary provisions and wait for you both outside." Then, with nothing more than a striking smile to shroud a lingering sadness, Tariq slipped through the tent flap.

*He left us alone.*

*Tariq left to give us time alone together.*

Either he had fully come to terms with the situation or Tariq was putting on a show worthy of Rey's finest street performer.

Could it be possible he was giving her his tacit approval?

*Tariq* was giving *Khalid* a chance to prove him wrong?

Momentarily shocked into silence, Shahrzad sat still on the edge of the raised bed pallet while Khalid moved to the nearby basin to wash.

"What happened between you and Tariq?" Shahrzad began without preamble. She dropped her voice. "And who has my father's book?"

"Tariq fired an arrow at you," Khalid intoned without pausing in his task. "And lived to tell the tale." He looked back at her. "As to the book, you needn't worry about it any longer. You've dealt with more than enough."

"Khalid."

Swiping his damp hands across his face and neck, Khalid remained silent for a time. "Tariq Imran al-Ziyad and I have come to a sort of understanding." He lifted the lid off a small wooden container beside the basin and shook a measure of ground mint and crushed rock salt onto his palm to cleanse his mouth of sleep.

"Then I should not worry?"

Finally Khalid turned to meet her gaze. "For Nasir al-Ziyad's son, I can make no promises. But for me, you should not worry. I promise."

The last word hung in the air with palpable meaning.

Shahrzad took in a slow breath.

Khalid would not seek reprisal for what had happened last night. Which hopefully meant he did not harbor any hidden resentment toward Tariq for trying to kill him. Nor did he wish him harm for injuring Shahrzad in the process.

The hope of reconciliation she'd dreamed of by the fire began to take shape once more.

"Will you not let me take you to Rey?" Shahrzad asked, seizing upon this newfound sentiment.

"No. I will not." He finished his ablutions without another word on the matter.

Shahrzad wrinkled her nose in frustration as Khalid wiped his chin of excess water. "I wish you would not be so stubborn."

"And I wish you had not jumped before an arrow last night. But wishes are for genies and the fools who believe in such things." The hint of anger in his words brought a rash of heat to her skin.

*Surely he's not angry with me for doing such a thing.*

"Do you think I *meant* to be shot with an arrow?" she accused. "You can't possibly be angry at me for this, Khalid Ibn al-Rashid. I certainly did not intend to—"

"I know." Khalid knelt before her, his hands coming to rest at her sides. "I didn't mean to imply otherwise. But"—he stopped short, the harsh lines on his face melting away—"you cannot do that again. I—cannot watch such a thing again, Shahrzad."

Her throat swelled tight at his pained expression. And her mind drifted back to the memory of a boy who had watched his mother die before his eyes.

Khalid brought a palm to the side of her neck, brushing a thumb along her jaw. "Do you know how close that arrow came to your heart?" he whispered. "To killing you in an instant?"

"If I hadn't pushed you, Tariq would have killed you," she replied, lifting her hand to cover his. To press the whole of his touch into her skin.

"Better me than you."

Her gaze hardened. "If you're asking me if I would do it again, I would. Without question."

"Shahrzad, you can never do that again." His words were muted and harsh. "Promise me."

"I can't promise that. I will *never* promise such a thing. Not as long as I live. As you once said, there isn't a choice in the matter. Not for me."

Khalid's chest rose and fell on a deep inhale. "I wish you would not be so stubborn." He echoed her earlier words as his thumb grazed her cheek.

As his eyes rippled with unfettered emotion.

Shahrzad smiled. "Are you a genie or a fool?"

"A fool. As I've always been when it comes to you."

"At least you can admit it."

"At least twice." One side of his mouth curled upward. "And only to you."

Shahrzad shifted both hands to Khalid's face. His stubble dragged across her skin as her fingers caressed his jaw. His eyes fell shut for an instant.

It was not the right time. Alas, it was never the right time.

But it did not matter.

Even the heaviness of the tonic did not dull the fire racing through her blood. She pulled him toward her, slanting her lips to his.

He tasted of water and mint and everything she ever hungered for in all her moments of remembrance. He smelled like the desert in the sun and the faintest trace of sandalwood. The palace at Rey and the billowing Badawi sands, coming together in perfect concert.

His touch was silk over steel. It made her hot and cold all at once. His kisses were the perfect mix of hard and soft. Practiced and unrestrained.

When she tried to tug him closer, Khalid was careful. Too careful.

As always, Shahrzad wanted more. She wound her fingers in the front of his borrowed *qamis*, wordlessly telling him so. He stilled her, capturing her face between his palms.

Shahrzad sighed, silently cursing her injuries. "I hate that I'm not going with you."

"And I hate that I'm leaving you behind. Leaving you amongst all this—chaos." Khalid's features tightened at the edges.

The reminder brought back another equally pressing matter she'd nearly lost sight of.

Her eyes drifted about the room. "Where is it, Khalid?"

*Her father's book. The reason for so much death and chaos.*

Khalid reached beneath the bed pallet, then lifted the small bundle her sister had been clutching by the well. "Irsa left it with me last night," he said quietly. "I kept it within arm's reach, along with my sword and your dagger."

"Irsa?" Shahrzad almost smiled at the familiarity. "She gave you permission to call her that?"

"In a fashion," he murmured, tucking her hair behind an ear.

"You once said you had no intention of being beloved by your people, Khalid Ibn al-Rashid. Yet you've managed to win over several of your harshest critics in a single evening." Shahrzad grinned without reserve.

"Irsa was one of my harshest critics?" He arched a brow.

"She's my sister. Of course she was."

The hint of a smile touched his lips. Shahrzad's heart warmed at the sight.

From beyond the tent, the loud bleating of a goat brought them back to the present.

"I should go." Khalid pushed aside the bloodied bandages on the floor to reach beneath the bed pallet a second time. He collected his sword and her dagger, placing them with her father's book, still wrapped in a length of coarse brown linen.

"And the key?" Shahrzad whispered.

Khalid tugged the silver chain from around his neck. The black key hung over his heart, alongside the jade talisman. The very sight of both sent a shiver down Shahrzad's spine.

She brought her hand to Khalid's chest to cover the cold metal. "Destroy it as soon as you can. Tonight, if possible. Waste no time."

He nodded once. "I'll ride through the day and destroy it as soon as the sun sets." Khalid rested his forehead against hers. "I'll return for you as soon as I can."

"No. I'll come to *you*."

Khalid smiled before pressing another heart-stopping kiss to her throat. Then he tucked the dagger into his *tikka* sash and disappeared beneath the tent flap.

An unexpected chill fell over the tent.

And Shahrzad realized how very dark it still was.

It was the cold that woke Jahandar.

He could not recall the last time he'd felt so cold.

His mind was battered and waterlogged, as though he'd been

tossed about at sea. His throat felt as though it had been stuffed with silk thread. Dry-mouthed and disoriented, Jahandar reached for the book atop his chest, seeking its reassuring warmth.

But it was not there.

In a sudden panic, his eyes flew open.

He sat up in his bedroll, his useless blankets peeling away like an onion's skin. His tent was still shaded in the cloak of night. Dawn had barely broken through the tent seams, trickling down in fractured beams of light.

Jahandar passed his palms across the bedroll. Then across the floor beside him. Then farther into the darkness.

Still he could not find the book.

His panic mounting, he reached for the key around his neck.

It, too, was gone.

Realization came crashing down on him in a flash of light.

Someone had stolen the book and key from him. His sluggish head and his swollen tongue were proof positive that someone had drugged him with a mind to pilfer his most prized possessions.

Someone had fooled him and fleeced him.

In a fit of rage, Jahandar bolted to his feet, kicking aside the brass lamp positioned next to his bedroll. The oil dripped from its innards in a slow dribble, filling the air with its pungent aroma.

Reminding him of the power lying dormant in the most innocuous of things.

Indeed, with a mere snap of his fingers, Jahandar possessed the power to set fire to the whole of this camp.

Or, rather, *had* possessed the power.

For he did not yet know the toll the storm had taken on his abilities. Nor did Jahandar know the full price he'd been forced to pay to wield such awesome ability.

He needed the book to restore himself back to his former graces.

*Needed* it to assist Reza with his efforts.

Jahandar paced from one end of his tiny tent to the other, his mind a constant flicker of thoughts, the thoughts piling one on top of another, turning tinder to flame.

There were only three people in the camp who knew of the book.

One of them had prepared his tea last night—the tea that had likely brought about his unusually restful slumber.

Another had been asking about the book for the past three days. Had asked to see the book, and learn of its contents. The book that had, until then, been of little import to anyone, save Jahandar.

Jahandar stopped pacing.

Had he been deceived by his own flesh and blood? Had his own children fleeced him? And then taken from him his one true chance to be a man of power and influence?

A man worthy of consideration.

Jahandar's hands clenched tightly into fists. He reached for his cloak, the rage building. Passing into his arms and chest.

Swirling through his mind in a storm of hot fury.

The last of these individuals would help Jahandar get the book back.

For this man had just as much to lose by its disappearance.

Just as much to gain by its use.

Jahandar may not be sure of much anymore, but of that he was certain.

Just as he knew he would do anything to get the book back.

Even beg, barter, or steal.

Even murder.

Shahrzad knew she should leave Tariq's tent.

She'd been inside almost all afternoon.

Though her shoulder was still sore and her body still weak from the past night's ordeal, it was time to return to her own tent. To proceed as though all were well. For if she spent another night in Tariq's tent, someone was bound to take notice.

And such a thing would not bode well for either of them, in the long run. Despite their feigned relationship.

She rose to her feet and winced at the sudden flare of pain that shot down one side of her body.

Her mouth and throat were parched. With a frown, Shahrzad reached for the tumbler of tonic by her bedside and nearly toppled over in the process. Cursing under her breath, she righted herself before taking a long swallow of the bitter liquid.

If she never again drank anything steeped in barley or willow bark, it would be too soon.

*I cannot remain so weak. Especially since I will need to journey to Rey shortly.*

Fighting to stand straight, she squared her *qamis* and wrapped her *shahmina* to conceal the thick wrappings banded about her shoulder. For a moment, she thought to wait until Irsa returned to help. Her sister had, strangely, disappeared after bringing the tonic to her bedside over an hour ago, and Shahrzad had no intention of continuing to lounge about in idle solitude.

"Shahrzad-*jan*?"

She almost dropped the tumbler. Trying to maintain her composure, Shahrzad tugged the *shahmina* even tighter about her. "Uncle Reza." She set down the tumbler, balling her hands into fists to conceal their sudden quaking.

"I didn't mean to startle you." He smiled with undisguised warmth, his brown eyes almost liquid in the afternoon sun shining from beneath the tent flap.

"I wasn't startled." Shahrzad swallowed. "Are you looking for Tariq?"

"No." Reza eyed the rumpled bed pallet. "I was looking for you. May I speak with you for a moment?"

"Actually, I was on my way back to my tent to meet Irsa. Is it a matter of import?"

"Somewhat." He stepped to one side. "I can walk with you, if you don't mind. My tent is on the way."

Though she felt discomfited by his persistence, Shahrzad could think of no reason to demur. "Of course."

Reza held open the tent flap for her. A guard stood outside, only to trail behind them at a distance. Shahrzad tried to mask her unease at both the guard's nearness and the lasting pain from her ordeal.

*How odd that Uncle Reza needs a guard with him at all times. Especially in his own camp.*

*As though he cannot trust those around him.*

"What can I help you with?" she began, striving to sound

lighthearted. Striving to tamp down how unnerved she felt. For it was clear Reza bin-Latief had known she was not in her own tent last night.

*Does he know anything more?*

Her heart hammered in her chest.

Reza smiled patiently. "I've noticed you're spending more time with Tariq."

"Yes."

"Is everything going well?"

"Yes." She glanced at him sidelong, unsure what he meant.

"Then you are no longer ill?"

Again, Shahrzad swallowed. "No."

"I've been worried about you of late. Word has reached me that you've been unusually tired during the day . . ." He trailed off, watching her all too circumspectly.

Shahrzad grinned, then bit her lip, affecting a sheepish expression. "I think the past few months have simply taken a toll on me, Uncle Reza. It's been a bit of an—adjustment here. But I'm much better now."

A single brow rose. "Truly? Your coloring leaves a great deal to be desired. Have you spoken with Aisha about your health?"

She waved a dismissive hand. "I don't wish to trouble Aisha with such things. In any case, Irsa has already made me a tonic that has helped a great deal."

"Irsa?" He paused in consideration. "So Irsa knows how to brew tonics, then?"

"Somewhat. I suppose you should try one first and then decide." Shahrzad widened her smile.

"I see." He stopped near his tent, his expression still dubious. Reza then reached for her arm, his touch light, but nevertheless not to be ignored. "Shahrzad? I do so wish to trust you, but I noticed something rather troubling . . . and I can no longer remain silent on the matter."

Shahrzad pulled back. "I'm sorry?" Her heart began to trip about in her chest.

"I saw the bloodied linen beside the bed pallet, Shahrzad-*jan*." He placed a gentle palm on her forearm, as though he meant to comfort her. "You are clearly injured. I'd like to send for Aisha to take a look at it." Reza turned to direct the guard behind them with a motion of his free hand.

"Uncle Reza . . . truly I'm not." She tried to pull away again, panic seizing her.

"I insist." He smiled, his grip tightening on her arm. If it were anyone else, Shahrzad would have felt beyond threatened. But this was her best friend's father. A man Shahrzad had known for much of her life. A man she had long considered a second father of sorts. "I could not in good conscience let you leave without first knowing whether or not you are well," Reza continued. "Please allow Aisha to care for your injury. If you don't mind, I shall wait with you inside until she arrives."

"Uncle Reza—"

"Shahrzad-*jan*"—his expression softened—"I've neglected you for far too long, and I was unjust when you first arrived. Though it was from a place of pain, there is still no excuse. Please allow me to make amends. Your condition is truly causing me a great deal of concern, and I cannot continue to go about ignoring it. Allow me this small indulgence. Please." He motioned with a nod of his head for her to proceed into his tent.

Reluctantly, Shahrzad made her way inside. For she could not see how best to extricate herself without drawing even further attention.

The tent was dark. Dark enough that it took her eyes a moment to adjust to the layers of shadow. Then, from the edges of her vision, Shahrzad caught sight of a hulking figure looming by the entrance.

It was the sentry she'd first met the day after she'd arrived at the Badawi camp. The one with the Fida'i brand seared into his forearm. The one who'd dealt her a rather rash judgment, only to be meted out one in kind.

He came for her in a blur of grey streaking through the dark.

Shahrzad spun back toward the entrance, a scream barreling from her lips. She looked to Reza bin-Latief for help. To Shiva's father. To the second father she'd so long trusted.

He watched, idly. A calm lethality about his gaze.

As the Fida'i assassin grabbed her by the throat. As a nauseating sweetness clouded her senses.

And everything went black.

# THE GREATEST OF ALL LIVING POWERS

O MAR AL-SADIQ WAS AFRAID.

It had been many years since he'd truly felt fear. He was far too old for fear. Far too at ease with life. Far too set in his ways.

But he could not find the Calipha of Khorasan. He'd searched for her all afternoon. And Irsa al-Khayzuran was nowhere to be found, either.

Omar had known something was afoot last night, when his most trusted sentry had come to him and reported that Shahrzad had not returned to her tent. Nor had that same sentry seen the calipha anywhere thereabouts this morning. Which was indeed cause for alarm. Before, when Shahrzad had disappeared each night, she'd always returned to her tent by dawn.

And now Omar was certain his worst fears had come to pass.

In truth, he'd known it was only a matter of time.

Which left Omar with a decision to make. It was obvious Reza bin-Latief had lied to him about his intentions, as Omar had suspected Reza might do. But it broke his heart to know the truth with such unequivocal certainty, for Reza had become a friend.

He'd been a good man once. A man who had loved his wife and daughter, and lived a life of simple desires.

But suffering had changed all that. For it was easy to be good and kind in times of plenty. The trying times were the moments that defined a man.

And love? Love was something that did much to change a person. It brought joy as it brought suffering, and in turn brought about those moments that defined one's character.

Love gave life to the lifeless. It was the greatest of all living powers.

But, as with all things, love had a dark side to it.

The darkness had overtaken Reza bin-Latief, as Omar had seen it would.

Omar had seen its shadow descend upon his friend, just as Omar had known his own tribe would fall into the clash of two kingdoms. Would be caught between the warring nations of Khorasan and Parthia. One a sovereign land of plenty, besieged by recent misfortune. The other its lesser in all ways, save for ambition.

The lands of the Badawi lay along the border between Khorasan and Parthia, and Omar had known it would be impossible for him to remain apart from any conflict that occurred between the two, however much he may have wished it could be so. His people were too close, his land too valuable.

But Omar had not known how best to proceed.

He had not known who would be his true enemy, and whom he could fashion into a friend. And Omar was not the type to choose sides without learning all he could first. Without seeing both faces of the coin.

He had hoped Tariq—the young nobleman from Khorasan who possessed such a pure heart—would help to guide him. The White Falcon from Khorasan, who would guide his kingdom from the darkness back into the light.

But now Omar was not so sure. For he'd not yet had the chance to speak freely on these matters with Tariq. And the boy's heart had not seemed to be in the recent raids made on neighboring strongholds. Omar was not certain Tariq had chosen right in following his uncle. Not certain Tariq knew how best to choose between right and wrong.

For Tariq had seen only one face of the coin.

It was time for Omar to share with Tariq all he knew. All he had learned from all his quiet observance. All he had long suspected.

It was time for Tariq to make a choice as well.

For Tariq's uncle had already made his. A path into darkness.

And now the Calipha of Khorasan and her young sister were missing. Omar need only hazard one guess as to where they'd been taken.

Which meant the two kingdoms were likely on the brink of war.

Which meant the al-Sadiq tribe would ride again.

But with whom?

With a mysterious boy-king who had murdered all his brides without seeming cause? Or with a power-hungry tyrant who had paid mercenaries to bide their time amongst Omar's people? The same power-hungry tyrant Omar suspected had allied himself with Reza bin-Latief long ago.

For Omar had seen the trunks of gold being spirited away under cover of night. He had seen the brigands with their scarab brands. It was why he had asked Reza bin-Latief's forces to relocate to the outskirts of his camp nearly a fortnight ago.

But which of these two kings was the true villain of this story?

For a story was only as good as its villain.

Indeed, it was time for Omar to make a decision. To pry back the worn wool from the desert's eyes.

For the desert did indeed have eyes. Eyes Omar had put in place many moons ago. Omar had always known how to watch and listen. This desert was his desert. A desert his people had ruled for six generations.

It was time for Omar to see if Tariq was made of more than muscle and mettle. To see if Tariq could handle the truth. Once Omar had confessed it to him, he would hear what the boy had to say. And his decision would be made.

Whether it would make the boy his enemy or his ally remained to be seen.

But Omar's people came first. Despite how much he'd come to care for the boy. Despite how much Omar longed to see the boy achieve all he'd set out to achieve.

How much he longed to see Tariq's love story win out.

Omar had said it to Aisha many times before. Though she'd harrumphed at him quite severely whenever she heard it, he knew it never ceased to make her smile.

"Give me a meaningful love or a beautiful death!"

Alas, Omar was a greedy man.

He'd always hoped to have both.

# LIFE AND DEATH IN THE PAGES
# OF A BOOK

K͟HALID RODE THROUGH THE DESERT UNTIL THE SUN
dipped low on the horizon.

It would take him two more days of hard riding to reach Rey.
By that time, his uncle would undoubtedly be at his wit's end. It
would not matter that Khalid was the caliph and therefore en-
titled to his own freedom. In matters such as this, General Aref
al-Khoury only saw an angry boy, alone in the shadows. The same
boy he had quietly cared for these many years.

Khalid could only hope the *shahrban* believed him occupied
by one of his many excursions into the city. Or that Jalal had been
willing to conceal Khalid's absence for a short while.

But Khalid doubted his cousin would be willing to do such a
thing.

For their exchanges over the past few weeks had been stilted
at best.

Downright hostile at worst.

As it was, Khalid did not know how he would ever explain

this particular disappearance to his cousin. And Khalid had been unable to find a trace of Despina or the Rajput. Anywhere.

He continued riding at a brisk pace through the umber sands until only a hint of the sun's warmth lingered across the sky. Then he dismounted from the borrowed steed and removed the pack of provisions from the saddle.

With only a moment to catch his breath, Khalid pulled free the book from its place in the worn leather folds of the pack. The book was still wrapped in a length of coarse brown linen. Tucking it beneath his arm, Khalid strode away from the horse, his hand shifting toward the dagger at his hip.

He did not know what to expect.

Though the strange sorceress in the eastern mountains had warned that the book would scream—would fight back—Khalid still did not know what it might bring about.

Nor did he trust her. Not in the slightest.

Which was why he'd waited to do anything with the book until he was far away from anyone or anything.

No one else would die for this curse.

Not if he could help it.

Khalid removed the jeweled dagger from his sash. Then he placed the book on a rise of sand before him. Once he'd unwrapped it, he studied it for a spell.

It was strangely unremarkable. Ugly, even. Bound in tattered, water-stained leather. Degraded at the edges. Rusted at the bindings. Sealed in its center by a tarnished lock Khalid felt certain even the most unskilled thief could open with a hairpin.

Strange that something so commonplace could signify so much. Could do so much incalculable damage to so many lives. To entire cities. To so many families.

Just a book. Merely scratchings on a page.

Khalid smiled a bitter smile. *The power behind words lies with the person.* It had always been one of his mother's favorite teachings. One of the more notable bits of wisdom Musa Zaragoza had ever imparted upon them both.

He narrowed his gaze on the worn volume below.

The words in this particular book would never give power to anyone again.

And, if the sorceress had not lied to them that evening in the mountain fortress, her words would spare Khalid from a life rooted in the past.

From a life spent atoning for his sins.

Khalid removed the black key from around his neck. And unlocked the book.

The pages sprang open. An eerie white light emanated from within. Sickly. The slashing text was indecipherable to him.

When Khalid reached out to touch the pages, a sudden flare of heat shot toward him, burning the tips of his fingers. He swore. With the burn came another flash of light, violent and vivid and bright. Wickedly so.

No more.

Khalid unsheathed the dagger.

The book pulsed in response. Rippled with a vital sort of menace.

He drew the blade across his palm. Dripped his blood onto

the metal. It began to glow a fiery red. Then he let his blood trickle onto the pages of the book.

The book began to scream. A high-pitched, keening wail. For a moment, its pages seemed to scorch. The smell took on a presence, heavy and thick in the air. The drops of crimson blackened as they struck the book's surface. Pale grey swirls rose above them, curling in sinister suggestion.

The wind bowed around Khalid, covering him in an eddy of dust and smoke. With the blooming gusts, the symbols the sorceress had worked into the blade began to shimmer as if in response to a threat.

Khalid lifted the dagger high.

But the smoke stayed his hand. It gathered a life force of its own and wrapped itself around his wrists in an icy vise.

What Khalid felt in that moment was like nothing he'd ever experienced in his life. It was not a vision, nor was it a memory. It was not a dream, nor was it a nightmare.

It was simply a feeling. A naked, exposed sort of feeling. The kind that ebbed from his center, drawing itself to the surface for all the world to see. The kind he'd spent so much of his life trying to deny, for fear it would make him appear weak. Would make those around him see past his skin into his very soul.

It was every moment he'd ever felt alone. Every moment he'd ever felt powerless. Every moment he'd ever wanted to disappear.

Every ugly thought and every empty feeling coursing through him, as though the book had reached within him and grasped every doubt—every insecurity—and brought it to the surface.

Brought it there to tell Khalid he was not worthy.

Of anything.

Not worthy to be a king. Not worthy of his uncle's faith. Not worthy of Jalal's loyalty. Not worthy of Vikram's friendship.

Not worthy of Shahrzad's love.

After all, what had he done to deserve any of it? He was the unwanted second son of an unwanted second wife. Everything to one person, then nothing to no one.

Nothing.

He'd been nothing but an angry boy in the shadows for so long. A boy who'd envied his brother from the shadows. A boy who'd watched his mother die from the shadows.

A boy who'd thrived in the shadows.

Now he had to live in the light.

To live . . . fiercely.

To fight for every breath.

Khalid grasped the dagger with both hands. But the smoke fought back. The jade talisman coiled about his neck. The screams rang louder around him. The sand swirled in a raging vortex, pressing in, tighter and tighter, trying to swallow him. Trying to make him disappear.

All he'd wanted for so long was to disappear. To take all the ugliness with him—all the vicious memories of his mother's blood spilling across blue-veined agate and silken cords at sunrise—

And vanish without a trace.

"No."

He squeezed the dagger tighter.

"No!"

Every letter Khalid had ever written, he'd written for a

purpose. Every apology he'd ever made, he'd made for a reason. Every journey he'd taken into Rey, he'd taken with hope.

Because he wanted to be better.

Here was his chance to be better. Finally.

A chance to live—to love—in the light.

Blood dripping from his hands, Khalid slammed the dagger into the book.

As the book let out a final, gut-wrenching scream, the sand closed in around him. Pressed in on him, biting into his skin.

Khalid couldn't breathe. Couldn't see. The wind and the sand strove to choke him. To steal away his last bit of purpose.

To fight for the book's last bit of strength.

His chest heaving, Khalid tore a scrap of coarse brown linen for tinder, then struck the flint to catch a flame. The wind snuffed out the tinder in the same instant.

It took five tries to light. Five tries to fight against the billowing silt. Five tries to cup the fire close and let the pages catch flame.

The book burned blue and foul for hours.

Until the sand finally swirled back to the ground. Until Khalid finally fell with it, exhausted. He stared up at the sky, his body broken. Every wound across his skin ached, the scars reopened in the struggle. Khalid's blood seeped into the sand. His eyelids began to droop.

He was losing consciousness. Losing blood. He would die here in the desert.

But it did not matter. If he took the curse with him. If he kept his people safe.

If he kept Shahrzad safe.

Nothing else mattered.

A strangely peaceful breeze ruffled his hair. It brought a sense of calm Khalid had only experienced around Shahrzad. That small measure of peace he always fought to keep. Like water cupped in his hand.

If Shahrzad was safe, he could be at peace.

His eyes drifted closed. Then Khalid slept.

With the jade talisman in pieces beside him.

# THE SANDSTONE PALACE

When SHAHRZAD WOKE, IT WAS TO THE SOUND of birds and the feel of silk.

Even the faintly scented breeze around her conveyed nothing but light and beauty.

Yet beneath it she felt nothing but the sense of being controlled. The sense of being imprisoned.

She was in a bower.

True, she was still dressed in the same rumpled *qamis* and dirty *sirwal* trowsers she last remembered wearing, but the chamber she'd slept in rivaled the finest rooms of the palace in Rey.

Indeed, it could be argued that it might even surpass them.

The open screens to her right were far more ornate in their carvings. Perhaps even a tad garish. The richly stained wood was inlaid with ivory, flecked by dark green jasper. Beyond the screens, Shahrzad could see a series of trellises shading a marbled balcony. Branches of flowering trees hung over the terrace, threading through the white latticework like drapery, their bright pink blossoms heavy on their boughs.

The walls of her chamber were sandstone. Where she could

see the walls, that is. Thick tapestries clung to every exposed surface. In the corner was a table fashioned from many bits of colorful tile. It was as though a crazed artisan had taken a hammer to a rainbow, destroying something beautiful in an effort to create something decidedly less so. The pillows tossed about were bold and fringed with tiny mirrors embroidered by threads of gold and silver. On the gaudy table was a basket of flatbread and a copper tumbler, along with a platter of fresh herbs, rounds of goat cheese, small cucumbers, and an assortment of sweet chutney.

When Shahrzad examined the tray of food more closely, she noticed her host had not provided her with a knife, nor was there a utensil or sharp object of any kind in sight.

Her suspicions as to her whereabouts mounting, Shahrzad rose from the mass of silken cushions and took a turn about the room. She could not see past the intricate screens at the edge of her balcony. Indeed, she could see very little outside this prison of sandstone and ivory. When she attempted to turn both handles of the double doors—which were presumably the chamber's entrance—they were firmly sealed from without, just as Shahrzad had expected.

Her shoulder still ached, but at least it no longer debilitated her. At least it would not inhibit her from fleeing were the opportunity to present itself.

*It's clear I've been "asleep" for quite some time.*

Shahrzad's thoughts turned more grim.

*How long has Shiva's father been planning to take me from the Badawi camp against my will?*

For it was now obvious Reza bin-Latief had been in league with the Fida'i assassins for quite some time. Had likely been the one to send the mercenaries to Rey those many weeks ago, in an attempt to either kill Khalid or kidnap Shahrzad with a mind to use her as leverage.

And now Shahrzad had successfully been taken unawares.

To a place she was certain would bring about a predictable turn of events. Especially since Shahrzad had a sinking feeling she knew where she had been taken.

Trying to tamp down her fears, Shahrzad made her way to the tray of food on the garishly colorful table in the corner. She dripped some of the water from the tumbler onto the silver edge of the tray, waiting to see if it would darken the tray's surface. When it did not change color, Shahrzad trickled some of the liquid onto her skin to see if it would do her any harm. Then she took a tentative sip. Her throat was terribly parched. She did not yet trust the food, but she knew she must at least wet her tongue if she meant to survive for any stretch of time.

When Shahrzad heard the sound of grating metal beyond the double doors, she knocked aside the herbs and smashed the platter against the edge of the mosaic table. Then she grabbed one of the larger shards of porcelain and wrapped a linen napkin around one end to fashion a rudimentary weapon.

At the very least, she would not face down her enemy without a fight.

One of the double doors swung open. Shahrzad concealed her weapon to one side of her sun-worn trowsers.

Only to watch her father breeze across the threshold—

303

Well-dressed and wearing a smile through the wisps of his neatly trimmed beard.

*Baba?*

When Jahandar saw Shahrzad—armed and crouched in an almost feral position upon the marble floor—he lifted his scarred hands in a placating gesture.

"Shahrzad-*jan!* You mustn't be afraid." He moved to her with a swift-footedness Shahrzad had not seen from him in quite some time.

"Baba"—she blinked, beyond confused to see him in such a poised and polished state—"where are we?"

"Dearest, please put down the weapon. There is no cause to be afraid!" He smiled again, even brighter. "The guards outside told me you'd tried the door not long ago, so I came straightaway."

"Where are we?" Shahrzad demanded again.

"I know you must be afraid, but he does not wish you any harm. No one does. Indeed, you will be safer here than you were in the encampment. And much better cared for. As befitting your status." His shoulders rolled back at the last, filled with a peculiar sort of pride. A pride that did not fit her situation at all.

"Baba!" she admonished, her frustration clear, for he had yet to answer the question she'd now twice posed.

His smile faltered. But only slightly. "Reza thought it best you be brought to Amardha."

As she'd suspected. Nevertheless, Shahrzad's heart lurched. For a moment, she could scarcely breathe. "You brought me to Salim Ali el-Sharif?"

"Of course!" Jahandar did not even flinch at her dangerous

tone. "He is your husband's uncle, is he not?" He spoke simply, though his expression indicated much more knowledge.

"How could you do this to me?" she whispered.

At her quiet accusation, her father's watery eyes wavered, then stiffened at the edges. In that instant, Shahrzad realized he would not be moved by her pleas.

Not this time.

He pulled straight. "Perhaps it is I who should be asking you this question, daughter."

Immediately, Shahrzad recoiled from both his charge and the cold light that had entered his eyes. Eyes that had always been a warm mirror to her own.

"What have you done with my book?" her father asked in a mincing tone.

"I don't know what you're talking about." She lifted her chin, trying to conceal her apprehension.

"Shahrzad. I've already spoken to Irsa. I know it was she who drugged me."

Shahrzad remained stone-faced, though her heart missed a beat at the mention of her sister.

"She refused to say anything further on the matter, but you know as well as I that Irsa is incapable of uttering a falsehood. And her attempts to avoid disclosing the truth belied her actions." His face screwed tight in frustration. "Therefore I must insist that you—" Though it took effort, her father managed to temper his reaction. "I am not angry, dearest. I know someone must have coerced you. Perhaps the caliph or someone with the desire to undermine—"

"No. No one coerced me to do anything. Because nothing has been done."

Again, a flash of cold light filled her father's gaze. "Do not lie to me, daughter."

Shahrzad steeled herself even further. "Where is Irsa, Baba?"

No response, save for a soft inhalation of breath. The barest of hesitations.

"Baba?"

He opened his mouth to answer, then paused a telling beat. A beat that made Shahrzad's throat swell tight with trepidation. Her father offered a kind grin. "You are still weak from the journey and your injuries. Allow the sultan's servants to tend to you, after which you should join us for dinner. The sultan's daughter has been quite worried about you. I promise all will be discussed tonight."

Shahrzad reached for him, unable to conceal her fear any longer. "Baba, please don't—"

"I have allowed you a great deal of freedom, daughter. Perhaps I have allowed you too much." Her father's tone was firm. He stood quite tall. Taller than Shahrzad ever remembered him standing. Indeed, she had not seen him act with such vim since before her mother had died. "You have defied me long enough, Shahrzad. I will not allow you to lie to me about this. You are toying with something far too dangerous and far too important. Rest for now. And we will discuss the matter later." Jahandar turned away.

"Please just tell me if Irsa is—"

"Rest. And we will discuss the matter tonight . . . when you are ready to tell me the truth." With that, Jahandar al-Khayzuran strode from the chamber in a whirl of fine silk.

Shahrzad sank back beside the shards of broken porcelain, still clutching her makeshift weapon.

The panic she'd been fighting since she'd first caught sight of her father—no, since the first inkling of where she was had begun to take root—washed over her with a dire sort of urgency.

The war she'd meant to end had now slipped beyond her control. Far beyond the boundaries of her worst fears come to pass.

For as soon as word reached Rey that Shahrzad was being held prisoner in Amardha—was now a "guest" of the uncle who most assuredly planned to use her as a pawn—Khalid would march on the city with a host at his back.

Of that, Shahrzad was certain.

And, though the truth of it would undoubtedly cost Shahrzad her father's trust and more, she was also certain of another thing: Khalid had already destroyed the book. Which left them nothing with which to bargain. Nothing to use as leverage.

Except her.

But Shahrzad was not a fool. She would not quail before the Sultan of Parthia. Would not beg for even one word of kindness from her enemy. Nor would she wait to be saved, like a child wailing in the wings.

She would do what needed to be done.

She would find Irsa. And uncover a way out of this cursed city.

Or die trying.

Her worry about Irsa made Shahrzad comply.

Even though she did not think her father would permit her sister to be harmed, Shahrzad no longer knew what thoughts swirled behind his power-hungry eyes.

So she said nothing when the servants entered the room to help her bathe and dress.

Strangely, the entire affair seemed eerily reminiscent of the day Shahrzad had first arrived at the palace in Rey, when the two servant girls had readied Shahrzad for marriage to a monster. When they'd scrubbed sandalwood paste on her arms and dusted her skin with flakes of gold before placing a heavy mantle upon her shoulders.

This time, Shahrzad's garments were nearly as elaborate as they'd been that fateful afternoon.

Vermillion. A rich red that reminded her of a setting summer sun.

Or fresh blood trickling from an open wound.

The *sirwal* trowsers were cut from the finest silk, embroidered in gilt thread. The fitted top was low across her chest. Much lower than Shahrzad was accustomed to wearing. The mantle was fashioned from a thin gold fabric. Not from the more typical damask. This fabric instead resembled gossamer. In the light, it hinted at everything beneath.

Shahrzad felt exposed. Vulnerable. Which she knew was not by happenstance.

The servants wove her black hair into a thick braid and wound strings of seed pearls around the shining plait. The bangles on Shahrzad's left arm and the hoops in her ears were of hammered bullion with matching seed pearls and tiny diamonds embedded throughout.

As her father had assured, Shahrzad had been well tended. Dressed to fit her station.

But she did not feel like a queen.

*For a prisoner can never be a calipha.*

*But a calipha is only a prisoner if she chooses to be.*

At these thoughts, Shahrzad threw back her shoulders and curled her toes within her pointed slippers. Her head high, she followed the servants into the corridor, where a contingent of armed guards stood at the ready, waiting to lead her toward the next destination.

Again, Shahrzad was struck by the overblown opulence of the sandstone structure around her. True, the palace at Rey had been marbled and polished past explanation, but there had always been a coldness to it. A kind of stark unwillingness to embrace all that it was. And now that Shahrzad saw all a palace could be, she was oddly glad Khalid had not appointed every corner with a gilt statue or every stretch of the eaves with a glittering tapestry. Indeed, it seemed every alcove in Amardha had been adorned in gold leaf or silver foil, every cusp framed with carvings and embedded with jewels beyond reason or taste, and the sight of it all made Shahrzad rather uncomfortable.

The only place where the palace at Rey outdid the sandstone edifice of Amardha was in its calligraphy. For Rey did boast an inordinate amount of elegant artistry. Of swooping flourishes and graceful swirls made in service to the written word. And Shahrzad knew it was because Khalid had a penchant for poetry.

While it was obvious Salim Ali el-Sharif had a preference for opulence.

*Give me poetry any day.*

Despite everything, Shahrzad almost smiled to herself at the thought.

The guards led Shahrzad down several more lavish hallways toward a set of beautifully carved doors as wide and as tall as any Shahrzad had ever seen. Of course, just as she'd come to expect in less than a day, the doors were coated in a layer of liquid gold, with handles of solid sapphire the size of her fist. Two guards pushed them open, and she followed the crush of soldiers down a series of polished sandstone steps into a cavernous room of pale pink granite veined with deep threads of burgundy. A single long table stretched through its center, lit by lengthy tapers perfumed in rose water and myrrh. The tablecloth looked to be spun from the finest spider-silk, gleaming lustrous in the warm light cast from the tapers' glow.

*Because the room could undoubtedly use more gold.*

As far as the eye could see, Shahrzad took in an altogether unnecessary display of opulence. Even the scent of the tapers cloyed at the back of her throat, for it was overwrought. Overdone.

Overmuch.

Shahrzad was the first to arrive.

Again, she was certain this was no accident.

A guard directed her to a richly appointed cushion of darkest blue near the center. While none of the soldiers were outright rude to her, she did notice a certain sort of amusement ripple through the throng when the one nearest to Shahrzad—a young man with a scar slanted across his nose—leered down at her chest as she bent to take a seat.

Shahrzad gazed up at him, fire in her eyes. "Is there a reason you're staring at me in such a manner?" she said, her snappish voice bounding through the cavernous hall. "Have you a death wish, or are you merely as senseless as you look?"

He dipped his head in a terse bow, his jaw taut.

"That is not an answer, you insolent fool. And it barely constitutes a bow," she continued, determined to make a point of this interaction.

Shahrzad could not let any man in this cursed city treat her poorly. Even for a moment. For if they saw even a trace of weakness in her, it would be her undoing.

A wave of laughter filled the air at her back.

Shahrzad's body froze at the sound of it.

*Salim.*

"Just as silver-tongued as ever, my lady." He clapped his hands as though he meant to applaud her. The sound rang in her ears, sharp and crackling.

Shahrzad did not turn around. Would not dare give him the satisfaction. Instead she faced forward and put on a show of affecting a lighthearted expression.

"Your soldiers could stand to learn a lesson in respect, my lord." Shahrzad grinned as the Sultan of Parthia came into view.

Salim returned her strident greeting by bowing with a flourish. "And I suppose you intend to give it to them?" He braced a hand on the gleaming hilt of his scimitar.

A hand meant to remind Shahrzad of her position.

"Well, someone should." She grazed her fingertips across her forehead as she emulated his mocking obeisance.

Jahandar al-Khayzuran followed the sultan, dressed in his silken finery, palms folded before him, his expression warring between pensive and perturbed.

Either her father did not know she and Salim had already established a troubling rapport or he was laboring to conceal the knowledge. Shahrzad refrained from meeting her father's gaze. The betrayal was still too fresh. And she did not want Salim to know how at odds they were.

How hurt she was by her father's treachery.

Salim moved to sit across from Shahrzad, a tranquil elegance to each of his movements. His heavily embroidered mantle and his beautifully tailored garments were just as overwrought as his palace. Like a simpering cat recently fed on the richest cream, Salim smiled at Shahrzad, his perfect mustache sloping above his wolfish teeth.

"I'm so glad you've come to visit us in Amardha, Shahrzad-jan. It's been long overdue."

"Visit?" Shahrzad peaked a brow. "That's a rather interesting choice of words."

Salim lounged, his elbow against the sapphire cushion to his left. "Surely you prefer it here to that tribal outpost you've been forced to bide your time in for the past few weeks."

"I couldn't say. My doors were never locked in that *tribal outpost*."

"Indeed." He aimed another spurious grin her way. "Do tents have doors?"

"Indeed they do not. But at least I had the pleasure of my sister's company there. I don't suppose you'd care to—"

"Of course! How inconsiderate of me. You must be quite hungry." Salim laughed, motioning toward the double doors behind her. Her father did not even bother turning as he fidgeted with the scalloped spoon beside his plate.

Shahrzad heard them swing open, and the scent of butter and spices wafted her way. Despite her resolve not to eat a morsel until she'd learned of Irsa's whereabouts, the intoxicating aroma made it rather difficult for her to stand firm in this conviction. When the servants placed a silver platter of spiced potatoes before her, along with a perfect mound of pistachio-and-pomegranate rice surrounded by skewers of saffron chicken, still-flaming lamb kebabs, and steaming tomatoes all heaped upon ornate serving trays, Shahrzad's stomach rumbled with hunger.

She could not remember the last time she had eaten so well.

Her mouth salivated at the smell of the simmering stew set before her—one of aromatic lentils and caramelized onions. The sweet scent of cinnamon and cloves called to her, the dates and the aubergines taunting her even further.

The last straw was the sight of the quince chutney.

Shahrzad sat on her hands.

"Are you not hungry?" Salim asked, a wicked gleam in his eye. "I've selected dishes I'm told are your favorites."

Her father frowned at her. "Shahrzad-*jan*, the sultan's daughter told the cook to prepare a special meal in your honor."

"I'm sure she did," Shahrzad muttered, gnawing the inside of her cheek.

"Perhaps my daughter can persuade you to eat." The light in Salim's eyes burned bright as he glanced over her shoulder.

Shahrzad did not look behind her, for the last thing she wanted to see at the moment was the perfect smile of Yasmine el-Sharif.

*If she attempts to bait me tonight, it will not be soot I smear on her teeth.*

No.

*It will be my fist.*

"Come, daughter," Salim called out. "Our guest is quite excited to see you."

*Indeed. Positively thrilled.*

Shahrzad pursed her lips and wrapped her fingers around the silken cushion at her sides as though it would imbue her with the strength to remain calm.

The soft shuffle of slippered footsteps on polished granite emanated nearby.

With obvious reluctance, Shahrzad lifted her gaze.

Eyes the color of a cerulean sky sparkled down at her.

Shahrzad's chin struck her collarbone in horror.

"Hello, Brat Calipha."

Despina.

Many things happened all at once.

First, Shahrzad bolted to her feet, intent on attacking her former handmaiden. A flurry of motion converged upon them.

Before the guards could reach her, Shahrzad stopped short.

Her reaction was not a result of the soldiers' unspoken threat.

Nor was it a result of some misplaced sense of propriety. Alas with Shahrzad, it was never that. It was something else entirely.

It was worry. Worry for a former friend. Worry for a child not yet born.

Just as soon as the worry coursed through Shahrzad, it was eclipsed by another tide of emotion.

Bitterness. Black and choking bitterness.

Her gaze flicked over the sweeping curves of the girl before her—always lovely—and now even more resplendent, in a dress of amethyst silk, gathered at both shoulders by copper cuffs forming shimmering folds. These silken folds fell to Despina's feet in streams of lilac and mauve. The deep cut of the garment only accentuated her beautiful shape, as did the high waist and the copper sash, embellished with brilliant gemstones of vivid purple and blush pink, encircled in rose gold. Her honey-walnut hair was piled atop her head in an ornate arrangement adorned with a band of glittering jewels.

A crown.

The bitterness swelled within Shahrzad.

Despina had been many things to Shahrzad once. She'd been a friend when Shahrzad had most needed it. A confidante where Shahrzad had had none. But it was clear everything Shahrzad had known about Despina had been cloaked in lies. For it was beyond evident she was even more things now. The secret daughter of Salim Ali el-Sharif. A princess of Parthia. A spy and a deceiver.

Above all things, it was clear Despina had never been Shahrzad's friend.

"Was there ever a moment in which you told me the truth?" Shahrzad demanded in a raw whisper.

Despina's lips gathered into a perfect moue. An all-too-familiar one. "Aren't you going to congratulate me? I'm married now. Or haven't you heard?" Her moue slid into a grin.

Over Despina's shoulder, Yasmine walked closer, with an uneasy laugh and a reticent gait. Amidst all the recent confusion, Shahrzad had not even seen the daughter she'd known about—the daughter she'd been expecting.

*At least Yasmine has the grace to feel embarrassed.*

For Yasmine el-Sharif did seem oddly out of place. Though she looked every bit as stunning as Shahrzad remembered—her mahogany hair a profusion of waves down her back, and her emerald skirt's gentle sway hinting at the sort of grace no amount of practice could ever perfect—the princess also did not seem to want to take part in this terrible unveiling. She continued glancing over her shoulder as though she meant to flee.

The girl seemed as though she wanted to be anywhere but here.

Shahrzad's eyes returned to Despina. "Married? What poor fool have you duped into marriage?"

Despina winked. "Wouldn't you like to know." She floated into the seat beside her father. "But congratulations are due, nonetheless. For it just so happens my husband is a good friend of yours."

Still inexplicably taciturn, Yasmine took the place next to Despina, while Jahandar sat beside Shahrzad. He shot her a nervous glance full of warning, which Shahrzad promptly ignored.

The feast before her forgotten in a sea of rage, Shahrzad

glowered at her devious former handmaiden, as moments from their shared past drifted hot and fast into her present.

*"A good spy would hide her identity."*

*"The best spies don't have to."*

So many conversations shared over so many cups of tea.

So many supposed confidences.

Despina's mother had been one of the most famous beauties in all of Cadmeia. Her father had been a rich man who'd left them both behind for a brighter future.

Or had he? What could Shahrzad believe of the tales she'd been told?

Of course Despina would not want to marry Jalal! Of course she would not want to marry into the family she'd been spying on for so many years! Of course she would flee! Only to return to her father's waiting arms . . . and all-too-eager ears.

Only to betray Shahrzad. And all those she loved.

*How could I have been so stupid?*

"How could you do this to us?" Shahrzad whispered. "I treated you as a friend. You told me Khalid was kind to you."

"The Caliph of Khorasan is kind to no one," Despina replied airily. "Or perhaps you've forgotten how you first came to be at the palace?" She snorted. "I daresay that's rather convenient."

The sultan laughed, rich and robust. Despina had the gall to simper in his direction. Now that they sat close to each other, Shahrzad could see it. Though it was not a resemblance readily apparent when they were apart. Despina must have acquired her coloring from her mother, but her bearing was much like that of the sultan. Haughty. Proud. Her bone structure was similar to his as well. A sharp brow and a high set of cheekbones. Indeed, Shahrzad could even see similarities between Despina and Yasmine. An ethereal sort of beauty. Regal in its manner.

No wonder Despina had slipped past everyone with such ready ease. Such brazen charm. It was born to her. She was meant to reside in a palace. To slither and snake her way into its inner circle, with the very best of the vipers.

In a mere six years, she'd managed to earn the trust of the Caliph of Khorasan.

And the heart of the captain of the guard.

"How could you do this to Jalal?" Shahrzad asked, her nails digging into her palms as she tried in vain to suppress her seething outrage.

Her expression unnervingly apathetic, Despina spooned some pomegranate-and-pistachio rice onto her plate. "Alas, Jalal al-Khoury's sentiments are no longer my concern." Then she smirked at Shahrzad, and the feigned sympathy behind it made Shahrzad want to tear the band of shining stones from her crown of curls. "But rest assured. The captain of the guard will have no trouble finding a willing girl to soothe his injured pride, of that I am certain." The last words savored strangely of bitterness.

Shahrzad clenched her teeth, willing herself to stay silent and still. She caught Yasmine considering her through half-lidded eyes.

It was unlike the princess to be so quiet. It surprised Shahrzad, but then Yasmine el-Sharif had surprised her on more than one occasion. Again, Shahrzad felt as though Yasmine wished to speak but perhaps had yet to form an opinion. Or lacked the necessary nerve in front of her father.

Nevertheless, Yasmine looked for all the world displeased. For an instant, Shahrzad thought to engage her. But the beautiful girl would not look her in the eye. Still refused to see her as anything but an enemy.

Not an equal.

Shahrzad continued glaring at Despina while the former handmaiden laughed and joked with the Sultan of Parthia—with her *father*—as though she had not spent years in a world of deceit.

In the midst of Shahrzad's roiling thoughts, a sudden realization rose quickly to the surface.

Despina could not have lied about being pregnant.

For Shahrzad remembered how Despina had fallen ill before her eyes.

Shahrzad let her shoulders relax. She reached for her jewel-encrusted goblet of wine. "Uncle Salim," she began in a cool tone, "are you aware of your daughter's pregnancy? Or did she fail to tell you that she is in fact with child?"

"Of course he is aware of it," Despina replied without missing a beat. "I told you, I am married. It stands to reason I might be with child."

*Even more lies.*

"Is that so?" Shahrzad clenched her jaw, then took a sip of wine, trying to steady herself. "And what did you do with your supposed husband? Toss him into the sea when you were done with him?"

"Oh, no." Despina's eyes shone bright. "He is safely stowed away, where he will cause me no trouble."

"Then you brought the poor lout with you?" Shahrzad all but sneered.

"Of course."

"What kind of fool husband is this?"

"The best kind. The type to say very little."

"Will you never stop lying?" Shahrzad said through her teeth. She turned with pointed intent toward Salim. "My lord, did you know the father of her child is—"

"The caliph's favorite bodyguard," Despina finished with a slow smile.

Shahrzad blinked once. Twice. "*What?*" she yelled, slamming her wine goblet onto the table.

Again, a pair of guards materialized from the shadows.

Despina aimed a cutthroat grin her way. "Vikram Singh is the father. Did you not know? And here I thought you two were rather close."

*The—Rajput? Vikram is here? I thought he had perished the night of the storm.*

Stunned into silence for the second time that evening, Shahrzad continued staring at her former handmaiden, trying to reconcile all she'd seen with all that had long been thought and said.

*No. That is not possible. Where is the truth in all these lies?*

"Don't worry, Shahrzad," Despina said. "Vikram is safe. Or, rather, he's as safe as he can be, given the circumstances."

Immediately, Shahrzad's most pressing questions melted away. "What have you done with Vikram?"

To her right, she heard Jahandar stifle a troubled sigh. A sigh meant to silence her questions.

"Father?" Despina looked toward the immensely pleased face of Salim Ali el-Sharif.

Salim took a deep breath, as though he needed time to consider how best to respond. "My nephew's most prized bodyguard is exactly where he should be—in a place reserved for those who fail to hold their tongues on matters that are no longer their concern."

"And what matters might those be?" Shahrzad asked in a furious whisper.

"Well, as my daughter's husband, he should care more for his family rather than for yours, should he not?"

"Forgive me, *Uncle Salim*. I thought we were one and the same."

A sharp pause. "No, Shahrzad al-Khayzuran. We are not."

Jahandar gasped quietly beside his daughter.

Again, Shahrzad wrapped her fingers around the silken cushions at her sides. "So then, we have come to it. Enough with the pleasantries. What do you mean to do with me?"

Salim leaned forward, bracing his elbows along the table's gilded edge. "What do you suppose I shall do?"

"That depends on what you expect Khalid to do," Shahrzad bit out.

"I expect him to come for you."

"And what do you think will happen when he does? Besides your utter annihilation."

Yasmine finally met Shahrzad's gaze. "Father—"

321

Salim did not even grace his daughter with a look. "I expect he will do what he's been too cowardly to do for years—meet me in the desert with a proper army. And fight to see who deserves to rule these lands."

Despite the fear that spiked within her—knowing Khalid still lacked a proper army—a scoff escaped Shahrzad's lips, its sound dripping with derision. "Khalid has never been a coward a day in his life. No matter how much you howl into the wind, it will never bow to you. And you're a fool if you think it will be that easy."

At that, Jahandar's body curved in on itself, as if preparing for the next blow.

Yasmine sucked in a breath, and Shahrzad could not help but glance her way. The Princess of Parthia aimed a look of warning at her.

Behind it Shahrzad saw a flash of sympathy.

"Easy?" Salim began, the word bursting from a caustic round of laughter. "Do you think this has been *easy*? Nothing about this has been easy. It has been years in the making. Years spent watching that sullen boy flout me at every turn. Years spent watching him deny my daughter!" A fist crashed beside his plate. "The only thing that saved him from being called bastard was his uncanny resemblance to his father."

Though Shahrzad caught the second look of caution Yasmine threw her way, she ignored it. "That and the fact that you were afraid of him."

Jahandar gripped her wrist beneath the table.

A rush of anger swelled across Salim's face. "I have never been afraid of him."

"You lie as your spiteful daughter lies." Shahrzad smiled. "You've always been afraid of him."

"Shahrzad!" Jahandar exclaimed, finally electing to speak out.

Only to side with Shahrzad's enemy.

"Baba, say nothing more."

"Daughter, you have defied me—"

At that, Shahrzad tore her arm from his grasp. "And you have brought me here against my will, to be used as a pawn by these despicable liars!"

"I thought to bring you here to negotiate a truce. To help ease these wounds!"

"To help *whom*?" Shahrzad accused. "For it seems as though the only person you sought to help was yourself!"

The color rose in Jahandar's face, first in a flush of red. Then in a wash of white.

He looked away.

But he did not deny it.

"How does it feel, Shahrzad al-Khayzuran?" Despina said in a melodious voice. "To be treated as a slave? To be the servant of people who see themselves as above you, when you know in your heart that you are the same?"

"Ask your father," Shahrzad retorted.

"I'd rather ask your husband. When I next see him . . . kneeling at my feet."

Without hesitation, Shahrzad splashed the remainder of her wine in Despina's face.

The guards rushed at her, hauling her to her feet and dragging her from the table.

"Where is my sister?" Shahrzad screamed. "Where is Vikram? What have you done with them?"

Despina wiped her chin with the edge of a linen napkin, utterly calm. "If she wants so badly to see her former bodyguard, then take her to him. And leave her there to rot."

Jahandar sat rigid at the table, burying his face in his shaking hands. He did not even glance her way as Shahrzad continued hurling obscenities into the air.

The guards dragged her through the lamplit halls. After a time, Shahrzad put up little resistance. For they meant to shame her as they hauled her along, like the carcass of a dying beast. And she would not give them the satisfaction. The arched corridors took on an even more garish look as she passed beneath their jewel-inlaid alcoves, going deeper into the sandstone palace. The scent of smoke from the guards' torches caught in Shahrzad's throat, causing her eyes to water.

They dragged her down a series of winding stone stairwells until they progressed into the underbelly of the palace, where the dank cold and the stench of decay took on a life of its own. Where it grew thick upon the walls as it seeped its way through the cracks.

The cells of the palace's prison were barred by large iron grates, shaped into crooked half-moons. The ceilings were low and the floors were covered in dingy straw. Mold saturated the space, musty and thick. At every other cell a single torch lit the lichen-covered walls, barely offering any light.

The scar-faced, leering guard from earlier yanked Shahrzad

against a wet stone wall. Its uneven surface rammed into the small of her back, jostling her injured shoulder and ripping a gasp from her throat.

"Not so silver-tongued now, are you?" he said, his sour breath hot against her skin.

Shahrzad punched him in the stomach.

"Bitch!"

Another guard lifted her off the ground as though to shield her from any resulting blows. Her eyes connected with his, and for a moment Shahrzad thought she saw a flash of panic. The first guard doubled over, clutching his middle and hurling curses her way. Then he straightened and came for her again, his face contorted with rage.

The second guard put a hand on his arm, worry etched across his forehead. "Be careful. I won't be fed to the crows in pieces. If the bastard boy-king discovers we've harmed her—"

"The bastard boy-king will never know. Especially after we've decimated his army and left his carcass to rot in the sands." He shot a disdainful glance at the smaller guard. "Unless you believe we are on the losing side?"

The smaller guard shook his head. And looked away.

"Besides," the first guard continued, "I won't harm her." With a wicked grin, he returned his attention to Shahrzad. "Not now, at least."

"Touch me again and the crows will be the least of your worries," she said.

He took her by the hair. "I doubt that very much." The guard pulled her closer. He yanked a hooked dagger from his sash. "Don't worry. I'll save the lasting damage for some other night."

With that, the guard sliced through Shahrzad's braid at the shoulder.

A shower of seed pearls crashed to the cold stone floor.

# THE TIGER AND THE FALCON

K HALID WAS EXHAUSTED.

He had not properly rested since his return from the desert late last night.

Upon Khalid's arrival, the *shahrban* had railed at him for quite some time. Khalid had let him, until he'd been forced to remind his uncle that he was under no obligation to report his whereabouts to anyone.

As he was in fact the *Caliph* of Khorasan.

After stating this, Khalid had promptly walked away.

Only to be accosted by Jalal within his antechamber.

His cousin, too, had been furious.

"I thought you were dead," Jalal had said without a single word of welcome.

"Would that not have pleased you, to a degree?" Khalid had replied. "It's much easier to hate a memory. I would know."

It was spiteful, without a doubt. But Khalid had always possessed a particular knack for spite. It was one of his many darker gifts. One of the numerous gifts passed down to him, father to son.

Jalal had called him a foul name before pushing past him into the darkness.

Khalid had thought to go after him. Had thought to apologize. But it was no use.

He'd tried for weeks to repair the damage. Tried to mend what had been broken between them that afternoon near the steps of the library. Alas, Jalal's heart had been lost the day Despina had vanished into the desert beyond the city's gates. And a lost heart was a dire thing, indeed. Especially since his cousin had never experienced true heartache before. Jalal al-Khoury had lived a life where precious little had been denied him. A boy who'd been blessed with a mother to love him from infancy into adulthood. A father who had always been at his side in support. For though it could be said Aref al-Khoury was a bit standoffish, he'd always loved his son and been quietly generous in showing it.

Indeed, Jalal had been denied very little throughout the course of his twenty years. His biggest loss in life had been the loss of his best friend.

The loss of Khalid's brother, Hassan.

Last night, after Jalal had stalked away into the cold corridors of the palace, Khalid had briefly recalled the time when Jalal had come to him after Hassan had died in battle. When Jalal had tried to find a common ground between them in shared loss.

Yet another time Khalid had retreated to the shadows, far from anyone and anything, even as a boy.

He'd spent so long concealing all from those closest to him that—even now—he did not know how to bring things to light.

How to mend matters with Jalal. For Khalid had only begun to feel what it meant to live outside the darkness.

This morning, Khalid had told his uncle, the *shahrban*, the events of the last few days. But he was still uncertain as to whether the curse was truly broken. For he was not one to believe in things without proof.

No. Only time would provide Khalid with that solace.

He had slept again last night. A fitful, restless sort of sleep. The kind that did not lend itself to dreams. But Khalid wanted to hope dreams would come in time.

Wanted to cling to the hope of dreams.

Alas, reality brought Khalid back to his covered alcove. Back to his ebony desk. Back to a teetering pile of scrolls, detailing the requests collected in his absence. He needed to work through at least a few before he could return to the desert for Shahrzad.

Just when Khalid had decided he could not possibly parse another page, a resounding knock struck at the doors.

"Yes?" Khalid looked up.

His uncle strode inside. As usual, it was difficult to read much in his expression. A family trait. In nearly all the men. Save for Jalal. And Hassan. Hassan had smiled a great deal. Especially at his younger brother.

Khalid raised his brows in question.

"*Sayyidi?*" his uncle began without stopping in his paces. "The captain of the guard has detained a rather—interesting party in the palace courtyard."

"Interesting?" Khalid leaned against one arm of his settee. "How so?"

"A Badawi sheikh wishes to speak with you. He rides with a small host at his back . . ." The *shahrban* hesitated. "And he is in the company of someone I'd advise you to avoid speaking with at all cost."

Khalid stood from his desk, letting loose a flood of scrolls to the floor. "Who is it?"

"The son of the emir Nasir al-Ziyad rides at his side."

At that, Khalid moved past his uncle without pausing for breath.

"Bring them to the royal audience hall immediately."


"Have you ever seen a room this large?" Rahim whispered as he gazed in awe at the diagonally patterned floor of black-and-white tile.

"Pick your jaw off the ground," Tariq said through gritted teeth.

Omar laughed loudly, and the sound echoed high into the ceiling, bouncing off the marble walls. All around them, intricate reliefs depicting warriors vanquishing their foes and winged women with hair streaming in the wind lined the cool stone surfaces. At the base of every column were two-headed lions with iron torches protruding from their roaring mouths.

Though the room appeared grand at first glance, Tariq could see chinks in its elegant armor—a crack through one wall, many small fissures through another—

The last remaining vestiges of the Great Storm.

It was a grand room, to be sure. But it was a room with a story to it.

At one end of the vast space was a raised dais with a low settee at its center. Behind it were a set of immense staircases shaped like open arms.

Tariq moved toward the raised dais, with Rahim and Omar in tow.

He'd seen this room before. The last time Tariq had been in it had been the night of a magnificent celebration, filled with food and drink and music and dance. The night the Caliph of Khorasan had introduced his new calipha to every nobleman in the kingdom.

Tariq recalled the moment they'd appeared at the bottom of the open-armed staircases, hand in hand. As though each were but an extension of the other.

He should have known then. Should have seen with his heart and not just with his eyes.

Tariq started from his remembrance when the caliph descended those same open-arm staircases in a sudden rush. This time, the caliph did not make a show of his entrance. He moved swiftly and without ceremony. Behind him followed the *Shahrban* of Rey, along with the captain of the Royal Guard.

"Why are you here?" The boy-king did not stand on even a semblance of formality.

A part of Tariq liked him a bit more for it. But only a little bit.

The *shahrban* flicked a glance toward Omar before drifting past Rahim and then back to Tariq. "*Sayyidi*, perhaps we should—"

"Shahrzad is gone," Tariq said in the same unceremonious tone.

The captain of the guard immediately reached for the front

of Tariq's *rida'*. "I knew I shouldn't have trusted you to keep her safe, you feckless—"

Without warning, Rahim's scimitar flew from its sheath, slicing toward the captain of the guard's throat. The *shahrban* tossed a sharp command into the shadows as he withdrew his own weapon.

Omar remained still, taking in the converging mayhem with an unnervingly agreeable expression upon his face.

"Enough!" the caliph said sharply. The command echoed through the hall.

The guards drew back as one.

Tariq nodded at Rahim, who dropped his sword at the same moment the captain of the guard released the front of Tariq's *rida'*.

"We are not beginning on a promising note, my friend," Omar said to Tariq with a slow shake of his head. "But I do see what you mean about the young caliph. He is not a man of many words." His eyes gleamed in the light of the lion torch to his right. "But he appears to be a man of the right ones."

The caliph let his eyes linger on Omar. Though he said nothing, unspoken questions abounded in his piercing study.

"I am Omar al-Sadiq." Omar stepped forward. "And I've been told you are a man worthy of earning my trust."

"By whom?" the caliph said.

"By Tariq, of course." Omar's smile was wide and gap-toothed.

A brow crooked into the caliph's forehead. "Did he use those words?"

"No. But it was implied in our conversation. In his choice." He paused. "And I believe he has chosen well, at last."

The caliph's eyes shifted to Tariq.

"You see, despite all your differences, the White Falcon has chosen you," Omar explained. "Thus, we are here to fight alongside you. It would be a great honor for you to earn my trust, as I quite like your wife and do not wish to see her come to harm."

The caliph's features hardened. Tariq watched his hands curl at his sides.

"Shahrzad has been taken to the seat of Parthia," Omar continued. "To the sultan in Amardha." Both the *shahrban* and the captain of the guard stiffened at the words, though the caliph remained still, his expression carved from stone. "I believe she was taken by hired mercenaries. Men contracted by Tariq's uncle Reza bin-Latief and funded by a sultan who wishes to see you fall from your throne." Omar tilted his head to one side. "So I ask you again—can I trust you?"

A small moment passed in which silenced engulfed the space. "What is it you seek by trusting me, Omar al-Sadiq?" the caliph replied softly. His knuckles had gone white.

Tariq knew the caliph was seeking a trust of his own. For Khalid Ibn al-Rashid did not yet know how to gauge the Badawi sheikh.

"The lesser of two evils," Omar replied without pause.

"That's a rather unflattering overture."

"I wish I had the occasion to offer better." Omar grinned. "For I have spent time in your wife's company, and she is delightful.

Moreover, she seems to have faith in you. Now it appears Tariq has faith in you. So I would like to follow suit. If you will leave my people in peace—and protect the lands on which we thrive—I will ride at your side."

The caliph considered this before glancing at Tariq. "You would turn your back on your uncle?"

Tariq's jaw clenched tight. "My uncle has lost sight of what it is I fight for. And I"—his lips caught on the words—"I am not certain I ever knew what it was I meant to fight for. But Omar speaks true; if Uncle Reza has taken Shahrzad against her will, then you are indeed the lesser of two evils."

The caliph nodded. "I cannot rally all of my bannermen in time. But I can send word to those nearby, and—" He stopped in consideration, looking to Tariq once more. "Do you know of the Fire Temple in the mountains by the sea?"

"I am not familiar with it."

Rahim stepped forward. "I know of it."

Again, the caliph nodded, this time to Rahim. "Would you send a message there for me through your falcon?" He looked to Tariq.

Though puzzled, Tariq agreed to the request. "Yes. May I ask why?"

"I know someone there who might be willing to help."

# THE BURNING BANYAN TREE

SHAHRZAD LEANED AGAINST THE COLD STONE WALL. A constant trickle of murky water passed by her slippered foot. The heavy chains around her wrists and ankles clinked with the smallest of movements.

She did not know how much time had passed.

Days perhaps.

It was impossible to tell, as not even a sliver of light seeped into the space.

The water in the filthy cup left by the grate was brackish. Even the smell of it turned her stomach. The bread beside it was stale and dry. She ate only enough to conserve her strength.

Her father had come to visit her twice. To beg her to apologize.

To see reason. To work alongside the sultan to achieve a lasting peace.

To surrender.

Both times, Shahrzad had turned her back on him. Had willed herself smaller, wishing she could disappear for just a moment, so she would not have to face him.

So she would not have to admit how he'd betrayed all she held dear.

Shahrzad knew she had betrayed her father by stealing his book, but a book was not the same thing as a life. Not the same thing as a future.

And with this book her father had taken so many lives that night in Rey. So many futures.

Now Shahrzad remained in near darkness. The single torch two cells over rarely wavered light in her direction.

At first, the guards had come to check on her regularly. To toy with her. To threaten her. To hurl intimations of unforgivable acts her way.

They'd pushed her. Shoved her face into the muck. Twisted her arms behind her back. Called her worse names than Shahrzad had heard screamed at wild animals.

She had believed their threats at first. Had steeled herself for their mistreatment. Had waited in the soggy gloom, shivering and alert . . . promising she would not cry.

Would not dare give them the satisfaction.

But beyond the first guard's cutting of her hair and the occasional crush of her cheek against muck, they did not press further. They did not inflict lasting harm on her.

Something stayed their hands.

Shahrzad was not fool enough to think it was respect. No, with men such as these, it was never respect.

Something was not right beyond these walls. And it was clear the guards were afraid of that something.

These thoughts gave her a measure of comfort. For once, they made her see the benefits of an unfavorable reputation.

A reputation forged in blood and fury.

*Let them fear what is to come. Let them know what it is to cower in the darkness, uncertain of their future.*

*Let them be afraid of Khorasan and its king.*

For Khalid would tear them limb from limb once he breached the city walls.

Once he learned Shahrzad was here.

*And when would that be?*

Again she was left to think about the perils of wanting too much. But little was served from wanting what she could not control. The past few weeks had taught her that.

Shahrzad swallowed drily as she pulled her knees in to her chest. Each passing hour took with it more of her resolve, and she could not allow her will to fade along with her strength. Refused to allow it.

She was a tree being lashed about in a storm. She would not break.

Never.

She had to find Irsa. And get far away from this palace.

At least now the soldiers were leaving her be. They had not come to harass her for quite some time.

At least now she was alone.

Shahrzad wrapped her arms around her legs. The sound of her wet sniffle seemed to leap from wall to wall. The torch beyond her cell flickered out.

Leaving her in utter darkness.

"You have not lost hope?" A gruff voice resonated from just outside the bars.

Shahrzad said nothing. She was not certain if it was another prisoner or a guard still trying to toy with her. Still trying to break her.

"You. Girl. Are you still alive?" the voice repeated in a dry rasp. It sounded like a pile of dead leaves gusting across granite pavestones.

Again, she said nothing.

*I will not break. Ever.*

"Girl? Are you alive?"

She sighed, loud and long. "I am, you ornery bastard. What of it?"

"Good." The voice coughed. Whoever it was, was old, bordering on sickly. "I've watched you these last four days. You've got courage."

"I suppose you think I should be flattered?"

Another cough. "No."

"Then what do you want?"

A pause. "I don't know yet."

"Then leave me be."

"Have you something better to do?"

"No."

"Neither do I." The strange old man waited for a spell. "You remind me of something."

Shahrzad shifted as she threw her eyes to the ceiling of her cell, her chains clanking around her. "And what is that?"

"The banyan tree I used to hide in as a boy."

Despite everything, Shahrzad's interest was piqued, for he was unlike any of the soldiers who had come to torment her thus far. "Banyan tree?"

The rustling sound from beyond the darkness made Shahrzad think her strange visitor had settled in for a while. He cleared his throat. "When I made mischief as a child, I would run to the hollow of a very old banyan tree on the edge of the jungle and hide within it before my father could punish me."

"And why do I remind you of this tree?"

"Because these trees destroy everything around them over time."

Shahrzad let out an unamused chuff. "Thank you for the lovely story, old man."

He coughed a low chortle. "I meant it as a compliment."

"Forgive me for not seeing it as such."

"Where I come from, we are raised to see things in a never-ending cycle. I saw that cycle in the life of the banyan tree. It grows big and tall and wide while providing shelter to those who seek it. Over time, it can grow too big for itself, destroying everything around it. But I've also watched it slowly feed its way to new life. Provide roots for the new trees. Seeds for the new flowers. You are a banyan tree because in you I see this story. The beginning and the end of all things. The hope for something to grow, even in shadow."

Shahrzad's pulse started to rise.

The old man's voice had begun to deepen as he spoke. Had begun to lose some of its raspiness. Had begun to roll like distant thunder.

"Be the beginning and the end, Shahrzad al-Khayzuran." A flare of light burst to life across the way. "Be stronger than everything around you."

The face of the Rajput shone bright in the flickering flame.

"Make all our many sacrifices worth it."

# THE HEAD OF A FLYING SERPENT

THE ARMY THAT MADE ITS WAY TO THE GATES OF
Amardha was an unusual one.

The like of which had not been seen in an age.

At its head rode a boy-king beneath a banner of two crossed
swords. His cuirass was of silver and gold, and his *rida'* was of
unrelieved black. By his side were his uncle and his cousin. One
wore a cloak with a griffin stitched upon its surface, and the
other wore a medallion signifying his status as the captain of
the Royal Guard.

At the young king's flank rode a boy in white, flying the banner of a falcon. A boy who had been his enemy mere days ago.

At this boy's shoulder rode a host of the finest horsemen this
side of the Sea of Sand. Horsemen who had not ridden to war for
a generation.

Above them flew a young man with a bald head glistening in
the afternoon sun. A young man with a gold ring through each
ear. A young man on a flying serpent with scales of darkest night,
rippling with each beat of its leathery wings.

A serpent that screamed through the heat with a sound like nails across stone.

The host moved in concert, led by this boy-king and the head of a flying serpent.

Again, it was a rather strange sight. But nevertheless a fearsome one to behold. A sight fueled by a tumult of emotions.

But oddly not by fury.

For the boy-king at its vanguard had mastered his rage even before he had begun the march from Rey to Amardha. Had leashed his control.

And his was a control even more deadly in such a state. A fury at its worst in such a case. When it could be shrewdly unleashed at a moment's notice.

Much like the head of a serpent.

The sight of Amardha's grey gates before him made the boy-king's eyes flash. Once.

No. He was not here to wreak revenge.

For revenge was trifling and hollow.

No. He was not here to retrieve his wife.

For his wife was not a thing to be retrieved.

No. He was not here to negotiate a truce.

For a truce suggested he wished to compromise.

The boy-king spurred his black al-Khamsa forward, its hooves kicking up a storm of dust and debris.

He was here to burn something to the ground.

## OUTMATCHED

THE SIGHTS AND SOUNDS OF CLANKING METAL AND whickering horses filled the desert air with an odd sort of anticipation. Though Irsa had not yet decided if it was the good kind. Nevertheless, she paced on the outskirts of the newly formed camp, trying to remain lighthearted.

"This is exciting, isn't it?" she began, glancing at Rahim sidelong.

He smiled, but it did not touch his eyes. "*Exciting* is perhaps not the right word."

Her expression fell. At that, Rahim reached for her hand. Irsa wrapped her fingers around his as though they were made for this, and only this.

They strolled through the bustling encampment. Members of the Royal Guard had already completed the work on Khalid's tent and had now turned to their own. Badawi soldiers were busy raising Omar's patchwork structure.

Their hands still entwined, Rahim and Irsa watched the men work in silent concert.

"Are you frightened?" Irsa asked.

He did not answer right away. "A bit. In most of the battles we've fought, we've had the advantage of surprise. And there is little chance for surprise when you march to the gates of a city and promptly set up camp." Rahim laughed softly. "But the caliph seems to be a sound strategist. And he doesn't seem prone to wasting life unnecessarily."

"You like him." Irsa grinned. "Don't you?"

"Not really." Rahim snorted.

But Irsa knew otherwise. She knew he at least respected Khalid a great deal more than he let on. "Don't worry. I won't tell Tariq."

"Tell him if you must." They rounded the shadowed side of a small dune on the edges of the encampment. "It won't change a thing. Tariq and I are kept beyond the inner circle for the most part." Rahim kicked a stone from their path. "Tariq is still incensed that he won't be allowed to go into Amardha with the caliph when he demands the sultan's surrender."

Irsa frowned. "I don't understand why he would want to go. To be honest, I don't even understand why Khalid wishes to go. That awful man will be unlikely to return Shazi just because he is asked to do so."

"Even so, I understand why both of them want to go into Amardha and try." Rahim came to a halt, then turned to shield Irsa from a gust of sand blowing their way.

Irsa shaded her eyes. "But you still disagree with Khalid."

"I think the caliph should take us with him," Rahim said firmly. "There's no finer archer than Tariq in the camp. The caliph is taking the young magus from the Fire Temple with him for protection, along with the captain of the guard. They'll definitely keep the caliph safe, but I don't know if they would risk his safety for Shazi's sake. I'd much prefer it if others were involved. Others whom I trust."

"Do you believe the sultan will actually surrender to Khalid?" Irsa looked up, her features dubious.

"It's less about demanding surrender and more about learning whether or not Shazi is still in the city."

"You're worried the sultan has harmed her." It was not a question.

Rahim sighed. "He would be foolish to hurt Shahrzad. For years, he's been outmatched in all ways. Though Parthia is a wealthy kingdom, it's never been able to hold a candle to Khorasan. Our armies, our coffers, our rulers have always been stronger."

"Until the storm," Irsa said quietly.

Rahim nodded.

Irsa turned her gaze toward the Sea of Sand. "Rahim . . . do you think he would hurt Shazi?"

His hands shifted to cup her face. "You know as well as I that Shahrzad can take care of herself." Rahim brushed his thumbs across her cheeks.

Irsa wanted to believe Rahim. But she could not forget the events of that terrible afternoon in the desert with Spider. That terrible afternoon she and Rahim had witnessed Shahrzad fall prey to hatred.

Had they not been there to help Shazi, something unspeakable might have happened that day. Had Rahim not been there, her sister might have died. Rahim had been Irsa's voice of reason through the turmoil. He'd never flinched from danger. He'd been swift and capable at all turns.

Irsa could not forget. And she could not help but remember that Spider had disappeared from camp the following day.

No. She would never forget that there were treacherous insects lurking where she least expected them.

Irsa lifted her chin. "I'll ask Khalid."

"What?" Rahim blinked.

"I'll ask him to take you and Tariq with him when he goes to Amardha. As a favor to me."

A mixture of surprise and gratitude washed across Rahim's features. "Thank you, Irsa-*jan*." He smiled. "Though I didn't plan for you to speak on our behalf, I thank you."

"Please," Irsa whispered. "Please bring her back safe." Again, Irsa recalled how Rahim had helped her rescue Shahrzad with very little bloodshed. "I know you'll think of a way."

He kissed her hand. Then they continued walking along the camp's periphery.

After a time, Irsa stopped. "We shouldn't stray too far from Omar's tent."

"No." Rahim laughed morosely. "For I don't wish to receive another one of his infamous lectures."

"You can hardly blame him. They looked for us for hours the day Shahrzad disappeared. And we worried them horribly." Irsa felt the weight of guilt settle upon her once more. Though everyone had assured her there was nothing she could have done to save her sister—that she, too, would likely have been taken—Irsa still felt guilty for having wandered off with Rahim.

They made the journey back toward Omar's tent in pensive silence. Aisha was standing outside, her expression warring between a smile and a frown.

Before a word of chastisement could be said, Irsa stood on her toes to speak in Rahim's ear. "Don't worry. I'll talk to Khalid." She felt the familiar warmth curl through her stomach when Rahim brushed his forehead closer. "I'll make sure he listens."

"I know." He looked at her with guileless eyes. "That's why I love you."


Tariq had not expected the Sultan of Parthia to invite them into his palace. He'd expected the ruler of the warring kingdom to meet them in the desert.

With a host of his own.

Instead, the sultan had sent a messenger, requesting to speak with the caliph in person.

So the caliph made the decision to ride into Amardha, under a flag of truce.

The *shahrban* had been staunchly against it. But the caliph had been adamant, citing the wisdom behind knowing his enemy's intentions. Understanding the game Salim Ali el-Sharif meant to play. The caliph had refused to show a hint of fear.

Tariq suspected the caliph wished, above all, to know of Shahrzad's whereabouts. Just as he did. Whether it was unwise or imprudent remained to be seen. But it would be difficult to lay siege to the city without first knowing whether Shahrzad was within its walls. Without first knowing whether they could rescue her.

Without first knowing whether she was safe.

So that very afternoon, Tariq, Rahim, the captain of the Royal Guard, a bald-headed boy from the eastern mountains, and a small contingent of guards accompanied the caliph into Amardha. Into a palace Tariq could only describe as beyond opulent. The marble fountains lining its courtyards were studded with jewels. The water itself seemed to sparkle as though it had been littered with the dust of discarded diamonds.

The caliph met the sultan in the main courtyard. For he'd refused to set foot in the palace proper. He did not speak when the sultan strode toward him, a wide smile cutting across his elegantly unctuous face.

"Khalid-*jan!*" the sultan began. "You've brought a larger party with you than we agreed upon. I thought it was to be just you and the captain of the guard."

The caliph did not respond. He merely stood still, cold and intractable.

A shadow crossed the sultan's countenance. "Such behavior could be construed as a threat, nephew—coming to my city's gates with a host at your back, only to disregard the simplest of my requests."

"I care not how you construe my actions," the caliph replied, his words a whispered barb. "I only care that you know this: you will pay for what you have done."

"Pay?" The sultan looped his arms across his chest, the sleeves of his lavishly trimmed mantle shimmering in the afternoon sun.

"I will not play these games with you, Salim. Where is she?"

Another smug smile. "Have you lost something of import, nephew?"

At that, Tariq took a step forward. The captain of the guard lifted a hand to stop him.

"I have not lost a *thing*, Salim Ali el-Sharif. You will tell me where Shahrzad is now. Before the words are forced from your tongue." A muscle worked in the caliph's jaw. "Before your city is reduced to ash."

The sultan's bodyguards flocked to his side, their hands upon the hilts of their swords.

"Bold," the sultan mused, utterly unmoved. "Especially in *my* palace. On *my* lands."

"This is your palace—these are your lands—at *my* discretion. As they always have been."

"Such arrogance." The sultan snorted. "If you believed so, why have you not taken them?"

"Out of respect. And because I did not wish to bring war upon us."

"Respect?" Disbelief registered on the sultan's face. "For whom?"

"For my brother's family."

"Misguided. If you truly thought Parthia so easily won, you would have taken it by now."

"I am not nearly as greedy as you may think," the caliph said with disdain. "I possess twice your bannermen, and you are out-matched in soldiers and weaponry by more than half. As to the pitiful force you tried to rally in the desert, do you think I could not have ridden through them in an afternoon, if put to task?"

"I think you are a conceited child of ridiculous words, just like your mother."

The caliph remained placid, even at the slight to his mother. "Then chance it. But I will raze this palace, stone by stone, as you waste that chance. And if you are still in it while I do so? Then so be it." He turned to leave without giving the sultan a chance to respond.

"I doubt you'll do that, you whoreson. I doubt that very much." With that, Salim tossed something in their direction.

It slid past the caliph's feet.

It took Tariq a moment to recognize it.

In the same instant he did, he wished he had not. Wished he did not know enough to recognize what lay strewn across the pavestones of the sultan's lavish courtyard. What it was to feel such a thing.

What it was to burn with fear and hate in the very same breath.

It was a length of black braid, wrapped in a broken string of pearls.

The party halted in their tracks.

"My soldiers tell me she smells like a spring garden," the sultan said softly, without a hint of emotion. Then he smiled. Slowly. Cruelly.

Tariq unsheathed his sword.

All he saw before him was blood.

Khalid had known his uncle Salim would try to provoke him.

But he had not known the depths to which the Sultan of Parthia would descend.

When Khalid first saw what his uncle had tossed across the stones, there had been a moment—less than a moment—where the world around Khalid had been reduced to cinder. Where all he'd wanted to do was crush something between his hands and watch it crumble to pieces.

But he'd realized in the next instant what Salim had done. What he meant for Khalid to do. And though Khalid wanted nothing more than to oblige him, blind rage would not serve a purpose beyond this moment.

Blind rage was the action of a boy who existed in the shadows. Not the king Khalid wished to be.

Salim wanted an excuse to attack Khalid in cold blood. To kill him in this courtyard, before a string of witnesses. To massacre Khalid in defense of himself.

For it was the best way to ensure a legitimate ascension to the throne. One that did not have the stink of treachery to it.

So Khalid remained still, the fury boiling in his blood, searing fast in his throat.

He did nothing. Said nothing. Made to turn away from the provocation. To stride back into the desert, with plans to rail at the skies later, when he was alone.

Khalid would make the Sultan of Parthia pay for what he had done.

There were a hundred ways to make him pay. A thousand.

But not now. Not in this moment.

Alas, Tariq Imran al-Ziyad did not know the things Khalid did.

So when the boy drew his sword and charged the Sultan of Parthia, Khalid knew what would transpire before anyone else did.

A legion of soldiers materialized from the shadows of the courtyard, ready to defend their sultan. Ready to strike down anyone who dared to assault their king.

Khalid ripped his *shamshir* from its scabbard without a second thought.

"Get back!" he yelled at Tariq, grabbing the boy by the shoulder.

Khalid swung his sword to defend the boy from the first blow. Tariq managed to deflect the next attack with an able parry of his own. He stood at Khalid's back as a swarm of soldiers surrounded them, wielding flashes of menacing silver. Soon, the sound of swords being torn from their sheaths emanated on all sides.

Though the blood raged through his body, Khalid felt his heart plunge like a stone in his stomach. This was not a battle they could win. They were grossly outnumbered. Outmatched, in all ways.

Nevertheless, Khalid separated his *shamshir* into two as a pair of soldiers charged his way. As all chaos broke loose. He glanced to his right, expecting to see Jalal there. As he always had been. Ever since Khalid was a small boy. Ever since Hassan died. But when Khalid looked to either side of him, he realized he fought alone. His cousin battled several soldiers far across the way.

Jalal did not even pause to look for Khalid. Just as he'd stated that afternoon before the steps of Rey's library, Jalal would no longer keep watch over Khalid's shadow. Would no longer worry unduly over his cousin.

Over the king who'd betrayed his confidences.

Khalid gripped the hilts of his swords tighter.

The soldiers were closing in on them. Khalid saw one of his men fall beneath the wicked slice of a blade. He knew they had to make it to the higher ground surrounding the sunken courtyard if they were ever going to have a chance to reach the gates.

"Jalal!" Khalid called out, trying to convey his intentions in a glance.

But his cousin could not hear him above the fray. Khalid whipped around one of Salim's soldiers, then slashed across his face and chest with both swords. Streams of crimson followed in his wake, staining the sandstone at his feet.

"Jalal!" At that, both his cousin and Artan Temujin, who was fighting to make his way through the crush of bodies toward Salim, turned in his direction.

Khalid saw his cousin's eyes go wide in the same instant Artan shouted a warning. For Khalid did not see the soldier from behind him until it was too late. He spun in an attempt to deflect the blow—

Then from his right, a figure emerged to repel the onslaught.

To save him.

It was the boy Khalid had fought that night in the desert.

Rahim.

Tariq Imran al-Ziyad's friend. Irsa al-Khayzuran's love.

Khalid saw in a crushing moment, as two more soldiers converged in their direction, as Khalid's swords swung to disarm the sentry before him . . .

That Rahim would not succeed in fending off the next wave.

A sword pierced through Rahim's stomach from behind.

Khalid cut at his attacker and kicked him away. Then slashed to defend Rahim. He pulled him close, yelling for help. No one could hear Khalid through the clanging of metal and the shouts of wounded men.

Then everything around Khalid came to a sudden halt.

At Salim's request.

For when Khalid looked up, he saw Artan Temujin a stone's throw from the Sultan of Parthia, the magus's palms wide by his shoulders—

And a halo of fire spinning about Salim Ali el-Sharif's head.

Salim stood motionless, his eyes bulging with fear.

"You will let us go," Artan said loudly. "You will not follow us." He began to back away, his hands widening as the halo of fire grew about the sultan's head. "And, in the future, you will seriously take to heart the meaning of civil discourse."

Shahrzad said nothing as Vikram lifted both hands to the metal grate of her cell. He breathed onto the iron in a slow exhalation of air, and the metal began to glow red.

She had long forgotten the demonstration in the training courtyard those few months ago. But in that instant, the memory returned; the Scourge of Hindustan had been a fire-breather.

Had set his *talwar* ablaze in a rush of air. Had finished the drill wielding a screaming dragon of a weapon.

Now she watched as he bent the molten metal without even the slightest singe to his skin. Once he'd widened a space large enough, he made his way into her cell.

"We haven't much time," Vikram muttered as he came to her side. "The soldiers may check on you again soon." A low oath passed through his lips when he saw the chains binding her wrists and ankles.

"How—"

"Now is not the time for such questions, little troublemaker." He grunted in frustration as he considered her manacles. "I can melt the links near to the cuffs, but you will likely make enough noise to rouse the dead when we move about. Which will be of no help to anyone. And these cuffs are heavy. Which is also quite unhelpful."

Shahrzad nodded, still at a loss for words. She'd never heard the Rajput say so many things in one breath.

In hindsight, perhaps his tale of the banyan tree qualified.

Vikram lifted a length of chain beside her feet. The sound of metal striking metal echoed with a thunderous *clank*. "When I melt the chain, the cuffs will become hot. They may burn you."

"I'd rather be burned than remain chained in this cell."

"As I suspected." He coughed with amusement. "Know there was a time not long ago when I would happily have left you to rot in this cell."

It took her only a moment to remember. The night of the

storm, Shahrzad had betrayed Khalid in Vikram's eyes. Had betrayed *him.* "I can explain—"

"That time has passed." Vikram wrapped both hands around the links by her ankles and let a slow whisper of air pass between his lips.

As the metal began to grow hot against her skin, the familiar tingling around Shahrzad's heart flashed to life. Taken aback by the sensation, she let in a sharp breath.

The feeling flared through her as the heat grew. As the chains began to take on a fiery glow.

In that instant, Shahrzad felt a thread take hold within her. A sudden, undeniable spark. For though she knew the chains were becoming hot, she felt little pain. Just a growing awareness. This thread called to her as she continued studying the metal. As she continued watching Vikram work to melt through the chains.

*Is it possible . . .*

Throwing all caution to the wind, Shahrzad placed both palms on the cuffs at her ankles. Just like the magic carpet.

"What are you doing?" the Rajput demanded in a guttural whisper, his black-as-night gaze cutting to hers.

She did not respond.

Just as she'd expected, Shahrzad continued to feel little pain, though she knew the iron was now hot enough to sear. At her touch, the magic Vikram had fed into the metal spread through her like a flame licking through oil.

Once she felt a link to it—felt that thread within her pull taut as it connected to the magic within her—Shahrzad willed the cuffs to fall away. Willed the magic to follow her unspoken directive.

The glowing cuffs dropped to the floor.

Not knowing what else to do in response, Shahrzad laughed.

Artan had been wrong. Yet he'd been so very right. True, she should not have run from his attempts to provoke her those nights on the beach. Yes, she should have faced her fears head-on. But not in the way Artan had imagined. For the magic within her worked on *touch*. Only when she willed those things around her—those things imbued with the same strange powers as she—could Shahrzad manipulate her power.

Just as she'd suspected. Shahrzad took in magic from what was around her.

Vikram teetered to one side at the sight, his massive frame coming to rest a hairsbreadth from the dirty trickle of water by her slippered feet. "How—"

"Now is not the time for such questions . . ." she began in an almost teasing tone.

He grunted in distaste, then righted himself. "Such a trouble-maker."

"That may be the nicest thing you've ever said to me." Shahrzad grinned. "Now help me with the bindings on my wrists so that we may find my sister and flee this godforsaken place."

# THE WHITE SHELL

THEY RODE FROM THE CITY IN A RUSH. A *CLATTER* OF hooves. A stream of wind. A trickle of sweat.

But not a single word.

This small band of battered men.

Khalid did not let his guilt for all that had transpired overtake him. Refused to let his regret deter him from his course. They had to flee the city. Far from the reach of Salim's injured pride.

So they soldiered on. Faster and faster through the alleys and streets and thoroughfares. A fruit stand was knocked to the wayside in their haste. Angry oaths were hurled at their retreating backs. Women pulled their children from Khalid's path, screaming and scurrying all at once.

Again, the guilt crept into his heart. Clawed at his insides.

It did not matter. How he felt in this moment did not matter. *He* did not matter.

There were far more important things at hand.

Khalid kept Rahim on the saddle with him. In moments of weakness, Khalid glanced down to see the boy's blood spill onto his palms. Onto his saddle. Onto his reins.

Soon, he slumped forward.

"Hurry!" Khalid yelled over his shoulder. He spurred Ardeshir even faster, the stallion's muscles slicking over with sweat.

As soon as they passed the city gates to break for the desert, Khalid yanked Ardeshir to a halt and dismounted from his saddle.

Tariq pulled Rahim onto the ground.

Even from a distance—even with only a cursory understanding of such things—Khalid could see there was little that could be done. The wound was too deep. The blood lost simply too much. Nevertheless, he looked back at Artan. When Khalid was a small boy, he recalled Musa Zaragoza using magic to tend to his injuries.

But those had been the scrapes of youth. Not the wounds of war.

Artan stooped above the boy. He tugged at an earring, then lifted his hands above the bleeding wound. A light flickered twice before fading out. With a glance and a grave expression, Artan confirmed what Khalid already suspected. Tariq Imran al-Ziyad ran a hand through his hair, slicking his forehead with his friend's blood. A line of crimson began to trickle from a corner of Rahim's mouth. He coughed and the blood spurted forth.

Nasir al-Ziyad's son bowed over him, clasping a bloodied hand in one of his own. "Rahim—"

Rahim shook his head once. "Me too." He had little voice left, so the words were more a whisper than anything else. Almost a broken sigh.

Khalid knelt at his side. Then placed a hand on his shoulder.

"Thank you, Rahim," Khalid said, meeting his dark blue eyes in a steady, unflinching gaze.

Rahim swallowed. His head moved in a feeble nod. A bow. "*Sayyidi.*"

Khalid's throat constricted. "Is there anything you need of me?"

Rahim's eyes misted, then cleared. "Irsa."

"Yes?"

"Make sure"—he coughed and the lines of blood at his lips widened—"she never feels lonely. That she always feels loved."

The knot in Khalid's throat grew. "I promise."

"Tariq?" Rahim clutched their joined hands tight.

"Yes." It was a strangled sound.

"Sometimes," he gasped, "the family you choose . . . is stronger than blood."

His chest rose and fell twice more.

Khalid looked away while the silent tears streamed down Tariq Imran al-Ziyad's face.

He did not move until they stopped.

No one did.

Irsa had been waiting in the tent with Aisha all afternoon. Every so often, Omar would leave to see if Tariq and the others had returned. The last time he'd left, Irsa had wanted to accompany him, but she'd decided it was wiser to stay in the tent.

Wiser to avoid causing any trouble.

After all, she'd been the cause of enough concern. What with all the searching the day Shazi had disappeared. And then with the march toward Amardha.

Toward possible war.

While Irsa had first thought this all to be rather thrilling, she was already tired of it. She longed to be back in one place. To know what tomorrow would bring.

To have those she loved back at her side. Safe.

For a time, Irsa had wondered if she should worry about what was taking place in the city today. After all, the men had been gone quite a while, but Aisha had reassured her that they'd left under a flag of truce. These sorts of negotiations were normal. A show of words that might lead to meaningful action.

Regardless, Irsa hoped they would return soon.

While riding through the desert the other day, Irsa had come across a white shell with a flower etched upon it. It had reminded her of the story she'd told—admittedly poorly—to Rahim that night she'd found her way to his tent.

The story of the little fish with his white petal wings.

In truth, Irsa believed that to be the night she'd begun to fall in love with Rahim.

So, when she'd come across the white shell, Irsa felt it only fitting that she place it within the folds of her cloak. She knew it was silly, but she thought to give it to him later. Perhaps when all these things had come to pass. For the shell was a ridiculously fragile thing. Apt to break at the slightest error. But at the very least she could show it to him. Perhaps make him smile.

She did so like his smile.

As Irsa found herself lost in its memory—in the way his smile made Rahim's eyes crinkle at the corners—the tent entrance opened, and a rush of dusky desert air washed back at her.

"Aisha."

Irsa turned at the name, though Omar had not spoken to her. His face was ashen.

The sight of it sent her blood on a strange course through her body. As though it were traveling rather fast, though the world around her seemed to have ground to a halt.

Shahrzad. Something had happened to her sister.

Irsa struggled to breathe. Struggled to think.

Aisha moved toward Omar, swift and certain.

Still, he said nothing beyond Aisha's name. Yet she seemed to understand. They'd always been connected in such a way. Omar's eyes wandered to Irsa, then back to his wife, speaking without words.

"Irsa-*jan*," Aisha said quietly, resting her hand upon Omar's chest to cover his heart. "Will you come with me?"

Irsa stood, her knees wobbling. Her *sister*. "What—what is it?"

"No." Omar took a steadying breath. He placed a gnarled palm over Aisha's hand. "I shall take her."

Irsa took a step forward. "Has something happened?" Her body did not feel like her own. Her voice sounded as though it were coming from beyond her—a muted echo from across the water.

Omar walked to her side. His eyes fell shut as he inhaled deeply. He clasped both her hands in his.

"Yes, dear one. Something has happened."

"Is—Shahrzad . . ." Irsa could not even finish the thought.

He shook his head. "No. A fight occurred at the palace." Again, Omar paused to steel himself. "And Rahim was killed."

*Rahim?* The ground beneath Irsa began to sway. "No." She shook her head, her voice sounding so strange. As though she were truly lost at sea. "That's not possible."

"I'm so sorry, Irsa-*jan*."

She did not believe it. Refused to believe it.

Rahim was not dead. The men had gone to speak under a flag of truce. Aisha had said so herself. Nothing bad was supposed to happen.

This could not be true.

"Where is he?" Irsa asked, her voice suddenly all too loud.

Omar's features folded into a grimace. "I don't think—"

"No. I want to see him."

"Take her, Omar," Aisha said in a grim tone. "She is not a child."

The Badawi sheikh sighed, then wrapped an arm about Irsa's shoulders. Irsa concentrated on blinking, on putting one foot before the other as they exited the tent into a beautiful desert sunset. The sky was awash in oranges and pinks. Brilliant colors that should have warmed her. Should have brought a smile to her face.

She'd always loved dusk. It was as though a hand in the sky had pulled the sun from its berth . . . only to have the sun fight back, resisting, leaving a trace of itself to fade amongst the stars.

Irsa stared at the desert sky as she walked. The sight before her blurred, and she ran a palm across her eyes.

No. She would not believe it.

Only this morning, Irsa had walked with him here. Held his hand here.

Watched him smile here.

Guards stood outside Khalid's tent. When they saw the sheikh, they moved to let Irsa pass.

Irsa strode inside, and immediately those within took to their feet.

The captain of the guard stepped before her. "I don't think it's wise—"

"Leave her be," Khalid said quietly.

The captain of the guard gazed down at her for a moment. He put a hand on her arm. Squeezed. Then moved aside.

Irsa stopped at the sight before her. Her heart lurched into her throat.

Tariq and Khalid stood around a raised bed pallet. Tariq's silver breastplate was dull, his expression lost. His face was covered with sweat and dirt. Khalid's hands were stained, his silver-and-gold cuirass marred by dark smears. Both their cloaks were bloody. Red over white. Crimson over black. Colors that could not be ignored.

Irsa knew then that this was not a lie. For blood did not lie.

But still she walked toward them as if in a trance, the warmth stealing from her very blood.

Rahim was lying on the bed pallet. So very still. If Irsa did not look closely, he could have been sleeping.

She halted an arm's length away.

"How—" Irsa cleared her throat. She would not be a mouse. She was no longer a mouse. Because of Rahim. Her chin rose. "How did this happen?"

"It was my fault," Tariq replied, his voice awash in misery. In undeniable self-loathing.

"No," Khalid said. "If it was anyone's fault, it was everyone's fault. And mine most of all." He moved toward her. "But he saved my life, Irsa-*jan*. And he thought of you, at the last."

Irsa nodded, her eyes wide and unblinking. "Rahim is like that. He always thinks of others first."

At that, the captain of the guard tore from the tent, a choked sound emitting from his lips.

"Do you want us to leave you with him?" Khalid asked, his eyes locked upon her face.

Irsa peered up at him. Only a few days ago, he had frightened her so when he looked at her that way. As though he could see through to her very soul. Now all Irsa saw was a searching look. A look that simply wished to understand.

To help.

"Yes, please," she whispered.

Khalid looked to the others. They quickly cleared the tent, save for he and Tariq.

Tariq came to stand before her, tall and wrapped in white stained with red. He pulled her against him in a gentle embrace.

"I'm so sorry, Cricket," Tariq said into her hair.

He did not seem quite so . . . much now. Before, Irsa had always thought of him as larger than life. So full of vim and vigor. So full of everything Irsa wished she could embody. So incapable of losing to anything or anyone.

Now he seemed like a boy who'd lost his best friend.

A boy who could lose.

Irsa could not reply with words, so instead she merely nodded. Once they had left, Irsa sat beside the raised bed pallet.

Strangely, she did not feel any pain. Again, it was as though she had moved beyond herself. Rahim still looked as though he might be sleeping. Someone had tried to clean him, but they'd missed a line of blood at his neck. But for that, Irsa could almost believe she might jostle him awake with nothing but her touch.

Instead she studied the line of blood in silence for a time.

Then Irsa reached into the folds of her cloak and pulled out the white shell with the flower etched on its surface. "I wanted to give you this."

She waited. As though she expected a response.

"*Oh.*" It was a quiet sob. Something tore behind her heart. Though Irsa wanted to fight back the sudden burn, she let it wash through her. She would not be weak. This was not a time to be weak. And fighting herself—fighting how she felt in this moment—would be weak.

Would be denying who she truly was.

"I—" Irsa took a careful breath to steady her words. "I have felt alone for most of my life. Until you." She placed the shell on his chest. "But I promise I won't feel alone anymore. I will never forget." She stood on shaky feet. "I will always remember."

"I love you, Rahim al-Din Walad. Thank you for loving me in return."

With that, Irsa turned and walked through the entrance of the tent, her head high, though her body had begun to tremble.

Khalid and the young magus from the Fire Temple were waiting outside, just beyond a pair of torches. The magus eyed her, his face softening. She started to walk by them. Then stopped.

The magus took a deep breath. He sent a sad smile her way

while placing a reassuring hand on Khalid's shoulder. Then, without a word, he left.

"Did he . . ." Irsa bit her lip, tears building upon the burn, threatening to converge at any second. "Did Rahim suffer?"

"Not long."

"I'm glad."

"As am I." Khalid studied her face. Studied the twist of emotions passing across her features. "Irsa—"

"How could you let this happen?" she asked, tears spilling down her cheeks. "Why didn't you protect him? Why didn't you—"

The Caliph of Khorasan pulled her in to his chest.

And Irsa cried until every last trace of the sun's warmth sank beneath the horizon.

# BARTERING, LIES, AND BETRAYAL

V IKRAM LED SHAHRZAD THROUGH THE UNDERBELLY of the sandstone palace, a single torch held high in his right hand. Though Shahrzad could not make out any sort of path before them, the mammoth bodyguard shifted and spun with a skill that suggested a prior knowledge of the space.

At the very least, he knew these labyrinthine hallways a bit too well for comfort.

Suspicion tugged at Shahrzad's core. "Exactly where were you this entire time?"

"In a prison cell," he grunted back. As curt as ever.

They passed into a winding set of stairs before branching off into another small corridor. With every turn, the halls seemed to constrict on all sides.

Shahrzad refused to be ignored. "Do you know where my sister is?"

"No."

"Then how is it you know your way around this palace?" she pressed.

"I told you: now is not the time for such questions."

At that, Shahrzad halted in her tracks. She had been betrayed one too many times of late. She would not be betrayed again now. "I disagree. Now is precisely the time for such questions. Especially if you intend for me to follow you a single step more."

Vikram pivoted in place. The flame in his hand flared bright as he cast her a look that would send a lesser man scurrying home to his mother.

Shahrzad tapped a slippered foot with impatience.

He frowned. Then huffed a sigh. "I was given a map."

"By whom?"

His frown deepened, though a brief flash of amusement wrinkled across his brow. "Who do you think?"

"By a palace rat," Shahrzad ground out. "How should I know?"

"Despina."

"Despina!" she sputtered. "You were fool enough to trust that turncoat?"

Vikram glared down at her, his torch almost close enough to singe what was left of her hair. "Bite your tongue. Despina is the only reason you have a palace rat's chance of escaping."

"A likely story. Since I suspect she's the reason I'm here at all."

He shook his bald head, grumbling unintelligibly. "There was no way to prevent that from happening, for she did not know of the sultan's plan. She only knew what would likely come to pass. She did everything possible to help you."

"Ha!" Shahrzad cut her eyes in disbelief. "You expect me to believe that the girl who smiled as she watched the palace guards drag me away intended to *help* me? There were a thousand things she could have done!"

"Such as?"

She flung an exasperated hand into the air. "She could have told Khalid who she was. What she thought would happen!"

"And confessed that she had been spying for the Sultan of Parthia all these years? That she was the sultan's daughter?" Vikram scoffed. "If you think your husband would have believed her following that, you do not know him as well as I think you do. Khalid Ibn al-Rashid is a most distrusting man. Though I cannot fault him for being so."

*Spoken like a friend.*

Shahrzad rested her hands on her hips. "Vikram, what is Despina trying to accomplish with all this deception?"

"It is not my place to divulge another's secrets." With an unbreachable finality to his voice, Vikram turned and began moving forward again, even deeper beneath the sandstone palace. Shahrzad had to quicken her pace to match his lengthy strides. For a time, she felt like a flea chasing after an elephant.

The walls around them continued to close in tight, the ceiling becoming rounded, less stone and more earth. As the silence passed, Shahrzad found herself considering Vikram's words.

Considering the whole of Despina's betrayal.

"She could have told Khalid everything," Shahrzad repeated, though with decidedly less vehemence. "He would have believed her in time. After all, you believed her."

"He would not have believed her in time." His words boomed through the semidarkness. "And he would never have trusted her. Even I took some . . . convincing." Vikram glanced over his shoulder. "And I swore if I caught her lying, I would slit her throat."

"I still may," Shahrzad retorted under her breath before nearly slamming into his broad back.

"Then I offer you that chance." With that, he threw open the ancient, creaking door before him, leading into a passage of sewers. The warm stench clogged Shahrzad's nostrils, curling in her throat and causing her to gag.

As did the sight of Despina waiting in the shadows.

Again, Shahrzad was possessed by the sudden urge to attack her.

The former handmaiden—now princess—stood wrapped in a dark cloak, with a crooked smile aimed Shahrzad's way. "You look awful." She leaned in close. "And you smell even worse."

"And you can go straight to hell."

Her smile widened. "As long as you'll be there, I think I might like it."

Shahrzad resisted the urge to scream. "I'm not going anywhere with you, Despina *el-Sharif*. First you are one thing, then you are another. At this point, my neck hurts from spinning about so fast. Just tell me this: Why have you been lying to me this entire time?"

Despina shrugged. "I was born to lie, Shahrzad. I ask you, how does one recover from such an inclination?"

"The same way one chooses to serve such a despicable father," Shahrzad replied sardonically.

"I suppose you would want to know about that." Despina cast her a thin smile. "Would you mind walking as we talk?"

Shahrzad crossed her arms and remained still.

*I will go nowhere with her. Not until she convinces me otherwise.*

"I can see these few weeks apart have not weathered your obstinance. Pity." Despina smirked. "Very well, then. I knew this had to happen eventually." She leaned back on a heel, her hands predictably akimbo. "On her deathbed, my mother confessed my father's identity. She presented me with a scroll as proof and told me to go to him, for she hoped he might care for me, now that I had no one left."

Though Despina spoke flippantly, a flash of pain—a glimmer of truth—rippled across her eyes. Despite the abhorrent smells and the sounds of dripping sludge around them, Shahrzad strove to maintain a posture of unmoved silence.

Despina continued. "After my mother's death, I journeyed from Cadmeia to Amardha, begging, bartering, and stealing my way there. When I arrived at the palace gates, the guards tried to toss me into the gutter. I was a skinny, scrawny, eleven-year-old girl. Eventually I found a sympathetic soldier willing to hear my plea. I presented him with the scroll bearing my father's seal. He disappeared within the palace and returned hours later."

"Forgive the slight," Shahrzad interrupted with a frown, "but I can't imagine Salim Ali el-Sharif putting a hand of welcome out to you. Especially after having neglected you for much of your life."

Vikram cleared his throat with a cough.

Though it had taken on a thoughtful bent, Despina held fast to her smirk. "You have to understand. When you've spent most of your childhood not knowing your father, only to discover him to be a charming, handsome king with wealth beyond your wildest dreams, there is little you would *not* do to win his affection." She lingered in a remembrance colored by anger. "He promised he would claim me as his own if I would help him learn the secrets of Rey's court. First it was to help Yasmine secure a husband. Then it was to usurp Khalid Ibn al-Rashid's throne. He found a slaver who would buy me and bring me to the palace in Rey, where I first started cleaning the queen's chambers. After Khalid Ibn al-Rashid became caliph, he freed me and offered me a position as a handmaiden. I rose in the ranks soon after. The rest you can surmise."

That Shahrzad certainly could. Despina had done her duty well.

Had served her father's purpose well.

"It's all a grand story," Shahrzad said, sidestepping a new trickle of questionable liquid. "But I still don't trust you."

"Fine." Despina sighed loudly, her frustrations coming to heel. "Then trust in this, Shahrzad al-Khayzuran: I would rather be a handmaiden in Rey than a princess of Parthia. As a handmaiden in Rey, I always knew who I was. I had pride in myself. In Parthia, I was denied my place time and again. Denied and denounced by my own father. In fact, if I had my way, no one would know of my lineage. All I want in life is to raise my child in the city I've come to love as my own. With the people I've come to love as my own. With the *family* I've come to love as my own." Her eyes flashed with an undeniable fervency.

Shahrzad swallowed. Then looked away.

With an exasperated huff, Despina moved closer. She hesitated only an instant before reaching for Shahrzad's hand. "The only family I know is the one I have in Rey. The friends I have. The love I have." Her voice grew soft. "They are without equal."

How well Shahrzad knew this. How well she had seen it. The wild look in Jalal's eyes the night of the storm. The warmth in Despina's now.

"Then why did you come back at all?"

"To preserve our family." Despina squeezed her hand. "No matter the cost."

Though a part of Shahrzad wanted to throw off Despina's touch—to deny the touch of a girl tied in any way to Salim Ali el-Sharif—Shahrzad did not.

For it was the touch of a friend. Beneath it lay the strength of family.

"You deliberately provoked me at dinner, did you not?" Shahrzad asked quietly.

Despina tilted her head in rueful fashion. "Well, I did have to get you down into the palace prison somehow."

"Somehow." Shahrzad sniffed.

"I knew you had a wretched temper and a deeply loyal disposition. The rest was only a matter of time."

Shahrzad paused in contemplation. "What you did was dangerous."

"Trust that I put the fear of the gods into the soldiers when it came to your husband." Despina snickered. "It's true not all of them believed it, but that did not stop me. Oh, the stories I told . . ."

"I meant for you."

Despina blinked. Her features softened. "Of course you did."

"What of Salim?" Shahrzad asked in an even quieter tone. "He will know what you have done."

"He will not realize it for a few days at least. He sent both Yasmine and me from Amardha earlier this afternoon in anticipation of what might occur."

"What do you mean?"

Despina smiled broadly. "Ah, I nearly forgot! The Caliph of Khorasan has brought quite an army to the city gates."

Shahrzad gripped Despina's hand tight. "Khalid is here?"

"That's what I've been wanting to tell you from the beginning." She rolled her eyes. "I planned on taking you to him, Brat Calipha. That is if you'll permit me. *Finally.*"

Another grunt from Vikram. One Shahrzad knew was meant to indicate agreement.

"Fine." Shahrzad pushed off Despina's hand. "What is your plan?"

"We make our way through the lovely sewers. These particular drains lead to a part of the city near the bazaar. I've paid men a great deal of money to wait for us there with horses."

Shahrzad nodded. "The only thing left to accomplish is finding my sister."

"Your sister?" Despina's perfect eyebrows gathered at the bridge of her nose.

"My younger sister, Irsa, was brought to the palace as well."

Despina's confusion intensified. "No. I would have heard as much. No one was brought to Amardha, save for you and your father."

Shahrzad paused in thought. Paused to remember how her father would not meet her gaze whenever she asked after her sister. Paused to recall his guilt.

*Is that why no one would tell me anything about Irsa?*

"Are you quite certain of this?" she said.

"Quite." Despina nodded. "For she would have been present at dinner. My father would have made sure of it. He enjoys toying with his prey."

Shahrzad spent another moment searching Despina's face for signs of artifice. Though she found none, she could not permit herself to feel at ease with this revelation. Not after so many lies.

After so many betrayals.

She looked from Despina to Vikram and back again.

Khalid had trusted them. And Khalid trusted no one.

*If I intend to escape, I will need to put my faith in someone.*

"If you are lying to me about Irsa's whereabouts, I will personally bring about your demise," Shahrzad said in a dangerously quiet voice.

"I expect nothing less, Brat Calipha." Despina grinned.

She let her shoulders relax. "Lead the way, Princess of Parthia."

"Call me that again and face my wrath." Despina hurled a cloak at Shahrzad.

Once Shahrzad had covered herself with the cloak, the trio moved deeper into the city sewers, Vikram leading the way. He prowled beneath the dripping stone channels with his body hunched forward, hands braced against the walls. Try as she might, it soon became impossible for Shahrzad to ignore the many-legged creatures scuttling through the darkness. A chill ran down her spine as one darted across her fingers.

They continued down the filthy conduit, skirting the edge of the flowing sludge. Shahrzad stumbled over crooked stones and misaligned pavers. Several times she heard the distinct squeal of rats. The cacophony of dripping water and echoing footfalls—in tandem with the waning of the torch fire in Vikram's hand—only heightened Shahrzad's distress.

When they reached the end of the passageway, they found a rusted metal grate sealed across the entrance. Vikram put out his torch and pushed open the creaking grate, his enormous muscles bulging beneath his stained *qamis*.

The trio alighted onto a deserted alleyway in the center of Amardha. Several streets over, the noise of late-night revelry tolled into the heavy summer air. A chorus of drunken merriment, tempered by riotous discord. Despina ignored the celebration and moved through the shadows at a sure-footed pace.

They passed by several backstreets close to the bazaar. Shahrzad followed Vikram and Despina toward a copse of lemon trees, their citrus scent wafting on the wind.

As they approached, Despina slowed. Then stopped.

"What is it?" Shahrzad asked in a whisper.

"They're not here," she replied.

Vikram halted in his tracks.

"What?" Shahrzad said.

"The men. Or the horses." Despina pulled her close, then swiveled to backtrack, tucking Shahrzad beneath an arm.

This close, Shahrzad could feel the rapid beat of Despina's pulse. The stutter of her breath. Though her former handmaiden's fear was becoming palpable, Shahrzad chose to remain silent, knowing words would not help matters at all.

Vikram stayed to the shadows, a dagger tucked inside his forearm.

After pausing midstep, Despina angled toward the revelry within the bazaar.

At their sudden change in direction, Shahrzad couldn't help herself. "Despina, why are we walking *toward* everyone?"

"The fools are already celebrating tomorrow's victory," Despina said under her breath. "If someone discovered our plans and is intending to catch us, it will be easier for us to disappear in a crowd."

The cheering before them grew louder as they crossed another dirt thoroughfare. Stragglers entering the main stretch of the bazaar pushed past them, while those who had long since had their fill lurched by. The scent of scorched oil suffused the air, thick and enduring.

"You! You there!" A drunken voice called to Despina's right.

Despina's hold on Shahrzad tightened. "Keep walking."

"You!" A group of bawdy young men stumbled into their path. One smiling boy slung an arm about Despina, knocking back her cowl in the process. "Come, have a drink with us!"

Shahrzad looked about in a panic. Vikram had vanished.

*If we draw unwanted attention . . .*

The boy's voice grew louder. "I said—"

"There you are!" A burst of feminine laughter filled the air behind them. "I've been waiting for you all night."

A soft hand brushed past Shahrzad to pull Despina free of the boy's embrace. Free of his protests. Though the girl was wrapped in a cloak of the finest silk, Shahrzad would recognize that hair anywhere.

Yasmine.

# UNWANTED ARRIVALS

Y ASMINE GESTURED TOWARD THE GROVE OF LEMON trees behind them, her hand firmly wrapped around Despina's wrist.

In response, Shahrzad took hold of Yasmine's arm, her threat clear.

"Remain calm, my lady," Yasmine said softly. She let her gaze drift past them.

To where three armed men stood. Watching.

"You evil hag." Despina's whisper passed through smiling lips.

Yasmine grinned in return. "Careful. Lest I start to believe your lies."

Shahrzad studied the beautiful girl standing a hairsbreadth from her. It would be the work of a moment for Shahrzad to knock her down. Had she a weapon, she would not hesitate to use it. Alas, all Shahrzad had was seething rage.

A rage that kept her trembling and silent.

"Come with me." Yasmine directed again with her chin.

"Like hell we will," Shahrzad seethed back.

"I was wondering when you would show your true face, Brat Calipha," Yasmine said. "For it's not like you to be so circumspect."

Shahrzad gritted her teeth. That nickname was reserved for Despina's use.

"For the last time, follow me, you ridiculous fools," Yasmine repeated with a silvery peal of laughter.

At that, Vikram slinked from the inky darkness behind Yasmine el-Sharif, putting his dagger to her throat in a silent threat. She froze for an instant, then began to struggle. The soldiers dashed toward her, drawing their swords.

"Step any closer, and you will bathe in her blood." Vikram's eyes flashed obsidian.

The soldiers stopped in their tracks.

"Drop your weapons," Shahrzad ordered the men.

When Yasmine nodded their way, the soldiers let their swords fall to the dirt.

Shahrzad bent to retrieve one of the blades. "And just like that, the tides of fortune turn." She assumed the fighting stance, as Khalid and Vikram had taught her.

Despina crossed her arms and simpered. "What do you suppose we should do with Parthia's favorite princess?"

"I'm not quite certain." Shahrzad contemplated the tip of her sword, keeping watch over the soldiers all the while. "What would you do?"

"I'd say she's an excellent bargaining chip."

Yasmine thrashed against Vikram. "You idiots. That's exactly why I came here."

"Careful." Shahrzad stepped closer. "Lest we start believing your lies."

Yasmine squealed with frustration. "Despina, tell your husband to release me this instant!" She continued struggling against the towering brute of a man. "He smells foul!"

"Vikram Singh is not my husband. He's under no obligation to me," Despina replied. "And I'd take care with whom you insult in this moment, little sister." She drew another, smaller dagger from her sleeve.

Shahrzad held back a sigh.

*It would have been nice to know about that weapon earlier, Despina.*

Ignoring Shahrzad's frown, Despina lifted the second blade before her half sister's beautiful face. "What are you doing here, you meddlesome imp?"

"I—I came to help," Yasmine stuttered.

"With the palace guards in tow?" Shahrzad jeered. "A likely story."

"It's true!" Yasmine elbowed Vikram hard. He grunted but did not move. "And they're not palace guards. They're sellswords, hired with my own coin. Do you think palace guards would hesitate to fight for my release? Besides, they're not even dressed as palace guards. Ask Despina."

Shahrzad exchanged glances with her former handmaiden and saw that Yasmine spoke the truth.

Nevertheless, Despina raised her dagger even higher. "How did you know where we'd be?"

Yasmine's perfect face twisted tight with frustration. "I knew you were up to something when you refused to leave the city with me earlier. That show you put on at dinner was simply too good, even for you."

"So you had me followed?" Despina pressed.

"No. I paid your handmaiden for information on your comings and goings. Money is a commodity in this city, as you well know."

"Did you tell the sultan?"

"Of course not." A wrinkle formed at the bridge of Yasmine's perfect nose. "Do you think you'd be alive now if Father knew what you've done?"

Shahrzad had stood by and watched this exchange long enough. "Why are you here, Yasmine? Tell the truth, if you value your life."

Yasmine's gaze traveled the length of Shahrzad's dirty figure. Buying time. "I came because I don't wish to see our kingdoms go to war."

"That's the reason you'd like to give. What is the truth?"

The Princess of Parthia inhaled with care. "Because I don't want to see my father die. Nor do I wish to see Khalid hurt. I love them both, and if we go to war, one of them will perish."

Shahrzad's eyes roved across Yasmine's face. "So then, what do you think we can do to prevent this?"

"I want you to take me with you." The princess did not hesitate in her response.

"What?" both Shahrzad and Despina said at once.

Yasmine's chin jutted forward. "I want to speak with Khalid."

"Why?" Shahrzad asked, cutting her eyes.

"Because I have an idea that might help end this war without shedding any unnecessary blood."

It was a bedraggled band of souls that trudged through the sands toward the Caliph of Khorasan's encampment.

Three young women—all dressed in torn finery, two of them smelling of sewage—made their way before the guards tasked with keeping watch over the camp's entrance at night. When a hulking warrior with skin of burnished copper came into view, the soldiers drew their swords. Two came to stand before him.

The smallest of the three girls spoke first.

"I'd like to speak to the caliph." She tucked a poorly shorn wave of hair behind an ear, smudging even more dirt across her face in the process.

At that, the leader of the night guard began laughing. "And I'd like a harem and a flagon of wine, while we're at it."

The girl's eyes flashed through a myriad of colors before settling on green. "Don't be a fool."

"Don't presume to lecture me, you filthy little—"

The brute of a warrior moved to strike. But was stayed by the smallest girl before he could proceed.

"Watch your words, soldier," the plump girl with the disheveled crown of curls said in an imperious tone. "That's the Calipha of Khorasan."

The soldier's sense of humor began to fade. "And I'm the *Shahrban* of Rey."

"I'm afraid you're not," the imperious girl replied. "He's older. And not nearly as stupid."

The other soldiers could not help but laugh at her rejoinder.

"Enough!" The last girl—the most striking one—finally stepped forward. "My name is Yasmine el-Sharif, and I demand to speak with—"

"And I demand a moment alone with you." The soldier in charge grinned before reaching to pull her in for a kiss.

Before the hulking warrior could stop her, the tiny girl with the badly shorn hair leapt onto him with the fury of a crazed monkey. She began pummeling him in the head and neck with both fists.

His soldiers laughed uproariously.

"It was just a kiss!" the soldier protested. When he failed to pull her off immediately, several other soldiers came to his aid.

In a blur of movement, the barrel-chested man accompanying them disarmed the soldiers. He blew onto one of their swords, setting it aflame. Then he held the burning weapon before their leader's face.

"Wait . . ." One of the soldiers staggered back.

Another tripped onto the sand in his haste to flee. "That—that's the Rajput!"

"Get the captain of the guard," the wielder of fire said. "Now."

Over the years, many interesting things had awoken Jalal al-Khoury in the middle of the night.

Many were to his liking. Some were not.

Being woken suddenly during a time of war did not strike him as a good thing.

He made a mental note to replace the fool in charge of the encampment at night. It was clear this idiot was not up to the task, for the wretch's lip was bleeding, and he'd clearly been in a recent fight.

Jalal armed himself, then traipsed through the sands after the unintelligible moron. The fool kept mumbling about fire swords and beautiful women smelling of the sewer.

If he was drunk while on the job, Jalal would be sure to find a way to punish him. A way that would involve spending a night in a thorny briar. Without his trowsers.

Once they neared the entrance to the camp, Jalal heard the distinct lilt of female voices.

At least the idiot had not been wrong about that. Though the thought of beautiful women dressed in sewage did not exactly spur Jalal to action.

A familiar, melodic laugh froze him in his tracks.

Without thought, Jalal began to run. He didn't care if he left the fool in the dust behind him. At that moment, he didn't care if he left all else in the dust behind him.

It wasn't possible. His mind was playing tricks on him. As it was apt to do of late.

Jalal turned the corner. And skidded to a stop, nearly tumbling into the sand.

Just like that. She was there.

He saw no one else save her.

All else could go to the devil save her.

Despina.

She smiled. Slowly. Catlike, her claws on her hips.

"Hello," she said. "Your family has missed you. Terribly."

"Where"—Jalal caught his breath, still incredulous—"have you been?"

Despina shrugged. "I'm here now. Are you very angry with me?"

"You"—his voice was choked—"you—have squeezed my heart dry."

"I know." She began to move in his direction. "And I will spend the rest of my life trying to fill it."

He walked toward her. Slowly. Catlike, his paws at his sides.

"Yes," Jalal whispered, nearing her, his pulse on a silent rampage. "You will."

Her smile widened. "Then you'll have me?"

Jalal took her chin in his hand. Despina wrapped both hands around his wrist.

"I will."

It was sealed with a kiss.


A rustling noise awoke Khalid from a restless sleep.

His tent flap had fluttered open. A shadow graced the entrance. Without hesitation, he reached for his sword.

"I am unarmed, *sayyidi*. This time."

Khalid could sense the smile behind her words. He did not move, certain that dreams had finally settled upon him.

And this was the dream from which he did not wish to wake.

Shahrzad moved through the darkness toward his bed pallet. She knelt beside him.

"Are you not going to ask me how it is I came to be here?" she said. He could hear the hint of recent sadness—the weariness—in her voice.

"I don't need to know that." Khalid reached for her hands. "Not now. Unless you want to tell me."

"Wanting and needing are two very different things. I always thought it before, but it's not the same as knowing it." Shahrzad leaned in to his chest and breathed deep. "My father's book?"

"Destroyed."

She nodded once, the tension leaving her limbs. The smell of *Nabulsi* soap clung to her skin. Soon Khalid felt the warmth of tears soaking through his *qamis*.

And he understood.

"You saw Irsa?" Khalid asked.

Shahrzad nodded. "Rahim . . ."

"Will always be remembered," Khalid finished softly.

"I haven't been here for her." The remorse on her face gutted him. "I haven't been there for Irsa when she's needed me. I was too busy wanting things I could not control." She pressed into Khalid. "I should have known better."

"As you said, wanting and needing are different. Now that you know, I trust you will do better." Khalid lifted his hands to her wet hair. Fury bristled within his chest when he touched the ragged ends. Ends that barely grazed her shoulder.

Ends that spoke of recent violence. Abuse at the hands of Salim Ali el-Sharif.

"Are you angry?" Shahrzad whispered.

Khalid steadied his rage. "Yes."

She looked up at him, her eyes still shimmering with tears. "Are you going to make him pay?"

"Many times over."

Shahrzad took a careful breath. "I have an idea." Her lips quirked to one side. "Well, it's not just mine. And we'll need your help."

"You have it, *joonam*. Always."

# THE GATES OF AMARDHA

I~~T~~ BEGAN AT DAYBREAK.

When Khalid sent his archers to fire a flurry of arrows at the city's battlements.

In response, the soldiers of Amardha—the ones tasked with guarding the gates—rained a shower of their own arrows down upon the string of archers below.

A warning. Proceed no farther.

Khalid's archers dashed back into the desert on horses faster than the wind. Badawi horses borrowed from Omar al-Sadiq.

Later, Khalid's archers returned.

This time with many more riders. And many more arrows.

Khalid had long known the sentiment that was undoubtedly roiling through the city of Amardha at this moment.

Khorasan had more soldiers. More money. More weapons.

All Parthia had was arrogance. An arrogance Khalid intended to use to his advantage.

The midmorning sun at their backs, his archers fired up into the sky. Alas, those in charge atop the wall could not see well, the sun shining too bright in their eyes. They could not issue the proper orders for their soldiers to fire down at the attackers. Their shots missed, striking dirt and sand and rocks and debris. The occasional shield. But never once striking their targets.

Then . . .

Khalid's soldiers took careful aim.

Not a drop of blood would be spilled in waste.

The soldiers tasked with issuing orders were felled in a single volley. Some slumped across the battlements. Others fell screaming to their deaths.

The arrows fired at them were marked with the standard of the twin swords. The al-Rashid standard.

A warning: Khorasan would take no mercy on those who continued to fight.

Khalid remained out of view, and his soldiers responded to Amardha's disorganized defense with a deliberate offense. Still no sign of the sultan. No words of inspiration. No leader at the vanguard.

The unconscionable coward.

A hailstorm of arrows fell toward the sultan's men. Arrows that continued to miss their marks.

Arrows that were promptly collected. And set to flame.

Khalid issued quiet orders. Only those in positions of power and influence should be targeted. After a time, his soldiers tipped their arrows in oil and set them afire. He watched the spark of chaos catch. Turn into flame.

Still the gates of Amardha remained shut.

Nevertheless, Khalid knew word of these events would spread through the ranks of Amardha's soldiers. The Sultan of Parthia watched from inside his jeweled palace as his city was set ablaze. And did not retaliate.

Salim Ali el-Sharif was afraid of Khalid Ibn al-Rashid.

That afternoon, Khalid ordered the ballistae to be brought forward. Ten giant crossbows armed with metal-studded arrows able to dispel over two talents' worth of wicked iron. Heavy iron meant to lay siege to a wall. Each ballista was positioned at a specific distance from the wall encircling the city of Amardha. At a point meant to inflict significant damage.

At a point made with an engineer's exacting eye.

The soldiers on the battlements began to scurry, cries of warning echoing through their ranks.

Fear running rampant.

Khalid waited to see if Salim would take action. When the sultan did nothing—as Khalid had expected—Khalid made ready to deliver another wordless message.

Structures filled with grain and other foodstuffs were targeted. Khalid hoped they housed very few people, if any. For he did not wish to be responsible for even more lives lost. The loss of any life in this war would be keenly felt. And Khalid did not wish to shed innocent blood.

The ballistae were loosed. They flew on a resounding current of air, crashing into their marks with rippling shudders.

Screams resonated throughout Amardha.

Several bodies fell from a collapsing turret, one impaled on a battlement. Khalid's chest grew tight. So many had already died so needlessly. For a moment he fought to take in a breath. Then Khalid hardened himself.

Such was the way of war.

Wait to feel when there is nothing left. Wait to feel after you've won.

He knew Salim Ali el-Sharif had never thought Khalid would truly attack Amardha. After all, Khalid had never done so. Not in all these years. Not after countless provocations.

But Salim needed to believe he would.

Needed to believe that Khalid would raze the entire city without flinching.

The ground at his back started to shake as the sun began to set. Khalid did not look behind. He knew what was on the horizon. Even Salim would be forced to take notice.

In the distance, a sea of Arabian stallions surrounded by a glittering cloud of sand marched toward the gates of Amardha. The men riding the horses were cloaked and masked, wielding wide scimitars and thick leather *mankalahs* on each wrist. They were people of the desert. Born and bred in the light of its scorching sun. Fearless and proud. Known to take few prisoners.

Known to have even less mercy.

They were led by a boy with a blue-grey falcon and an old man with a long beard.

The son of emir Nasir al-Ziyad. And the sheikh of the al-Sadiq tribe.

They stopped a quarter league outside the city gates. Tariq Imran al-Ziyad raised his scimitar into the sky. An echoing ululation rippled through their masses. The men lifted their swords as the whooping reached a feverish pitch. As the sand around their stallions' hooves rose into a dusky haze, mingling with the flashes of steel above.

Khalid could feel the fear amassing above the city. No longer a spark about to catch flame. It spread like wildfire, deep into the darkest alleyways of Amardha.

For just as Artan had said yesterday, wars were won before they were even fought.

Then, as the sun set below the horizon, the winged serpent appeared, bearing a bundle beneath its wings. Artan sat astride him, sporting a wicked grin and a darkly punishing gaze.

The winged serpent screamed as it swooped toward the city gates. The men along the wall began frantically firing arrows at it. Arrows that rebounded off its armorlike scales. In response to the arrows, the winged serpent screamed even louder, and Khalid watched the men below clap their hands over their ears, yelling to one another in terror.

Then the winged serpent dropped its bundle over the city gates. The thick liquid splashed down the grey wall, coating it in a shining viscous fluid.

Oil.

The serpent screamed once more and disappeared into the night sky.

With a *click* of his tongue, Khalid spurred Ardeshir from the shadows. His battle regalia was encrusted with silver and gold, and his *rida'* billowed behind him. A full battalion of the Royal Guard marched at his back.

Several sentries on the battlements above shouted warnings. The soldiers there began scrambling once again.

A quarter league away, Tariq dipped an obsidian arrow in oil. Omar put a flame to it. Then the son of Nasir al-Ziyad fired it straight at the city gates.

When they caught flame, the ululations began anew.

Khalid watched the gates of Amardha burn from astride his black Arabian. Watched the dark wood glow in flashes of blue and white. Dancing flames of umber and orange.

Behind the walls, the city descended into pandemonium.

When Khalid heard the screams and the shouts and the sounds of rising panic, he glanced down at the waiting messenger beside him.

"Deliver the letter."

The moon hung high in the sky when the Sultan of Parthia rode into Khalid's camp. He dismounted before the largest tent in silence, the rage on his face as plain as day. Behind him rode Jahandar al-Khayzuran and the two most senior generals of the Parthian army.

As Salim stepped toward the canopy leading inside, the captain of the Royal Guard detained his party. And asked that they leave all weapons outside.

At this, Salim balked in open protest.

Jalal smiled at him with bladed serenity. "Feel free to return to your palace." He offered him a flourishing bow. "In any case, we shall see you soon."

With a disdainful sneer, the Sultan of Parthia threw down his sword and the curved dagger at his hip. His men followed suit before they were permitted to enter the Caliph of Khorasan's tent.

Once they made their way inside, they found Khalid and his party waiting for them, seated at a long, low table. Lamps hung from iron posts at either end, and behind the table stood an intricately carved screen dividing the tent in two.

Khalid was positioned at the table's center. To his left sat the *Shahrban* of Rey. Beside the *shahrban* was Tariq Imran al-Ziyad. At Tariq's side sat Omar al-Sadiq. The captain of the guard took the space to Khalid's right.

"Sit." Khalid gestured to the silken cushions across from him.

Barely managing to conceal his scorn, Salim sank down, his generals at either side of him. Jahandar al-Khayzuran shuffled to a corner of the table, under the watchful gaze of Tariq.

Khalid regarded Salim in silence for a moment. "Now that I have your attention—"

"Where is my daughter, you bastard son of a whore?" Salim said.

"Daughter?" Khalid paused, his disdain all too evident. "You should at least have the decency to say *daughters* by now."

At that, Salim's jaw fell open for the briefest instant. Then his gaze narrowed with sudden wariness.

"For you do count Despina amongst your children," Khalid continued, stone-faced. "Especially after all she's done for you?"

The silence hung in the space like a specter. Jalal's fists were balled tight, his body coiled as though he were ready to lunge at any moment.

Ready to render justice.

"I do." Salim's response was sharp.

"Good," Khalid said. "At least you've done right by her in one matter."

"Don't pretend you care for Despina," Salim replied. "Not after she lived as a slave in your palace all those years." He shifted in his seat. "In any case, I knew you would not treat her poorly." His smile was caustic. "After all, you reserve that behavior for your wives, not your servants."

Though Jalal uttered an oath beneath his breath, Khalid did not react to the words. Nor did he bother to defend himself. "You do as you always have done—blame others for your transgressions. And in doing so, you reap the same reward—nothing."

Salim snorted. "I did not come here to be lectured by a boy. Let us come to it—in your letter, you told me you had Yasmine."

Khalid nodded, then leaned back, placing his hands on the table. He waited a moment. "Did you bring Shahrzad?"

Salim's expression hardened. "I will give you what you love in exchange for what I love."

Another pause. "Again, it is good to know you care for something. Besides yourself."

"Don't toy with me, you arrogant—"

"And don't lie to me, you specious coward." Khalid's eyes burned bright.

"How dare you—"

"He does dare, Uncle Salim," a voice echoed from behind the carved screens. "He dares quite often."

At that, Khalid's lips curved in a dark smile as Shahrzad glided into view. She was dressed in simple clothing. A cream *qamis* and pale grey *sirwal* trowsers. Her wavy hair fell to her shoulders, and she was unadorned, save for the jeweled dagger at her hip.

But she was, as ever, a queen.

Khalid watched as Salim tried in vain to conceal his shock.

"Are you surprised?" Shahrzad asked, her hazel eyes lambent. "I suppose you've tasked many soldiers with finding me. Or perhaps you did not think I would manage to find my way out of your city?" She took her seat beside Khalid.

The Sultan of Parthia managed to mask his shock with admirable speed. He tried to smile at Shahrzad, but his smile lacked the odious surety of before. "I continue to be impressed with you, Shahrzad al-Khayzuran. But it's clear you had assistance in escaping. Perhaps you could regale me with the story one day, so that I can be certain to address the lapses in my security."

"Oh, it's *quite* the story." Shahrzad grinned. "And I did have a great deal of help. But if you don't mind, I think I'll let your daughters tell you the story."

# THE ROSE

$S$HAHRZAD WATCHED WITH BITTER SATISFACTION WHILE Salim Ali el-Sharif was undone by his daughters. First one, then the other.

As his plans were utterly routed.

Though it did little to fill the hollow left in her chest after Rahim's death, Shahrzad did feel a shadowed sort of satisfaction to see Salim fall at the hands of women. Especially at the hands of those he'd been so willing to cast aside or use as pawns.

It was time for Salim to learn that his daughters were much more than objects to be used and discarded at his whim.

But the true difficulty had come when Salim had been faced with Yasmine.

It was easy for him to disregard Despina. He'd done so for most of her life. But Yasmine? Yasmine was the daughter Salim had loved. The daughter he'd prized.

She had been his future.

"What would you have me do, Yasmine?" Salim asked once he'd realized the full breadth of her treachery.

Yasmine's lovely eyes welled with tears. But she did not cry. As

Shahrzad had long suspected, there was an undeniable strength to her, even in the most trying of times. "I would have you stop this, Father. Stop this endless fighting. This endless unrest."

"I did this for *you*. To ensure your future."

"No." Yasmine shook her head. "You did it for many reasons, but if you'd ever paused to hear my thoughts, you would know this was not what I wanted. You do not know what I want."

Salim's features hardened. "What do you want?"

"I want to go through life and not regret all that I am."

"I have never—"

"You have." She sat tall. "Had you not been who you are, perhaps I would not have repelled those I truly care for. Perhaps then I could have found the happiness I sought."

Shahrzad saw Yasmine's eyes flit to Khalid for less than an instant. It was not intentional. And Shahrzad did not resent it, for she understood. Yasmine had known all along that her father's deplorable actions had been a hindrance to her union with Khalid.

Yasmine took a deep breath. "Perhaps then you would not have had to resort to such base means to achieve your goals."

Anger lighted Salim's gaze once more. "And now that we are here, what is to become of us, daughter? For in doing what you have done, you have abased our family. Would you have me surrender? Would you have us lose all for your childish hopes?"

She did not respond.

"You may do as you please, Salim," Khalid replied instead. "You may turn and walk from this table now, if that is what you wish to do," he continued. "But the gates of your city will burn until dawn. And once they are gone, there is nothing to stop us from laying siege to Amardha." Khalid leaned forward. "But I would rather not. I would rather not kill so many people for my pride and your conceit."

"Then you would have me surrender?" Salim bit out in a wrathful whisper.

"You surrendered the moment you appeared before my tent."

A wave of fury passed across the sultan's face. "And what of the others involved in this? Many of your bannermen have supplied arms and funds to this cause. What of them?" His voice grew louder. "What of Reza bin-Latief?"

It was Tariq who spoke in response to this charge. "Make no mistake: my plotting uncle will be dealt with. As will the others aligned with him. There is much to be discussed." He exchanged a knowing glance with Shahrzad. A glance she was glad to share. Glad to understand. Finally.

"What is it you want, Khalid Ibn al-Rashid?" Salim demanded. "My death?"

Khalid let his eyes linger on the Sultan of Parthia in pointed consideration. "I should kill you for all you have done. For all the pain and death and destruction you have brought on those dearest to me."

"You do not have the courage." Though Salim said the words in sharp retort, Shahrzad could sense a trace of fear beneath them.

"It does not take courage to kill. It takes courage to live."

"Then what do you want of me?"

"I want you to abdicate your throne," Khalid replied. "I will give you a home outside Rey in which you will reside, with guards to stand watch at all times. Guards I will appoint."

Rage contorted Salim's features once more. "And I suppose you will become ruler of Parthia? Ruler of all my family has held for over five generations?"

"I told you before. I have no interest in taking control of your kingdom."

"Then who is to rule?"

Khalid looked to Shahrzad. She glanced back at him, relishing how he gave her leave to divulge the best secret of all. The agreement they'd come to last night. Together.

Shahrzad held Khalid's gaze. "I think Yasmine el-Sharif would make an excellent Sultana of Parthia, my king."

"As do I, my queen."


Jahandar sat at his corner of the table in the caliph's tent and watched his world unravel like a skein of silk.

He had chosen wrong. He had thought Reza bin-Latief would be the one to help him find a way back into the book's graces. Back into power. Back into influence.

He'd thought the Sultan of Parthia would help him find a way.

Jahandar had been horribly, horribly wrong.

He had not realized how much enmity existed between Shahrzad and Salim Ali el-Sharif. He'd foolishly thought Shahrzad would help to win the sultan over to his cause. After all, his daughter was married to the sultan's nephew. Though Jahandar knew the sultan intended to dethrone the caliph, Salim had assured him no harm would come to Shahrzad. It was why Jahandar had been so willing to go along with Reza's plan to steal away Shahrzad to Amardha.

But everything had fallen apart that awful night at dinner.

Jahandar had realized then that the boy-king—the Caliph of Khorasan—had already won this war. Had already grasped the power Jahandar needed to succeed. For the caliph had already taken control of everything Jahandar held dear.

When Jahandar had tried to find Irsa in the desert, he'd been unable to do so. Now he'd learned from the captain of the guard that she was amongst the caliph's soldiers. Safely ensconced in his camp. Beyond Jahandar's reach.

When Jahandar had tried to enlist Shahrzad's help in retrieving his book, it had been clear she'd already agreed to work alongside the caliph to take it from him. The caliph who'd stolen the book from Jahandar while he slept.

The caliph who'd used Jahandar's own children against him.

Where was his book?

He'd lost his wife. He'd lost his standing in Rey.

Now he'd lost his daughters.

Irsa was nowhere to be found. Shahrzad would not even look at him. She had not gazed his way even once.

His elder daughter had eyes only for the boy-king.

When everyone stood from the table to leave, Jahandar rose to his feet as well. He watched the caliph's guards follow the sultan and his generals from the tent. Then all who remained began to move about, disregarding Jahandar's presence.

Just as before. Just as always.

Then, as Shahrzad and the caliph drew near, Jahandar leapt at the chance to speak. Leapt at the chance to act. And be noticed.

"Where," he began, his voice wavering, "where is the book?"

"Is that truly all you care about, Baba?" Shahrzad asked softly.

"N-no."

Her face pulled tight. "Why have you not asked after Irsa?"

"Does Irsa have need of me?"

Shahrzad glanced away. But not before Jahandar saw the expression of pain on her face. The caliph stepped closer. He regarded Jahandar through steady, piercing eyes. The look all but shriveled him.

Jahandar resented it. For though this boy was his king, he was still a boy.

A boy who had taken so much from him. Had taken everything from him.

"Your book is no more," the caliph said in a cold tone.

"What?" Jahandar whispered.

"It is gone. Destroyed."

The very air around Jahandar stilled. Turned hot. "How?"

"I destroyed it myself."

Jahandar clasped his hands before him, the blood rising in his neck. "Why?"

The caliph stared at him once more in silent censure.

Then turned away.

Judging him. Dismissing him. As so many had always done.

As all would continue to do. Because of this boy. This boy who had no right to do such a thing. This boy who had taken so much from Jahandar.

His daughter. His book.

His respect.

Anger spewed from Jahandar in a blistering torrent. In a hot flood of rage. Without thinking, he reached for the dagger at Shahrzad's waist. Immediately the caliph stepped between them to push her aside, but Jahandar was not trying to hurt his daughter. *Never* his daughter.

Jahandar raised the dagger high.

The caliph lifted his arm to deflect the blow. Shouts of alarm rang out from the guards.

Oblivious to all, Jahandar slashed downward with vicious precision. The blade sliced across the caliph's face as he tried to shove Jahandar away.

But the dagger found its final mark.

In the heart of the Caliph of Khorasan.

# THE DAGGER

KHALID HAD OFTEN THOUGHT HOW HE WOULD MEET his end. He'd often wished he'd been given the choice to die before Ava's father. To die instead of foisting his curse on his people.

But this?

He had not foreseen this. Not at the hands of Jahandar al-Khayzuran.

For an instant, Khalid's gaze locked on Shahrzad's father.

His murderer.

But Khalid did not have time for hatred. Did not have time for retribution.

His eyes met Shahrzad's.

No. In the end, there is only time for love.

Khalid staggered to the ground, shock rippling through his body in waves of hot and cold.

The room fell silent.

Pain coursed through Khalid's chest. An ache without end. He knew the wound was mortal. His vision shimmered, then cleared as hot blood trickled beside him. He heard Jalal slam Shazi's father to the floor and kick the dagger free from Jahandar's grasp.

The tent went still. Not a sound could be heard.

Khalid gripped Shazi's hands, his touch strong.

Fading.

"No." Shahrzad began to scream. She clutched his weakening body lying on the ground before her. Watched the blood flow from his chest.

Watched as Khalid gasped for breath, his mouth filling with blood.

The last thing he saw was her face.

In the end, there was only love.

So much more than he deserved.

# THE POWER TO LOVE

His ELDER DAUGHTER'S SCREAMS BECAME SOBS.

No one else around them moved. The princess of Parthia's hands were clasped over her mouth, her blue eyes wavering with unshed tears. Her younger sister had buried her face in her shoulder to stifle her cries.

Yet no one looked Jahandar's way. No one even uttered a word in his direction. Not his daughter. Not even the *shahrban*. Not a single word of hate or fury or retribution.

All were lost in the sight before them.

And Jahandar did not feel different. Did not feel any better for having done what he had done.

Instead, Jahandar slowly came *un*done at the sight of his proud daughter breaking before him. She had never broken before. Not when her mother had died. Not when she'd had to take control of their home when Jahandar had been lost to grief. Not even when Shiva had been taken to the palace.

Not once had Shahrzad faltered.

But now, she was breaking. Jahandar saw it. Saw her shimmering eyes. Heard her mournful sobs, each louder than the next.

His heart missed a beat. Then crashed through his chest on a rampage.

Jahandar could not stand the sight of his daughter breaking. For he'd never meant to hurt her.

Not Shahrzad. Never her.

The caliph's blood flowed toward him. Toward Jahandar's hands, curled in the ground.

And Jahandar knew then what he had to do. He'd memorized every spell in his precious book. Every line of text he'd translated was seared into his mind.

And this spell?

It would be his last. His finest.

The blood that touched his fingertips was still warm.

In that moment, Jahandar recalled the day in the palace when he'd given Shahrzad the last rose from his garden. A budding flower of cream and blushing mauve. He'd wanted to give her a lasting remembrance of home.

He'd killed the rose to give her one moment of beauty.

With the caliph's blood on his hands, Jahandar began to mutter the spell. He let his wrist turn in the slowest of twists.

His vision started to blur. From the tips of his fingers bloomed an unsteady light. A wave of cold tugged at his center, only to roll down his spine. His sight lightened, then darkened, as though a drop of ink had splashed within his eyes, only to fade into nothingness.

Pain began to collect in his heart. Began to blossom into an open wound.

But it did not hurt. Not truly. Not in the slightest. Jahandar began to smile.

For here . . . here was the true power. The power Jahandar had wanted all along.

The power to speak without words.

The power to love.

Reza watched dawn slowly break in the west. Slowly blur from a night still filled with stars. He had long been a man of infinite patience. It took patience to build relationships. Patience to fortify trust.

Patience to bring down a king.

Reza waited in the desert, watching the gates of Amardha burn. It alarmed him that the sultan's army had yet to retaliate, but he knew it would come in time. And Reza refused to show the mercenaries around him he had anything but the utmost faith in his cause.

Men with a loyalty bought and sold could not be trusted around a questioning heart. For questions could be sold at auction to the highest bidder.

When Reza saw the swirl of rising dust from an approaching rider, he sat taller on his steed. The horses of the men around him whickered as his men drew near.

The Fida'i messenger said nothing while reining in his stallion before Reza. The animal shone with sweat, the messenger's eyes were grim.

"The sultan has surrendered to the caliph," the messenger said without pausing for breath.

Reza concealed his surprise. But not his fury. "How is that

possible? A battle was never even fought. Did you speak with the sultan?"

The messenger did not reply. He exchanged a brief glance with the other men around Reza.

Even before he felt the first blow, Reza understood what was happening.

It came from behind. The slash of a sword.

Reza fell forward on his horse. The stallion reared back at the second blow to Reza's side.

With a gasp, Reza collapsed into the sand, clutching his wounds.

He rolled onto his back, wheezing for air.

The messenger rode closer, his bloodied blade glittering against the sky. "I have a message from the son of Nasir al-Ziyad. He says the next time you send a mercenary to kill someone he loves, make sure she does not live to tell the tale."

The last thing Reza bin-Latief saw was the flash of a sword.

# EPILOGUE

THE BOY BOUNDED THROUGH THE DOUBLE DOORS
into his father's waiting arms.

"Baba!" he cried. "Uncle Artan is going to teach me to fly on
his winged serpent!"

The Caliph of Khorasan gazed down at his son with thinly
veiled amusement. "I think your mother may have something to
say about that."

"No!" The small boy shook his head. "You can't tell Mama.
Uncle Artan made me promise."

"Again, your mother may have something to say about that."

The boy made a sweep of his room with his large, amber-flecked
eyes. "Where is she?"

"I believe she is in the solarium with your aunt."

"But she's coming soon?"

"Of course."

Eagerness alighted the boy's gaze. "She said she has a new
story tonight."

"I heard." Khalid smiled.

At that, the boy raced to the center of his platformed bed and grabbed his favorite green cushion. Khalid came to rest beside him.

Cautiously, the boy reached up to place a hand on the scar marring his father's face. "Does this ever hurt?"

"Sometimes."

"Uncle Artan fixed my knee the other day after I fell. Maybe you should ask him to fix it."

"That's not necessary."

"Why is that?"

"I don't mind it."

"Why?"

Khalid smiled again. "Because it reminds me that all things come at a cost. That every decision we make has consequences."

The boy nodded slowly, as though he were very sage for all his five years. "I just don't like that you're hurt." His small fingers remained pressed to his father's cheek, grazing the edge of the scar ever so gently.

"Just as I would not like for you to be hurt either. Hence the worry regarding the flying serpent."

The boy grinned, his pert nose wrinkling. "I love you, Baba."

"And never forget my heart is always in your hands, Haroun."

The doors to the chambers opened, and Shahrzad walked through them in a flurry of wild hair and jeweled silk.

Haroun raced to the edge of the bed to greet her.

"Mama, don't tell Uncle Artan I told you, but he said once I learn my lessons this week, he will teach me how to fly!"

Khalid narrowed his gaze. "Haroun-*jan*, you told me you promised Uncle Artan you wouldn't tell your mother."

The boy side-eyed his father with a sheepish glance. "I forgot."

Shahrzad laughed. "You must learn to keep your promises, my star. For a man who cannot keep his promises is nothing." She brushed back his tangle of wavy black hair. "And what's this about you flying?" Shahrzad reached for one of the wilted roses beside her son's bed. "If you're so interested in flying with Uncle Artan, then perhaps I shouldn't be telling you the story I intended to start tonight. It might only encourage you." With a twist of her hand, Shahrzad brought the flower back to life.

"No!" Haroun leapt back to his place in the center of the cushions. "I won't learn to fly." He smiled, and it was so wide and bright and perfect that it turned up the edges of every feature on his perfect face. "Even though Amira said it wasn't scary, and—"

"Sometimes Amira al-Khoury likes to embellish the truth. Just like her mother." Shahrzad held back a sigh.

"I know. But I trust her because she's my best friend." Haroun's smile widened. "Don't worry, Mama. I won't fly . . . yet."

With a wide smile of her own, Shahrzad settled beside the most beautiful ones in existence. Her husband and her son. The small boy lying alongside her was a tiny mirror of Khalid, save for having her nose and her wild waves of hair.

Save for the white scar across Khalid's cheek.

One of the marks from the night her father had given his life for their love. One on his face. One at his heart. These marks that made her thankful, each day, to be alive. To share this life with those she loved.

She thought for a moment about Shiva. A warmth settled upon her.

All Shahrzad wanted was before her. All Shahrzad needed was within her.

She woke to each dawn with a grateful heart.

"Did all go well with Irsa?" Khalid asked as Shahrzad leaned against a cushion.

"Yes," Shahrzad replied, lifting the rose to take in its scent. "She's still busy in the solarium studying medicinal herbs along-side Artan. But she might accompany Tariq when he next visits Amardha."

Khalid raised a brow. "Still trying for a match? Both you and Irsa are worse than the gossips on the street corners of the souk. Always plotting something." A warm light gleamed in his eyes.

"I'm not doing anything!" Shahrzad threw up her hands. "Tariq travels to Amardha on his own accord. If he manages to spend an inordinate amount of time with Yasmine while doing so, then . . ."

One side of Khalid's mouth slid upward. "Indeed."

"Mama?" Haroun cleared his throat, looking between his parents. "The story?"

"Ah, yes. Of course!" She pulled him close. "Since my most esteemed *effendi* is so enamored by the idea of flying, I thought I would begin this tale in a land not so far from here. Our hero begins his journey on a dark night, where he slips from his bedroom window into a garden, with naught but a small rug under his arm. An ugly, blemished rug, with a medallion at its center and scorch marks along its sides."

"A rug?" Haroun asked, a furrow lining his forehead.

"Yes. A rug." Shahrzad's eyes sparkled. "But this is no ordinary rug! It is a rug that can take our hero wherever he wishes to go. To any time and any place. His imagination is the only thing that binds him. Should he wish to see the magical creatures that swim in a blue sea a thousand leagues away, he can, if he but wishes so. If he wishes to know what the snow at the top of the highest peak tastes like when mixed with the finest honey in the markets of Damascus, he has but to ask. Alas, these are not his chief concerns. For he has but one dream, and one dream only."

Shahrzad paused, staring down at the boy at her side. Then she glanced up at the man across the silken cushions.

Her heart was as boundless as the ocean. As vast as the sky.

"Do you want to know more about our hero?" she asked.

Haroun's eyes danced. "Yes!"

"Then we begin with the first tale . . . 'Haroun and the Magic Carpet.'"

# ACKNOWLEDGMENTS

I FEEL AS THOUGH I ONLY YESTERDAY PENNED THE acknowledgments for *The Wrath and the Dawn*, and here I am with a finished series in my sights. Trite though it may sound, time certainly does fly.

As always, I could not make this dream of mine a reality without the tireless support of my brilliant agent, Barbara Poelle. B, only Cookie could begin to compare. Also—good luck, stupid.

To my editor, Stacey Barney: thank you for always, always challenging me and never allowing me to settle for anything less than excellence. Working with you is one of the greatest gifts this amazing career has afforded me. Thank you for loving these books and these characters as I have—from the beginning to the end.

To all the fantastic people at Penguin: there are no words to express how much your support and enthusiasm mean to me. Special thanks to the indomitable Kate Meltzer and my wonderful publicist Marisa Russell—thank you for never shying away from my endless questions and forever having my back. Also huge thank-yous to Carmela Iaria, Alexis Watts, Doni Kay,

Anna Jarzab, Chandra Wohleber, Theresa Evangelista, Marikka Tamura, Jen Besser, Catherine Hayden, Lisa Kelly, Lindsay Boggs, Sheila Hennessey, Shanta Newlin, Mia García, Erin Berger, Amanda Mustafic, Colleen Conway, Judy Parks Samuels, Tara Shanahan, and Bri Lockhart.

To the 2015 Bat Cavers: here's to many, many more shared critiques and even more shared laughter in our near future. Thank you to Alan and Wendy Gratz for making this magic possible. Gwenda Bond, your voice narrates my life.

To all the wonderful bloggers, librarians, YouTubers, and book lovers who champion books everywhere—I thank you, from the bottom of my heart.

To my writing sisters—Joy Callaway, JJ, Traci Chee, Sarah Lemon, Ricki Schultz, and Sarah Henning—thank you for being there every step of the way.

To Marie Lu: there are not enough thank-yous in the world. I am so grateful to call you my friend. There will be many more pots of tea in our near future, and I look forward to them all.

To Beth Revis and Lauren DeStefano: never, ever stop being the wondrous souls you both are. It is glorious thing to witness, and I am beyond thankful to have each of you in my life. Lauren, there are no emojis left. We've used them all. Also Eva says hi. Revis, that liner is on fleek.

To Carrie Ryan: thank you so much for every lunch, every text, every laugh, every tear. I don't know who first said it, but when you find someone who hates the same things you do, cling to them; therefore, I shall cling to you. Always.

To Marie Rutkoski: for the beautiful critique of *Rose,* for the advice, for the emails, for everything. But mostly just for being you, wonderful you.

To all the amazing friends I made my debut year—to Sona Charaipotra, to Dhonielle Clayton, to Victoria Aveyard, to Adam Silvera, to David Arnold, to Becky Albertalli, to Valerie Tejeda, to Nicki Yoon, to Melissa Grey, to Virginia Boecker—it was such an honor to go through that maelstrom with you.

To Brendan Reichs because I promised. And also because he rocks a tangerine suit like no other.

To Sabaa Tahir: you are my rock, and I have no idea how I would have written this book without you. *None.* I thank every seven for bringing us together.

To Heather Baror-Shapiro and the entire team at IGLA: every time I see a foreign cover, I have to pinch myself. Thank you, a thousand times over.

To Elaine: for understanding me as no one else does. Also for putting up with me after the fact. Thank you, thank you, thank you. To infinity.

To Erica: being your sister is one of the best things about being me. Also there's a hole in your jeans. You should probably look into that. To my brothers, Ian and Chris—I am certain you both will read this book. There are characters in it inspired by each of you. Mwahahaha. To Izzy: thank you for being so awesome and supportive. To my dad: thank you for instilling in me the love of the written word. To my umma—thank you for telling people in the grocery line to buy my book. Never, ever stop doing that. Also thank you for being so proud. To Mama Joon and Baba Joon: I hope when you read this book, you feel what I feel when I'm around you—deep and abiding love. To Omid, Julie, Navid, Jinda, Evelyn, Isabelle, Andrew, Lily, and Ella: thank you for the rich gift that is our family. And for always being there, no matter what.

And to Vic—

To not belonging to anyone. But belonging together.